D1026288

Ryder paused a long moment. "Very well. I will see that Lady Claire gives up any thought of marrying me . . . on one condition."

"Condition?" Eve said cautiously.

"Come here, sweeting."

She tensed with sudden wariness. "Why?"

"Because I asked you to."

His gaze was a bold and steady challenge, capturing hers and holding it without effort. When he simply waited, Eve reluctantly obeyed, moving to stand before him. Ryder tucked an errant tendril of hair behind her ear, letting his fingertips skim the outer rim with the gentlest of caresses.

Eve stood perfectly still, suddenly unable to move. He left off toying with her ear and shifted his hand so that his thumb stroked along her jaw. Eve became aware of an abrupt weakness in her limbs. "*What* condition?" she forced herself to say in a voice far huskier than she would have liked.

"That you spend one night with me."

By Nicole Jordan

Paradise Series:
Master of Temptation
Lord of Seduction
Wicked Fantasy

Notorious Series:
The Seduction
The Passion
Desire
Ecstasy
The Prince of Pleasure

Other Novels:
The Lover
The Warrior

Fever Dreams

A Novel

Nicole Jordan

BALLANTINE BOOKS • NEW YORK

Fever Dreams is a work of fiction. Names, characters, places, and incidents are the products of the author's imagination or are used fictitiously. Any resemblance to actual events, locales, or persons, living or dead, is entirely coincidental.

A Ballantine Books Mass Market Original

Published in the United States by Ballantine Books, an imprint of The Random House Publishing Group, a division of Random House, Inc., New York.

This book contains an excerpt from *Touch Me with Fire* by Nicole Jordan. This excerpt has been set for this edition only and may not reflect the final content of the forthcoming edition.

ISBN 0-345-46787-6

Cover design: Carl D. Galian
Cover illustration: Jon Paul

Printed in the United States of America

www.ballantinebooks.com

OPM 9 8 7 6 5 4 3 2 1

In memory of
my dear friend Gin Ellis.
I'll miss you terribly.

Prologue

The Isle of Cyrene
March 1815

The dream returned unexpectedly, more vivid than ever. Sunlight pouring over the meadow where he lay. Lady Eve in his arms, enveloping him with her warmth and scent and softness.

The waiting was over. She was his bride at last.

She belonged to him.

Cradling her possessively, Ryder shifted onto his back and pulled her body flush against his, making her hair spill down in a gold curtain around them. When she bent to press an ardent kiss on his bare chest, he uttered a harsh groan. In response, Eve smiled her soft, beguiling smile.

Delight filled him, while all his muscles clenched in anticipation of their joining. As their gazes locked, the very air shimmered with raw passion.

Bending again, she kissed the line of his jaw, the vulnerable hollow of his throat, his breastbone, searing the flesh that concealed his hammering heart.

"At last I am yours," she whispered.

The husky warmth of her voice stroked him as

tenderly as her lips did, caressing him, setting him aflame. Needing to satisfy his fierce hunger, he guided her down until he was buried deep inside her. His blood pulsed feverishly as Eve sheathed him in wet, silken heat. She was bound to him now in the most primal way possible.

His back arching, Ryder began to move. The sweet surge of her hips matched the thundering of his blood as he drove himself inside her, hard and deep, branding her, claiming her, marking her as his, until their whole world dissolved into hot, pulsing brightness. . . .

Alex Ryder woke hard and throbbing, his heart's rhythm slowing as he recognized his familiar surroundings. He lay alone in his bed, bathed in a pool of sunshine. Early morning rays streaming through the tall French windows of his bedchamber flooded him with warmth, yet the heat suffusing his body had far more to do with his erotic, futile dream of Eve.

One he should have conquered long ago.

With a quiet curse, Ryder kicked off the tangled sheets—a testimony to his restless fantasies during the night—but continued to lie there, letting the hot sunlight play over his skin while memories burned in his mind.

His remembrance of Eve was so intense, he could still feel her body's shape in his arms. He could picture her without closing his eyes, could recall every vibrant detail of her.

Lady Eve Montlow . . . now Eve Seymour, Countess of Hayden.

She was the golden girl of his dreams. Living,

breathing sunshine. Indisputably his life had changed because of her.

His fascination had begun the moment they'd met, when he was sixteen and she was barely eleven. He'd thought her a princess in some imagined fairy tale, with her honey-gold hair and rose-red lips. And then she had smiled at him. He'd felt as if someone had slammed a fist into his gut. Eve had an enchanting smile, so warm it had the power to take his breath away. One smile and he was lost.

For all the good it did him.

As the daughter of an earl, Lady Eve was forbidden to him. He'd been a wild, rebellious youth then, and worse, a poor commoner; his late father was a mere soldier. Even though his mother had been a gentlewoman, Eve's patrician family had considered Ryder dangerous and entirely beneath notice. Indeed, the first time he and Eve met, her noble father had threatened to thrash him for simply daring to help the young lady down from her mount.

Two days later, Ryder remembered, Eve had boldly escaped her groom and ridden halfway across the island, expressly to seek him out.

She'd discovered him in his favorite meadow, sprawled beside the stream where he was fishing. She rode a horse far larger and more spirited than was wise for a girl her age, but she easily controlled the prancing bay as she drew rein.

"Oh, good, I found you. I had almost despaired and thought I would have to return tomorrow—but I knew my groom would never willingly let me out of his sight after the trick I played on him today."

Still smarting from his humiliation at her father's

hands, Ryder practically snarled at her. "What the devil are you doing here, my lady? Come to gloat?"

"Certainly not! I wished to apologize for my father's unforgivable rudeness to you. Papa has been a bear of late, ever since we were compelled to move to Cyrene from London to escape his creditors. He still clings to the notion that we are socially superior to everyone here on the island, and he won't countenance anything that threatens his consequence, as you were audacious enough to do yesterday."

Ryder stared at her, surprise and wariness battling in his mind. But all he could think to say was "How did you know where to look for me?"

Young Eve flashed her beguiling, impish smile. "That was easy—I merely listened to gossip and asked questions of the servants. You are the wild boy everyone has warned me about." But her smile took the sting from her words, Ryder's first indication that she was as charming and kind as she was beautiful.

That day not only had cemented their clandestine friendship. From that moment on, he'd set his sights on winning Lady Eve for his own.

He refused to accept that he couldn't aspire to her hand because of his lower station. He knew, however, he would have to change his wild, hell-bent ways. And of course he would first have to wait for Eve to grow up. Meanwhile, he would go off to seek his fortune, to make himself worthy of her. . . .

Uttering a sharp laugh at the memory, Ryder rolled over to bury his head in the pillows. Upon leaving the island two years later, he'd indeed eventually made his fortune. But from Eve's family's perspective, his means of acquiring his wealth as a mercenary soldier was yet another strike against him. And his newly won riches had made no difference in his suit. By the time he was able to return to Cyrene, Eve was lost to him. She was being sold in marriage to a wealthy nobleman in order to save her family from destitution.

That summer, when she was eighteen, Ryder had forcibly taken one savage, unforgettable kiss from her, and that was all he would ever have. As the wife of the illustrious Earl of Hayden, she was morally beyond his reach. She'd spent the past six years in England, and during all that time, Ryder had studiously avoided her.

He'd resolutely put Eve out of his mind. She was a youthful obsession, merely that—a boyish infatuation that he'd thankfully outgrown.

Yet in the dark hours of morning, he still sometimes found his dreams filled with the fantasy of Eve becoming his bride. And unconsciously he continued to hold her up as his ideal.

It was amusing, really. He was thirty years old now, and rich enough to buy almost any bride of his choosing. But he'd never found any other woman he wanted to marry. He had no permanent mistress, either. Oh, he took his pleasure with various ladies of the evening, but he'd never desired one enough to give her a long-term place in his bed or his life.

Flinging aside the pillow, Ryder ran a hand down his black-stubbled jaw. He would do better to find a willing siren to regularly slake his passion. Perhaps then he could finally banish his feverish, unwanted dreams of Eve.

Just then a tentative rap on the door interrupted his dark reverie. When Ryder impatiently bade entrance, the door was opened gingerly by his manservant, Greeves.

"Begging pardon for disturbing you, sir," Greeves said, "but you have visitors below."

"At this hour?" Ryder asked. It was barely seven, and any of his fellow Guardians would have come straight to his bedchamber to rouse him if the problem was serious enough to warrant calling so early in the day.

"Yes, sir. It is Mr. Cecil Montlow and Lady Claire. They say they have urgent news of their sister."

Ryder's heart gave a reflexive jolt. "What has happened?"

"They did not say, sir. Shall I tell them you are at home?"

"Yes, I'll be down directly."

Trying to stifle his apprehension, Ryder rose and threw a dressing gown over his nude body. Not bothering with trousers or even slippers, he left his bedchamber and swiftly descended the stairs to the drawing room to greet his unexpected guests.

Eve's younger siblings, Cecil and Claire, were twins, both tall and fair-haired with elegant, aristocratic features. Yet in personality, they could hardly have been more different. The Honorable Cecil Montlow was outgoing and lively to the point of brashness, while Lady Claire was gentle and shy, and at eighteen, a pale imitation of her older sister, Eve.

Cecil was currently pacing the carpet while Lady

Claire sat primly on the settee, her gloved hands folded in her lap. As Ryder entered the room, she rose and her brother halted in his tracks.

"What has happened?" Ryder asked, managing a measured tone. "I understand you have news of Eve?"

"You won't believe it," Cecil burst out. "Hayden has kicked the bucket."

"Cecil," Lady Claire chided softly, "you know you shouldn't use such vulgar cant."

"Well, it's true," her brother insisted. "And Mr. Ryder understands cant perfectly well."

Perhaps he did understand cant, Ryder thought, yet his whirling mind couldn't quite grasp those particular words. He would swear Cecil had said *the Earl of Hayden had died.*

Claire, searching his face, expounded in a quiet voice. "We had a letter from Eve last evening—it came on the packet. His lordship was tragically killed last month in a riding accident."

"What she means is," Cecil added with a touch more remorse than previously, "Lord Hayden crammed his horse at a stone wall during a hunt and broke his neck."

Which meant . . . Ryder felt his heart stop, then slowly begin to thud again. *Eve was now a widow.*

He should not be glad to hear of another man's death, and in truth, he wasn't. Yet an aching sensation gripped his chest, a strange, quiet burgeoning of emotion that he couldn't quell.

Vaguely Ryder realized the twins were still speaking, although he heard only one word in three.

Cecil apparently was lamenting their unexpected

turn of fate. "It isn't fair that we must suffer simply because Hayden croaked. But now London is out of the question for either of us."

"Eve will be in mourning for a full year," Lady Claire explained, "so my comeout must be postponed until next spring."

"But *I* was to spend this Season in London with my sisters," Cecil griped, "and gain some town bronze before I head off to university. Now there is no chance. I'm to go straight to Oxford this fall while Claire remains here on Cyrene with Mama and Papa. She'll join Eve in Hertfordshire next February to begin preparing for her entrance into the marriage mart."

"To be honest," the young lady admitted in a low voice, "I don't at all mind the delay. Eve is quite skilled at matchmaking and has promised to make my search for a husband as painless as possible, but I still dread being put on display for the London ton to scrutinize."

"You are just afraid to be courted by any beaux."

Claire flushed while sending her brother a cool glance. "I am not *afraid.* I am simply nervous among strangers."

She tended to stammer when she became nervous, Ryder recalled, so the respite from a formal presentation would undoubtedly be welcome to her. The boy's disappointment was understandable, however. For the past year and more, Cecil had been champing at the bit to get away from Cyrene—a small island in the western Mediterranean not too distant from the coast of Spain—and have a taste of the glamorous London social life.

Ryder shook himself and entered the fray. "Mind your manners, halfling. Lady Claire will do very well in London. She'll have countless beaux eating out of her hand, I have no doubt."

Cecil had the grace to look apologetic. "Yes, sir, I am sure you are right. But meanwhile, I have a favor to ask of you, Mr. Ryder."

"What favor?"

"Will you look after Claire while I am away at university? We have never been separated for long, and I would feel better knowing you were championing her. Escort her to the island assemblies, stand up with her at dances, that sort of thing. Help her to become more at ease in company to prepare for her eventual debut. I will worry myself sick otherwise."

Ryder returned a wry smile. To the boy's credit, he cared deeply for his twin and would let no one but himself plague her. The twin's parents, however, were another matter entirely. "Your parents will object to my associating so intimately with Lady Claire."

"No, they won't, sir. They consider you almost respectable now, since you are a hero and command such distinguished patronage."

"I suppose I should be gratified," Ryder murmured sardonically. He had recently performed a valued service for the British Foreign Secretary, which had earned him several high-powered advocates in the government. But even that couldn't make up for his notorious past with high sticklers such as Eve's father.

"Besides," Cecil added sincerely, "Claire may need help in standing up to Papa while I am away, and you are not the least afraid of him."

Ryder eyed Lady Claire curiously; she in turn was studying him. It surprised him that she remained mute while her brother arranged her future. Claire might be sweet and shy, yet she possessed an unexpected backbone hidden beneath her quiet demeanor, Ryder knew.

But he smiled graciously and gave her a gallant bow, saying he would be honored to stand her champion while her brother was away in England.

When he then offered the twins breakfast, Cecil accepted with alacrity, exclaiming that he was famished, but Lady Claire suddenly became aware of Ryder's state of undress. Her cheeks turned pink as she stammered a polite refusal, insisting that they had imposed long enough. She then marshaled her brother from the drawing room, leaving Ryder alone with his dazed thoughts.

Crossing to the window, he stared out at the foothills in the distance, which were covered with spring wildflowers. If Eve was now a widow, was it possible she would eventually remarry? And if so, did he want to put himself in the running for her hand?

She might not welcome his suit. At their last meeting, his behavior had been less than admirable, for he'd practically assaulted her when he claimed their first kiss.

The image was burned into his mind. It was the summer he had returned to Cyrene in order to court her.

For two months he'd taken advantage of Eve's habit of riding daily over the island, journeying out every morning in order to encounter her in some measure of privacy. He'd managed to renew their friendship and make progress in his campaign to gain her trust and affection. But then came a week when he saw nothing of her. He knew an English earl was visiting her family, but when he began hearing rumors about Lady Eve's possible betrothal, Ryder sent a servant to her with a message, asking her to meet him in the meadow where he regularly fished.

He waited impatiently for Eve to come, and when she did, the oddly guilty look on her face told him without words that his dreaded suspicion was correct. Until then, he had never believed she would accept a proposal from anyone but *him*.

"So it's true?" he rasped, his stomach clenching with a feeling of betrayal. "You intend to marry that damned earl?"

As if to equalize their levels before delivering her answer, Eve dismounted to join him. "It *is* true that my parents have arranged a marriage of convenience for me."

"Whose convenience? *Theirs?*" Ryder replied savagely.

"Ryder, it isn't like that. If you only knew how close Papa is to debtor's prison . . ." She broke off, biting her lip. "Lord Hayden means to settle all of our debts, to provide a dowry for Claire, and to fund Cecil's university schooling as well. And it is considered a brilliant match for me."

His anger and frustration spilled over. "What I see is that you're being sacrificed in order to keep your wastrel father in horses and carriages and fund his ruinous gaming habits."

Dismayed, Eve tried to placate him. "Surely you understand that I must marry well, Ryder. I've always known that it is up to me to repair our family fortunes. That I would never have the luxury of making any kind of match but one of convenience."

"You could marry me instead."

She stared at him as if stunned, and Ryder stared back—fiercely. He hadn't meant to declare his intentions so baldly, but her announcement had forced his hand.

"If you were to wed me, you wouldn't be pressed into a marriage repugnant to you. I'm wealthy enough now to care for you and your family in style and comfort."

"Oh, Ryder," she whispered softly. Her eyes lowered. "That is exceedingly kind of you, but I could not accept."

"Why not?"

When she made no reply, Ryder took a step closer. "I could take you away from here, Eve. We could elope."

She managed a faint smile. "The thought is tempting, I admit." She shook her head and gave a quiet laugh. "It is foolish for me to even contemplate, especially now that it is too late. Papa has already accepted a settlement from Lord Hayden, and he cannot go back on his word."

She offered him another smile, this one bright and brave. "Come now, Ryder, you needn't feel pity for me. It won't be so bad, being the wife of an earl. Certainly not repugnant. Lord Hayden is considered a prime catch. He is handsome and charming and moves in the first circles of society, and he has vast estates in Hertfordshire and a mansion in London. I intend to make the best of it. I will make a fine countess, don't you think?"

She was trying to lighten his savage mood by teasing him, but it had the opposite effect; Ryder wanted to strike out at something.

"Is that why you won't accept my proposal?" he demanded. "Because I cannot make you a countess?"

"Mama is set on my marrying a title, true, but it is not merely that—"

"It's because your parents consider my gains ill gotten."

Eve gave a helpless shrug. "I could not create a scandal by eloping with you, Ryder. My family would be devastated, and my sister and brother would only suffer for it."

He understood all too well. She could not buck her family—indeed, all of society—and run away with a lowly mercenary, no matter how wealthy. It would brand her a social outcast and taint her family in the process.

His resentment was unfair to Eve, Ryder knew, but it galled him to see her being forced to pay the price for her damned father's excesses, and his bitterness couldn't be controlled. He took a final step toward her, closing the distance between them. He'd always been careful to resist touching her, to avoid temptation, but now he reached for Eve and pulled her into his arms, hard against him.

He intended to kiss her, *needed* to kiss her in order to express his helpless rage. He couldn't stop himself; it would have been easier to stop his own heartbeat.

Eve's lips parted in a gasp an instant before Ryder brought his mouth crashing down on hers. Her body went rigid with shock at his unexpected assault, but he went on ravaging her mouth, his tongue thrusting deep into her warmth, as if by sheer force of will he could compel her to change her mind and accept his offer of marriage instead of the one her parents had decided for her.

For a long moment, she remained frozen, paralyzed. And then suddenly, miraculously, she melted against him, reaching up to clutch at his shoulders. She returned his kiss with fervor, stunning Ryder to his core. At last, after all these years she was in his arms, surrendering to his passion.

Devouring her mouth, he sank with her onto the grass, struggling for breath as he strove to control his primitive urges. He felt desperate, hungry for the taste of her, for the incredible feel of her. Helplessly, he moved his hand over the jacket of her riding habit and covered her breast. She moaned at his touch, responding as passionately as he'd known she would.

The husky sound ignited a raging fire inside him. Driven by the need to possess her, he reached for the hem of her riding skirts and pushed up the fabric, dragging his palm along her bare thigh. Somehow he hoped to prove to Eve that she didn't want a cold-blooded marriage to a rich lord. That she wanted *him*. But when his hand reached the naked juncture of her thighs, she went rigid with shock.

"Ryder, no! We can't . . ."

Frantically she shoved his hand away and squirmed to break free from beneath his heavy body. When he released her, she scrambled to her feet, looking dismayed.

"Eve . . . God, Eve, I am sorry."

She clapped a hand over her passion-bruised mouth and shook her head. "We can't," she whispered again.

Turning, she practically ran to her horse and pulled herself into the sidesaddle. With one last despairing glance at Ryder, she spurred her horse into a canter and fled the meadow, leaving him staring after her retreating form, a cold knife blade twisting in his gut.

Cursing the memory as he stood at the drawing-room window, Ryder ran a hand raggedly through his dark hair. If Eve hadn't stopped him, he would have taken her there in the meadow like a common doxy, with no thought for her innocence.

He should have been flogged for acting so savagely. Perhaps, he'd brooded afterward, he didn't deserve her after all. And not merely because he had blood on his hands.

Society deemed him a killer with a tarnished soul, yet the state of his soul had never seriously troubled him before. He couldn't honestly regret his choice of becoming a mercenary, since it had been his way out of poverty. He'd sold his services to various private armies, true; his father had been a grenadier in the British army and had taught him the principles of explosives from a young age. Ryder had purposely become an expert at firearms and in devising explosive weapons—valued skills in the deadly art of warfare.

He knew a hundred ways to kill . . . yet he also knew how to protect. Foreign royalty paid well to remain safe from the threat of spies and assassins. It was while acting as personal bodyguard to a Russian prince that Ryder had earned his first lavish reward, which had become the seed for his future wealth.

But haughty aristocrats such as Eve's parents could never accept a former soldier of fortune for their precious daughter. And Ryder had seen the wisdom of moving beyond his mercenary past, at least in the eyes of society.

It was his behavior toward Eve that day, however, that had jarred him and left him with a driving need to make something more of his life. To become a better, worthier man. As a result, he'd turned his skills to a far greater cause than protecting rich royalty: He'd joined the Guardians of the Sword, a centuries-old order dedicated to a noble ideal, which publicly operated as a minor arm of the British Foreign Office headquartered on Cyrene.

Ryder had been grateful for his new purpose, more grateful still to be given his first mission and a reason to leave the island, for he refused to stay and watch Lady Eve wed another man.

In the six years since, he'd dedicated his life to serving the order's cause. He had found fulfillment with the Guardians, and his avocation had become a passion.

In all that time, he'd worked hard to convince himself that Eve no longer meant anything to him.

Yet if he were entirely honest, he would admit that his longing for her had never fully diminished.

And now she had become a widow. *And everything had changed.*

Ryder couldn't deny the heavy thud of his heart or the restless ache welling in his chest.

He still wanted Lady Eve for his bride.

And he meant to win her. She epitomized everything he'd ever yearned for. Symbolized everything he'd had to fight for all his life because of his common origins and questionable past. He intended to prove to her aristocratic world that he was good enough to aspire to their elite ranks.

Most important, with Eve as his wife, he could finally satisfy his long-held desire for her.

Yet he would have to proceed carefully, Ryder knew. Eve would likely offer him resistance. But he *would* succeed this time.

Abruptly Ryder turned to stride from the drawing room. He had plans to make.

He would allow Eve a proper period of mourning, of course. But in the meantime he would do everything in his power to clear his path. To remove any outward objections to his suit. He would make certain that he was not only welcome in polite society but moved in her same vaunted circles.

He would call in every favor ever owed him, take advantage of every obligation, all his wealth, ill gotten or not.

And then nothing and no one would stop him from winning Eve Seymour for his bride.

Chapter One

London
April 1816

"What I cannot understand, Eve," Cecil said, spearing a kippered herring on his breakfast plate, "is why you don't wish to marry again. Since we arrived here for the start of the Season, I must have counted at least a dozen gentlemen who are eager to court you."

Caught off guard by her brother's unexpected choice of topics, Eve drew a sudden breath and regrettably wound up choking on her morning coffee. Blindly setting down her cup, she groped for her napkin and pressed it to her lips to stem her fit of coughing.

But if she hoped to avoid answering, she was doomed to disappointment, for Cecil waited with stubborn patience for her to be able to speak again, even to the point of ignoring his forked kipper.

"One marriage was enough, thank you," she finally rasped.

"Seriously," Cecil prodded with a frown, "*why* don't you want to remarry?"

"If you were a woman, you might understand why a widow would cherish her independence," Eve replied vaguely.

"But I'm not a woman—*or* a widow—so it doesn't make any sense to me unless you explain."

Holding back a smile at his earnestness, Eve busied herself with taking a bite of soft-boiled egg. Cecil regularly puzzled over the "inexplicable workings of the female mind." But because it would be impossible to make her younger brother understand how she felt when he had no concept of what some married women endured, she wouldn't even begin to attempt to explain.

Thankfully, though, Eve reminded herself with joyful relief, after six interminable years of marriage and one of widowhood, she finally had a glimpse of freedom and independence. And she would allow nothing and no one to spoil it. She would never, ever marry again.

"It does seem a contradiction," Claire said in her soft, melodic voice, "since you are insisting that *I* marry."

Eve cast her sister a sympathetic glance. "Because marriage is the only viable option for a young lady of quality. But I promise you, dearest, no one will force you to accept any man who is not your ideal match. We will find you a husband who can make you happy. You have my most solemn word on that."

Claire gave a rueful sigh. "Doubtless you will, since you are such a splendid matchmaker. But it does seem a trifle ironic that you delight in arranging suitable matches for everyone but yourself."

"I am perfectly content to remain a widow," Eve insisted, managing a careless smile.

At her declaration, she spied the twins exchanging a long, meaningful glance. "Why this sudden interest in my remarriage?" she asked, her smile fading to a frown.

"Oh, no reason," Claire replied, her tone perfectly innocent.

Eve's gaze narrowed as she looked from one twin to the other. Her siblings were up to something, although what she couldn't guess. Before she could probe further, however, she heard the sound of carriage wheels outside the breakfast-room windows.

Fortunately her brother's attention was similarly diverted, and he turned his head to glance out.

"Look, there is Sir Alex at last!" Cecil exclaimed, tossing down his fork. Jumping up from the table with no thought whatever to gentlemanly behavior, Cecil crossed to the window for a better view. "I told you he intended to take residence today."

With effort, Eve controlled the urge to leap from her chair and rush to the window herself. Her heart had suddenly quickened, but she refused to be seen gawking like her nineteen-year-old brother.

She and the twins were alone in the breakfast room, which overlooked Bedford Square. Sipping her coffee, Eve contented herself with glancing casually across the tree-shaded, grassy expanse that separated her elegant town house from the others in the square. A dashing curricle had just driven up and halted before the imposing mansion opposite hers.

"What a bang-up rig that is," Cecil declared, admiring the red and yellow sporting vehicle. "I cannot wait to try it. Sir Alex promised to take me for a drive this week and let me handle the ribbons."

Ignoring the curricle, Eve instead found her gaze riveted on the driver, who was dismounting and tossing the reins to his groom. Even from a distance she recognized Ryder's tall, hard-muscled form. His shoulders filled out his bottle-green coat to perfection, while his buff breeches and polished Hessian boots molded his long, powerful legs.

It was her first sight of Alex Ryder in seven years, but there was no excuse for the sharp little leap her heart gave. Perhaps it was merely the surprise of seeing him dressed as a fine gentleman. When she'd known him on Cyrene, he had rarely worn a coat or cravat, just shirt and breeches, since the Mediterranean island was far warmer and much less formal than London.

Or perhaps her quickened pulse was due to anticipation at again encountering the handsome rebel who had at one time both fascinated and unnerved her.

Like his body, Ryder's face was lean and hard, possessing a dangerous masculine appeal. It was the face of a man who didn't cater to anyone—utterly compelling and perhaps a little sinful. What she remembered most about Ryder, however, was his smoldering intensity. He possessed a pair of breathtakingly intense eyes, the hue of dark mahogany, just like his hair. And the air of danger that surrounded him only added to his forceful impact.

Eve thought she had prepared herself to contend with Ryder again, but seeing him in the flesh was more of a jolt than she'd bargained for. And so were the unexpected feelings her remembrances of him aroused.

Silently scolding herself, Eve brought her coffee cup to her lips to hide her deplorable flush. She should have banished her memories of him long before now. It seemed a lifetime ago when they had been friends on Cyrene. A lifetime ago when she'd harbored a girlish infatuation for him during their final summer together.

Then again, she doubted that any woman could ever forget Alex Ryder. Certainly any woman who had ever been fiercely kissed by him, as she had.

Ryder had already created quite a stir in the short time he'd been in London. Mercenary turned hero. The papers were full of gossip and speculation about him.

It was strange to think of him as Sir Alex, though. He'd always been simply Ryder to her.

Even more strange, they were to be neighbors again, since he had hired the house directly across the square from hers for the Season. Workmen had been traipsing in and out all week in preparation for his arrival.

She suspected her brother had something to do with the odd coincidence, but she hadn't wanted to seem overly interested in Ryder by asking about his plans.

"Do sit down, Cecil," Eve told her brother as Ryder disappeared inside his house. "There will be plenty of time to admire Sir Alex and his curricle *after* you finish breakfast."

Cecil gave an impatient sigh but complied with

her request, much to Eve's relief. She was well aware that Ryder was her brother's idol.

Admittedly, Cecil's obsessive case of hero worship worried her a little. A whirlwind of energy, he was capable of getting into enough mischief and mayhem on his own, without having a former soldier of fortune to pattern his behavior after. Cecil was here now only because he'd behaved so outrageously at Oxford that he'd been sent down for the rest of the term. In his defense, he had wanted to be with his twin when Claire made her bow to society—to offer her moral support and provide her with an escort if she couldn't manage to find any beaux on her own.

It was exasperating, trying to rein in Cecil's admirable but misguided chivalrous instincts, yet Eve had cherished having both her siblings with her during her final months of mourning.

She had lived quietly in Hertfordshire for the past year, not merely out of respect due her late husband Richard, but because she much preferred the freedom offered her in the countryside to the starched formality of town life. Then three weeks ago, she had opened the London house for the Season and moved in with the twins, to begin Claire's society debut.

Richard's widowed aunts—Drucilla, Baroness Wykfield, and Lady Beatrice Townley—had accompanied them. The aunts were elderly dowagers of exalted birth and fortune and influential enough with the ton to significantly aid Claire's comeout.

Since their arrival, Eve had spent much of the time commissioning a wardrobe for Claire, sparing no expense to outfit her sister in the height of fashion in the hope that beautiful gowns would bolster the girl's confidence when she faced the judgmental arbitrators of the *ton*. Additionally, Eve had found it necessary to refurbish her own wardrobe, since she'd finally put off her black and gray widow's weeds.

She had also spent time renewing old acquaintances and was gratified to be welcomed back enthusiastically, more for Claire's sake than for her own. Richard had been very popular with London's fashionable set, for his public persona was far more congenial than his private one. Eve was planning on resuming her place in society in order to give her sister every possible chance at success.

At Claire's pleading, however, they had forgone a formal court presentation. Instead, the aunts had held an elegant dinner earlier this week in her honor, so Claire was officially "out" now. They had not yet attended many evening functions, but invitations were pouring in, and Eve expected to have a full social calendar for the next several months.

She was listening with only half an ear when Cecil addressed his twin with his usual youthful enthusiasm. "Mr. Ryder has invited us to tour the London sights with him, Claire. He wants to see the Tower tomorrow. I mean, Sir Alex. I sometimes forget to call him by his new title."

The girl brightened. "Oh, I would enjoy that immensely."

"What would you enjoy?" Lady Wykfield questioned as she swept into the room. Tall, elegant, and silver-haired, Drucilla was the elder and more sharp-tongued of Richard's two aunts. Trailing in her wake was Lady Beatrice—a softer, fluttery version of her sister.

Two footmen entered directly behind the aunts. Drucilla was a stickler for proper form and wished to be waited on every morning rather than to fill her own plate from the sideboard as Eve and the twins did. The servants proceeded to pour coffee and serve breakfast for the ladies, while Cecil answered Lady Wykfield's question.

"We were speaking of Sir Alex Ryder, Aunt. Claire and I mean to see the London sights with him."

Drucilla's elegant features turned disapproving. "Certainly you will not. It would be highly inappropriate for Lady Claire to jaunt around town escorted by a bachelor, particularly one of that man's infamous reputation."

"An outing would be acceptable if Cecil accompanies her," Eve interjected evenly.

She wasn't wild for the idea either, since Ryder's notoriety could do Claire little good. But the twins shared a long friendship with Ryder, and Eve had no intention of forbidding the relationship. Nor did she care for the way Drucilla tried to rule every aspect of her sister's life. Claire was timid enough without being ordered about until she was too frightened to have a thought of her own.

Cecil also objected to Drucilla's opposition. "There is nothing wrong with Claire's accompanying me, Aunt Drucilla. We've known Mr. Ryder—Sir Alex—for a donkey's age, since we were out of leading strings. He taught us how to fish and to swim and all manner of—"

"That is hardly a recommendation," Drucilla

stated airily, not hiding her scorn. "He is nothing but a pretentious upstart who has attempted to acquire respectability by purchasing himself a knighthood."

Cecil bristled. "That is a complete lie!"

Seeing her brother's welling anger, Eve quietly dismissed the two footmen, not wanting them to witness a family argument. "Cecil," she remarked then, knowing she had to set a good example even if she agreed with him in this instance, "you will apologize to Aunt Drucilla for your outburst."

"Sorry," the young man muttered, though with little contrition. "I did not mean to imply you were a liar, Aunt."

Drucilla, who still looked coldly offended, deigned to give a brusque nod.

Quelling the urge to smile at the baroness's indignant countenance, Eve took the opportunity to smooth over the contretemps. "Sir Alex did not purchase his title, Drucilla. He was knighted for valor, for his exemplary service to the Crown."

Drucilla gave an elegant "Humph!" and applied herself to her coffee.

"Indeed, Aunt," Claire spoke up. "Sir Alex is a true hero. He saved the life of Lord Castlereagh, as well as several other Foreign Office diplomats."

"He is still no better than a mercenary."

At that accusation, Cecil couldn't hold his tongue, although at least this time his tone was more respectful when he declared, "Even as a mercenary Mr. Ryder saved the lives of countless people, protecting them from assassination. And he gave up his military post to assist our government. He has honorably served the Foreign Office for years."

That had surprised Eve—to learn Ryder had worked for the Foreign Office, under the leadership of Sir Gawain Olwen. The elderly baronet was a revered figure on Cyrene, and a man for whom she had great affection. She knew that Sir Gawain ran a small department of the British Foreign Office headquartered on Cyrene, and her respect for Ryder had only deepened upon hearing that he'd joined Sir Gawain's endeavors.

She had always admired Ryder's boldness, and more, his staunch determination to challenge his fate. Yet it troubled her to know he had blood on his hands. Apparently he'd made a concerted effort to redeem his dark past and wild reputation—and in the eyes of Cyrenean society at least, he had succeeded.

Indeed, Sir Gawain himself had sponsored Ryder and recommended him for knighthood to the Prince Regent. Now he was wealthy *and* titled.

They had never discussed his circumstances, but even when she was young, she'd known that he chafed at his poverty and the social divisions that relegated him to the lower classes. It could not be pleasant to be disdained for the vagaries of birth and fortune.

But Drucilla shared the same haughty attitude as her noble peers. Her aquiline nose rose in the air as she eyed a fuming Cecil. "Hero or not, his fortune was earned through blood, selling his sword to foreign princes. There is no possible justification for that."

"Not *all* of his fortune," Cecil insisted in passionate defense of his hero. "Most of it was earned by perfectly respectable means, investing in the Company. Hayden did the same, as have any number of lords."

Eve couldn't help but smile at this rational argument. Her late husband had indeed increased his fortune substantially by investing in the East India Company's lucrative shipping trade. From what Eve understood, Ryder had done the same, taking the rich rewards he'd earned in his service to foreign royalty and investing wisely. Reportedly he had multiplied his investments a hundredfold, quietly becoming as wealthy as some of the British nabobs who'd amassed their staggering fortunes in India.

But Lady Beatrice chimed in then, echoing her elder sister, although less stridently. "An accumulated fortune and awarded title cannot compensate for lack of birth and breeding. He is indeed an ineligible connection for a young lady like Claire."

Of course she would agree with Drucilla, Eve knew. The aunts were daughters of an earl, born to aristocratic privilege and highbrowed notions of superiority. They would not readily accept anyone into their blue-blooded ranks.

"I don't believe the connection is ineligible," Eve replied, managing to repress her own growing impatience. "Sir Alex's mother came from a good family in Kent, and he was educated as a gentleman's son. In fact he shared a tutor with the son of a local viscount on Cyrene."

From what Eve had gathered, Sir Gawain had arranged Ryder's schooling to try and curb his rebel tendencies, while his mother had taught him refined manners, how to speak properly and such—the sort of critical education that defined a gentleman.

"But he is *not* a gentleman's son," Drucilla parried. "Who was his father? And if his mother was genteel, why did she marry so far beneath her?"

"I understand it was a love match," Eve murmured, although she knew that changing the aunts' minds was a hopeless cause.

"Well," the baroness pronounced, "he will have difficulty finding a bride from the Quality, given his encumbrances."

Refraining from disputing the observation, Eve fell silent. The rumors that Ryder was in the market for a genteel wife had surprised her even more than his new title. The Alex Ryder she knew had never cared much for polite society or sought their good opinion, and his disdain for the nobility's pretensions was fierce. But she supposed it made sense that Ryder would want to shop the Marriage Mart during the Season now that he'd been knighted.

Cecil had intimated as much, and Eve had no reason to doubt her brother's reports. The twins knew far more about Ryder than she did, for they had both regularly written to him since joining her in Hertfordshire in February. And Cecil had called on Ryder at his bachelor's lodgings several times since their arrival in London, so Eve had kept somewhat abreast of his plans.

Moreover, she'd heard various tales about Ryder from her own set of friends, in addition to the gossip in the newspapers. Speculation was rife regarding what sort of bride he was seeking and what his chances were for attracting one from among the nobility.

Her own opinion was that Ryder's obvious encumbrances might not overshadow his advantages of acquired title and enormous wealth. She doubted, however, that he would make good husband material. Although even the most refined ladies would find him fascinating, with his combination of smoldering vitality and dark, charismatic charm, "fascinating" men rarely made admirable mates.

Still, Eve well understood how appealing a man such as Ryder would be to a young lady of marriageable age. The summer he'd returned to Cyrene from his adventures abroad, she had been eighteen and ripe for his masculine admiration.

Admittedly, she'd been shockingly attracted to Ryder, with his sensual dark looks and forbidden allure, although a little unnerved by his fervent intensity. If her circumstances had been different, she might have let herself be swept away by her longings for him. But she hadn't been free to choose her future or indulge in dreams of handsome, dangerously improper suitors as other young girls were.

Regrettably, however, that hadn't stopped her from responding with wanton abandon when he'd kissed her so ruthlessly that day in the meadow, Eve remembered with chagrin.

Feeling herself grow warm at the memory, she returned to the discussion at hand. "I think it unexceptional for Cecil and Claire to accept Sir Alex's invitation."

Her brother's mulish expression faded. "Capital! You are a trump, Eve."

Claire smiled contentedly. "It will be a pleasure to see Mr. Ryder—Sir Alex—again after these past few months."

The aunts, particularly Drucilla, were not happy with Eve's permissiveness, but she wisely steered the conversation to Claire's wardrobe, a subject the elderly ladies found dear to their hearts. The modiste was coming at ten to give Claire another fitting, and Eve felt confident in leaving the aunts to supervise. Not only did they need to feel useful by contributing to her sister's debut, but both ladies had superb taste and an excellent eye for the styles and colors that would show a fair-haired, pale-complected girl like Claire to best advantage.

Thus breakfast ended on a congenial note after all, with the aunts accompanying Claire upstairs for her fitting and Cecil haring off to visit some friends who were nearer his own age.

Eve, on the other hand, went to the kitchens and asked Cook to make up a fresh batch of scones, to be ready within the hour. She intended to send a basket of provisions across the square to Sir Alex, since it was only polite to welcome him to the neighborhood.

After relaying her instructions, Eve proceeded to the morning room, where she attended to her correspondence and reviewed household and estate accounts. As the hour wore on, however, she found herself distracted, staring out the window at Ryder's newly acquired house across the square when she should have been sorting through and replying to invitations.

Seeing him again after all these years had brought

back wistful memories of her last summer on Cyrene, when she'd felt the first sweet stirrings of passion. When her growing attraction to Ryder had led her to dream about what might have been.

That summer she hadn't been eager to marry a strange nobleman and move to England, far away from her family and friends. She would much rather have remained on Cyrene, where she was permitted a fair measure of independence, far more than that allowed in well-bred English society. But for the sake of her parents and her two younger siblings, she'd been willing to do her duty, agreeing to the kind of bargain women had been making for centuries—trading beauty and breeding for financial security and a loveless marriage of convenience to a wealthy aristocrat.

It had warmed Eve's heart when Ryder offered to wed her himself to save her from making such a sacrifice. It had stunned her when Ryder kissed her. Shaken her to her very core.

She would never forget that incredible kiss. The intense passion behind it, the ravishing hunger of his lips. Even now she remembered the hard press of his body as he drew her down among the wildflowers. The burning heat of his embrace, his devouring mouth.

His tender savagery had kindled a response in her that was basic, primitive, wholly feminine: the fierce yearning to surrender to her primal needs as a woman, to give herself wholly to Ryder, heart and body and soul.

Thankfully she'd come to her senses at the last possible instant and fled the meadow. But his sensual assault was still branded on her memory. And admittedly, those few unforgettable moments in his arms had been more erotic than any spent with her husband during their six cold years of marriage.

For her, marriage had been a rude awakening to reality, shattering all her budding dreams. The heated promise she'd felt in Ryder's kiss had died a swift death on her wedding night.

She had not seen Ryder since that scandalous embrace, when he'd given her her first and last taste of desire. Eve sometimes wondered if he remembered that passionate kiss. She hoped he had forgotten about it long ago, just as *she* should be doing.

Certainly she would never refer publicly to that brazen moment between them. No one need know about their past, other than the innocuous fact that they had once been friends and neighbors on Cyrene. *And I refuse to be intimidated now, simply because he is living across the square.*

She was determined to repress any lingering inappropriate feelings of attraction for Ryder. She was a mature woman now, Eve sternly reminded herself. Perfectly capable of dealing with him—

"Sir Alex Ryder to see you, my lady."

Her butler's unexpected pronouncement gave Eve such a start that she jerked back her quill pen and promptly turned over the inkwell, spilling black ink across the surface of the letter she'd been trying to compose.

Giving a gasp, she jumped up from her chair and hurriedly righted the well. At the same time, she was keenly aware that Ryder had crossed the room to her side. Drawing out a linen handkerchief, he tossed it over the spill before the stain spread across the marquetry surface of her writing desk.

Turning to look up at Ryder, Eve froze as she met his dark gaze. He stood frozen as well, his eyes riveted on her.

He looked lean and male and dangerous, she thought, feeling her heart race wildly. And he was still as breathtaking as ever.

His eyebrows were heavy and straight, his lashes a tangled fringe over eyes the shade of midnight. Her scrutiny took in his lean cheekbones, his chiseled jawline, his firm, sensual mouth. His skin was deeply tanned as usual, and his hair—so dark to be almost black—was cut longer than the current fashion and curled a little. Moreover, his eyes still held that intensity she found so unsettling . . . like a physical touch.

The thick rim of lashes lowered as slowly his gaze swept down her figure, then lifted again so that his stare captured hers.

"Lady Hayden," he said. "Forgive me for startling you. I've come to pay my respects . . . and to gain your permission to take your brother and sister on a sightseeing tour of London tomorrow."

"Yes. . . . They told me of your invitation."

Odd that she found breathing difficult when she had no reason to. It was merely the pleasant shock of seeing him again that unsettled her.

Ryder was still as dynamic and imposing as she remembered, with heat and vitality radiating from his body in waves. But he had changed subtly. He was all man now, all traces of youth gone. She could see the hard life of a soldier in his striking features, along with the alertness that was second nature to him. He reminded her of a wolf she had once glimpsed in a forest—lean, primal, potentially deadly.

Except that she doubted she would ever be this keenly attracted to a *real* wolf.

Eve promptly scolded herself, yet she couldn't seem to break the heated tension that vibrated between them.

"May I take this away, my lady?"

Vaguely she realized that her butler was speaking to her. He had cleaned up the ink spill and was carefully holding the sodden handkerchief and her half-written letter in his cupped palms.

"Thank you, Dunstan," she said gratefully. "Will you see that Sir Alex is given a replacement for his handkerchief?"

"That won't be necessary," Ryder responded lightly, "since I caused the accident."

Eve's gaze was drawn back to him. She wished she could think of something clever to say. Instead, she settled for addressing her butler again. "Dunstan, please send for my sister and tell her Sir Alex is here."

"I already have done so, my lady. Lady Claire asked to be informed should Sir Alex call."

So Claire had expected him, Eve thought with a twinge of annoyance. She wished *she* had known Ryder was coming, for she might have been less flustered upon seeing him again.

But in fact she should be glad he was here now. She would rather get their first meeting over with in private, so there would be no awkwardness between them when they met in public.

"Very well, Dunstan. Then will you have Cook prepare a tea tray for our guest? And tell her she may bring Sir Alex's basket here to the morning room when it is ready."

"As you wish, my lady."

"Basket?" Ryder repeated when the butler had bowed himself out.

"I asked my cook to do some baking for you. I thought to welcome you to the neighborhood."

A gleam entered his dark eyes. "Playing lady of the manor, are you, Countess?"

Eve glanced at him uncertainly, wondering if his remark was a gibing reference to her marriage. "I have a good deal of experience with the role. Being mistress of a large estate holds obligations. For your information, I requested hot scones. You were once very fond of them, if I recall."

Suddenly he gave her one of his rare smiles—a slow, charming, devilish grin that seared all her nerve endings. "You remembered."

"Well, yes."

"That happens to be one of my fondest boyhood memories. How you used to sneak me scones from your kitchens, kept warm by a heated brick."

She tried to repress her flush of warmth at the remembrance. "There will be strawberry preserves also, freshly made from the forcing houses at Hayden Park."

"Thank you, Countess. I'm certain I will enjoy them."

Eve gestured toward the sitting area at one side of the room. "Will you take a seat, Sir Alex? I will see what is keeping my sister."

When she retreated a step toward the door, the smile in Ryder's eyes deepened. "Running away so soon? I never took you for a coward."

Eve found his perceptiveness disconcerting, but she instantly halted, a spark of exasperation flaring in her own eyes. "Of course I am not a coward."

"Yet I seem to remember you disappeared just as quickly the last time we met."

"I *hoped* we might ignore that unfortunate incident, Sir Alex. It happened a long time ago and is best forgotten."

A slashing black eyebrow lifted quizzically. "Do you think I could possibly forget that day? You were my first proposal—in fact, my only proposal. A man never forgets a thing like that. Not to mention our kiss."

Feeling color flood her cheeks, Eve returned a measuring glance, taken aback to think she was the recipient of Ryder's only proposal . . . even though she'd always suspected he was not the marrying kind and had proposed to her that day only out of altruism. She opened her mouth to reply, then shut it again promptly, deciding it wiser to ignore both his admission and his pointed reminder of their kiss.

At her muteness, the gleam in Ryder's eyes intensified. "You needn't fear a repetition of that incident, sweeting. I've given up assaulting beautiful young ladies. Some people even mistake me for a gentleman now."

"It is not gentlemanly," Eve countered, "to remark on our . . . that kiss. My behavior that day was not in the least ladylike, and I would like to forget it ever happened."

"I fancy I was a trifle more at fault than you were," Ryder replied dryly. "But I am willing to overlook our past if you wish it."

"Thank you," Eve said in gratitude. "I do wish it. I thought we could simply be friends, as we once were."

"Friends." Ryder stared at her for a moment, then shook his head. His sudden laughter was soft, unexpected, charming. "Very well, if you insist."

Casually he turned and strolled over to the sofa, where he settled himself comfortably. Eve moved forward and sat in a wing chair opposite him.

"It has been a long time, Countess," he said finally, still studying her.

"Yes, it has."

"I gather Lady Claire's comeout is proceeding well under your auspices?" Ryder mused.

"Thus far it is. But I'm afraid she finds the whole process intimidating. I was much the same when I first came here—a green girl just out of the schoolroom."

"That is not what I've heard. By all reports, you were the Belle of London your first Season."

Eve's smile was self-deprecating. "Hayden's popularity had much more to do with my success."

"You have grown up into a magnificent woman. Your hair is a richer gold than I remember."

There was something intimate, almost possessive, about Ryder's scrutiny, and Eve once more found herself remembering what it felt like to kiss him, remembering the heat and hardness of him . . .

before she caught herself in exasperation. "Sir Alex, I will thank you to refrain from making such remarks. I don't desire your flattery, however well meant. And it is not appropriate between mere friends."

"Very well, my lady," he agreed amiably, although he scarcely looked repentant.

Eve cleared her throat and sought a new topic of conversation. "I should congratulate you on your new knighthood. The honor is well deserved, I understand."

That glint returned to his eyes, but this time it held an edge of cynicism. "I believe your father would disagree. He always thought I was born to be hanged."

"Yes, well . . . Papa always did consider it a crime to be born with any blood other than blue."

"Cecil tells me that Hayden's aunts are even worse."

That comment elicited a pained smile from Eve. "Indeed, we regularly battle over their notions of superiority. But despite their disdain for anyone not of the peerage, they are lovely ladies."

"Doubtless they wonder how you came by your radical views."

"I suspect *you* had a great deal to do with my radical views," Eve conceded with a laugh.

Ryder flashed her a grin. "And you had a great deal to do with altering *my* views, I admit. I turned over a new leaf because of you—actually more than once. But that summer, after you rejected my offer, I decided to put my mercenary past behind me and become respectable."

Eve eyed him in surprise. She was a little amazed

to think she'd had that much influence over Ryder, and flattered as well. "Is that why you joined the Foreign Office?"

"In part."

Her smile turned faintly teasing. "Does that mean I can take some of the credit for your becoming a celebrated hero?"

"I would say so," Ryder answered in the same vein. "And if you follow that line of argument, you can also claim some credit for the fact that I was knighted. I realized a title would aid me in gaining respectability, so I allowed Sir Gawain to put forward my name for the honor. I could never have stomached the absurd formalities of court otherwise."

Eve glanced toward the window at Ryder's mansion across the square. "I suppose you hired your new house for the same reason?"

"Yes. If I'm to set up as a knight and marry a well-bred lady, I must have a suitable address."

"Then the gossip is true? You are looking for a wife?"

Ryder hesitated.

Just then Claire entered, a delighted expression on her face as she crossed the room to him. "Sir Alex, how good it is to see you again! I have missed you."

"I have missed you too, Lady Claire."

When Ryder rose to greet her, she gave him her hands in a gesture of friendship. "It is wonderful news about your being knighted."

"Thank you, my lady. You are looking quite enchanting. Have you taken London by storm yet?"

She laughed, and Eve was struck by how animated her sister's face was. Claire was indeed looking fresh and pretty in a new yellow dotted-swiss gown, and she was gazing up at Ryder with genuine fondness. A fondness he seemed to return.

Distracted by the sight, Eve barely heard a throat being cleared until she realized that Beatrice had joined them.

The elderly lady sent Eve an apologetic glance as she stepped into the room. "Drucilla wishes me to act as chaperone, Eve."

Which doubtless meant, Eve thought, that Drucilla herself refused to honor their visitor with her presence, but believed the ladies of the house required protection from the likes of a former mercenary.

Beatrice was eyeing him with great curiosity, so Eve made the introductions. Ryder's bland look held politeness as he offered her a formal bow.

He had just straightened when Dunstan appeared with the tea tray. Lady Beatrice settled in a chair with her needlework while Eve busied herself pouring tea.

Claire sat next to Ryder on the sofa.

"Now, Sir Alex," the girl continued, "what were you saying when I interrupted? Something about the gossip being accurate? Are you truly looking for a wife?"

When Eve felt Ryder's glance fall on her, she returned an inquisitive gaze, very curious to hear his answer.

"Yes, I intend to marry," he acknowledged. "It's the chief reason I've come to London."

"Did you know that Eve is known for her matchmaking abilities?" Claire asked.

His eyebrow lifted. "Is that so?"

"I have had some minor success," Eve admitted.

Claire smiled as she sipped her tea. "You are far too modest, dearest sister. Sir Alex, she can claim credit for at least a dozen marriages."

From Ryder's expression, Eve could tell he seemed surprised. "Are you so interested in promoting the institution of matrimony, then?"

She gave a light shrug of her shoulders. "Truthfully, no. I have no fondness for matrimony. But if a young woman *must* marry, I believe she ought to find someone with whom she can live happily. So each season I make it a point to help several of the new debutantes."

"Help? How?"

"Oh, nothing exceptional. I advise them on finding the right sort of husbands and try to pair them with suitable prospects so they can make good matches and avoid bad ones."

The amused glint in his eye had returned. "And just what do you consider a good match, Countess?"

"One where the couple shares compatible character and temperament. And of course social and financial considerations are important. A union is not likely to succeed where there is a great disparity between husband and wife."

"Perhaps you should consider asking Eve to help you find a suitable match, Sir Alex," Claire suggested. "She really is quite skilled at it."

"Oh, no," Eve said at once. "I wouldn't dream of offering Sir Alex advice."

"I think it a grand idea," Claire insisted.

Frowning, Eve sent her sister a questioning look, wondering why in the world Claire was being so adamant about the issue.

But Lady Beatrice spoke to Claire before Eve could. "Pray, don't be absurd, my dear. It would be inappropriate for Eve to become involved in this gentleman's matrimonial affairs."

Eve felt herself stiffen. It was true, she did not want to involve herself with Ryder, but she felt obliged to defend him. "Beatrice, there would be no question of propriety if I were to aid him, since Sir Alex is a longtime friend of my family."

Ryder, who was the subject of their discussion, smiled slightly. "It won't be necessary for you to aid my search, Lady Hayden."

"Why not?" Eve asked, her curiosity piqued even further. "You don't think I could?"

"Perhaps you could, but I don't want you to trouble yourself. I already know the kind of bride I want."

"Oh? Do you have someone in mind, then?"

"In fact I—"

"Wouldn't you care for tea, Sir Alex?" Claire interrupted.

She leaned forward and picked up the teacup Ryder had left sitting on the table. But as she turned to hand it to him, the cup slid off the saucer straight into his lap.

Chapter Two

Wincing, Ryder let out a reflexive oath under his breath and grabbed for the cup at the same moment Claire also dropped the saucer in his lap.

"Oh, no!" she exclaimed, looking utterly dismayed as she brought her hands to her mortified cheeks. "I am so very sorry, Sir Alex! How dreadfully clumsy of me."

Dismayed as well, Eve quickly rose and snatched up a napkin from the tea tray. Moving to his side, she bent over Ryder and began urgently wiping the hot liquid from his breeches.

Yet the buff-colored fabric was already thoroughly soaked, she noted with chagrin. No matter how hard she pressed, her efforts were not helping.

Then she moved the linen cloth higher to the juncture of his thighs, and Ryder sucked in a sharp breath. With a jerky movement, he caught her hand, holding it away from his lap. "You had best leave that to me, my lady."

He was grimacing in pain, Eve realized as she met his gaze. Or perhaps not pain. . . . His eyes had gone very dark, she saw, while his voice held a strange huskiness.

But what did she expect, when she had been fondling his *loins,* for mercy's sake?

Her cheeks flushing scarlet at the realization, Eve dropped the napkin as if it were on fire and backed away. "Yes . . . of course . . . please forgive me. I just thought that s-since you had sacrificed your handkerchief earlier, that you would want a n-napkin."

Realizing she was stammering like a flustered schoolgirl—or like Claire at her worst—Eve forced her mouth closed and stood watching ineptly as Ryder took up the napkin and gingerly began patting at his lap.

Swallowing hard, Eve made a valiant effort to compose herself. "I cannot believe how clumsy we both were today, Sir Alex. First I spill ink all over my desk, then Claire drenches you with tea. Do please forgive us."

Ryder's strained smile held no anger as he returned the cup and saucer and napkin to the tray, then rose to his feet. "Pray, think nothing of it—it was a mere accident. But I had best excuse myself and return home to change. Your servant, ladies."

He offered them all a polite bow before turning to the door.

Watching him stride away, Eve remained where she stood, wanting to sink through the Aubusson carpet. She couldn't ever remember being so mortified.

"I am truly sorry, Eve," Claire said in a small voice behind her.

"Don't worry about it, dearest," she replied absently. "Of course you didn't do it on purpose."

Claire's pink face turned an even brighter red,

and she mumbled another apology before she went scurrying from the room.

Her sister, Eve realized, looked as flustered as she felt.

Amazingly enough, however, Beatrice was still calmly attending to her needlework. "I confess, Sir Alex is not what I expected," the elderly lady said rather thoughtfully.

Her pronouncement caught Eve's attention as she moved to ring for Dunstan to clear away the tea tray. "What *did* you expect, Beatrice?"

"Someone less gentlemanly, I suppose. He is not quite the uncivilized brute that Drucilla predicted, even if he *is* an ungodly mercenary."

"No, Sir Alex is not quite a brute," Eve replied, feeling a prick of amusement break through her chagrin.

She supposed Beatrice's reluctant admission was something, even if the rest of the morning had been a complete disaster.

In the aftermath of his visit, Ryder stood on the front steps of Eve's mansion, gritting his teeth as he waited for his overheated pulse to cool. For the past year, Lady Eve had figured prominently in his erotic dreams, but to have her slim fingers pressing against his cock, stroking him just as he'd always imagined. . . .

Ryder closed his eyes, nearly laughing at the irony of it. The delightful shock had almost unmanned him.

Hell, just seeing Eve again after all this time had been a shock, no matter how much he had prepared himself. When he'd walked into the room and spied her sitting there at her desk, his carefully worded speech had fled his mind. And then Eve had looked up at him.

For a moment he'd been deafened by his own heartbeat. His gaze had riveted on the perfect oval of her face sleekly framed by a gold chignon, on her searching blue eyes, and his breath had lodged in his throat.

It had taken a supreme effort of will to pretend a casualness he didn't feel. Eve was still tall and slender and graceful. Yet now instead of merely a beautiful, spirited girl, at twenty-five she was a mature, beautiful, spirited woman. Poised, elegant, infinitely lovely.

And more desirable than ever.

Her enchanting siren's smile, quick and bright as the sun, had brought sharp hunger leaping forth in his body—and forcibly reminded Ryder why he'd fallen so hard for Eve in his youth. The moment he'd seen her, he'd felt as if his heart had suddenly started beating again after a long sleep.

"Devil take it, get hold of yourself, man." Muttering the oath, Ryder pushed away from the door and bounded down the short flight of steps to the street, heading for his house across the square. He halted, however, when he heard Claire calling him.

"Sir Alex! Wait. I need to speak to you."

Turning, he watched as she carefully shut the front door and remained waiting for him on the landing.

Retracing his path, Ryder mounted the marble steps to where Claire stood looking flushed and breathless. "What is it, Lady Claire?"

"I wished to apologize again."

"I told you there was no need. It was merely an accident."

"Well, you see . . . that isn't quite true." Her guilty expression surprised him, as did the way she twisted her fingers together. "I truly didn't *want* to spill tea all over you. I just didn't know what else to do. I had to distract you."

"Distract me?" Ryder's gaze sharpened. "Do you mean to tell me your clumsiness was no accident? That you doused me deliberately?"

Claire hung her head. "I am afraid so. I honestly am sorry, but I didn't want you declaring your intentions, you see."

Ryder took a slow breath. "I confess I don't see, my lady. Why don't you explain it to me?"

She looked at him earnestly. "You cannot propose to Eve just now. It would be a dreadful mistake."

"What makes you think I want to propose?"

"It has been obvious to me for years that you have a tendre for Eve. Whenever you merely speak of her, you get this certain look in your eyes. . . ."

With effort, Ryder managed to keep his features impassive. He'd suspected Lady Claire had been quietly observing for some time, but he hadn't realized she knew.

Just then a carriage went by on the street, the rumble making speech impossible.

"You must understand about Eve, Sir Alex," Claire continued in a low voice when the vehicle had passed.

"What must I understand?" Ryder asked, trying to control his impatience.

"Why she never intends to marry again."

He gave Claire a penetrating glance. "Why?"

"Well, you see . . . even though her marriage to Lord Hayden was considered a brilliant match, I think she was terribly unhappy."

"You *think*?" Ryder demanded, his tone reflexively gruff.

"Well, I don't know for absolute certain, but little things Eve has let slip have painted a picture of despair."

A scowl snapped his eyebrows together. "You don't mean to tell me that bas—" He cut off the foul name he'd started to call the late earl. "That Hayden abused her?"

Claire shook her head. "Not so evil as that. But Eve was miserable all those years of being wed to him, I don't doubt. Hayden was the essence of charm in public, but to Eve, he was cold and heartless. When I came to live with her at Hayden Park, I made friends with the servants, and her abigail told me something about how it was for Eve . . . how Lord Hayden treated her like some exotic songbird in a golden cage, to be forever kept on display. He required her to be perfect at all times. The perfect lady, the perfect wife and hostess, so she would reflect well on him. And his temper turned violent whenever she dared slip."

Claire bit her lip. "You can't imagine how awful that made me feel, knowing the sacrifice Eve made for me . . . for our entire family. She only married Lord Hayden in order to save us from destitution.

It's solely because of Eve that I can even afford a Season and that I have a generous dowry provided by her marriage settlements."

"So you believe she never plans to wed again," Ryder repeated in a rough stranger's voice.

"I *know* it, since she told me so in no uncertain terms. We were discussing my comeout, and when I mentioned the possibility of Eve finding another husband for herself, she was adamantly set against it. Indeed, she only came to London for my sake, to find a good match for me. I have the feeling Eve doesn't care much for the ton or all the trappings of her rank. She is far happier living in the country, setting Hayden Park to rights after Lord Hayden practically let it go to ruin."

"And you are telling me all this because . . . ?"

Taking a deep breath, Claire gazed intently up at him. "Because I felt I *had* to offer you a warning, Sir Alex. If you mean to court Eve, you must approach it subtly. Telling her she is the bride you want is the surest way to frighten her away."

"Thank you, sweetheart," he said after a moment, neither confirming or denying her supposition. "I will keep your warning in mind."

Claire hesitated, clearly wanting to say more. "I just wished you to see why the very thought of another marriage is so distasteful to Eve. That's also why she has devoted herself to matchmaking . . . so other young women don't end up in her situation, in a repugnant marriage of convenience. Especially *me*. Eve is determined that I find a suitor who will make me happy because she was not able to find happiness. The real point, however, is that it will not be easy to persuade her to give up her independence, now that she finally has some measure of it. In marriage, husbands have all the power, and Eve will never subject herself to that powerless state again."

"I see," Ryder said quietly.

"*Do* you see, Sir Alex? Then perhaps you understand why I suggested that you ask Eve to help you find a suitable match."

"You were actually serious about that?"

"Yes, I truly do believe it your best option. If Eve makes it her mission to find you a bride, she won't be able to avoid you. And you will become her pet project—so you won't be so threatening to her."

His eyebrow shot up. "You think I threaten her?"

A sheepish dimple appeared in Claire's cheek. "Well, you must admit you are very . . . forceful. And accustomed to having your own way. You would never be as domineering as Lord Hayden was, but Eve is too skittish even to give you a chance to prove it."

Ryder felt his mouth twist in a dry smile, though he felt little amusement.

"You must allow Eve time to know you better," Claire went on. "I'm certain she will come to care for you as Cecil and I do, but she needs time."

Sweeping off his tall beaver hat, Ryder raked a hand through his hair in frustration. "So you want me to play games with Eve," he stated finally.

"I don't see any other way. She would never allow you close enough to court her otherwise."

Ryder felt his fists clench as he stared off at the distance.

"Well," Claire said, interrupting his dark thoughts. "I had best return inside, or everyone will wonder where I have gone. But please . . . promise me you will at least think about it, Sir Alex."

"I will, sweeting." He made himself look at Claire. "And I do appreciate your warning."

With an uncertain smile, she opened the door and disappeared inside the house, leaving Ryder standing there on the front steps, silently cursing the fact that all his carefully calculated plans had just gone completely to hell.

His frustration was still simmering by the time he reached his bedchamber to change out of his tea-stained breeches.

He sure as the devil hadn't counted on this unexpected setback. Not after plotting his strategy with the care of a military campaign.

For nearly a year now, he'd bided his time, waiting to begin his courtship until Eve was out of mourning. Then finally in March he'd come to London for the express purpose of wooing her.

He had spent the past month reconnoitering and laying the foundations for his entry into the ton, setting himself up for the leisurely life of a gentleman. He'd hired a house directly across from hers, even though he didn't need such luxury or extravagance.

Hell, Ryder thought crossly as he tugged off his expensive, highly polished boots and damp breeches, he'd grown up in a three-room cottage, and he was accustomed to bivouacking in barns and barracks and open fields. But this exorbitant mansion offered close proximity to Eve.

Yet now all his best-laid plans had been thwarted. The only woman he had ever wanted to wed was resolved on remaining husbandless.

Ryder cursed softly. Somehow he would have to change Eve's mind.

He knew he intrigued her; all his male instincts told him so. This morning she'd done her damnedest to appear unaffected, but the lady had been as intensely aware of him as he was of her. Yet that was a far cry from accepting his marriage proposal.

And if Claire was correct about Eve seeing him as a threat . . .

His manservant, Greeves, entered just then. "You rang for me, sir?"

"Yes." Ryder indicated the stained breeches he had tossed on a chair. "I suffered an unfortunate accident with a teacup."

"I will have these cleaned and pressed, sir," Greeves said, picking up the breeches and taking them away.

Alone once more, Ryder finished dressing in fresh pantaloons and went to stand before the cheval glass. Instinctively he knew Claire was right. He couldn't show his hand by baldly declaring his matrimonial intentions to Eve or risk driving her away with an open chase. Instead, he would have to change tactics.

Very well, Ryder decided, turning to purposefully stride out of his bedchamber. He would ask Eve's help in finding him a suitable match, for it would give them time to become more intimately acquainted.

Although it bothered him to conduct his courtship clandestinely, he would cloak his pursuit in the trappings of proper convention, claiming that he was searching for a wife. It was the utter truth, even if Eve was the only wife he would ever want.

Asking her help in finding him a bride from among the haut ton would provide him with a valid reason to be in her company so he could woo her without raising all her defenses.

And the resumption of a simple friendship between them was a good start. If it made Eve feel safer, he would treat her with the same brotherly affection he lavished on the twins.

Even if you feel not at all brotherly toward her.

Ryder let out a harsh chuckle at that vast understatement as he bounded down the sweeping staircase of his new mansion. Eve was a hundred times more vibrant in real life than in his dreams. He could see why she was sought after now by any number of gentlemen. A beautiful, wealthy, noble widow would be an alluring matrimonial prize.

But *he* intended to be the winner. He would pay any price to possess her. Make any sacrifice.

His jaw hardening with determination, Ryder headed for his front door, intending to cross the street again and pay another call on Eve.

Now he just bloody well hoped he could marshal his acting talents enough to hide how he felt for her for the duration of his secret courtship.

To Eve's gratification, she was able to receive Ryder with much less sensation this time. When he was announced, she rose calmly from her writing desk, refusing to be as flummoxed as she'd been during his first call, even though she was again alone in the morning room.

"Sir Alex," she said politely. "I did not expect to see you again so soon."

He waited until her butler had withdrawn before saying, "I've thought about your offer, Countess, and I would like to take you up on it."

"My offer?"

"I want your assistance in finding me a suitable bride."

A ripple of surprise ran through Eve. She had made no such offer; the idea had been solely her sister's. But Ryder did not appear to be jesting, Eve noted as he steadily returned her searching regard.

Warily moving to the sitting area, she offered him a seat. When he resumed his place on the sofa, Eve settled in the armchair across from him, a safe distance away. "Perhaps you should tell me what sort of assistance you had in mind."

With a casual nod, Ryder relaxed against the sofa, stretching his muscular arms out along the high back. "I'm interested in making a marriage of convenience to match my new station. I want to become better accepted by society, and I believe the right wife will aid me."

When Eve frowned, he asked with a half smile, "What, you don't think I can find a genteel lady to be my wife?"

"No, I am merely surprised that you would even wish one. You are the last man I would expect to seek a society marriage."

"At my age, it's time I considered settling down and setting up my nursery."

Eve felt her frown deepen at the thought of Ryder's actually settling down . . . and the more startling concept of his siring children and raising a family. She just couldn't picture it. Nor could she immediately picture the sort of bride who would appeal to him and make him happy.

Still, that didn't explain her instinctive resistance to the idea of Ryder taking a wife.

"I realize," he continued, "how much I could benefit from your aid. My chances of acceptance would increase significantly if someone of your station were to sponsor me—a wealthy lady of rank who moves in the highest circles. You are quite popular with the haut ton. If you were willing, you could ease my way into your set—introduce me to the right people, help me garner invitations to functions where I could meet suitable marital candidates. That sort of assistance."

Eve hesitated to reply, wondering why she felt so discomfited at the thought of helping Ryder. Possibly because if she was to do as he asked—aid his entree into society and assist his search for a bride—she would be in his company far more than was wise.

Yet he was asking very little of her, after all. And he had been such a stalwart champion of the twins all these years that she owed him her allegiance. Of course, Drucilla and Beatrice might raise objections.

"I suppose I could try," Eve said slowly, thinking

ahead to how she could circumvent their opposition.

"If it is too much trouble—"

"No, it isn't that." She would be attending countless entertainments and functions in her role as Claire's sponsor, so it would not be much trouble to include Ryder in their plans. "I was merely considering how I could best handle the aunts."

The corner of Ryder's mouth curved mockingly. "They won't approve of your having anything to do with me."

Eve couldn't help but laugh at that understatement. "True. But then I don't permit them to rule my life or attempt to rule theirs. We rub along well enough—and this will be no exception."

"You would have my profound gratitude," he said lightly.

Still contemplating, she gave an absent nod. There would be other advantages to helping Ryder that weren't apparent at first glance. For one thing, her sister was more comfortable in his company than in any other gentleman's. And he could provide a male escort when needed. As long as the aunts didn't refuse altogether to participate if Ryder joined their party. . . . But she would persuade them, Eve pledged to herself.

"I might be able to help you," she replied finally. "Didn't you say this morning that you have a candidate in mind? Who is the lady?"

Ryder shrugged his broad shoulders. "No one in particular. I expect most any well-bred woman will do."

Eve winced at that. "No, it will *not* do, Sir Alex.

If you must enter into a union of convenience, there is no reason you shouldn't try to make the most harmonious one possible. You don't want to be miserable for the next thirty or forty years of your life, do you?"

"No, certainly I don't," he agreed, obviously amused.

"As I told you earlier, I try to pair couples who have something in common, but . . ."

"But what?"

She eyed him thoughtfully. "I expect it will be something of a challenge to find you a suitable mate."

His eyebrow rose. "Why?"

"You have a rather . . . forceful personality. You will be difficult to match with the young ladies on the marriage mart today."

"You mean that young ladies want a tame lapdog for a husband." Ryder was watching her with that laughing gleam in his eye. "I can play the role of tame lapdog if I put my mind to it."

Tame? Ryder? Her glance turned dubious as it moved over his lean, handsome face, then lower, over his lean, powerful body. That last summer together, she had once spied him without his shirt, and a vision of Ryder as he'd looked then, all corded muscles and bronze bare chest, came to her unbidden.

Feeling her pulse quicken again in a deplorably wild rhythm, Eve forced her gaze back up his face. She doubted Ryder could ever be the least bit tame. Even relaxed, he seemed dangerous, with his smoldering eyes and air of barely leashed male energy.

"I would never liken you to a lapdog," she said

wryly. "You are more like a tiger, and possibly just as dangerous. Some young ladies will find you fascinating, no doubt, just as they would any exotic species. But unfortunately, I expect more will be a bit afraid of you."

His expression sobered. "Is that how you see me, Countess? As someone to fear?"

Eve paused. "Not fear, exactly—because I have a long acquaintance with you. In any event, it doesn't matter how *I* see you. What matters is how you appear to your prospective brides. You will have to tone down the intensity of your manner if you don't want to frighten them away."

"I can manage that. I will be the soul of amiability."

"Amiability is an estimable quality in a husband," Eve said, smothering a smile. "But you must be willing to conform to society's expectations of a gentleman as well."

"Of course. I have already made a concerted effort on that front."

"And you will have to do everything I tell you to, Sir Alex."

"If I do, will you take on my case?"

"Well . . ." Eve hedged.

"You are up to the challenge, aren't you, sweeting? I should imagine it would be a matter of pride, seeing if you can arrange a successful marriage for me. Think what satisfaction you would derive if you were able to find me the perfect mate."

At his deliberate provocation, Eve felt another twinge of exasperation, even as she wondered what sort of woman would make Ryder the perfect mate. He had once proposed to *her,* although he hadn't actually meant it. Would he want someone like her for his bride? But she was confident in her own matchmaking abilities.

"*Yes,* I am up to the challenge," Eve responded archly. "But in return I expect strict obedience from you."

"Very well. I swear to obey your every word." The dancing light returned to his eyes. "Shall we draw up a formal contract?"

"That won't be necessary. As long as you heed my advice, I promise to do my best to find you a bride."

"Good," Ryder said with satisfaction. "Then it is settled." As if unwilling to let her change her mind, he rose to his feet.

Following suit, Eve suddenly shook her head, amazed that she had just agreed to introduce Ryder to society and, more astonishingly, to help him achieve a good match. But she couldn't back out now. "I will see what arrangements I can make and keep you informed."

"Thank you, Countess." He stepped forward to take her hand.

There was nothing in his action she could take exception to, yet her heart suddenly began beating much faster, and it was all she could do to keep from retreating. The mere feel of Ryder's strong, warm hand around hers unsettled her. He was so very male. Eve was keenly aware of him, of his heat, his masculine scent, the dark intensity of his eyes.

For a lingering moment, those eyes rested on her face with a dangerous intimacy. Eve felt her stomach tighten, a natural reaction to being this close to

Ryder. She had a sudden memory of his hard body stretched full length over hers—

With a reflexive shiver, she slid her hand from his grasp and moved to ring for her butler.

"Do you still mean to take the twins to see London tomorrow?" she asked Ryder, striving for a light tone.

"Yes, I am looking forward to our outing. Tell them I will call at eleven in the morning and we will make a day of it."

To her relief, Dunstan appeared just then, carrying a large wicker basket. "These are the foodstuffs Cook prepared for Sir Alex, my lady."

Eve nodded before addressing Ryder. "Would you care to take the basket with you, or would you prefer I have it delivered by a servant?"

Ryder's mouth curved in a grin. "Oh, take it with me, most definitely. I wouldn't want my scones to grow cold."

Eve drew a sharp breath at his infectious smile, holding it in her lungs as Ryder politely took his leave and followed Dunstan from the room.

She stood waiting a moment longer, listening for his departure from her house. When eventually she heard the front door shut, Eve slowly let out her breath, yet she chastised herself as she returned to her writing desk.

The way Ryder's simple nearness affected her was absurd. There was no reason at all for him to unsettle her, since he seemed content to treat her merely as an old friend, just as she'd asked.

Yet dismayingly, being alone with Ryder had stirred long-buried, decidedly dangerous feelings for him.

She found herself unnerved not only by his smoldering intensity but also by her own powerful attraction to him.

Amazing, considering that she had never felt a remotely similar attraction to any other man, including her husband. *Particularly* her husband.

It was inexplicable that she would feel physical longing for Ryder. She was no longer a green girl, as she'd been that summer. She understood precisely what occurred between a man and a woman when they made love, and she had no desire ever to repeat the experience. For her, the marriage bed had been not only unpleasant but painful.

Just as inexplicable was the vague discontent she felt. She didn't regret agreeing to help Ryder find a suitable bride. Yet if she was entirely honest, she would admit to being strangely disappointed that he had no interest in pursuing *her*.

Utterly ridiculous. It was mere vanity on her part, of course. She absolutely did not want Ryder considering her a candidate in his search for a bride.

She would never again enter into the loathsome state of matrimony. She'd been utterly miserable as Richard's prize possession, living under his dictatorial thumb, more chattel than partner.

Eve's jaw tightened as she picked up her pen to resume her correspondence. Her future would be different, she vowed. And freedom was in sight at last.

First, however, she had to focus on getting the twins—especially her sister—happily settled.

Claire would never, *ever* be sold into marriage as she had been. Eve was fiercely determined to give her sister more choices for her future than she herself had been given. If it took the last breath in her body, Claire would have the chance to choose her life's mate. Someone who could make her happy.

The girl's reticence was a drawback on the marriage mart, undeniably. Most gentlemen did not mind her soft-spoken, gentle manner, but her occasional nervous stammer tended to put off potential suitors. She would need a great deal of support and encouragement to make a successful match. But Eve intended to find Claire a husband who would love and cherish her as she deserved.

Eve also hoped to keep her brother out of trouble long enough to get through the Season without scandal and see him safely returned to school in the fall. Perhaps afterward she might be able to use her late husband's connections to find Cecil an occupation that would satisfy his lust for adventure.

Until then, she was willing to subjugate her own personal desires a little while longer.

Once she had Claire safely wed and Cecil settled, however, she intended to live exactly as she pleased. For her entire life she'd done precisely what everyone else wished her to do, bowing first to her parents' dictates and then to her husband's. And for the past year, she'd been confined by the strict conventions of mourning. But soon she would be entirely independent. She would have sole control over her own decisions, could make choices wholly for her own sake, unlike during her dreadful marriage.

But not just yet, Eve reminded herself. Widows were allowed much more liberty than wives, but for the time being, she would have to remain circumspect in all her actions.

Even if she sometimes dreamed of being a little wild and scandalous, she had no intention of indulging her longings. Her obligations as a sister were far more important just now.

She would do nothing to jeopardize Claire's chances of making a perfect match, and that meant not harboring highly dangerous, utterly inappropriate feelings of attraction for Sir Alex Ryder.

Chapter Three

When Ryder returned home, he went straight to his study, intending to enlist the aid of another of his friends and fellow Guardians—Christopher, Viscount Thorne.

Sitting down at his desk, Ryder drew out a sheet of vellum to write a message to Thorne and his beautiful wife, Diana. He might have managed to persuade Eve that he wasn't an immediate threat to her, but he would need more help if he had any hope of winning her for his bride.

For a moment Ryder paused, his pen going still. His mind was full of vibrant images of Eve. Her warm laughter, her tempting smile, her purely feminine response to him. Remembering how she had shivered when he took her hand, Ryder couldn't prevent his body from tightening with hunger.

He shook himself and began to write. He wasn't looking forward to trying to sleep tonight, however.

Now that he had seen Eve in the flesh, had touched her and felt her touch in return, he knew his dreams of her would be all the more vivid—which, damnably, would only make slumber an exercise in torment.

* * *

That night, to Eve's dismay, she dreamed of Ryder and woke in a restless tangle of sheets. She lay there in the early morning light, attempting to ignore the throbbing warmth that suffused her body and the improper, vivid images of Ryder that still lingered in her mind. Growing vexed with herself, she rose and dressed without calling her abigail.

She breakfasted alone, since no one else was up yet, and did her best to avoid glancing out the windows at Ryder's house across the square.

As soon as possible, Eve escaped to the morning room. She'd always taken pleasure in working here, attending to her correspondence and accounts. The room offered a brightness that cheered her even on London's frequently gray days—days that reminded her how much she missed the brilliant sunshine of Cyrene. The fact that Richard had rarely joined her here was an added benefit that Eve acknowledged only to herself.

Since the twins shared her love of sunlight, the family tended to congregate here during much of the day and even entertained casual visitors.

Settling comfortably on the settee, Eve picked up the morning paper and immediately let out a mild oath. Her eye had skimmed over the society column and a name had leaped out at her: *Sir Alex Ryder.*

"It seems you cannot escape him," she muttered before proceeding to read about the gala event that Sir Alex had attended the previous evening in the company of his intimate friends, Lord and Lady Thorne. Ryder apparently was a delicious topic of gossip for the Beau Monde.

Last night Eve had experienced a similar reaction when she'd taken the twins to a small rout party. She'd been questioned relentlessly by her own friends, who had discovered she was a longtime acquaintance of Ryder's and who wanted a firsthand account of him.

She used the opportunity to speak highly of him, and soon had at least a dozen ladies and gentlemen asking to meet him. Surprisingly enough, it seemed Ryder was already considered a prime target for matrimony, in part *because* of his exotic past.

Even more oddly, Eve had felt a twinge of what absurdly could only be called jealousy, seeing the flashes of interest and even excitement in the eyes of her female acquaintances.

Jealousy would never do if she was to assist Ryder with his bride search; she would have to avoid emotional entanglements of any kind.

Eve finished perusing the rest of the newspaper just as her butler brought her three gilded cards of invitation that had been hand-delivered by a footman rather than by the morning post. All three were from Viscount and Lady Thorne.

The nobleman and his lovely wife, Diana, were holding a soiree to honor the knighthood of Sir Alex Ryder the following Friday. Also included was a personal note from Diana, saying that she would be delighted if Eve and the twins would attend.

The other two cards were addressed to Lady Wykfield and Lady Beatrice Townley. Apparently the aunts had each received a personal invitation, a fact that brought a smile to Eve's lips. It was a clever strategy, since the elderly ladies would be less likely to refuse if they were accorded the respect they believed was their due.

She had underestimated the strength of their convictions, however. Eve was folding her invitation when her family joined her after having finished breakfast.

Cecil practically pounced on the cards and waved them in the air with glee before recollecting his manners and formally presenting the aunts with theirs. "Sir Alex told me we would be invited to Lady Thorne's party to celebrate his knighting."

Claire smiled. "We will be attending, won't we, Eve?"

"I wouldn't miss it," she replied, watching the aunts peruse their invitations. "Will you accompany us, Drucilla?"

"Certainly not." With two fingers, the elderly lady dropped her card on the side table as if it bore an unpleasant odor. "I have no intention of honoring that upstart with my presence."

Beatrice, wearing her habitual air of distraction, nodded in agreement, as usual following Drucilla's lead. "It would set entirely the wrong example."

"Indeed," Drucilla added. "You are making a grave mistake, Eve, with this foolish scheme to find him a bride. Your reputation will only suffer for it."

Eve bit back a sigh of exasperation. "I should hope my standing is secure enough to risk it," she said sweetly.

She had broken the news to the aunts yesterday afternoon, declaring her intention of conducting a bride search for Ryder. Drucilla had vociferously tried to talk her out of it and refused outright Eve's request to present Sir Alex to society under their auspices.

The twins, on the other hand, had expressed delight and even offered to help.

"Perhaps Lady Thorne could act on his behalf," Beatrice said to Eve now, "instead of you, my dear."

Eve shook her head. "Lady Thorne is fairly new to London herself and is much less familiar with the debutantes who would make suitable candidates than I am. She also has a flourishing career as an artist, which occupies most of her time."

At the word *artist*, Drucilla sniffed in disdain, yet she could hardly protest Lady Thorne's vocation, since the viscountess's remarkable talents as a portraiturist were in great demand by the ton.

"I thought we would do well to begin immediately," Eve said. "I sent Sir Alex a message, asking him to arrive a bit early this morning before he takes Cecil and Claire on their excursion."

Drucilla's eyebrow arched in disdain. "What time does he intend to call?"

"Ten o'clock."

"Very well. But if you insist on this mad scheme, Eve, then Beatrice and I will remain here with you. You will not entertain that man alone."

"You are welcome to join us," Eve said pleasantly, refraining from arguing, since Drucilla's remaining would allow her the opportunity to meet Ryder and judge him for herself.

It was precisely ten when Eve heard the faint rap of the door knocker. All her muscles tensed while her siblings looked around eagerly.

The twins had already changed clothes for their outing and had gathered with her in the morning room. As usual, Claire was quietly reading while Cecil paced the floor. Both aunts were occupied with their tambour frames, and both studiously ignored Ryder when he was shown into the room.

Eve, however, felt her pulse leap inexplicably at the sight of him, while her body became instantly aware.

She was glad when her brother advanced to greet Ryder and pump his hand with enthusiasm. She and Claire rose, smiling in welcome, but both aunts remained rooted to the settee. When Eve made Ryder known to the elderly ladies, Drucilla lifted a lorgnette to her sharp blue eyes and surveyed him coldly.

Ryder certainly looked the part of a gentleman. The tailoring of his charcoal-gray coat was clearly Weston and fitted elegantly across his strong shoulders, his silver-gray pantaloons were spotless, and his starched cravat was artfully arranged. Yet he still appeared a little dangerous, his tanned skin and dark eyes a stark contrast to the pristine white linen at his throat.

Giving the aunts a formal bow, he offered one of his rare, sensual smiles. "I am honored to meet you at last, Lady Wykfield. Cecil and Lady Claire have told me much about you. And my patron, Sir Gawain Olwen, sends you his regards. Sir Gawain knew your esteemed late husband and spoke highly of him."

With the coldest of nods, the noble dame gave a derisive sniff and returned to her embroidery, making it clear that Ryder was not considered worthy of notice.

Eve stiffened, chagrined and embarrassed by Drucilla's rudeness. Ryder did not seem to take umbrage, however, but merely pressed on. "How kind of you to permit Lady Hayden to assist me in my bride quest."

Drucilla raised her chin regally to look along her nose at him. "I most certainly have not given my permission for this mad scheme."

"Even so, your condescension is much appreciated, my lady. You could make it very difficult for me if you chose to."

There was no sign of mockery in his bland tone, but Drucilla eyed him with suspicion. "Flattery will get you nowhere with me, sirrah."

"I did not imagine it would. You are set against me from the start—a natural reaction, to be sure," Ryder said in a lazy drawl. "I can fully comprehend your reservations and even commend you for your defense of Lady Hayden and the twins. But you could not be more protective of them than I am, Lady Wykfield. I can promise you, I would rather cut off a limb than bring them harm."

"Then you should reconsider dragging Lady Hayden into your affairs," Drucilla retorted, keeping her spine rigid. "It will do her reputation immense harm."

Ryder's smile held a disarming charm. "I am loath to contradict a lady, particularly one of your venerable years. So I will merely beg to disagree. I understand that I must win you over, Lady Wykfield—which is why I have brought you and Lady Beatrice these."

He held out the two parcels he was carrying, both wrapped in gold tissue. "I would be pleased if you would accept this token of my esteem. Lady Claire advised me on what you might like."

"I do not accept gifts from perfect strangers," Drucilla announced scornfully.

Eve sucked in a breath at her virulence. Snobbery was one thing, but this acid scorn from Drucilla was totally uncalled for.

Yet Ryder merely smiled into her eyes with cool aplomb. "Ah, but we are hardly strangers, my lady. Considering my close relationship with the twins, you and I are practically like family." Moving forward, he placed the gifts on the table in front of the aunts. "Moreover, Lady Hayden holds you in great affection. I understand that your company has made her year of mourning bearable. So I intend to do everything in my power to make myself agreeable to you."

The elderly lady remained unbending, even when Beatrice sent her a nervous glance.

Eve was about to intervene when Claire said softly, "Aunt Drucilla, Sir Alex went to a great deal of trouble to search for gifts that you would enjoy. I do think you will like them."

"Yes, Aunt Dru," Cecil chimed in, "you should at least open your presents."

The scathing look she sent the boy was withering. "Pray do not address me in that vulgar way, young man."

"Beg pardon," Cecil replied unrepentantly as he waited for the aunts to act. "Well, I will open them if you won't."

Lunging for the gifts before anyone could stop him, Cecil tore open both packages and laid them on the table in front of the aunts. Ryder, Eve saw, had brought an assortment of silk threads for Beatrice and a small pair of gold scissors on a chain for Drucilla—practical gifts as well as lovely and thoughtful.

Beatrice gave a secret smile of pleasure at hers, but Drucilla merely scowled.

"If Eve wishes to recklessly risk her reputation by participating in this absurd plan, I cannot stop her. Nor will I attempt to argue with her further. I have said all I intend to on the subject."

"I highly doubt that," Ryder returned with a murmur of laughter.

"I'll thank you to show proper respect for your betters!" the lady ground out. "I request that you leave this house at once."

Eve had had enough. "Drucilla, we mean to discuss a few matters regarding Sir Alex's requirements for a bride, but you must have more pressing matters to attend to. Pray don't let us keep you."

"Yes, Lady Wykfield," Ryder seconded. "I understand if you choose to go. But I would be pleased if you would remain and offer your assistance."

"You cannot possibly expect me to support you!" she exclaimed in astonishment.

"Expect, no. Wish for? Yes. And before you wash your hands of me, you might consider the benefit to Lady Hayden if you are seen to be behind her efforts."

"It is hardly proper for her to be involved with you so intimately, widowed or not."

"All the more reason for you to throw your weight behind her. Surely your consequence will shield her from the tarnish of my reputation."

"It is not merely your reputation that alarms me, but your character. You cannot scrub such blackness and turn it to lily white simply by purchasing a title!"

"Of course not. But you might examine all the evidence before condemning my character out of hand. If you mean to judge me, then surely you can attempt to be just and fair and allow me a chance to earn your good opinion."

The noble lady stared, clearly seething. Eve had to bite back a smile. Drucilla had obviously met her match in Ryder. Of course the elderly dame had no intention of surrendering, but she was still determined to remain in order to chaperone. She sat in tight-lipped silence as Eve graced Ryder with a smile and invited him to be seated across the room.

When the twins had settled near him, Eve fetched the lists she had been working on, then joined them.

"If we are to find you a suitable match," Eve said, pencil poised to write, "I think we should begin by listing your requirements in a wife. I need to understand what type of lady you are specifically looking for."

Ryder pursed his lips thoughtfully. "I expect I will be satisfied with anyone who meets your standards."

"But surely you have some requirements—age, appearance, fortune, rank?"

"I'm not too particular. I leave it to you, my lady." Ryder paused before offering Eve an apologetic smile. "Actually, I do have one stipulation. Ideally I would like a wife who isn't obsessed with social status or overly concerned with appearances. My mother comes to mind. She was a gentlewoman, but she gave up her position in society to wed the man she loved—a common British soldier. I would be fortunate if I could find a woman like her."

At that Drucilla gave a disdainful sniff, although she kept her penetrating gaze focused on her embroidery.

Ryder's smile grew cool. "I fully understand the difficulty any bride of mine will face. My own mother suffered because she married beneath her—which is why my bride must have the courage to defy the ton for my sake."

Eve felt herself go still, wondering if Ryder was alluding to her. She had not been willing to defy society for him all those years ago. But then she'd had little choice, with her family facing disaster.

"You would be satisfied with someone like Eve, I expect," Cecil interjected into the silence.

Ryder eyed Eve thoughtfully. "Your sister does resemble the type of bride I am looking for." When Eve suddenly froze, he flashed a grin. "That was not a proposal of marriage, Countess. I was simply stating my preferences, as you asked. I doubt I will find any lady who could compare to you."

"That is likely true," Claire said quickly. "Eve is considered a diamond of society."

"But that isn't her best quality," Cecil added. "She makes a fellow feel comfortable, that's what."

"True," his twin agreed. "No one has her flair for

setting people at ease or her polish among company."

"Please stop, you two," Eve said, feeling a blush rise to her cheeks. "I am hardly the paragon you are describing."

Claire replied with a sigh, "I wish I had even a tiny bit of your ease and polish, Eve."

"You will. It simply takes practice. I have had years to hone my drawing-room skills. Now enough about me. We are here to discuss finding Ryder a bride." Eve glanced down at her lists. "I should also like to review your qualifications as a prospective husband so I can be certain to present you in the best possible light when I introduce you to marital candidates."

Ryder's eyebrow shot up. "You can hardly expect me to boast about my laurels. How ungentlemanly that would be."

Cecil gave a snort of laughter while his twin hid a smile. "I think Sir Alex has admirable qualifications," Claire said firmly. "He is very handsome and manly, for one thing."

Eve sent Claire a curious glance, surprised that her demure young sister would have the nerve to comment on a man's physical endowments.

"You can add courageous," Cecil broke in. "He's a genuine hero. And filthy rich. He's the possessor of an immense fortune."

"And kind," Claire added softly, favoring Ryder with a sweet smile.

Eve paused in her writing, her expression bemused. She had not included kindness on her initial list, but it was indeed one of Ryder's best qualities.

His warm friendship with the twins was clear evidence of his genuine kindness. He spoke to Cecil as an equal, with none of the condescension that would have mortified a young man of nineteen. And Ryder drew Claire out of her shell so that she lost her shyness—which no male except her brother seemed able to do.

"Ah, yes, I am a virtual saint to children and animals," Ryder admitted, his voice smooth and amused.

"And bold," Cecil added. With a swift glance across the room, he lowered his voice in a stage whisper. "How many chaps do you know who would go up against Aunt Drucilla?"

At that, Drucilla's head came up, and she shot the boy a regal glare, but Cecil only flashed an innocent grin.

Boldness was indeed a cornerstone of Ryder's character, Eve acknowledged, contemplating him thoughtfully.

"What?" he asked, interrupting her reflections. "I have to temper my boldness as well as my intensity?"

Eve hesitated. She herself admired Ryder's boldness, but then she'd been reared in the less sheltered society of Cyrene and had known him since she was a girl.

"You should attempt it," she said seriously, "since boldness can be intimidating to young ladies fresh out of the schoolroom. There is an *art* to courting, Sir Alex," Eve added more lightly. "The most appealing suitor is a model of devotion and charm, dancing attendance upon the ladies as if they were the sole reason for his existence. And you will have to learn to conduct a polished flirtation in the accepted style of London drawing rooms."

Ryder feigned a shudder. "My soul shrivels at the prospect."

A smile curved her lips. "But you promised to heed my advice," she reminded him.

"So I did."

Still smiling, Eve gathered her lists and rose to her feet. "Well, I think that is enough for one morning. I should be able to make up a list of suitable candidates to review with you. Now, why don't you and the twins go on your outing?"

Cecil jumped up with alacrity, already having grown restless with the lack of activity. Eve knew how eager he was to escape the household of females, and more keenly, to appear a man about town.

She hoped he behaved himself, and that he would remain close to his sister to ensure propriety. Since Ryder was to be their sole chaperone for the day, she had arranged to have her own abigail, Janet, attend Claire for the afternoon, but she wanted the chance to tactfully phrase her concerns to Ryder.

When Claire went to fetch her bonnet and pelisse and Cecil his hat and gloves, Eve accompanied him to the front door.

"It is kind of you," she murmured then, "to pay Cecil and Claire such attention and take them sightseeing when you must have more important matters to occupy your time."

Ryder shook his head. "Kindness has little to do with it. I am glad for their company. I have few acquaintances in London whom I really enjoy, as I do the twins. Are you certain you won't come with us?"

She wished she *could* accompany them, since it was sure to be pleasurable. "I cannot, I'm afraid, since I am already pledged to make several calls with the aunts. But I hope you will keep a close eye on Cecil. He is always ripe for trouble."

"I promise I will watch over them like a mother hen," Ryder said.

Eve hesitated. "And I trust you will have a care for Claire's reputation. It will not do for her to be seen alone about town with you."

A wry smile flickered at the corner of Ryder's mouth. "How well I know."

Just then the twins joined them with Janet in tow.

"Eve is more protective than any mama hen," Cecil apologized to Ryder, evidently having overheard her warning.

"Perhaps so," Eve retorted lightly, "but I am acting in place of your mother. Mama conferred the duty on me when she sent you here."

"I am old enough to take care of myself," Cecil complained.

Reaching up affectionately, Eve smoothed an errant lock of her brother's blond hair back into place. "Then pray devote your efforts to looking after your sister."

"I know," he said, rolling his eyes. "Claire is exactly my age, but she's a *girl.*"

" 'A lady's reputation is a fragile thing,' " Claire quoted their mother in an arch tone before wrinkling her nose. "Mama does not wholly approve of my friendship with Sir Alex, either, but I would not shun a friend simply to accommodate society's stuffy opinions—any more than Eve would."

Ryder shot Eve an amused glance. "It seems your radical notions have rubbed off on your sister," he remarked.

At the devils dancing in his eyes, Eve felt her breath falter, while her heart did another deplorable little somersault. She took a reflexive step back, unable to manage a reply other than to wish them a good outing.

She watched as Ryder, after giving her a brief bow, whisked the twins and maid out of the house to his waiting town carriage. Then Eve returned to the morning room.

She was glad he was gone, for she felt absurdly unnerved by his intense masculinity, even when he was behaving with perfect propriety.

"At last he is gone," Drucilla echoed when Eve entered the room. "I cannot believe you entertained that man longer than the correct fifteen minutes, Eve."

"He seems quite well spoken, at least," Beatrice observed. "His manners are most amiable."

Drucilla shot her sister a sharp look. "Surely you have not allowed yourself to be taken in by that sly devil."

Pressing her lips together stubbornly, Beatrice clipped a thread with her sister's new gold scissors. "I suppose I have at that. I may be getting old and dotty, Drucilla, but I can still appreciate a fine figure of a man. And you must admit Sir Alex is that. He is a striking fellow—in a dark, rakish sort of way."

"I will admit nothing of the kind," Drucilla said,

stiffening. "But I can see there is to be no reasoning with you. *Either* of you."

With a disdainful glance at Eve, Drucilla rose and swept from the room.

Muttering mutinously under her breath, Beatrice made a face at her sister's retreating back, then caught herself and sent Eve a sheepish look. "After this morning, Eve, I am no longer certain you are making such a grave mistake with Sir Alex, as Drucilla believes. But of course my opinion matters little. You had best determine a way to win her over, for we will have no peace in this house otherwise."

"I know, Beatrice," Eve said solemnly, though finding it hard not to smile.

Her rebellion short-lived, Beatrice gathered up her embroidery, including Ryder's gifts, and stood.

When Beatrice had followed her sister from the room, Eve couldn't help laughing softly to herself as she resumed her place at her writing desk. Ryder had made a conquest, she was certain. Even the elderly Lady Beatrice was not immune to his masculine appeal—any more than *she* was.

Drucilla, on the other hand, was a force to be reckoned with, for once she had made up her mind, it was difficult to change. She was just as opinionated as her only nephew had been, perhaps more so.

Eve's smile suddenly faded at the thought of her late husband. Richard, for all his vaunted rank and power, had been a cold, unfeeling man, focused only on his own desires. He'd purchased her as a broodmare and hostess and expected her to be nothing more than an ornament for his arm, pretty but entirely useless.

Granted, he took pride in her social skills and found great pleasure in showing her off to his peers. For the Earl and Countess of Hayden, London had been an endless glittering round of balls and dinners and fetes, a milieu in which Eve excelled, since she had been raised from birth to be a nobleman's wife. At the Hayden family seat in Hertfordshire, she was allowed to play lady of the manor, delivering jellies and dispensing small boons to the tenant farmers.

From all outward appearances, her life of grandeur and gaiety had seemed perfect. But it was a facade, an empty existence that had no heart, no soul, no meaning.

Since Richard's death, Eve had tried to make up in small measure for all those wasted years, striving to make a contribution that would benefit people other than herself.

Richard had never understood or condoned her longing to achieve something of more value than planning the next party. To him, her worth had been measured solely by the social consequence she had brought him. That, and her ability to carry on his bloodline by giving him a son and heir—which sorrowfully had never happened.

It was a failure that Richard had never let her forget. She'd endured his haranguing in silence, but her biggest regret was that she had never conceived.

Remembering how her hopes had ultimately shriveled and died, Eve stared blindly down at the notes in her hand. She had always wanted children, but she was likely barren. Thus there was no sound reason for her ever to reenter the prison of matrimony.

She had resigned herself to reality—that the best years of her life were over, devoted to a marriage of convenience that had been infinitely more convenient for her husband than for her.

Stop it! Eve commanded herself silently. *You cannot spend the rest of your life dwelling on the past.*

She had vowed that she wouldn't look back or punish herself for making the only choice possible at the time, even if sometimes she ached for what she had given up.

Eve suddenly shook herself out of her morose thoughts. The sudden quiet of the house had left her feeling a bit blue-deviled, that was all.

She was perfectly content with her life now. She had Richard's aunts and the twins to keep her company. She had no reason to feel lonely, even if the twins were a little too young and the aunts a little too old to be kindred spirits. She had numerous acquaintances, many of whom she called true friends. And she could keep herself occupied with an estimable ambition, giving her sister the life she herself had missed: the opportunity to make a match based on mutual respect and caring.

Now she also had to inventory prospective brides for Ryder. The task might actually be enjoyable if she could manage to quell her unwonted attraction for him.

From now on, though, she would maintain a proper reserve between them while she focused solely on fulfilling her pledge.

Fortunately there was no reason for her to become more intimately involved with Ryder than she already was. She had defended him to the aunts this morning, even when he hadn't needed defending, but he'd proven he was perfectly capable of fighting his own battles.

It remained only for her to identify suitable marital candidates and introduce him. Then she could step out of the way and let him pursue a courtship on his own . . . no matter the hollow, unsettling pang of discontent that prospect gave her.

Until then, she intended to keep her guard up with Ryder, so there would be no repetitions of these ridiculous feminine yearnings he stirred in her.

"I think you have made a good beginning with Eve," Claire murmured softly as she stood with Ryder at a parapet wall of the Tower of London.

Thus far, Cecil had failed to properly chaperone his twin sister as he'd promised, having raced off numerous times to investigate sights that caught his interest. At the moment the lad was pointing out the River Thames below to the awed maidservant, Janet, leaving Claire alone with Ryder. Yet they were surrounded by a crowd of sightseers, so there was no real impropriety.

"Good enough, I suppose," Ryder agreed, smiling without humor. All during his interview with Eve this morning, he'd felt himself chafing at the game he was being forced to play with her. "It goes against the grain, though, to enact such a deception on your sister."

"But it is for a good cause," Claire replied. "You will never win her otherwise."

His humor improving, he glanced down at Claire.

"You are very wise for a girl of your age, aren't you, my lady?"

She dimpled prettily. "I think I might be, at least in this instance. But I know you will make Eve happy in the long run, unlike her first husband, who saw her only as a prize possession. You want Eve to be happy, isn't that so, Sir Alex?"

"Yes, of course I want her to be happy."

"Well then, you must try to be patient and let things take their course."

With those quiet words, Claire moved away to join Cecil and Janet, leaving Ryder rooted to the spot. Emotion came to him in an uncomfortable flood as he stood mired in his own reflections.

Before hearing Claire's confidences yesterday, he had never really considered how Eve had fared in her marriage—whether or not she was happy. He'd been too virulently jealous to allow himself to contemplate her life with another man. It galled him to think that the bastard who'd purchased her had treated her as some prize possession.

And yet haven't I done the same? Ryder reflected, his chest constricting with unfamiliar guilt.

For nearly half his lifetime, he'd been driven by a primitive need to possess Eve. Admittedly, he'd always thought of her as a golden princess in an ivory tower, an object to be won. Not a mortal flesh-and-blood woman with hopes and desires and dreams of her own. Dreams that had been shattered when she was compelled to marry to save her family. As bitter as he'd been at the time, Ryder acknowledged, he'd had to respect her for making such a sacrifice.

But had he ever really considered *her* happiness? What *she* wanted?

His fingers gripped the parapet as he realized how badly he wanted for Eve to be happy. And for the first time ever, he was feeling qualms about his own selfish motives for winning her hand in marriage. He'd been determined to prove his social legitimacy, and more keenly, to satisfy his physical desire for Eve. Both reasons made him no better than her bloody late husband.

A soft oath escaped Ryder's lips at the guilt knifing him. He didn't want to push Eve into another marriage of convenience. He wanted her to wed him of her own free will. Yet his task would be far harder than he'd ever imagined, given the substantial defenses Eve had erected around herself.

Just then Claire glanced over her shoulder, her searching gaze meeting his. Ryder sent her a faint smile of reassurance before his jaw knotted.

Despite his reservations about the deception, he knew how critical it was to camouflage his pursuit of Eve and was indeed glad that he'd agree to a clandestine strategy of courting her.

One thing was certain, though. If he hoped to win Eve for his own, he would have to begin by showing her that he wasn't like her bastard husband or any of the other covetous men who were avidly pursuing her now that she was widowed. But for damned sure, he had to start figuring out how he could achieve Eve's happiness rather than simply trying to realize his own.

Chapter Four

The dream was different this time. Eve's pleasure was his only purpose.

Laying her down on the sun-warmed grass, he used his hands and mouth until she was gasping for breath, pleading with him to take her. He felt a tantalizing gentleness wrap around his heart when she responded so ardently. Eve was panting for him, clutching fiercely at his shoulders, throwing her head back in wild abandon, sobbing with joy as he plunged inside her. Moments later she cried out, a high, keening pleasure sound. Desire surged through him, as intense as any he'd ever felt—

Ryder woke suddenly, his heart racing, his body pulsing, his erection throbbing. When he recognized his new bedchamber in the gray light of dawn, he grimaced and let his head fall back against the pillows.

His body still ached with hunger for Eve. A fire still smoldered low in his belly, swelling his groin, while beneath the sheets, his manhood strained in hot, unrelieved arousal.

With resignation, Ryder wrapped his fingers around his heavy shaft and stroked in hard, quick rhythm, at the same time recalling his dream: how he had made Eve sob with ecstasy, how he had given her happiness.

The fantasy took him by storm, and in only a moment he was shuddering with physical release, his hot seed spurting violently into his hand as he spent himself in scalding bursts.

Yet the relief was only temporary, Ryder knew, gritting his teeth to contain his ragged breaths. The explosion powerful but not fulfilling. His desire for Eve was undiminished.

Because nothing would ever satisfy him except having her for his own.

When he was admitted to Eve's house across the square three hours later, Ryder was surprised to be shown not to the cheerful morning parlor but to the formal drawing room, which bespoke elegance and wealth from the gilded plasterwork to the excellent paintings to the brocade and gilt furniture.

It was because Eve already had a caller, Ryder deduced, feeling his hackles rise. A tall, beefy, fair-haired gentleman sat on the settee next to her, attempting to hold her hand, even in view of her entire family.

She rose immediately when Ryder entered and came forward with a smile that was tinged with relief.

"How good of you to join us, Sir Alex," Eve declared, her greeting holding genuine warmth. "I wanted to thank you for taking Claire and Cecil on their outing yesterday."

Once again Ryder felt struck by a gut-clenching awareness. Eve looked impossibly bright and fresh, wearing a rose-colored morning gown that flattered her perfect figure, with her gleaming mass of tawny hair swept up casually and held in place by a ribbon.

"I trust you won't mind the imposition, Lady Hayden," Ryder said truthfully. "The workmen at my house are creating such a racket that I hoped to take refuge here for a while."

"But of course."

After Ryder had been welcomed by the twins (eagerly) and acknowledged by the aunts (barely), Eve introduced him to the other caller. George, Viscount Gyllford, owned the vast estates adjacent to Hayden Park in Hertfordshire, Ryder was aware. Both twins had warned him that Lord Gyllford had been trying to woo Eve for months, even before she had left off mourning—"to get a jump on the competition," in Cecil's words.

Ryder disliked the nobleman on sight, his reaction stemming primarily from jealousy but partly from distaste. Eve's country neighbor was dressed as a tulip of fashion, in blindingly bright colors with shirt points so absurdly high, he could barely move his head.

After staring at Ryder dismissively and waiting for him to be seated, his lordship returned to the subject they had been discussing, adopting a tone of simpering charm. "As I was saying, Evelyn, you must come for a drive with me and try out my new prads. You will enjoy them, I have no doubt."

Ryder saw her wince at Gyllford's casual form of address. "Evelyn", he knew, was her full name, but she'd always preferred to be called Eve.

"I am certain I would, my lord," she replied lightly, "since you have such excellent taste in horseflesh. But I fear my schedule keeps me so busy of late that I have not a single moment to spare. I hope you will forgive me," she added with a smile so winsome that Gyllford obviously found it difficult to protest. "In any event, the weather does not appear to be cooperating with your desire for a drive." Tilting her head toward the windows, Eve called attention to the chill drizzle trickling down the panes.

She did not return to the settee to sit beside his lordship, but instead moved over to the bellpull to ring for fresh tea and then stood near the hearth fire, holding out her hands as if seeking warmth.

She was uncomfortable with Viscount Gyllford's proprietary air, Ryder realized.

Recognizing his own possessive instincts, he repressed the urge to go to Eve's side, as if guarding his property, and forced himself to settle casually back in his chair. When the aunts, who as usual were busy sewing on their tambour frames, took up the topic of the weather, with Lady Claire chiming in softly now and then after controlling her initial stammer, Ryder let the conversation flow around him, content to watch Eve.

Her natural setting was a drawing room. Yet underneath her elegant, gracious air, he sometimes caught a tantalizing glimpse of another woman entirely, a woman of passion and courage and fire.

All his muscles tightened as he remembered the rawly sexual dreams he'd experienced for most of the past night. Feeling heat spread through him to pool in his groin, Ryder shifted uncomfortably in his seat. It was with a sense of relief that he realized a footman had entered the drawing room, bearing a fresh pot of hot tea.

Claire courteously poured tea for Ryder and more reluctantly for Lord Gyllford when the viscount held out his cup. At least another twenty minutes passed before Gyllford finally took his leave.

The nobleman made a great show of gallantry, lauding the aunts before moving over to the hearth to corner Eve, bending over her hand to kiss it and ignoring her subtle attempts to pull free.

Ryder felt a savage urge to plant his fist in the fawning peer's face, but with effort, he managed to tamp it down and remain civilized.

Cecil, however, was not so sanguine. The moment Gyllford left the drawing room, the boy gave a snort of disgust. "Of all the insufferable toad-eaters . . . how can you bear to let him simper over you like that, Eve?"

Lady Wykfield spoke before Eve could respond. "His lordship has exquisite manners, young man. You would do well to emulate him."

Scowling, Cecil jumped to his feet. "Exquisite—hah! Surely you noticed that he overstayed his welcome by more than a half hour, Aunt Dru. We could not get rid of him. How is that mannerly—for him to refuse to take the hint that he is not wanted here?"

"Do not be impertinent!" Drucilla snapped.

Cecil had obviously taken a violent dislike to the viscount, Ryder realized. But it was Eve's opinion that concerned him most.

"Has Gyllford been in London long?" he asked casually.

"He just arrived this week for the Season," Eve replied.

Cecil snorted. "He is mainly here to court Eve. His lordship won't stop hounding her," he explained to Ryder. "It's no wonder she brought us to London early—to get away from that man-milliner. She has already refused one marriage proposal from him, but he's oblivious to the fact that she wants nothing to do with him."

"Cecil, that is quite enough," Eve said with an edge of embarrassment. "You need not air our personal affairs in front of Sir Alex."

"Well, he already knows Gyllford is courting you, because I told him so. And I think you would be wise to use Sir Alex to help you fend off that popinjay's unwanted advances."

Drucilla intervened then. "Eve will do no such thing. Lord Gyllford is a highly respectable suitor."

"Oh, yes," Cecil agreed with a revolted grimace. "He has an excellent pedigree and vast estates. Too bad he so sadly lacks brains."

At Drucilla's haughty stare, Cecil finally fell silent, apparently realizing he had gone a step too far in his denunciation of the viscount. With a dismissive sniff, the elderly dowager turned her attention to Eve. "His lordship would make a good second husband for you, my dear."

It was Eve's turn to wince. "I can understand why you might believe so, Drucilla, but I have no intention of marrying Lord Gyllford or any other man."

A frown appeared between Lady Beatrice's eyes.

"You are still young, Eve. Of course you will marry again."

Eve gave the younger aunt an exasperated smile. "I know you only wish my happiness, but I assure you, I am perfectly content to remain a widow."

"Well, I am glad you are here in London now," Beatrice said, "where you can mix in proper society for the Season. Who knows? You might find a gentleman who can persuade you to change your mind."

"I am glad as well," Drucilla observed. "London will be safer for you than the country, I sincerely trust."

"Safer?" Ryder asked curiously.

"It is nothing," Eve replied. "I met with a mishap or two in Hertfordshire shortly before leaving to come here."

Beatrice frowned again. "They were more serious than mere mishaps, Eve, you know very well."

Ryder glanced at Eve, waiting for an explanation, but it was Claire who responded in a troubled tone. "The first was a wolf trap set in the path where Eve frequently walks. And then a stray gunshot in the woods came close to hitting her while she was riding."

"They were simply accidents," Eve said. "They could have happened to anyone. I was never in any real danger."

Cecil gave another snort, this one of disbelief. "That trap was deadly enough to maim you for life. And the shot could have killed you."

"I expect a poacher was at work," she insisted. "No doubt he took himself off as soon as our steward initiated a search for the culprit."

Ryder felt himself frowning, not quite satisfied with that explanation. Both incidents could indeed have been lethal, and the thought of Eve maimed, or worse, dead, made his blood run cold.

Apparently Cecil concurred. "They might," the boy murmured to Ryder, "have been mere accidents, but I confess they worried me. I have been keeping a closer eye on Eve ever since, and I would be obliged if you would do the same, Sir Alex."

"Of course," he agreed, all his own protective instincts aroused.

Eve had heard her brother, however, and immediately protested. "There is no need for anyone to watch over me."

Cecil shook his head. "It won't hurt for Sir Alex to be on the lookout. Protecting people is his profession, after all."

Lady Beatrice eyed Ryder thoughtfully, and even Drucilla turned to scrutinize him with something other than disdain.

"Very well then," Eve said with a hint of exasperation. "You may both play at guarding me, if it will comfort you. But perhaps now we could change this morbid subject?"

"What subject might we discuss?" Ryder asked amiably.

"I thought we might plan your social debut."

Ryder's eyebrow shot up. "My debut? You intend to treat me as a debutante?"

Eve responded to his wry question with an arch smile. "Of course. The strategy we employ for you will be scarcely any different than for a young lady such as Claire. We must make certain you are introduced to appropriate candidates in a setting that will show you to best advantage. The ideal time to launch your campaign to win a bride, I suspect, will be Lord and Lady Thorne's soiree this Friday. What better way to show you off than at a gathering to honor your knighthood?"

"I can see your point," Ryder said, amused. "I just never thought of myself in the same league as Lady Claire."

Cecil snickered while Claire's eyes began to dance as she met Ryder's gaze.

Ignoring her brother and sister, Eve went to a side table to fetch her notes. "Every successful match-making mother since the beginning of time has learned the wisdom of plotting a careful strategy," she said lightly. "I have made a list of suitable candidates and want to make certain that as many as possible are present at the soiree. I hoped we could review my list this morning, Sir Alex. You could then give it to Lady Thorne so she can see that all the ladies and their chaperones are invited."

"As you wish," Ryder murmured, holding back his laughter. "I am at your disposal, Countess."

Moving back across the room, Eve handed him a sheet of paper. "As you can see, there are eleven names in alphabetical order."

"This is the new crop of debutantes on the marriage mart this Season?" he asked, perusing the list.

"These are the ones I consider most eligible. Have you met any of these young ladies thus far?"

"No, I'm not familiar with any of them."

"Who is on the list, Sir Alex?" Claire asked. "Perhaps we could offer our opinions as well, so you will be better able to judge. We have met a number of debutantes these past few weeks in the course of my comeout."

"Miss Abercrombie," Ryder read out loud.

Claire nodded. "I have met her. She seems quite congenial."

"The Honorable Miss Doddridge."

Cecil grimaced. "She is pretty enough but a featherhead. You would be bored to tears within a week, Sir Alex."

Refraining from commenting that a featherhead would be his very last choice, Ryder continued down the list. "Miss Gouge."

"Don't know her," Cecil said bluntly.

"Miss Gouge," Eve said, "is possibly the most promising candidate in appearance and fortune. But she has no title."

"That doesn't concern me," Ryder said mildly. "Lady Hannah Irwin."

Claire wrinkled her nose. "I am afraid she is not very kind."

"Miss Leeson."

"Know her brother," Cecil said. "Fine, sporting chap. And I hear his sister is a bruising rider to hounds."

Glancing at Eve, Ryder saw her bite back a smile. Of course Cecil would approve of any young lady with excellent horsemanship. "The Honorable Miss Nisbett," he went on.

"Don't know her either."

He waited for Eve to comment, which she did. "Miss Nisbett is a bit plain in appearance, but very clever. I think you might like her."

"I would be pleased to meet her," Ryder said. "Miss Pittard."

Eve hesitated. "Miss Pittard is a little on the common side but a beauty and exceedingly wealthy. I added her because she will doubtless be the most sought after young lady of the Season."

"Yes," Claire observed rather mournfully. "Miss Pittard is regarded as the chief competition this Season."

Ryder gave a contemplative nod. "Miss Robson."

From across the room, Lady Beatrice interjected her opinion. "Miss Robson is nearly penniless, but then you don't require a fortune, do you, Sir Alex?"

"No," Ryder agreed. "I don't need a rich wife." He glanced further down the list. "Lady Susan Rumbotham."

To his surprise, Drucilla spoke. "Lady Susan is a duke's daughter. Her lineage is impeccable."

Glancing again at Eve, Ryder saw that she was managing to keep her expression impassive, but the amused light in her eyes acknowledged one small victory: The elderly dame had unbent enough to at least enter into the conversation, and with none of the snideness that usually characterized Drucilla's remarks regarding him.

"Miss Smythe."

"She squints," Cecil offered. "She needs to be fitted with a decent pair of spectacles, but she is too vain to be seen wearing them."

Eve gave her brother a look of exasperation. "If you only mean to point out defects, Cecil, then you may take yourself off. We don't need your discouragement."

"But Sir Alex should know the defects of the lady he will be making his wife," Cecil protested. "After all, he will have to live with her the entire rest of his life."

Ryder smiled. "True, but I value your sister's opinion, Cecil. If she thinks I should consider all these candidates, then I certainly will."

"Well, don't blame me if you wind up with a bride who will make you miserable, sir. And remember I tried to warn you."

"I won't blame you, cawker," Ryder said, amused. "And I thank you for your advice. Miss Waters," he added, naming the last lady on the list.

Beatrice's eyebrows drew together in a frown. "She is quite young . . . nearly a child, it seems. I should think a man like Sir Alex would prefer a bride nearer his own age to a green girl barely out of the schoolroom. Perhaps one with more . . . experience."

Ryder found himself momentarily staring at Lady Beatrice, surprised by her perceptiveness that he preferred a bride with less innocence and more passion. But when the lady's cheeks turned a becoming pink in embarrassment at her forwardness, he immediately recalled his manners and favored her with an appreciative smile. "I might indeed, my lady. Is there anyone," he asked Eve, "nearer your own age who might be a suitable candidate?"

"Well," Eve replied reluctantly, "there are one or two more who might fit your requirements, but they are both widowed, and I thought you wanted a young lady."

"A widow would be acceptable," Ryder said.

"Then I will add Lady Keeling. Lydia is elegant and charming, and she happens to be a close friend of mine."

"Lady Keeling has excellent ton," Drucilla agreed.

"And perhaps Mrs. Ferris-Jones might do," Eve continued.

Cecil huffed in appreciation. "Whoa, she is a prime looker, no mistake."

"Don't be vulgar, young man," Drucilla commanded with a dark look.

"Yes, pray control your tongue, Cecil," Eve seconded, but less sternly. "Mrs. Ferris-Jones is a beauty, true," she told Ryder, "but she is best known for her wit."

"I am rather fond of sharp wit," Ryder said blandly.

In response, Eve gave him a searching glance, then averted her gaze as she took back her list from him. "Very well, I will add their names so that you may give this list to Lady Thorne."

While Eve scribbled with her pencil, Cecil moved to look over her shoulder at her list, murmuring quite seriously, "I say, this courtship business is hard work. Even after Sir Alex chooses a particular lady, he will have to persuade her to consider his suit. If you ask me, it would be easier if he simply flung a sack over her head and carried her off to Gretna to be married over the anvil. He could save himself the bother of wooing a lady who might turn him down."

At the suggestion that Ryder abduct his choice of bride over the Scottish border, where they could be married without approval of parents or church, Eve's mouth dropped open. When she glanced back and saw the mischievous gleam in her sibling's eye, however, she couldn't help laughing.

"Cecil, you are positively outrageous. Abducting young ladies is out of the question, as surely even you know. But hopefully by the time you are ready to pursue a wife, you will understand the rules governing courtship."

Cecil made a face. "My courting anyone will be a long time in coming. I have a great deal of wild oats to sow before I even think about getting leg-shackled."

"That is fortunate, since no woman would have you if you intend to treat her like a sack of potatoes."

Watching Eve's teasing warmth with her brother, Ryder felt something vibrate through him, a sensation that was part laughter, part physical desire. He couldn't help but admire her relationship with her younger siblings. Eve was more than simply supportive toward them; she was protective and nurturing, fostering a feeling of family that was rare among the nobility. She made Cecil feel as if he were almost a man rather than a callow youth. She made shy, insecure Claire believe she could accomplish anything. She even made the aging aunts feel useful and wanted.

Just then Eve met his gaze, and Ryder went very

still, his muscles clenching with renewed awareness. She had the power to turn him inside out with no more than a look.

Then her smile slowly faded, as if she were unnerved by the intense way he was staring at her. Ryder swore silently at himself, forcibly remembering that he was supposed to treat Eve as merely a friend.

She seemed to recall their pact at the same time he did, for she briskly folded the list and handed it to him. "Now that is done, it will be up to Lady Thorne to see they are invited."

"Thank you," Ryder said sincerely. "I'm certain Diana will be agreeable."

Eve hesitated. "If you would rather not return home just yet, you are welcome to stay for Claire's dancing practice. The twins have been tutored by a dancing master since they came to England, but they both need the practice, particularly with the dance from the Continent that swept London last year, the waltz. Drucilla usually plays the pianoforte while I advise."

Cecil gave a mock groan, and Claire looked less than happy. "I am not particularly graceful, Sir Alex, so you may not want to watch."

Eve answered before he could. "You are a lovely dancer, dearest. And it will benefit you to have an audience now so you will be more comfortable when you perform the waltz in public for the first time."

"Very well." With a resigned sigh, Claire rose and crossed to the open space at the far end of the drawing room, near the pianoforte, and stood waiting for her brother.

"I don't know why we must endure this torture," Cecil complained as Drucilla took her place at the instrument.

"Because you care that your sister succeeds," Eve said firmly, moving closer to observe.

Lady Beatrice remained occupied with her needlework, but as Drucilla struck the opening lilting bars of the waltz, Ryder joined Eve on the sidelines, where together they watched the first half of the dance. Cecil performed with the gangly awkwardness of a leggy colt, but his twin was surprisingly accomplished, as elegant and graceful as a swan.

"Your sister is right, Lady Claire," Ryder said over the music. "You are a superb dancer. I have no doubt you will cast your competition in the shade."

Claire looked up from her intense concentration to give him a brilliant smile, and Eve murmured in a soft undervoice, "Thank you, Ryder. Claire's dancing has always been excellent. It is her self-esteem that is lacking."

"I don't think you need worry. She will dazzle her audience in her own quiet way."

Eve cast him a diffident glance. "I would like you to dazzle your audience as well. You are my protégé, so to speak, and I want you to put your best foot forward." Eve took a deep breath, as if girding herself for a difficult task. "I could show you how to waltz, if you like. I am considered a fair teacher."

"I remember," Ryder replied lightly. "You taught me how to dance the cotillion when I was as awkward as Cecil is now."

He saw her reluctant smile at the memory. It was during their one summer together on Cyrene. He'd known Eve had felt sympathy for him when he'd admitted he had no idea how to dance, so they had spent one entire afternoon laughing and cavorting in the meadow with only their horses for an audience.

He'd learned a good deal about dancing since then, including how to waltz, but Ryder didn't correct her. Eve had likely offered to teach him just now because she didn't want him to be embarrassed by his shortcomings. He in turn wanted a legitimate excuse to take her in his arms. Dancing was the only socially accepted means of touching a lady, and one of the few ways to increase the intimacy of his clandestine courtship without driving Eve away.

Thus Ryder answered quite truthfully, "I would like you to show me how you waltz, Countess."

At her brisk nod, Ryder understood that Eve regarded her offer of instruction as purely a business proposition, as part of her role as matrimonial guide. While the twins finished their first dance, Eve explained the rhythm and the steps, raising her skirts a trifle so he could see her slippered feet move in time to the lilting rhythm. Ryder fixed his gaze on her trim, stocking-covered ankles and tried not to fantasize about her slender limbs wrapping around his hips in the throes of passion.

When her siblings concluded, Eve lavished them with praise and suggested more practice. She waited until Drucilla struck up the next waltz before moving onto the floor and positioning Ryder. She showed him the proper stance—where to put his hands and feet and how to hold her.

They began the steps in slow motion, but Ryder

immediately recognized his mistake. He'd wanted an excuse to touch Eve, but torturing himself with the brush of her body against his, the warm, ripe feel of her in his arms, was not the wisest thing he could have done.

Eve was entertaining similar chaotic feelings. As Ryder gazed down at her with his dark, smoldering eyes, she shivered with awareness, a common occurrence whenever she was in his presence. She could never ignore her body's natural response when he merely shared the same *room* with her, and being this close to him now—her fingers clasped in his warm ones, his hand resting lightly, possessively, at her waist—made her positively breathless.

It had been a mistake to offer to teach him, Eve knew. And she was so distracted that several moments passed before she noticed Ryder had increased their tempo effortlessly to keep pace with the music, and that he was leading.

He danced with the lithe easy grace of the natural athlete, she realized.

Her eyes widened, then narrowed suspiciously. "You know perfectly well how to waltz," she said, her tone accusatory as she snapped out of her reverie.

Ryder's mouth curved in that appealing lazy smile he gave so rarely. "I made it a point of learning the waltz when I decided to come to London for the Season and enter the matrimonial lists."

Eve felt like writhing in embarrassment. "I presumed you didn't know how, but you let me go on and on with my instruction without saying a word."

"You offered to teach me if I liked, and I very much liked. As you said, it never hurts to practice.

And I couldn't pass up the chance to dance with a beautiful woman, now could I?"

His smile was disarming; it gave her an achy little sensation deep in the pit of her stomach, as well as the urge to kick him in the shins for leading her on that way.

"You should have told me, you wretch. And you won't mollify me by showering me with empty flattery."

Ryder's shoulders lifted in an innocent shrug. "Now you wound me, sweeting. You specifically told me I needed to learn how to conduct a polished flirtation, and I was merely being obedient—attempting to use you as my sparring partner. How else am I to improve my skills if not on you? You want me to be polished enough to impress a prospective bride, don't you?"

"I suppose so," Eve admitted grudgingly.

As if to prove his point, he whirled her around in an intricate move that left her feeling a little lightheaded and filled with the desire to laugh.

"You are shameless, you know."

His grin was slow and wicked. "Not at all. I am merely intrepid, taking advantage of the opportunity you presented."

How tempting he was, how impossibly tempting, Eve thought.

She was barely aware that their steps had slowed . . . and that the dance eventually came to an end. Yet he didn't release her; quite the contrary. Eve wasn't certain if Ryder drew her closer or if her body leaned toward his of its own volition. But either way, she found herself pressed lightly against him, cradled against his body that was rock hard and lean.

She stood riveted in the heat of his embrace, her heart pounding, her pulse racing. The way Ryder looked at her made her hot and shivery. He was staring down at her mouth, reminding her of their one passionate kiss on Cyrene. That single kiss had awakened hungers in her that she had never forgotten . . . or satisfied.

Without conscious thought, Eve raised her mouth closer to his. . . .

A throat being loudly cleared—Drucilla, perhaps—made Eve suddenly recall her surroundings.

Keenly flustered, she stepped back out of Ryder's embrace and averted her gaze, hiding her flushed cheeks. How inexcusable to become so carried away by her attraction that she had almost kissed Ryder right there in front of her family!

The man was pure danger, lethal to her senses.

Clearing her own throat, she managed to say in a tart voice far huskier than she liked, "I think that is enough practice for one day."

Avoiding Ryder's gaze, Eve crossed the room, trying to compose herself. Yet her knees felt ridiculously weak. She could still feel Ryder holding her, feel the residual tingle of her skin, the humming of her nerves.

She was very glad she had added two more names to his list of prospective candidates. Lady Keeling and Mrs. Ferris-Jones were both sexually experienced widows who should appeal to him. And once Ryder was fully occupied with wooing his future wife, then surely she wouldn't have such difficulty controlling her own brazen feelings for him.

But the soiree couldn't come quickly enough for her, she reflected as she took a deep, calming breath before turning back to face him.

The sooner she found Ryder a bride, the better.

Chapter Five

By any normal standards the soiree should have been considered a smashing success, Eve thought as she observed the crowded gathering over the delicate lace web of her fan.

The drawing room of the Thorne mansion in Cavendish Square glittered with the light of myriad chandeliers, a perfect setting to honor the hero of the hour, Sir Alex Ryder.

His friends, Viscount and Lady Thorne, proved the ideal aristocratic sponsors—gracious and charming and lavish in their praise of Ryder. And any number of dignitaries were also present to vouch for him, many from the British Foreign Office, including the foreign undersecretary.

And to assure Ryder's triumph, the Prince Regent himself had put in an appearance to offer congratulations and then remained for some time afterward.

In addition to the distinguished company and scintillating conversation, their hosts had provided dancing and cards and a light supper for the guests' entertainment. Eve, however, felt she could also take partial credit for the success of the evening, for she had thrown herself into championing Ryder and introduced him to perhaps two-thirds of the ladies on her potential bride list.

So why did she feel so dissatisfied? she wondered as she stood to one side of the drawing room, plying her fan and waiting for another of Ryder's friends, Mr. Beau Macklin, to fetch her a glass of punch. She should be proud to see Ryder so fawned over. Across the room, he was surrounded by a gaggle of beauties, all laughing and chatting and vying for his attention.

"But you knew he would be successful," Eve muttered to herself.

Ryder looked infernally handsome tonight, dressed in an exquisitely cut black tailcoat and pristine white cravat, just as many of the other gentlemen wore. Yet he stood out boldly from the crowd, for there was an unmistakable air of danger about him that made every female head turn.

Women would find his smoldering eyes and raw masculinity, combined with that hint of dark charm, irresistible, Eve knew very well. She understood the secret excitement of being near a dark, dangerous man with a questionable past. And she suspected that any number of ladies were fascinated by the notion of trying to tame him.

Even the aunts were starting to warm to Ryder. He'd succeeded in charming Beatrice quite thoroughly during the past week. And while Drucilla still pretended to view him with a measure of disdain, declaring that the sooner they concluded this nonsensical bride search, the sooner they could get Ryder out of their lives, the haughty dowager's comments were becoming less disparaging by the day.

But then Eve had expected nothing less. Ryder was so completely unlike any man the aunts had ever known that she felt sure he would surmount their defenses in the end.

He had worked on doing just that all week, escorting the family to various functions, including tonight's soiree. But tonight he had earned Eve's undying gratitude with his treatment of her sister.

Ryder had simply worked wonders with Claire. When they'd first arrived, the girl had seemed as timid as a mouse surrounded by hungry cats, and her stammer returned with a vengeance. But Ryder claimed he was terrified to face the intimidating list of bridal candidates alone and insisted that Claire remain by his side. Thus for the first hour of the evening, she had gamely followed his lead while he endured the social obligations of exchanging polite greetings, accepting good wishes, and receiving introductions.

Claire's stammer soon disappeared. Then when the dancing began, Ryder had claimed her as his partner for the opening minuet. Claire looked so animated, smiling and laughing up at him, her steps so sure and graceful, that she dazzled her audience.

The sight had brought a hot sting of tears to Eve's eyes, making her feel so grateful to Ryder for his kindness that she could have kissed him.

After that, her attempts to pair Claire with suitable partners had required no effort at all, for numerous gentlemen had eagerly solicited her hand for a set of dances. Even better, for the remainder of the evening, Claire had lost her usual awkward reserve among strangers.

And when Ryder escorted them into supper, Claire had actually responded to his teasing question "How does it feel to be such a heartbreaker?" with a coquettish smile and a toss of her head.

"It feels exceedingly pleasant, thank you. In fact I think I could become quite addicted to such popularity."

Claire was dancing now with a young nobleman who appeared fascinated by her. She did indeed look lovely tonight, Eve thought with a surge of sisterly pride, in a gown of blue net over a white satin slip, with a string of pearls around her neck and a garland of damask roses entwined with pearls in her hair.

Eve herself wore an evening gown of silver-shot gauze over rose satin with a choker of small diamonds at her throat, but she was overjoyed to have Claire outshine her. She didn't really mind, either, that Ryder had paid her almost no attention all evening long.

She herself had never lacked partners, even though she'd tried to maintain a congenial but polite distance from all her potential suitors. She'd also been sought after by various female guests. All evening long the ladies on her list had come up to her to find out more details about Sir Alex, which Eve found unaccountably vexing.

When she saw Lady Keeling approaching just now, however, Eve smiled with genuine warmth. A good friend, Lydia was near her own age, as well as being blond and tall and widowed just as she was—although Lord Keeling had not left her with much of a fortune to speak of, unlike Richard had done for Eve.

"So tell me, Eve," Lydia said after they had pressed cheeks, exchanged affectionate greetings, and made small talk for a few moments, "do you have prior claim to Sir Alex?"

"No, not at all," Eve answered, trying to repress an inexplicable twinge of regret at her disavowal. "Sir Alex was a neighbor on Cyrene and is close friends with the twins. And workmen are redecorating his house across the square, so he has spent more time than usual with us the past week. But he is merely an acquaintance."

"So you won't mind if I consider throwing my cap at him?"

Absurdly, she *did* mind that her friend was romantically interested in Ryder, but she could hardly say so. "Of course not. I could think of nothing more delightful than having you fix his interest."

"The competition will be fierce," Lydia said thoughtfully, glancing at Ryder as he led yet another young lady onto the dance floor.

"I have already put in a good word for you," Eve assured her.

"Thank you—you are a dear."

Before either of them could say another word, an arch feminine voice spoke behind them. "I am afraid you don't stand a chance against *me,* Lady Keeling. Neither of you do. So you might as well save yourself the bother of pursuing him."

Eve turned to find Mrs. Ferris-Jones smiling cattily. The beautiful widow had evidently been eavesdropping, but she wasn't the least embarrassed by the fact. On the contrary, she seemed to be deliberately throwing down the gauntlet.

The lady's confidence was well placed, Eve acknowledged with distaste. Mrs. Ferris-Jones wore an exquisite gown of emerald lustring, with emeralds sparkling in her flame-colored hair. And her low décolletage showed off a scandalous expanse of creamy white bosom.

Eve felt rather prudish by comparison, but she managed to say airily, "Oh, I am not in the competition for Sir Alex, Phoebe. I am merely helping an old friend—doing my small part to bring him into fashion."

"That is fortunate," the beauty replied. "A man like Sir Alex will doubtless prefer someone with more . . . sophistication in the bedroom. And from all reports, neither of *you* fit the bill."

The remark stung, as it was meant to, but Eve would rather have chewed nails than allow that cat to see it. Forcibly relaxing her grip on the spines of her fan before they snapped, she plied it back and forth in a careless display of indifference while offering a cool smile. "Actually, Sir Alex has confessed to me that he is looking for a bride out of the . . . *common* way. Someone with refinement, such as Lady Keeling."

"We shall see," Phoebe declared, giving a sharp laugh before she turned and glided away.

Eve and Lydia exchanged eloquent glances.

"Well, that was certainly pleasant," Eve said wryly. "But I don't think you need worry overmuch. Ryder is intelligent enough to realize that she simply wants him for his fortune."

"His person is nothing to scoff at either" was Lydia's amused reply. "I vow he quite makes my heart flutter."

At her friend's frank admission, Eve couldn't quell a sharp pang of jealousy. Honestly, she should be very happy that Lydia was attracted to Ryder—and that the feeling might be mutual. Over supper, he had casually mentioned that of all the candidates he had met thus far, he liked Lady Keeling and Mrs. Ferris-Jones best.

And it was patently absurd, Eve rebuked herself, to feel the least bit possessive toward Ryder. She had no claim to him whatsoever. She simply didn't like the idea of that witch Phoebe sinking her claws into him. To think of Ryder wooing her left a sour taste in Eve's mouth. She would do her best to steer his attention toward Lydia as the more suitable bride.

But if he chose Mrs. Ferris-Jones . . . well then, she would simply have to get over it, Eve told herself resolutely.

She made some noncommittal reply to Lydia's observation about Ryder's heart-stirring appearance, but she was glad when his handsome friend, Mr. Macklin, returned to her side.

Determinedly planting a smile on her lips, Eve accepted her cup of punch and drank, vowing to enjoy the rest of the evening and put Ryder and his matrimonial dilemmas out of her mind.

Ryder considered the evening a marginal success, for on the drive home, he was able to tell Eve that personally meeting her candidates had helped him narrow down the field and that she could cross off several—the youngest and flightiest—from her list.

Once his town carriage had deposited the ladies and Cecil on their doorstep and then continued around the square to set him down at his own house, Ryder repaired to his study, where he poured himself a stiff brandy.

It was perhaps an hour later when he was interrupted by a footman from Hayden House, who delivered a handwritten message.

Ryder's heart jumped, but upon reading the note he realized it was from Lady Claire.

You must help me, Sir Alex, for I fear Cecil may be involving himself in grave trouble. Will you come to my window as soon as possible, please, so that I may explain? I have left a candle burning.

Puzzled and frowning, Ryder dismissed the footman and then waited a short time before following the servant across the square. Keeping to the shadows, he slipped around the house until he spied a female form at a dimly lit second-floor window. Most of the other windows were dark, indicating that the rest of the household was abed.

Claire leaned out at once and waved a handkerchief at him. She was still fully dressed in her pretty evening gown, Ryder saw as he moved to stand directly beneath her window.

"Oh, thank you for coming, Sir Alex!" she whispered down to him.

Her secrecy concerned him, admittedly. He might

have expected such cloak-and-dagger schemes from Cecil, but not from Claire.

"What seems to be the problem?" Ryder asked, keeping his own voice low.

"It's Cecil. He has disappeared. He sneaked out of the house, I believe, shortly after we arrived home. Oh, Sir Alex, I think he meant to visit a *gaming hell*."

The disgust and anger in Claire's plaintive tone was underlain by a note of sheer dread. "I fear he means to gamble all his funds away! He will land us all in debt again, and Eve will have to pay the price. It isn't fair, Sir Alex, it just isn't fair, but I don't know what to do!"

"Lady Claire, take a deep breath," Ryder said to calm her, "and slow down so I can understand you."

Obediently she took a shuddering breath, then said more slowly, "Please, you have to help me stop him!"

"Of course I will help. I'll go in search of Cecil at once. But I'll do it alone. London gaming hells are no place for a young lady. Do you know what club he might have chosen?"

"No, I haven't the least idea. But I doubt it was White's or Brooks's or any of the respectable gentlemen's clubs, for they wouldn't let a green youth in without a sponsor, would they?"

"No," Ryder agreed.

"I would not even know where to start looking for him, but I hoped you might."

"I know of a dozen clubs I can try, and I have

friends who can tell me about a hundred others. I'll find him, I promise you."

"Oh, *thank you,* Sir Alex."

Ryder smiled reassuringly. "Don't mention it, my lady. Now go to bed and try to get some sleep. It may take me a while to find Cecil and bring him home."

"I don't think I could sleep a wink," Claire whispered passionately.

"You need to try. You don't want to alarm your sister, do you?"

"No. . . . Very well, I will *try.*"

Ryder waited until Claire had retreated into her bedchamber before returning to his house and calling for his carriage. He armed himself in case he ran into trouble, and then he and his coachman and two sturdy footmen set out to search London for the Honorable Cecil Montlow.

He spent the next two hours making the rounds of gaming hells and pleasure clubs, attempting to quell his concern. Cecil was nowhere near the rebel Ryder had been in his own youth, but the boy was eager to sample the delights London had to offer and wouldn't be satisfied with the tame, proper entertainments his sisters enjoyed. Ryder had every intention of keeping the boy out of trouble, if he could.

He eventually found Cecil at a shabby hell near St. James Street, hunched over the faro table, three sheets to the wind and more than a thousand pounds in debt.

The relief on Cecil's face when he saw Ryder,

however, clearly exposed his knowledge that he'd gotten in over his head. Several other young gentlemen about his age were present, all looking guilty as sin, so it wasn't hard to deduce that the lad had come here with his friends.

Sauntering up to the table, Ryder amiably clapped a hand on Cecil's shoulder. "I was just making my way home when it occurred to me that I should offer you a ride."

Cecil shook his head drunkenly. "Can't leave yet, Shir Alex . . . not till I recoup m' losses."

"I would enjoy your company, old chap."

"But . . . that fellow there woan take my voucher." He pointed unsteadily at the dealer who held the faro bank.

"No problem."

Ryder calmly drew out his purse and paid the dealer, then put a firm hand under Cecil's arm and helped him rise. "Would your friends care to accompany us?"

The oldest of the young men answered for the rest. "*We* are winning, sir. But a flat like Cecil should never have come here."

"You might have considered that before you brought him to a hell that regularly fleeces young gulls," Ryder returned icily before guiding his drunken charge away from the gaming tables toward the entrance.

The bruiser who stood guard took one look at Ryder's expression and gingerly stepped aside to let them pass.

When he'd supported Cecil down the stairs and

onto the street, his footmen helped him load the boy into the waiting town coach, then shut the door behind them and jumped on the footboard.

Almost immediately the coach rolled forward. Ryder settled back, silently watching Cecil, who lay sprawled on the seat groaning.

He suspected that remorse was nagging at the boy's fogged brain, and he was right. Two minutes later, Cecil mumbled an apology while covering his face with his arm as if ashamed.

" 'M sorry, shir. 'Twas a damn fool thing to do."

"I won't disagree," Ryder said coolly.

"Eve'll kill me if she fines out . . . send me to the country for shure. . . ."

"If you plan to act like a country bumpkin, then perhaps you belong there."

Cecil pried one blurry eye open and tried to sit, as if the threat had partially sobered him. "No, please! I've learned m' lesshon . . . shwear it. Doan tell Eve . . . beg you, sir. I'll pay you back every penny."

Ryder hid his smile and paused a long while before finally saying, "When we reach your home, we'll slip you inside and up to bed. Hopefully your sister will be none the wiser."

Cecil let out a heavy sigh of relief, then promptly groaned again and clutched his temples.

"Your aching head in the morning may be punishment enough," Ryder added with unsympathetic amusement.

"Aye, it will," Cecil mumbled. "But I promise . . . you won't regret it."

"I trust not, halfling," Ryder said levelly.

* * *

The entrance hall of the Haydon mansion was dimly lit by a candle wall sconce, and so was the upstairs corridor. Ryder managed to support Cecil all the way to his bedchamber door before the boy stubbed a toe on the carpet and painfully turned his ankle.

When he let out a vivid oath that could be heard halfway across London, another door opened and Claire peered out.

Ryder winked at her and gestured with his head for her to go back to bed. With a grateful smile, she obeyed, shutting the door softly behind her.

But then a third door opened farther down the hallway, and Eve stepped out.

"Ryder? What are you . . . oh, my word," she said, taking in the sight of her brother clinging to Ryder, both still dressed in the evening clothes they'd worn to the soiree.

Caught red-handed, Cecil froze. His slurred plea "Now, doan be mad, Evie," was followed quickly by Ryder's remark, "There is nothing to worry about, Lady Hayden."

Eve obviously jumped to her own conclusions. "I cannot believe it, Ryder! You got my brother *drunk*?"

"Wuzzen his fault," Cecil muttered. But when he started to expound further, Eve lowered her voice to a whisper and cut him off tartly. "Not here in the hall where everyone can hear. You will wake the entire household!"

Moving forward, she pushed open the door to Cecil's room, then made a sound of disgust as she caught a whiff of him. "You smell like cheroot smoke and cheap perfume. Honestly, Cecil, get inside. I won't have Aunt Drucilla seeing you in this odious state."

Politely elbowing Ryder aside, Eve put her shoulder under Cecil's arm, trying to take his weight, but when she immediately stumbled, Ryder took over again, guiding the boy inside the dark room to the bed and helping him lie down.

Eve lit the bedside lamp, then stood with her arms crossed over her chest, watching in grim disapproval as Ryder pulled off Cecil's shoes and form-fitting coat. "I am severely disappointed in you, Sir Alex, corrupting him this way. You should know better than to take a mere boy to a place that would allow him to become so disgustingly foxed."

"Yes, I should," Ryder replied calmly.

At her scolding, Cecil clutched his head and tried to shake it at the same time. "Sir Alesh wasn't to blame at all, Eve. He didn't take me to that gaming house. Fact, he saved me."

"You went to a gaming house?" Her voice rose in dismay. "Cecil, how *could* you?"

"I know. I'm sorry, believe me. I'm not like Papa, Evie, I shwear it. Just wanted to play in t' shame league with the other chaps. Thank my shtars Sir Alex came to fetch me. That bloody dealer was a shark, Eve. Took all my blunt and then some."

Eve fell grimly silent, and Ryder could sense the effort she was making to hold back her wrath. After a moment he could feel her gaze shift to him. "Well, we will discuss this later, Cecil, but it seems that I must eat my words." She cleared her throat as if embarrassed by her obvious mistake. "I owe you an apology, Sir Alex."

Ryder glanced back over his shoulder and froze at the picture Eve made in the lamplight. She was directly behind him, dressed in nothing more than a long-sleeved cambric nightdress, barefoot, with her bright mane of tawny hair tumbling about her shoulders in disarray. A beautiful siren just risen from her bed, God help him.

Desire clenched in his gut—a damnably inappropriate reaction for the moment, considering how distressed she was about her brother.

Cursing himself silently, Ryder tried to crush his response, even as his gaze roamed helplessly over her form, from her flowing gold hair to the sweet curve of her breasts barely concealed by cambric to her long slender limbs.

At his intent scrutiny, Eve's cheeks suddenly flooded with color as she apparently became aware of her scanty state of dress. "Will you await me downstairs while I finish putting Cecil to bed, Sir Alex? I would like to speak to you in private."

Carefully straightening, Ryder stepped away so he didn't have to breathe in her scent and nodded his assent so he wouldn't betray the sudden huskiness of his voice.

Another nod acknowledged Cecil when the boy mumbled, "Thank y' again, sir."

Letting himself from the bedchamber, Ryder made his way downstairs to the library, choosing the most severe room of the house for his late-night interview with Eve. He lit a lamp and perused an old history tome as he waited, but his mind kept reviewing images of her in her nightclothes while his body hardened at the thought of taking her back to her bed.

The oath Ryder swore at himself was soft and potent. If he was wise, he would leave here this instant and wait for the bright light of day to face Eve. The entire evening had already been something of a torment. He'd watched her during the soiree, charming her way through the crowd of beautiful, elegant people. Even in the glittering company, Eve caught the eye. Gentlemen had danced attendance on her without pause, eager to do her least bidding. It was all Ryder could do to curb his jealousy.

He was in no mood to be wise just now, though. He wasn't about to give up his one chance to have Eve alone. Perhaps he could even use the opportunity to chip away at her defenses—*if* he could manage to control his own lust.

When she finally appeared some five minutes later, she had thankfully donned a wrapper and slippers, but Ryder had to remind himself to unclench his teeth at the provocative sight.

When Eve paused in the doorway, he averted his glance and returned his attention to his book, pretending to be absorbed in the text. She seemed a little hesitant to face him alone, but then took a deep breath, as if bolstering her courage, and crossed purposefully to where he stood before a section of leather-bound volumes.

"I want to apologize, Ryder," Eve said somewhat sheepishly. "It was absurd of me to accuse you of corrupting my brother. I should have known you would never allow him to become so drunk, let alone take him to a gaming hell."

He gave a casual shrug. "It was an honest mistake."

Her smile was wry. "I'm surprised you didn't tell me to go to the devil. You would have had every right."

"Very well, if it will make you feel better, sweeting: Go to the devil."

She laughed, as he'd meant her to do to break some of the tension between them. "Well, thank you for bringing Cecil safely home. I owe you my sincere gratitude."

"You needn't thank me. I care a great deal for your brother, even as reckless and maddening as he can be occasionally."

"He told me how much he owed you. I intend to repay you at once."

"No." Ryder shook his head firmly. "Any debt is between Cecil and me. He needs to understand there are consequences for his actions, or he'll never learn to take responsibility when he gets himself into a scrape. I will hold him accountable for his debt, one way or another."

Eve nodded in fervent agreement, then gave a small shudder. "This was far worse than a scrape. It could have been disastrous. I can't bear to think of Cecil following in our father's footsteps—becoming infected with gambling fever."

"I don't believe he will. Cecil is merely doing what every normal young man does at his age—sowing his wild oats."

Eve studied Ryder with a faint smile. "You were not still sowing oats at his age."

"Because I had to earn my living. I sowed whole

fields when I was younger. This was a good lesson for Cecil, though. And I'll keep a closer watch on him from now on."

"Thank you. He responds so well to you, much better than he does to me."

"It's the least I can do, considering all your help in finding me a bride."

Ryder returned the volume to the shelf, then eyed the other rows of books, as if looking for something else to read. "To be truthful, I'm glad for the chance to speak to you privately. I have a question I hoped you might answer."

Eve eyed him in surprise. "Certainly . . . if I can. What question?"

"Well, it's a rather delicate matter."

"Yes?"

Turning to face her, Ryder leaned one broad shoulder against the oaken bookshelves. "I want your advice, actually. On how to woo a woman."

Eve felt her heart give a sudden leap. "I'm not sure I understand. What do you mean, 'to woo a woman'?"

"You see, I've changed my mind. Or rather, my marital ambitions have changed. I'm no longer interested in simply buying a convenient bride. I want something more."

"More?"

"For some time now I've wondered about the possibility of making a love match."

"You want to make a love match?" she repeated weakly, blinking at him.

"Yes. Or at least to increase my chances of making one."

She stared up at Ryder, finding it hard to believe that he actually wanted love in his marriage. Or that he would go to the effort of trying to make his future bride come to love him. The sentiment was so different from her experiences with any other gentlemen, especially her late husband.

But Ryder seemed perfectly serious. There were no traces of cynicism or hardness on his chiseled face. Instead, his dark eyes were keen and watchful.

"So," he said softly, "how do I woo a woman so that she will come to love me rather than my fortune?"

Eve couldn't manage a reply. In the hushed quiet of the library, her heart was drumming warnings against her rib cage. The intense way Ryder was looking at her made her shiver. And his velvet-edged voice had a stark effect on all her feminine nerve endings.

Thankfully he had no idea how her body had warmed at that sound. She was safe as long as he didn't realize how vulnerable she was to his potent masculinity. Even so, she took a step back, putting more distance between them as she shook her head. "I'm afraid I am not the right person to advise you."

He cocked his head at a lazy angle and folded his arms across his chest, giving her a perceptive glance that was disconcertingly thorough. "No? Why not?"

His eyes had become very warm, Eve realized, the irises dark and brilliant—which only intensified the shivering rush of awareness that swept through her.

Disturbed by the way her body flared in response

to his scrutiny, Eve tried to make light of the moment. "You must realize I have no experience with love matches, Ryder. I wouldn't have the faintest idea how a man should woo a woman to win her heart. My late husband never attempted to woo me. There was no need for him to, since ours was a union purely of convenience."

She saw Ryder's jaw harden for an instant before he smiled blandly. "But you can tell me what appeals to you. What you would want in a suitor . . . in a lover."

The question both flustered and dismayed her. Eve fought the urge to wrap her arms around herself. Perhaps it was pride, but she didn't want Ryder knowing the sordid details of her marriage. "I cannot help you, Ryder. I have never had a lover, only a husband—so I have no way to judge what is appealing and what is not."

Ryder made a low scoffing sound. "Your husband evidently was a terrible lover."

Eve gave a careless shrug. "But then I hardly have the right to complain. What is the saying? If you make your bed, you must lie in it? My bed was not . . . exactly pleasant, but I knew from the beginning that the bargain I made came with obligations."

Her tone was light, but there was considerable dignity in that quiet declaration. Even so, Ryder wasn't about to let her comment pass without an explanation. "What do you mean, your bed wasn't pleasant?"

The emotions on her face were too complex to

sort out. "Most wives do not enjoy the marriage bed, I understand."

"Perhaps not, but there's no reason for it. A man should be concerned with his woman's pleasure."

Her amused laugh held the tiniest hint of bitterness. "Richard never subscribed to that particular theory, certainly."

"Eve, don't talk in riddles," Ryder said with impatience. "What the hell did he do to you?"

She paused. "Nothing, really."

"I don't believe that."

Her cheeks flushed as she averted her gaze. "If you must know . . . Richard always considered me merely a receptacle for his seed in order to sire an heir. He always . . . finished quickly, but it was still painful. To be truthful, I was grateful that he satisfied his usual carnal needs with his mistresses."

Something clutched at Ryder's heart, made his chest go tight.

Eve must have misinterpreted his silence, for her chin rose. "Don't you *dare* pity me, Ryder."

"I'm not pitying you. I'm angry as hell. I would like to strangle that bastard for causing you pain. It's fortunate he's already dead, or I might be tempted to speed his demise."

Her wry smile made his chest hurt. "Did no one ever tell you it is sinful to speak so scathingly of the dead?" she teased.

"I don't give a damn. That bloody boor made you afraid of physical intimacy, didn't he?"

She didn't reply.

"I could change that," Ryder said softly.

Her eyes flashed back up to his, full of vulnerability.

It was a long time before she spoke. "You know very well this conversation is wholly improper."

His glance lowered to her elegant hands, with their long delicate fingers. She was twisting them together unconsciously, betraying her agitation. That and her prim reply only confirmed his suspicions: that despite being married for six years, Eve was still sexually inexperienced.

"It's clear you know little about passion," Ryder said finally, taking a step closer. "Lovemaking can be remarkable with a man who cares enough to give you pleasure. I want to show you, Eve."

She stared up at him, her eyes blue pools of uncertainty. Heat and desire and tenderness stung Ryder's body at the sight. Yet he forced himself to remain still, letting Eve make the first move.

His heart contracted when slowly, with trance-like gentleness, she reached up and touched his cheek. "You are such a kind man, Ryder."

Ryder clenched his fists to contain the emotions knotting inside him. "I'm not particularly kind."

"Yes, you are. You were always kind to me from the moment we met. But what you are suggesting now . . ."

She stood very still, looking vulnerable and soft and more beautiful than any woman had a right to be, her hair gleaming in the low light like molten gold. He imagined the incredible pleasure of touching it, of tangling the tresses in his hands.

Ryder took another step closer. He wanted to hold Eve. Wanted to fill his hands with the textures of her. Even more, he wanted more to show her the pleasure she had never known.

What if he yielded to his desires? an insistent voice prodded. It might be too soon to act. He might frighten her away. Then again, if he took great care, her response might be everything he had dreamed it would be.

The thought sent tenderness and desire warring brutally in his midsection, making his whole body burn for her.

Yet he could tell Eve was wondering something similar. Even without touching her, he knew she was trembling. His senses registered each shiver of her body, every pulse. And he felt the deep primal response in his own body. The ache in his gut grew deeper and sharper.

Of its own volition, his hand lifted to touch that shining fall of golden hair. It was indeed as silky as he imagined, the strands caressing his skin and curling around his fingers, tantalizing him with their softness.

Gliding slowly, he reached higher and traced Eve's ear with his fingertips, then her delicate jawline. His desire to hold her had become a need so powerful, he wasn't certain he could control it.

Watching him helplessly, Eve sensed Ryder's struggle, saw it in his midnight eyes, yet she had no idea how to respond. As his long fingers grazed her jaw in the lightest caress, her every instinct cried danger, but she couldn't seem to move, couldn't speak. She was spellbound by his tenderness.

Shifting his hand, he brushed her cheek, his lingering fingers startlingly hot against her skin. The simple intimacy of the caress made her tremble, and she fought the need to turn her face into the cradle of his palm. Her heart was pounding madly, her body vibrating with currents of excitement.

Did he know how swiftly, how fiercely, her heart was beating?

As if wanting to discover for himself, he shifted his touch lower, along the column of her throat. When his fingers found the beat of her pulse there, she saw Ryder's mouth curve with the faintest hint of satisfaction.

Of course he knew how he was affecting her.

Defenselessly Eve gazed up at his dark face, seeing the slash of hard lines that made his features so virile and arresting, the vibrant obsidian eyes that held her captive. A woman could get lost in eyes that black and deep.

But it would be a colossal mistake to let this continue.

"Ryder . . . I cannot." Tearing her gaze from his, Eve turned away.

His fingers closed gently over her arm, holding her fast. "Don't go."

A moment later she felt Ryder's arms fold around her from behind. Eve went rigid, suddenly unable to breathe.

His lips pressed against her hair, making her heart gallop even faster.

"You know I would never hurt you. Don't you, Eve?"

She couldn't speak, so she gave the barest of nods.

"You needn't fear me."

She didn't fear Ryder in the least; she feared what

he made her feel. Tremors coursed through her body, making her weak.

She knew she should put an end to this madness, yet she couldn't seem to pull away. She was surrounded by his strength and warmth and arousing male scent. Unable to resist.

For a long while he simply held her, his hard frame pressed against her back. His body radiated heat even through their layers of clothing; she was keenly aware of the feverish sensation.

She had never expected to experience Ryder's embrace again, but the feel of his muscular arms around her was incredibly arousing. Just as it had been that summer day in the meadow. She still remembered his embrace, how it felt to lie beneath his hard body, hot and vital and strong.

He was infinitely more gentle now, though. One arm rested just beneath her breasts while the other curved lightly around her waist. Then barely moving, he splayed his hand to cover her abdomen. He held it there, letting her feel his touch through her nightclothes.

When she didn't protest, he slid his hand even lower to the juncture of her thighs, caressing her woman's mound.

Her heart leaped in alarm, as did her body, but his embrace never faltered. "Does this frighten you, Eve?" he murmured against her ear.

Yes, it frightens me. Yet she didn't want him to stop. "I . . . don't know," she whispered.

His voice was the texture of rough velvet as he nuzzled her temple. "Do you trust me, Eve?"

"I . . . yes," she answered truthfully.

"Good."

Slowly he unbuttoned her silk wrapper and slipped it off her shoulders to pool on the carpet.

His hands slid around her waist again, but this time he reached upward, skating his palms over her thinly clad breasts, stroking her through the fine cambric of her nightdress. A soft gasp escaped her as her nipples budded instantly at the delicate pressure.

Ryder went still, waiting. Fearing he might stop, Eve arched slightly, pushing against his palms, wanting him to touch her more.

Obligingly he cupped the quivering mounds of her breasts with both hands, his thumbs slowly circling her nipples. "Does this feel pleasurable?"

There was no need for her to reply, since he already knew the answer. She felt a bright, warm stirring of pleasure that rippled though her entire body. A delicious sensation of weakness, a sweet restless ache that pulsed deep inside her, centering in the feminine recesses between her thighs.

And Ryder seemed to know exactly what she was experiencing—as if his instincts were finely tuned to her every desire. His caresses moved again, down over her midriff, then lower still, seeking her most sensitive woman's flesh.

When a whisper of cool air brushed her legs, Eve realized that Ryder was raising the skirt of her nightdress. Shock flickered through her, yet she did nothing to stop him. Her hands hovered at her sides, as if not knowing what to do with themselves.

When he had raised the fabric to her hips, baring all her feminine secrets, Ryder nuzzled her hair again. "Close your eyes, Eve. Don't think. Just close your eyes and feel."

Helpless to fight her own desire, she did as he commanded. She felt Ryder at her back, his body pressed fully against her, making her aware of the hard length of his erection beneath his satin evening breeches. She should have been alarmed, should have been cringing from the shocking contact, yet she only pulled in a deep, shuddering breath.

His fingers caressed her naked thigh as he whispered in her ear, "Your skin is so soft."

His touch is so soft, Eve thought dreamily. His warm hand on her flesh was gentle, searing, filling her body with a tight, hot longing she had never before known.

His embrace engulfed her with tenderness. She wondered how a man so hard, so dangerous, could be so tender. His hands were arousing sparks everywhere he touched, yet gentle enough to make her feel as fragile as spun glass.

Then his fingers slid along her cleft, spreading slowly to cup her sex. At the fiery sensation, Eve gasped sharply, her eyes flying open.

He held the hot center of her in his palm, setting her athrob. "Hush, sweetheart. This will be pleasurable, I promise."

She had no doubt Ryder was speaking the truth. She had never felt anything like the swollen, pulsing ache between her thighs. But it unnerved her enough that her hands clenched into fists at her sides.

Behind her, she felt Ryder slowly shake his head. "No, don't become so tense, Eve. I want you to relax and help me."

"H-Help you?" she rasped, her voice unsteady.

"Hold up your nightshift," he ordered softly.

Eve felt a flush scald her cheeks at his insistence that she participate in her own seduction. Even so, she obeyed him, clutching at the cambric as if she might shred it.

"Eve, I won't hurt you. Just lean back and give yourself over to me."

She forced herself to do as he said, trying to ease the tension from her rigid muscles. It was difficult, though. She caught her breath as his gentle fingers probed her naked center, parting her folds, lightly following the contours.

All her senses had flared to painful life, yet Eve struggled to hold herself still and closed her eyes again. In the silence of the library, she could hear Ryder's soft breaths mingle with her own harsher ones.

His fingers continued to move over her delicate flesh in the most intimate investigation, rubbing slowly, exploring. She had to bite back a whimper as liquid heat rushed and throbbed between her legs.

He was casting a sensual spell over her, Eve realized sometime later. The silence had lengthened, holding her rapt and breathless.

This moment did not even seem real. Rather it was an erotic fantasy, encompassing her in a dream of vibrant awareness.

Time flowed around them. Every brush of his fingers against her skin spread heat and hunger until finally she whimpered, "Ryder, I am so hot. . . ."

"I know, love. Just let it take you."

His middle finger teased her silky crevice, already

slick with her own moisture, then slid inside her. The invasion was unbearably intimate, yet he had scarcely begun, Eve realized.

His thumb stroking the exquisitely sensitive bud hidden in the folds of her sex, he slid another finger inside her to join the first. Then both withdrew, slowly plunging in and out in a lingering, impossibly arousing rhythm.

In response, her hips began to move, seeking something she couldn't even identify. Her entire body had gone taut with fever, with longing. Somehow Ryder was kindling a firestorm inside her, and she wasn't certain she could bear it. She felt a savage need she had never imagined, a desperation that claimed every nerve in her body.

Helplessly Eve arched against his hand, the surge of desire so fierce she thought she might die of it.

Suddenly all her inner muscles clenched around his fingers. She uttered a strangled scream as an unexpected sob ripped from her, and she gripped his forearm, shaking at the explosive burst of pleasure inside her, jagged and intense and flame-hot. Her knees would have buckled except that Ryder was holding her up, enfolding her as if she were a precious treasure he wanted to protect.

When her powerful climax was over, Eve sagged in his arms, shaking with awe, trembling with the wonder of it.

It was a long, long moment before her gasps slowed, before the tremors faded. Longer still before Ryder trusted her to stand on her own. But then he turned her to face him, his hands curling about her arms, warm and strong as he steadied her, his gaze searching.

She couldn't look at him, though. Instead Eve buried her face in the curve of his shoulder to hide her keen embarrassment, her emotions so raw and intense, she could barely breathe. She felt like a dreamer who had awakened from a deep sleep.

Ryder must have understood, for he continued to shower her with tenderness as he held her—his lips moving against her hair again, his fingers gently stroking the tresses with the same gentleness he had used to set her on fire.

The very thought of what he had done to her made Eve's face go scarlet. When her ragged breath was finally under control, she uttered a rueful, self-deprecating laugh and mumbled into his shoulder, "You must think me a complete wanton."

"No, I think you a lovely innocent. One who is startled to realize she can feel such deep physical pleasure."

"I never knew," she breathed with wonder.

"Of course you didn't. How could you unless someone showed you?"

Her nose burrowed further into his coat. She was grateful to Ryder for his kindness, for awakening her to passion, but she wanted to squirm, she felt so exposed to him, so completely vulnerable. "I suppose . . . I should thank you."

"It was my pleasure, Countess." She heard the smile in his voice as he rested his chin on the top of her head. "There is much more I could show you, but I think that is enough for one evening."

"There is *more*?"

His low laugh held a strangled note. "Much, much more."

Suddenly Eve became aware of the heat of his body, the coiled tension of his muscles, and realized that the incredible passion he had shown her had all been one-sided. Ryder had made her shiver and tremble with fire, but he was still burning.

She drew back to look up at him. "But what about you, Ryder? You didn't . . . take any pleasure."

His eyes were dangerously dark and distinctly possessive as they traveled over her face. "Giving you pleasure was enough for me."

At his reply, she shook her head in bewilderment. She could tell from the bulge at his groin that Ryder was physically stimulated; the arousal that had branded her back was definitely sexual. But apparently he was content to remain that way out of concern for her sensibilities.

His restraint shocked her, even more than the carnal experience Ryder had given her, even more than the wondrous feelings he had kindled in her. Her late husband had never shown the least concern for her sensibilities.

But then Ryder was a vastly different sort of man from her husband. Or perhaps he merely didn't desire *her.*

Eve searched his gaze, which had grown darkly enigmatic.

He wanted her sexually, she was fairly certain about that. But it was a normal male reaction to a barely clothed female body. Any woman could satisfy his physical needs—and in fact would satisfy him far better than she could.

The thought left a strange ache in her chest.

Before she could examine the emotion, however, Ryder drew a shallow breath. "I had best go."

Bending, he lightly kissed her forehead as he might a child. Then he pulled free of her and stepped back. "Sweet dreams, Countess."

Mutely Eve watched him turn away, disappointment and something else she could only identify as dismay knotting inside her. Perhaps Ryder meant to seek physical release with his mistress as Richard had done.

Did Ryder have a mistress?

The ache in her chest actually became painful.

Impossibly, she wanted to ask him to stay. But she stood unmoving as he strode to the library door and disappeared.

It shouldn't matter to her if Ryder was leaving to find carnal gratification in the perfumed arms of his mistress or some other ravishing lady of the evening.

It meant nothing to her. She had no business dwelling on the intense, sexual feelings he had aroused in her. Ryder had merely done her a kindness, showing her that there was more to lovemaking than pain and loathing.

Still nonplussed, Eve shook her head. He had asked her how he could woo a lady in order to please her, but instead *he* had been the one to enlighten *her*. His tutelage had been enough to make her woman's heart yearn and her body ache.

But she had to crush those dark desires for Ryder,

Eve told herself staunchly, before they got entirely out of hand.

Even so, when she lifted her hand to her bare throat, she couldn't help remembering how fiercely gentle his touch had been or stop herself from longing again for the kind of caresses Ryder had given her. Caresses that for a breathless moment in time had made her feel cherished and desired.

Ryder let himself out of the house, grateful to escape with his control barely intact. He needed a long walk in the cool night air to lower the fever that had taken over his mind and body.

Desire still knifed through him, sharp and insistent. His own throbbing arousal wasn't solely to blame, though. Eve's response to his caresses wrenched him to his soul. That sob of surprise and pleasure she'd given had nearly brought him to his knees.

It had required all of his strength to pull back, almost brutal fortitude to refrain from carrying his lovemaking further. But he hadn't even kissed her.

Holding back had been sheer torment, leaving him burning with an ache so fierce, he felt on fire. And restraining his desire in the future would be an even greater torment, now that he knew how soft her skin felt, how sweet and ripe her breasts were, how perfectly they fit his hands, how inviting and tempting her woman's flesh was.

Yet he would do it all over again. He had relished every tremble and shudder of her response, relished knowing how right he'd been about Eve. She might appear coolly elegant on the outside, but she was searing, passionate heat on the inside. If only he could uncover it.

He would have to go slowly, he knew damned well. Her late husband had given her a fear and disgust of lovemaking, a revulsion that would take great patience to overcome. Her sensual awakening was merely the first step.

Ryder forced himself to exhale slowly, girding himself for the protracted battle ahead. For the time being, he would have to keep a savage rein on his desire, even if it meant continuing to endure this gut-twisting hunger that turned him inside out.

Chapter Six

Eve was determined to forget that forbidden interlude with Ryder in the library. The difficulty was, she had to face him late the next afternoon, when he called to take her brother and sister to supper and an evening performance of the circus at Astley's Royal Amphitheatre. Or rather, Eve *forced* herself to face him.

When Ryder was admitted to the entrance hall, she drew him aside for a private word while the twins donned their evening cloaks and summoned Janet to act as chaperone.

Eve could scarcely meet his gaze. Even though Ryder gave every appearance of nonchalance and did nothing overt to remind her of their scandalous tryst, the burning memory of his embrace wouldn't leave her. She thought of his hands touching her secret flesh and felt her stomach quiver.

Chastising herself, Eve cleared her throat and kept her voice low. "Whatever you said to Cecil this morning seems to have had a positive effect."

Ryder's reply held a wry note. "I don't believe it was what I *said* that influenced him. Cecil was still suffering from his bout with the port bottle when I required him to take a drive with me in my curricle. It was a tame sort of punishment, but it will make him think twice about getting sotted again, especially when he's in proximity of a card table."

"I sincerely hope so," Eve said with a shudder.

"We also discussed the details of how he was to repay me," Ryder added. "Since his quarterly allowance is nearly depleted, I intend to put him to work performing some secretarial tasks."

"He told me of your agreement," she confirmed. "And astonishingly enough, he claims to be looking forward to it. Or at least he prefers working for you over being banished to the country."

Fearful of that threat, Cecil had groveled appropriately and vowed solemnly that he would never again enter a gaming hell, at least not until he filled his pockets and could hold his liquor better. Eve had accepted her brother's apology, although knowing it was only a matter of time before he got into more mischief. She quelled her impulse to keep him on a tighter leash, though, realizing it would be best to let Ryder handle her brother man-to-man.

"Thank you for dealing witn him, Ryder," Eve said sincerely. "And for what you did for Claire last evening. The door knocker has practically fallen off its hinges today with callers and servants delivering flowers." She indicated a side table, where a vase of daffodils rested. "She's received posies and bouquets from half a dozen young gentlemen, all of whom called this afternoon. Claire is in alt with her success."

Ryder nodded in satisfaction. "I knew it wouldn't take much to make her finer qualities known."

"As long as you are here," Eve said, "I wanted to suggest a slight change to our Vauxhall outing." Ryder had invited the family to Vauxhall Gardens one evening this week to enjoy a lavish musical entertainment and supper, culminating in a grand fireworks display. Both aunts were to accompany them.

At his raised eyebrow, Eve explained. "I thought we might expand the party to include two or three of the young gentlemen who are interested in Claire—the ones she favors most—to give them a chance to become better acquainted under less formal circumstances."

"Of course. Invite whomever you would like."

"If you mean it, then I would like to ask my friend Lydia, Lady Keeling, to join us, so you can come to know her better."

A glimmer of amusement lit his dark eyes. "You are taking your role of matchmaker fully to heart, aren't you, Countess?"

Eve had no idea why she should feel like blushing, particularly when Ryder had requested her matchmaking services. "Well, yes, Lydia is by far the most agreeable candidate on your list, and you did say she was your favorite."

"I also said I was partial to Mrs. Ferris-Jones."

Eve hesitated, trying to hide her distaste. "Certainly we could invite her as well."

"You don't approve?"

"It isn't my place to approve or disapprove of your choice."

"Then I would like her to come also."

Just then the twins joined them and there was no

chance for further conversation in the bustle of seeing them off.

When the front door closed behind them, Eve was left pursing her lips in frustration. Mrs. Ferris-Jones was acceptable enough, if a bit scandalous, so if Ryder wanted the beautiful widow in his party, there was no reason not to include her.

Indeed, Eve told herself irritably as she mounted the stairs to dress for a boring levee the aunts wished to attend, she should be trying to encourage the attachment. The best way for her to avoid temptation was for Ryder to become fully occupied in courting his chosen bride, for then he would have no time to indulge in late-night forbidden trysts in the library with *her.*

And that was precisely what she wanted, Eve reminded herself firmly. Wasn't it?

Eve continued to remind herself of her goal at Vauxhall Gardens three nights later as she watched Mrs. Ferris-Jones flirting outrageously with Ryder. Thus far the flame-haired beauty had monopolized his attention nearly the entire evening.

His party was a large one, consisting of Eve, the twins, and both aunts; Eve's friend Lady Keeling; Phoebe Ferris-Jones; three young suitors whom Claire favored; and Ryder's friend, Mr. Beau Macklin.

Upon arriving, they had strolled the grounds of the lavish pleasure gardens, along graveled, tree-lined walkways illuminated by colored lanterns of crimson and gold. And as a group, they had playfully explored the Dark Walk, which unlike the other unexceptional pleasure walks at Vauxhall, had gained a reputation for infamy. Its shadowed alcoves and romantic hideaways had been designed for lovers, but more than one young damsel's good name had been ruined there.

The widow, Eve had noted, hung back with Ryder, clinging to his arm like a limpet and laughing huskily up at him.

Eventually they all settled in his hired box for the music concert, which boasted a sizable orchestra and vocal performers. Phoebe immediately seated herself next to Ryder and proceeded to exert her charm in an effort to claim his sole attention, while the other guests enjoyed a lively conversation of their own.

During the intermission, they left the box to view a magical extravaganza of a cascading waterfall. When they returned, they dined on paper-thin slices of shaved ham, sparrow-sized chickens, pigeon pie, and potent Vauxhall punch, followed by strawberries and cherries and flavored ices. After the concert, they would walk down to the riverbank to watch the spectacular fireworks and view the rockets bursting overhead in a reenactment of Napoléon's defeat at the Battle of Waterloo.

It was a gay evening, and Eve tried hard to appreciate the musical entertainment and the delicious supper. And she did enjoy the company of her friend Lydia. It was the other beautiful widow that Eve found hard to stomach.

Watching Ryder's head bent toward the lady, Eve was conscious of a nameless dissatisfaction. She didn't want to call it longing, yet she couldn't help wishing she were in Phoebe's shoes at that moment.

She could see why such a woman would appeal to him. The beauty oozed a sensual confidence that had every male within a hundred yards lusting after her, including Cecil, who was clearly moonstruck.

That Ryder would lust after Phoebe was to be expected. A virile man like him would have appetites that could be satisfied much better by an experienced widow than by a young debutante.

Despite her own widowhood, Eve knew she didn't fit that bill, since she had almost no carnal experience at all, other than forcing herself to lie passively beneath her husband's rutting body and trying not to cry out from the pain while he performed his duty.

She had never felt sexually attractive or alluring, either, and wouldn't know the first thing about pleasing a man in bed. Even if she were to consider having an affair with Ryder—which she couldn't possibly—he would never see her as an object of desire, as he obviously saw Phoebe Ferris-Jones.

Phoebe was evidently wary of her competition, though. A short while later, when the concert ended, the party rose from their chairs and began to file out of the box in order to view the fireworks. When somehow Mrs. Ferris-Jones stumbled right into Ryder's arms, his reflexes were swift enough that he caught her with ease, but not before she had flung the entire contents of her punch cup down the front of Lydia's silk gown.

Lydia gasped at the drenching while the other guests froze in shock.

"Oh, I am so *terribly* sorry, Lady Keeling," Phoebe exclaimed. "How clumsy of me."

Eve gritted her teeth, knowing the accident had been deliberate, despite the woman's effusive apologies. "It was indeed clumsy of you, Phoebe," she replied coolly as she swept up a cloth napkin and gave it to her friend. "But your aim was perfect."

"I cannot think what you mean."

"No, of course not." Eve smiled supportively at Lydia, who was wiping futilely at the dripping stain. "I will accompany you to the ladies' retiring room, where we can try to repair the damage to your gown."

"No, please go ahead," Lydia protested. "I wouldn't want you to miss the fireworks and spoil your evening."

Eve cast a darkling glance at Phoebe, thinking that her evening had been spoiled long before this. "It's no bother, truly, Lydia. I've seen similar spectacles numerous times on previous visits to Vauxhall," she said aloud before murmuring under her breath so that only her friend could hear: "You would be doing me a service, for if I remain here, I might just cause some fireworks of my own."

In the carriage ride home, however, Eve let Ryder know of her objections. "You do realize that spill was deliberate?"

Beside her, Claire looked shocked, while Drucilla nodded sagely.

"I had my suspicions," Ryder replied in a mild tone.

"That sort of cattish behavior is precisely why I didn't want Mrs. Ferris-Jones on your bride list."

"You're right, of course. Consider her stricken."

Eve stared at him warily, wondering at his easy capitulation. "Do you mean it?"

"Certainly. I gave myself over to your talented hands, so if you advise me to drop her, then I will do so."

"It is for the best, Ryder," Eve felt compelled to explain. "If you wish to move in the highest circles, then you will want a bride whose reputation is spotless."

"That is exactly what I want," he murmured blandly.

When Eve continued to scrutinize him in the light of the carriage lamp, Ryder flashed her a smile that took her breath away.

That smile could prove lethal to her senses, Eve realized, feeling a shiver of heat slowly slide down her spine.

She was very glad when his town coach stopped before her house and set them all down so she could part from Ryder without making a fool of herself by fawning over him as a certain other obnoxious widow had done.

The incident at Vauxhall proved typical of the competition for Ryder's notice. For although he had scratched several ladies off his list, there were others eagerly vying to be his choice of bride.

Eve witnessed one particular altercation herself. It occurred in Hyde Park, during the fashionable hour of five, when the ton congregated in order to see and be seen. She was acting as chaperone for Claire and a prospective suitor when their phaeton came upon Ryder and two of the debutantes on his list.

He clearly had his hands full, Eve realized at

once. Apparently he had taken up the stylish, wealthy Miss Gouge in his curricle for a drive. But Miss Pittard, the reigning beauty of the Season, who was currently riding with friends, had lost her seat when her horse suddenly shied and had conveniently tumbled off directly in front of Ryder's equipage.

Eve's gasp turned to a sigh of relief when she saw Ryder expertly bring his spirited pair of grays to a halt in time to avoid the fallen damsel.

Dazed, Miss Pittard pushed herself up and looked around her, her gaze immediately latching onto Ryder. "Oh, Sir Alex, thank heavens it is you," the raven-haired beauty exclaimed. "No one else could have reacted so splendidly. You saved my life."

When she added forlornly, "I know you will help me," he sat debating for the barest instant. To his credit, there was only the slightest edge of dryness to his voice when he replied, "Of course I will help you, Miss Pittard."

When he handed the reins to Miss Gouge beside him, however, that young lady gave a startled protest. "But I don't know how to drive."

"Just hold the horses steady and don't saw on their mouths," Ryder said patiently before going to Miss Pittard's rescue.

"I seem to have sprained my ankle," the girl complained, her lower lip trembling dramatically.

Eve considered helping Ryder deal with the spoiled beauty, but seeing the difficulty Miss Gouge was having in controlling his grays, who were nervous from the spectators and the unexpected commotion, she decided that the horses needed her more. Climbing down from the phaeton, Eve went to their heads and spoke to them soothingly while Ryder gingerly examined Miss Pittard's ankle.

"You see, Sir Alex, how swollen it is? I vow, it is painful enough to make me swoon. I would be ever so grateful if you would take me home in your curricle." Without even waiting for his response, she shamelessly put her arms around his neck.

"But there is no room," Miss Gouge objected coldly.

Miss Pittard tossed her head. "I am certain Sir Alex will make room. He would never be so ungallant as to leave an injured lady lying on the ground to fend for herself."

By now a crowd had gathered to watch, so Ryder had no choice but to comply, and Eve had difficulty swallowing a laugh at how easily he had been maneuvered by the little hussy.

He seemed to share the sentiment, for his expression held sardonic amusement as he met Eve's gaze over the girl's head. Visibly quelling his exasperation, however, he lifted Miss Pittard in his arms and carried her to his vehicle, where he settled her on the seat beside her fuming rival, Miss Gouge.

Miss Pittard's escorts—two dashing young bucks riding spirited mounts—were clearly not happy to lose her, and both threw Ryder dark looks beneath the brims of their tall beaver hats.

Ignoring them as well as the other gawkers, Ryder climbed into the driver's seat—a tight squeeze with himself and two passengers—and resumed control of the reins.

"Thank you, Lady Hayden, for your presence of mind," he said solemnly to Eve.

"It was nothing," she replied, stepping aside. "Indeed, it was fascinating watching you play the hero, Sir Alex."

The gleam sparking in his eyes promised retribution, but he merely gave her a bow and snapped the reins, sending his pair moving briskly forward.

The gossip columns delighted in recounting the incident the following day, and the *Morning Chronicle* even displayed a cartoon showing two ladies squabbling over Ryder in a fistfight.

Eve was reading the paper in the morning room when Ryder was shown in. "Ah, the conquering hero returns," she remarked, not hiding her amusement.

"Vixen," he murmured without heat. "That was a low blow yesterday, scoffing at my heroics."

"I do beg pardon, Sir Alex. I don't mean to disparage your gallantry in the least. Indeed, I am quite impressed to see the competition for your favors heating up."

Ryder settled himself comfortably in a chair near Eve. "Perhaps you were a bit *too* successful in finding candidates willing to wed me."

"Oh, no, I cannot take credit for the fact that damsels are swooning over you and throwing themselves at your feet. However, I'm not certain this sort of publicity is productive to your campaign." She waved the cartoon at him. "The mamas who are high sticklers will not be pleased to see their precious daughters engaging in fisticuffs."

"It hardly seems fair when I did nothing to provoke it."

"Ah, but you did, Ryder. Your charm is to blame."

He raised a sardonic eyebrow. "My charm?"

"Certainly. You can be devilishly charming when you put your mind to it. It has made you an even more inviting matrimonial prize. But perhaps you should restrain yourself a little if you don't wish to put off the more modest candidates," Eve commented with an impish version of her bewitching smile.

Ryder froze, caught by that smile, feeling bowled over, just as he'd been the first time he'd met Eve. The golden warmth of it still had the power to stun him. He was glad when the twins entered the morning room just then. After responding to their enthusiastic greetings, Ryder settled back to watch Eve interact with her brother and sister, content simply to listen to her melodic, slightly husky voice.

He had practically run tame in her house the past week, although he'd rarely had Eve to himself. The door knocker at Hayden House sounded at least a dozen times a day to announce callers and admirers. Yet Ryder had found himself eager to be a part of it.

He cherished the laughter and familial feeling that was so prevalent in this house. Such emotions had been quite rare in his life—and nonexistent since his mother's death when he was seventeen, when he'd left Cyrene in search of a bold new future.

He was a loner by choice, but the career of a soldier of fortune was harsh, completely lacking in warmth and softness. Even his years as a Guardian, though fulfilling and filled with the special camaraderie of a brotherhood, had been austere, dedicated to duty and noble ideals, not the tenderness and devotion of siblings who truly cared for one another.

Perhaps that was why he found himself drawn here. Why part of him hungered for the kind of warmth and affection that was second nature to this family.

Eve had roused that longing in him, Ryder knew. She was a joy to be around. Whenever she was near, he was filled with an acute awareness of her presence. More than ever he wanted to win her. He could remain here forever, basking in her smile, her scent, her softness.

Yet shopping was on the agenda for today. He and Cecil were to escort the two sisters to Bond Street. He didn't mind in the least, Ryder reflected wryly, as long as he was in Eve's company.

They set out in the Hayden town coach, with one of Eve's footmen accompanying them to carry packages. They spent the next three hours visiting various shops and merchants, primarily searching for accessories for Claire's wardrobe.

Ryder had promised them luncheon and ices afterward, however, so they were headed for the Clarendon Hotel, having sent the footman back to the carriage with all their parcels, when they passed a shop that sold tobacco and snuff.

Cecil stopped cold, peering in the window at the display of pipes and enameled snuffboxes and beautifully carved cases to hold cheroots. "Hold a moment, Sir Alex, will you?" he called to Ryder, who had moved ahead with the ladies to the street corner.

The busy thoroughfare was bustling, crammed with carts and drays and carriages, and the sidewalks were crowded with pedestrians. Ryder asked Eve and Claire to wait for him before crossing, then retreated the short distance to the tobacco shop.

"Your friend Macky is fond of cheroots," Cecil explained, "so I thought I might purchase a box for him. Can you advise me on what kind he might like?"

Beau Macklin had begun to develop a friendship with Cecil, and Ryder thought it wise to encourage the acquaintance. He was trying to recall the brand Macky favored when behind him he heard Claire scream over the din of iron wheels and horses' hooves, followed by sudden shouts of alarm.

Ryder spun around and his heart jumped to his throat. Eve was sprawled halfway into the street, facedown on the cobblestones, directly in the path of a heavily laden dray drawn by four massive draft horses.

Claire stood frozen on the curb, watching in horror at the dray's swift approach. The next moment she started forward, apparently intent on rescuing her sister from the imminent peril of being run over.

Reacting on sheer instinct, Ryder raced toward them, shoving pedestrians out of his way in his frantic effort to reach Eve.

In a desperate burst of speed, he yanked Claire back to the curb and lunged for Eve, catching her beneath her arms and literally dragging her out of the path of the deadly hooves an instant before the horses thundered past, the driver still hauling fiercely on the reins in a futile attempt to stop his team.

Ryder ended down on his knees with Eve sprawled partway beneath him. His heart pounding, his mind roiling, he lifted her carefully so that she was half sitting on the pavement, half clinging to his forearms. His trembling hand brushed tendrils back from her face as he scrutinized her for injuries.

"Are you hurt?" he demanded, his voice hoarse with fear.

"I . . . don't think so," Eve replied, her own voice tremulous with shock, her expression still stunned.

It was only then that Ryder could breathe again. His arms tightened convulsively around her for a moment, until he realized they were still in the busy street.

Cecil had moved to stand guard over them and was frantically waving his arms to halt traffic.

Ryder helped Eve up and led her back to the curb, where he continued to support her.

"My God, Eve," Claire rasped, "are you all right?"

"Yes . . . just shaken a bit."

Claire gave her sister a fearful hug. "Dear God, you could have been killed."

At the reminder, Ryder found himself muttering a prayer of relief. Seeing Eve lying there helplessly, about to be crushed, had almost stopped his heart.

"What the hell happened?" he demanded, his voice still rough with emotion.

"I'm not certain," Eve replied. "One moment I was standing at the curb, waiting to cross, and I felt my arm being jostled. The next, someone in the crowd shoved me into the street. I barely caught myself with my hands, or I would have landed on my face." Dazedly, she glanced down at her gloved hands, finding the palms soiled and scraped. "Then you came to my rescue, Sir Alex." Eve gazed up at him with a forced smile. "Despite appearances, I promise I was *not* throwing myself at your feet."

Ryder couldn't manage to respond to her wan attempt at raillery, since he could find no humor whatsoever in the situation. When Eve shuddered, he raised his unsteady fingers to rest comfortingly on her cheek.

"Falling on your face was the least of the danger, Evie," Cecil broke in. "If not for Sir Alex's quick thinking, you would have been mincemeat."

"Yes. Thank you, Sir Alex. You saved my life."

"Still don't know how you managed it," Cecil said admiringly. "I could only stand there gawking like a simpleton."

Ryder brushed off the boy's compliment without comment. He had reacted in time only because his reflexes had been honed to a razor's edge after years of surviving as a mercenary and carrying out the clandestine enterprises of the Guardians.

Instead he turned to address Claire. "Did you see who pushed her?"

Claire shook her head. "No, I saw nothing. It all happened so suddenly."

At the grim note in his tone, Eve gave Ryder a searching look. "Surely you don't think it was deliberate?" she asked faintly.

"If you ask me," Cecil interjected, "it is the work

of that cursed villain. The one who nearly killed you twice at home."

Ryder's jaw hardened as he recalled learning of the two other accidents that had befallen Eve before she'd come to London—a deadly wolf trap and gunshot—both of which she had blamed on poachers.

Before Cecil could go on, however, they were joined by Eve's footman, who took one glance at his mistress and let out a worried exclamation. "Is something amiss, my lady?"

"A mere mishap, Ned. I am all right."

"You still look shaken, Eve," Claire said. "Perhaps we should go home at once."

"Not a good idea," Cecil objected, shaking his head. "It'll put the aunts in a quake if Eve returns early looking like she was dragged through the streets, which is precisely what happened."

"I just need a moment to compose myself . . . preferably out of the public eye," she added, glancing around to see that they were still the center of attention.

Ryder wasn't about to send Eve home alone, certainly not before questioning her. He'd spent too many years living by his wits to brush off this third incident as mere coincidence. He wanted to know who might bear Eve enough animosity to try to kill her. Somehow she had developed an enemy, Ryder was certain. A cowardly enemy furtive enough to be difficult to identify.

To think someone would dare try to harm Eve filled him with fury, while her vulnerability touched him with an unfamiliar fear. He wanted to hold her safe from everything that could hurt her. He wanted to wrap Eve in his arms and never let her go.

Yet that was impossible at the moment, since they were surrounded by dozens of observers, including her brother and sister and servant.

He could take her to his house across the square, however, where they would have a moment of privacy.

"I think it best if I accompany you home now," Ryder told Eve. "We can stop first at my house, so you can repair the damage to your gown and pull yourself together before facing the aunts. How does that sound?" When Eve nodded, Ryder turned to Cecil. "You escort Lady Claire to lunch, and I will send the carriage back for you."

"If you are sure you don't need us, Eve," Claire said tentatively.

"I will be fine," she replied. "Ned," Eve added, speaking to the footman, "will you accompany Mr. Cecil and Lady Claire?"

"Aye, milady."

When the twins had set off for their luncheon, Ryder took Eve's arm and steered her toward a side street, heading for her town coach.

Still feeling light-headed, she allowed herself to be guided. It was some while before the fact of Ryder's grim silence penetrated her daze. When she glanced up at him, she winced at the dark expression on his features. The set of his jaw suggested fury and steely determination.

"You realize of course," Eve murmured as they reached the carriage, "that the gossip rags will devour this new tidbit? And when w-word of your heroics get around, it will only increase y-your appeal."

Realizing how weak her attempt at teasing sounded, Eve clamped her lips shut. She had been trying to make light of the situation, but the tremble in her voice shocked her. She was grateful for Ryder's support as he handed her into the coach, for fear suddenly clutched at her midsection.

Perhaps it was a delayed reaction to the accident. She had escaped serious injury or even death because Ryder had dragged her out of harm's way barely in the nick of time.

He still made no comment but merely gave orders to the coachman as Eve sank back against the squabs. Ryder followed her in and shut the door, and immediately the vehicle lurched forward.

She ought not to let herself think about it, Eve scolded herself. Yet the jolting experience had left her cold and shivering with a need to be held.

As if he understood, Ryder silently and possessively put an arm around her shoulder and drew her close, tucking her against his chest. "I'm not about to let anyone harm you," he breathed roughly in her ear.

The protectiveness in his voice felt strangely wonderful. Except for her brother, no man had ever been so intensely protective of her. Turning into Ryder, Eve pressed her face in the hollow of his neck and shoulder and breathed in his warmth. It was the smell of comfort, of safety.

She had never before leaned on anyone, and she had no desire to start now, especially with Ryder. She didn't want to show her fear to him, to let him see how frightened and vulnerable she felt. He'd always been so strong, and she didn't want to appear weak or cowardly in his eyes. Just now, however, the temptation was too great to fight. It was a relief to have Ryder to depend on, to rely on the strength that seemed to radiate from him.

Eve sighed, realizing how safe she felt with him. She could stay like this forever, wrapped in his arms, pressed close to his lean, hard body, his heat and strength engulfing her.

All too soon, however, the carriage halted in front of his house. As Ryder whisked her inside through the entrance hall, Eve glimpsed wealth and good taste in the decor. Shortly she found herself in his large, masculine study, where he made her sit on the couch.

He poured her a brandy, then sat beside her and gently urged her to take small sips. Eve obliged, feeling the potent burn of the liquor all the way down to her queasy stomach. When she could feel the color returning to her face, she pushed the snifter away.

"Are you prepared to talk about it now, Eve?" Ryder asked.

"I suppose I must," she said reluctantly.

"You do realize someone is out to do you serious injury or worse?"

Her response was a faint huff of laughter. "The thought did occur to me . . . although not until I was lying facedown on the pavement with those massive beasts bearing down on me."

A humorless smile pulled at his lips. "As long as you now understand the danger you are in."

Eve nodded slowly. "The first attempts were likely not accidents either, were they?"

"It's unlikely."

"I didn't want to believe it," she murmured. "I thought I was safe in London. But I was deliberately pushed in front of that dray."

"I believe so. Someone followed you this morning and waited for the opportunity to strike."

The notion that an assailant was stalking her was unnerving. An enemy was intent on killing her, or at the very least, frightening her out of her wits. And he had certainly succeeded. The swiftness and unexpectedness of the attack terrified her.

Eve shuddered and then quickly took another gulp of brandy for courage.

Ryder smiled his grim, enchanting smile. "Don't worry. From now on, you will be under my protection."

Her gaze flickered to him. He did look supremely dangerous at the moment, even though his violence was leashed. But if Ryder said he would protect her, then she had no doubt he would.

"That is a comforting thought, Ryder. I've heard tell that royalty has paid exorbitant prices to purchase your services. But how do you protect someone from an unknown assailant?"

"We start by trying to identify him. And to do that, we need to discover who might want to harm you."

"I don't have the faintest idea."

"We'll go over everyone you might have ever angered or slighted. And I want you to tell me in detail everything you remember about the first two accidents. We will get to the bottom of this, Eve, but until we do, I intend to put some of my men in your house to guard you when I can't be there."

"In my *house*? But won't that alert whoever is threatening me?"

"Servants will be unobtrusive. I'll send some of my own over to join your staff. And I have someone else in mind who is trained in hand-to-hand fighting. He can pose as one of your footmen. We must be better prepared next time."

And there would be a next time, Eve suddenly realized. Shivering, she rubbed her aching temple. "What about my sister and brother and the aunts? They could be in danger as well."

Ryder's slashing brows drew together. "Of course we'll keep a watch on them, although there's no evidence we should be concerned. You're the one suffering the accidents."

"But if something happens to me, how will they go on?"

Ryder surveyed her with amazement. Eve had nearly been killed today, yet she was more worried about her family.

"Nothing will happen to you, I promise," he vowed solemnly.

And he meant it. He would protect her or die trying; it was as simple as that.

When she was silent, he took the snifter from her and set it on the side table. "You have to trust me, Eve."

She smiled feebly, a picture of courage that squeezed hard at his chest. "I do trust you. Of course I do. It is only . . ."

"Only what?"

Shivering, she clasped her fingers together and sat there staring down at them. "I cannot seem to stop shaking."

Her air of vulnerability frightened him almost as much as the force of his own feelings. Then she lifted her shimmering gaze and his heart stumbled. The trembling he could handle; it was the tears in her eyes that were his downfall. The protective tenderness that rushed through him left Ryder shaking as much as Eve was.

Needing to touch her, he raised his hand to her face, brushing back the tendrils around her pale cheeks and strained eyes.

"Ryder," she whispered.

His gut tightened, locking the air in his chest. Helpless to stop himself, he leaned closer and brought his head down. When he kissed her softly, her mouth instantly turned warm and yielding beneath his. Joy and pleasure leaped within him before he could arm himself against them.

Forcibly he drew back and rested his forehead against hers. The next moment, he felt Eve reach up to entwine her fingers in his hair.

He breathed her name against her fevered skin, murmuring it like a caress, a curse, a warning. But then suddenly she was kissing him ardently, her fingers tightening in his hair, clinging.

The desire that lurked just below the surface exploded to life. Ryder buried his hands in *her* hair and kissed her fiercely, his lips slanting again and again over hers. The heat suddenly pouring through him was as intense as any he'd ever known. Desire ran through him like torch fire, making him ache and burn.

He craved the feel of Eve, the touch and taste and smell of her, all the things he'd denied himself for years. He wanted her more than he wanted his next breath, to lose himself inside her and never find his way free. The storm in him was nearly uncontainable.

Yet somewhere in his dazed mind, he realized that she was pushing at his shoulders with her hands. She had fallen back upon the sofa and he was sprawled half on top of her.

With a savage growl, Ryder broke off and sat up, damning himself for losing control. Eve needed a protector, not a lover, yet he had practically assaulted her.

Reaching down carefully, he helped her up, his chest burning with each labored breath.

Her own breath was coming in gasps as she rose shakily to her feet. "I need to leave."

"No!" Ryder exclaimed. When he saw her startled look, he added more softly, "No, you can't go home looking like you've been ravished. I'll have my housekeeper show you to a room upstairs, where you can tidy yourself."

Pushing himself to his feet, he went to ring the bellpull and stood waiting there until the cheerful-looking elderly woman appeared. Eve remained silent as he gave orders to show her to a room, and then she followed the servant out without a word.

Ryder stood there for a moment, eyes closed, his expression savage. Then he made straight for the brandy decanter, cursing himself all the while.

* * *

Eve was still shaking when she reached the bedchamber upstairs, but the cause had little to do with the threat to her life and everything to do with the dangerous man she had left behind in the study.

She was grateful when the housekeeper withdrew, saying she would fetch warm water for her ladyship to wash with and a damp cloth to remove the stains on her gown.

When Eve sat down at the dressing table to take off her soiled gloves, however, she winced at the image of herself in the mirror. Her cheeks were flushed, her mouth was red and glistening, and her hair hung in wisps around her face. She did indeed look as if she had been ravished.

She felt precisely the same way.

She raised her fingertips to her still-tingling lips. She had always been a little unnerved by Ryder's intensity, but this time it had overwhelmed her. Eve let out a shaky breath, remembering how he had looked at her. The emotions in those turbulent dark eyes had held her riveted. And then his lips had touched hers.

The heat and tension radiating from him was frankly shocking. She'd felt seared by his heat, by the hunger burning in his kiss, and suddenly it was too much. Lying there beneath him she'd felt helpless, overpowered by his ardent sensuality.

Eve closed her eyes now, recalling how her heart had pounded in her chest, how she had fought for breath. She had frankly panicked.

Yet it wasn't simply fear of Ryder that had made her bolt like a frightened doe. It was fear of her own feelings. She was bewildered by the fierce yearning he made her feel. She'd never felt such savage need, such craving as the hot ache that had come painfully to life between her thighs. She'd been swept away by the same fire, the same passion as when he'd kissed her in the meadow all those years ago . . . except that this time the sensations were a thousand times more powerful.

It would *have* to stop, Eve vowed to herself. She wanted control over her feelings, not chaos and uncertainty and helpless desire. She had spent her entire existence with no power or control over her life, and now that she'd finally gained some measure of control, she was determined never to lose it. She would never again be at the mercy of some man, no matter who he was.

Pressing her lips together, Eve yanked the pins from her hair so she could brush it out and start all over with a new coiffure.

She would start anew with Ryder as well. He had turned her own senses against her, but she wouldn't let it happen again.

Yet that meant she could never again allow herself to be alone with him, Eve told herself fiercely. She had barely escaped this time, and she might not be so fortunate the next.

Chapter Seven

If Eve hoped to avoid Ryder, she immediately realized the impossibility, for he made clear his intention to remain underfoot—beginning that very afternoon when he escorted her across the square to break the news about her mishap to the aunts.

As soon as he returned home, Ryder sent two of his own footmen over to join her staff, and promised a third in the morning. And that evening he insisted on squiring the family to two different balls.

At both events, he kept Eve in his sights the entire time, even when his attention was formally engaged by the various beauties vying for his hand.

Eve was profoundly grateful for his support, despite her determination to keep her distance from him, for she still felt jittery and vulnerable. Whenever she caught Ryder's eye, it was like a reassuring touch in the dark. She didn't want to admit her fear, even to herself, yet she found herself staring at shadows and looking over her shoulder, searching for nonexistent villains.

The aunts were no help in calming her nerves, either. As predicted, they were shocked and appalled by the attack on her life and offered to cancel all their engagements for the indefinite future. Eve refused, however. She wanted nothing to interfere with her sister's Season or chance to make an ideal match. She was determined to control her trepidation and go on as normally as possible, even if she was in danger.

It was easier said than done. Eve had a nightmare that night and woke bleary-eyed and uneasy the next morning. Breakfast was a subdued affair, even though Cecil kept up a cheery monologue throughout the meal, supported now and then by Claire.

When afterward Eve retired directly to the morning room, intent on taking refuge there, she was immediately followed by her family, who were resolved to provide her company and keep her mind off her troubles.

Moments later, she heard the rap of the door knocker. Her nerves still on edge, Eve felt all her muscles tense—until she realized that the visitor was likely Ryder, since it was too early for normal callers.

She set aside the book on agriculture that she was reading and strove for poise, although she felt at a disadvantage wearing an old gown, with her hair piled carelessly on top of her head. Then Ryder strolled into the room and sent her a quiet smile before greeting the others. Absurd how his presence instantly comforted her.

Amazingly, he was welcomed warmly by both Drucilla and Beatrice.

At least some benefit, Eve thought wryly, had come from her near death. Because Ryder had saved her life, the aunts had amended their opinion of him somewhat, and he was tentatively established in their good graces at least for the moment.

"I promised you another footman, Countess," Ryder said when the aunts were done expressing their gratitude once more. He gestured toward the door, and immediately a handsome chestnut-haired man entered and moved to stand before Eve.

Her eyes widened when she recognized Mr. Beau Macklin, for oddly enough, he was dressed as a footman.

Although his stance was appropriately humble for a servant and his expression solemn, his eyes twinkled at her. "Good morning, my lady. Macky, at your service."

Cecil bounded to his feet, looking astonished. "Macky, is that really you?"

"Aye, lad, 'tis I," he responded with a bold grin.

"What the devil are you doing dressed as a servant?"

"It is my costume, of course—to support my new role. I will be posing undercover as a footman in your house." He gave Eve a formal bow. "I was formerly an actor, my lady, so I have experience playing roles other than that of gentleman about town."

Ryder spoke up. "As I told you, Countess, I want someone to protect you when I cannot be here, and this is the most expedient way. Consider Macky your new shadow. You will take him with you everywhere you go, and I mean *everywhere*. You are not to leave the house without him."

"Very well," Eve said slowly, "if you think it necessary. But won't Mr. Macklin be recognized?"

"Probably not by anyone in your household,

since your servants have never seen him before. And it's unlikely your peers will make the connection, since gentry rarely glance twice at servants."

Ryder turned to address the aunts. "Lady Wykfield, Lady Beatrice, I hope you won't hold Macky's former profession against him. He is well qualified for the task of keeping Lady Hayden safe. I would trust him with my life—and have done so on more than one occasion. He is sometimes employed by the Foreign Office, as I am."

When Drucilla gave Macky a cold scrutiny, Eve could tell she was offended that they'd been duped into assuming Macky a gentleman. But for once Drucilla stifled her class prejudices in favor of more practical concerns and nodded regally. "We will all be grateful for his presence, Sir Alex. I scarcely slept a wink last night, worrying about Lady Hayden. I feared that she—indeed, we all—could be assaulted in our very beds."

"I say!" Cecil exclaimed. "Never knew you were an agent of the F.O., Macky. It must be exciting. I hope you will tell me about some of your adventures."

"Certainly I will," Macky agreed. "But you will need to keep my identity a secret. We don't want to alert our villain and spoil the chance to catch him, now do we?"

Cecil chuckled, and Eve could tell her brother considered it great fun to support the hoax. Even Claire was smiling softly. The twins had grown fond of Ryder's friend in the short time they'd known him, and Eve enjoyed his company too, for Macky could be counted on to liven any gathering and frequently made them all laugh with his wit.

With another bow, Macky withdrew from the room to stand guard just outside the door, but Ryder settled beside Eve on the settee, saying he wanted to question them about who might want her harmed.

He was deadly serious about protecting her, Eve knew, consoled by the thought. It was Ryder himself, however, who made her feel safe. For him, defending others against potential violence was commonplace. It was his profession, after all. He was a man comfortable with danger, and his self-assurance and air of purpose bolstered her own confidence and made her believe that eventually they would discover the identity of and thwart her unknown assailant.

Ryder appeared all business when he asked her again to recount the two incidents that had occurred in Hertfordshire. Then his inquiry turned to possible suspects—anyone with whom she might have had altercations during the past year.

"There is only one person I can think of," Eve said pensively. "The former steward of Hayden Park, Tobias Meade."

"Yes," Cecil agreed. "Meade would have good reason to dislike you—although not enough to murder you, I should think."

"Why would he dislike her?" Ryder asked.

"Because Evie fired him six months ago."

"I let him go for poor management," she explained, "and for gravely neglecting the estate tenants. I didn't believe Meade was crooked, merely lazy and incompetent. But after my husband died, I could no longer tolerate his ineptitude. So I fired him and hired a better steward to take his place."

Ryder raised an eyebrow. "Did you have the authority to fire him? I thought the estate was entailed."

"It is," Eve replied. "Hayden's elderly uncle, Laurence Seymour, inherited the title and all the entailed property, but he lives in Bath and has no desire to take up residence at Hayden Park."

"A crabby skinflint if there ever was one," Cecil interjected scornfully.

Drucilla intervened, her tone haughty as usual. "You will not speak so of your betters, young man. The new Lord Hayden is my cousin, and you will show him proper respect."

Cecil grinned. "Didn't mean to be improper, Aunt Dru. I only meant that he doesn't concern himself with anything but profits. Before he died, Evie's earl did his best to let his ancestral seat go to rack and ruin, and now your cousin is following his lead."

Eve couldn't dispute her brother's contention. Richard had neglected his estates whenever possible, for he had no interest in farming, and tolerated his tenants only for the income they brought him. And the new Lord Hayden was so miserly, he refused to care for his tenant farmers or to pour any of his inherited assets into making the Park a productive estate. Which was why she had taken a greater role in running affairs there.

"Come to think of it, Evie," Cecil said thoughtfully, "the new earl isn't happy with your nagging. Wonder if he has it in for you."

"I hardly think Lord Hayden would stoop to

murder," Eve said wryly, "simply because I have pressed him to acknowledge his obligations."

"But your interference isn't making him happy. No doubt he would be glad to be rid of you."

Beatrice spoke up in her gentle tone. "Laurence may be a skinflint, but he would not exert himself to do murder. It would require too much effort."

Eve couldn't help but smile. "It is absurd to consider him a suspect, Cecil."

"What have you done that is so vexing?" Ryder asked her.

"I've merely tried to oversee the estate in his place, since he won't trouble himself."

Drucilla grimaced. "You have troubled yourself to the point of obsession, Eve. You never take your nose out of that almanac or some other publication on agriculture."

When she pointed at the book lying on the table before Eve, Eve saw Ryder glance down and read the title: *The Farmer's Calendar* by Arthur Young.

His eyebrow lifted in surprise, and she felt a need to explain. "I cannot judge how an estate steward is performing if I am totally ignorant about agriculture, so I've tried to learn about land management and more productive methods of farming."

Drucilla scoffed at this. "It is bad enough that you delve into such unladylike matters as crop rotation and drainage and the impact of the Corn Laws. But I don't know why you insist on spending so much of your widow's jointure on repairs of tenant cottages and such. It is not your responsibility in the least."

"Perhaps I have no formal responsibility, but

morally I feel obliged to make amends for Richard's neglect. And Lord Hayden refuses to become involved."

"No doubt," Beatrice pointed out, "he would be delighted if you simply remained in London and never returned to the Park."

That much was true, Eve reflected. The London house belonged to her, willed to her by her late husband. When Richard was alive, they had spent most of their time in London, for he had relished the whirl of town life. But Eve much preferred the country. She was glad the new earl had declined to assume residence at Hayden Park—the family seat of the Earls of Hayden. But even if he did eventually claim his seat, he could not evict her entirely. She had the right to remove to the nearby dower house, which was a rather large, comfortable manor specifically built for the widows of the Hayden earls.

"I have no intention of leaving Hayden Park," Eve replied lightly. "I cannot simply abandon the tenants there. They need someone to champion them, so for the time being, I have appointed myself to the role."

"I think it quite admirable of you, Eve," Claire said loyally.

"So do I," Beatrice seconded.

Feeling Ryder's eyes on her, Eve glanced at him. He was studying her as if she were fascinating to him.

She looked away as a blush rose to her cheeks. "Whatever contribution I've made to their welfare is merely their due. The tenants welcomed me as their mistress seven years ago, and I merely want to repay them. And truthfully, it is satisfying to be able to help. There is so little ladies are allowed to do, but this is one way I can make a difference."

She strove to keep her tone light, although it was difficult. She'd been helpless to aid the tenants much when Richard was alive, for he wouldn't countenance her involvement in estate affairs beyond the superficial. But she had tried to make up for it since.

"I think you make too much of your perceived limitations, Eve," Drucilla said. "Ladies are permitted a great deal of independence within the boundaries of their station."

Eve winced and couldn't help but respond to what was such a sore subject for her. "I beg to disagree, Drucilla. Ladies, even more than most women, have little control over anything in their lives. And wives are hardly more than chattel. The law doesn't even consider them persons, but rather the property of some man. And a woman with no fortune is utterly powerless."

She couldn't control the edge of bitterness in her tone, and Drucilla objected just as vociferously. "It is simply as God ordained. Yet any lady of birth and breeding wields a great deal of authority."

"Not without the permission of her husband," Eve retorted. "Some are expected to be nothing more than a possession, a pretty, useless ornament for a nobleman's arm. Richard considered that my proper role."

Seeing Ryder's frown, Eve realized how sharp her tone had become. She shook herself, wondering how she could have let herself get so carried away.

She hadn't meant for the discussion to lead to her own views on female independence.

"But never mind that," she said, softening her tone. "We were discussing what enemies I might have made—unconsciously or otherwise."

"Well, it is unlikely to be any of the estate tenants," her brother commented. "They all think you a saint. But there is always Viscount Gyllford," Cecil added, referring to the owner of the neighboring estate who had been pestering her to wed him. "He could still be angry at you for rejecting his proposal."

"Enough to kill me?" Eve asked dubiously.

"He is eager to marry you, Evie. Perhaps he doesn't want anyone else claiming you."

She shook her head, and a long silence followed while they all stewed over who the culprit might be.

Eventually Ryder broke the silence. "I think for now we can put your former steward at the head of our list of suspects. Certainly enough to warrant investigating him."

The aunts went on to speak in Lord Gyllford's defense, repeating their arguments regarding his eligibility for Eve's possible remarriage. Ryder listened with only half an ear while contemplating the feelings Eve had let slip about her late husband—her bitterness and resentment.

He understood clearly now that she hadn't relished her vaunted position as a nobleman's prize possession. That even now she hoped to make a difference in the lives of her former estate tenants, despite the fact that they were no longer her responsibility.

What shamed Ryder was knowing he was guilty of striving to acquire Eve as *his* possession. For years he'd viewed her as a living, breathing symbol of all the things he'd never had, all he'd ever wanted.

Yet now that he was coming to know the real woman behind the image, he'd discovered she was even more captivating than the golden girl of his dreams. Her generosity of spirit, her caring nature, were more irresistible than her beauty or her alluring siren's smile.

And his desire for her was far more than carnal. He craved her company, her conversation, her thoughts. Learning more about Eve, truly knowing her, had become as much of an obsession as making love to her. He wanted to know everything about her: her longings and fears, the joy and pain in her life, the things that made her Eve, the woman he loved.

Ryder suddenly went still as his heart slammed hard in his chest. He had refused to put a name to the feelings he'd always had for Eve, but he could no longer deceive himself.

He had fallen in love with her.

Not a mere boy's yearning, either, but an adult love, powerful and vibrant and terrifying.

For a long moment Ryder sat stunned as the emotion he'd denied needing all his life abruptly swamped him. God help him, he loved Eve. He would have no defenses against her now at all.

Not that he ever had. He'd never had any choice in loving her. Certainly not since coming to London and meeting her again.

Beside him, he felt Eve shift slightly. When he

turned his head, their gazes locked and Ryder's breath caught in a hard knot in his throat.

He yearned to reach out and clasp her hand, just for the pleasure of touching her, yet he didn't dare. He had shocked her yesterday with his overwhelming passion, when he'd lost complete control. He couldn't acknowledge the violent flame around his heart to her now, for fear of driving her away.

Eve wasn't ready to hear of his feelings yet. He could tell by her sudden stillness as she became aware of him, of his nearness. Her lips had parted, as if she was remembering the feel of him against her.

Forcibly Ryder tore his gaze away to keep from unnerving her any further.

At least now, however, he knew exactly what he wanted. He had vowed to win Eve for his bride, but he yearned for far more: He wanted to win her heart.

His life had held little softness or warmth, and little love beyond a small circle of treasured friends. But he wanted to change that. He wanted to come out of the shadows, where he had lived for too long. He wanted a future with Eve—with love, with warmth, with laughter. The kind of life he'd seen others have.

His mother had known true love with his father. Some of his friends did as well. Caro and Max. Thorne and Diana. Deverill and Antonia. Ryder wanted that kind of love for himself. He understood now why seeing his friends' happiness had left him feeling hollow inside. Because of sheer envy.

He wanted fervently to believe his dream of a future with Eve could someday come to fruition. The vision stirred a longing that made him ache inside.

It was a tiny glimpse of heaven. One that for now was out of reach, Ryder reminded himself grimly.

Keeping Eve safe had to be his main objective. It had made his heart hurt to see the anxiety behind her bright smile. Since the assault yesterday, he'd known he would have to set aside any other aspirations in favor of stopping her assailant. Winning her heart would have to wait.

When he heard his name being called, Ryder shook himself out of his somber musings. "I beg your pardon, Lady Claire," he murmured. "What did you say?"

Claire gave him an understanding smile. "Only that I am glad you are escorting us to the Sudbury ball this evening. I much prefer your company to any of my other suitors."

"I am honored," Ryder replied politely, realizing that he had missed half the conversation.

"To be truthful," Claire asserted, "I wish we didn't have to attend. I would be perfectly happy to spend the evening quietly at home. In fact, every evening for the rest of the Season."

Eve took exception to Claire's pronouncement. "You won't be able to find a husband if you remain at home."

"I know, but it is all so wearying." She sighed. "I have met countless marital prospects, and they have all bored me to tears."

Looking puzzled, Eve scrutinized her sister. "There are at least three gentlemen whom you said interested you."

"I have since changed my mind."

"I think you simply have not given them much of a chance."

"But I *have,* Eve. And I cannot see that any of them will improve with time. They are all so . . . superficial, with no substance. I cannot admire them . . . not the way I admire Sir Alex."

When Claire smiled at Ryder, Eve pressed her lips together in a worried frown. "Perhaps you merely need the opportunity to come to know them better, Claire. I could arrange a day's outing to Richland for a picnic, for example. Or better yet, a house party at Hayden Park. It would allow you to become acquainted under less formal circumstances."

Claire shook her head. "I doubt that familiarity will do more than breed contempt. No, the trouble is that I cannot even *like* them very well, Eve. I certainly can't imagine myself falling in *love* with any of them. And I have grown utterly weary of the marriage game. Aren't you weary of it yet, Sir Alex?"

Ryder hesitated to answer, not knowing where she was leading the discussion.

Thoughtfully Claire put a finger to her lips as she surveyed him. "You know, Sir Alex, it would be so much easier if we could simply marry each other. You would be spared all the bother of choosing a bride, and I would be saved from utter boredom. And Eve would be grateful to have my future secure, wouldn't you, Eve?"

Ryder's eyebrow's shot up while Eve stared blankly at her sister. Wondering what the devil Claire was up to, he feigned a smile. "The offer is tempting, but you have no desire to wed me, Lady Claire."

"Oh, but I do. I am quite fond of you. And you are fond of me too, I know it."

"Of course I am."

"Well, if I must marry someone, I would far rather it be *you*. What objections would you have if I were to throw my cap at you?"

When she gave him a flirtatious look from under her eyelashes, Ryder was struck with the suspicion that Claire was trying to rouse her sister's jealousy.

Rather than exhibit jealousy, however, Eve looked troubled. "Claire, your jest about throwing your cap at Sir Alex is not particularly amusing."

"But I am not jesting," her sister replied innocently. "Oh, I know that the pinnacle of any young lady's matrimonial aspirations should be to land a wealthy nobleman, but I don't need wealth or a title. I want a husband I may be comfortable with. Sir Alex fits that bill. And at least he could be confident that I don't simply want him for his fortune."

Ryder cast a glance at the aunts. Both ladies had stopped their needlework and were staring at Claire as if she had grown two more heads. They might be grateful that he had saved Eve's life, but not enough to entertain the idea of his marrying into their family.

Looking agitated, Eve rose suddenly to her feet. "Claire, may I speak to you alone?"

Her guileless expression never changed as she said, "Certainly." Rising as well, Claire followed Eve from the room.

Ryder sat unmoving for a long moment, torn between dread, amusement, and the urge to shake Claire for her interference, no matter how well intentioned. If she was trying to rouse Eve's jealousy, he sincerely doubted it would work. Instead, it would likely only raise her defenses further.

"You don't mean to marry Claire, do you, Sir Alex?" Cecil asked, looking puzzled.

"I doubt it will come to that," Ryder said evasively.

"Good," Cecil said in relief. "Can't think what maggot has gotten into her head. You two wouldn't suit in the least," he added, shaking his own head at the vagaries of the feminine mind.

Chapter Eight

"You would not seriously contemplate marriage to Ryder, would you?" Eve asked as soon as she guided her sister into the library and closed the door behind them.

"Why wouldn't I?" Claire replied sweetly.

"Because you are wholly unsuited to each other," Eve said, feeling an inexplicable anxiety. She couldn't picture her reserved young sister entering a marriage of convenience with her undeniable opposite—a dangerous, intensely passionate man like Ryder. Claire was no match for him.

Claire, however, merely gazed back serenely. "You were the one who insisted he would make a splendid husband, Eve. His qualifications far surpass any of my other suitors, you know it. Sir Alex is a wonderful man, like a dear brother to me. I am much more comfortable with him than with any of the London bucks who are courting me."

Unable to dispute that assertion, Eve found herself struggling to reply. She couldn't fathom why she felt such a desperate need to protest her sister's wild notion, except that it felt entirely *wrong*. She could understand how Claire would be drawn to

Ryder. His devilish charm and wicked allure might appeal to other women, but his chief attraction for Claire was that he set her at ease, treating her like a cherished younger sister.

"I know you are fond of each other, but simply because you are comfortable together is not always the best basis for marriage. Sir Alex clearly doesn't regard you in a romantic light, and brotherly affection is unlikely to lead to love."

"Perhaps love isn't so important after all," Claire responded. "As Mama is fond of saying, love isn't necessary to a prosperous union."

Eve winced, hearing the echo of their mother's voice remarking disdainfully, *People of our class cannot let themselves be swayed by love.* She shook her head. "Love is not necessary, true, but you must have at least some interests and aspirations in common to sustain a marriage over the long years ahead."

"You are worried I will be miserable wed to Sir Alex."

Eve fell silent. It was true that she fervently wanted Claire to marry the right husband and be spared the loneliness and misery she herself had endured in her cold marriage. But that wasn't her only objection.

Claire spoke before she could marshal her chaotic thoughts. "I don't believe I would be miserable, Eve. In fact I imagine I would be perfectly happy with Sir Alex. And I would do my utmost to make him happy as well. If he proposes, I think I should accept."

Eve felt her stomach knot. She stared at her sister in dismay.

"Besides," Claire went on as if she hadn't just

dealt a painful blow, "marriage to me will help Sir Alex become accepted by society. Isn't that what you want for him?"

Certainly she did. But it was one thing to help Ryder find a bride; it was quite another for that bride to be her younger sister. Eve didn't want to think of him marrying Claire and becoming such an intimate a part of their family, for it would be impossible to keep any real distance from him then.

What was more, she didn't want to envision Ryder touching Claire or showing her sister such intimate pleasure as he'd shown *her.*

Which was ludicrous when she had no claim to Ryder herself.

She certainly couldn't share her irrational arguments with her sister, however.

"I do want acceptance for him," Eve finally replied, "but I want more for you to be happy with your chosen partner in life. And I don't want you making an irrevocable mistake simply for the sake of expediency."

"You cannot keep me wrapped in swaddling forever," Claire said softly.

Eve took a deep breath, striving for calm. "Very well. Perhaps I am being overprotective. I won't press further just now. But there is no need for you to make any hasty decision. Promise me you won't accept any proposals for the time being, from Sir Alex or anyone else. I want you to have adequate time to make a suitable match, and two weeks are not nearly enough to judge." When her sister hesitated, Eve's tone sharpened. "Promise me, Claire."

"Very well, I promise. But I very much doubt I will find anyone I would rather wed than Sir Alex."

Watching as Claire let herself from the library, Eve stood quite still, feeling a desperation far out of proportion to her sister's pronouncement. In the eyes of society, Claire and Ryder would make an acceptable match. And admittedly Claire would be lucky to have a husband like him.

Yet she couldn't bear to think of it, Eve acknowledged, biting her lower lip.

She raised a hand to her aching brow. Somehow she would have to change Claire's mind about wanting to marry Ryder—or alternatively convince Ryder not to propose.

Ryder was waiting for Claire at the end of the corridor when she emerged from the library. Upon seeing him, she gave a guilty start and took a step in the opposite direction, as if hoping to slip away. But he crooked a finger at her, and with a sigh, she went to meet him.

"Just what in the devil are you up to, minx?" he asked, keeping his voice low to prevent his words from carrying down the hall to where Macky stood performing his footman duties.

"I am only trying to help you win Eve," Claire admitted in a whisper. "I thought you could pretend to court me and I would pretend to return your interest."

"Forgive me," Ryder said dryly, "if I fail to see how that would help anything."

"Why, by shaking Eve out of her complacency, of course. She is much too indifferent about your other marital candidates, but if she thinks you are considering *me* for your bride, she will eventually realize that she wants you for herself."

Able to follow her logic but suspecting her scheme had backfired, Ryder had difficulty biting back his exasperation. "I appreciate your concern, my sweet, but I prefer to fight my own battles."

Claire dimpled. "Well, it did provoke a reaction from Eve. She is highly disgruntled at the thought of us marrying."

"I don't doubt it. She will defend you like a mother tiger, only now she will see *me* as the villain."

Claire instantly sobered. "She only wants my happiness, Sir Alex, so that her sacrifice won't be in vain. She gave up her future for us, you know."

"I know," Ryder said grimly.

"And I was afraid to wait much longer, since Eve doesn't seem to be responding to your subtle wooing." Claire gave him an intent scrutiny. "You *do* still want to win her, don't you, Sir Alex?"

"Certainly I do, but I'll thank you not to interfere from now on."

"I am sorry. I merely thought I could help. If you like, I will tell her that I have changed my mind."

"No," Ryder said sternly. "Pray, don't do me any more favors. Although . . ." He frowned thoughtfully. "You may have given me an opportunity to shake your sister out of her complacency, as you termed it."

Claire clapped her hands together with delight. "Then you have thought of a new plan! I knew you would."

"Enough, minx." Placing his hands on Claire's

shoulders, he spun her around and aimed her back toward the morning room. "Now, go join the others and leave me to handle my affairs my own way."

When she returned to the morning room, Eve was glad to learn that Ryder had taken his leave. And eventually her family dispersed, leaving her in privacy.

An hour ago, Eve would have felt uneasy being alone, knowing that her life was menaced by a furtive assailant. But now Mr. Macklin was standing guard just down the hall. And Claire's recent declaration was worrisome enough to keep her from dwelling on anything else.

She hadn't yet managed to arrange an ideal match for her sister. The slow pace thus far, however, was not due to a lack of appropriate suitors. The dowry provided Claire by Richard was adequate enough to entice all but the poorest candidates. And Claire seemed to have lost much of her shyness, in large part due to Ryder.

Which was perhaps the real difficulty. Claire had had no opportunity to become comfortable with any of her other prospects.

Determined to redouble her efforts, Eve put her mind to solving the dilemma. Her notion of a house party was actually a good one, for it would give several young gentlemen the chance to seriously court her sister. And the sooner, the better.

She could hold a weeklong gathering at Hayden Park, Eve decided, beginning next week. But she would have to hurry and make up the guest list right away in order to give everyone enough advance notice. And perhaps she could ask the aunts to help her write out the invitations this afternoon.

She would not invite Ryder, though. And not simply because she was afraid of her own feelings for him, but because she wanted to keep him away from her sister. Eve had little doubt the aunts would support her, for they had been appalled at the idea of Claire marrying Ryder. She could use the excuse of Drucilla's birthday next week as a valid justification for the party.

Eve spent the next half hour at her desk, composing a long list of prospective guests for the house party. Besides her family and suitors for Claire, she would have to provide a proper mix of people to ensure the right atmosphere. Some elderly ladies to keep the aunts company and to act as chaperones for the younger crowd. Perhaps some young ladies Claire's age and some friends of Cecil's—

"Do you want to go riding with me, Evie?" her brother asked from immediately behind her.

Starting violently, Eve clasped a hand over her heart and glowered at Cecil. "Will you please give me some warning before sneaking up on me?"

"Beg pardon," he said contritely. "Should have known you were still jumpy after yesterday."

Eve couldn't dispute him; even though she had something else to preoccupy her, her nerves were still fragile as glass.

"I merely came to ask you to ride," Cecil explained. "You have been cooped up in the house since the mishap yesterday."

"Thank you, but I cannot spare the time. I must speak with Drucilla and Beatrice to gain their approval for the house party and then get off the invitations this afternoon."

"What house party?"

"The one we are holding next week at Hayden Park, to give Claire a more comfortable setting in which to be courted. I've made up a list of potential guests. You might review it to see if I have included the friends you would like to invite."

Surprisingly Cecil didn't argue. Instead he took the list from her and sprawled in a nearby armchair to read. "Yes, these chaps will do. But I see you left off Sir Alex's name."

"Because I don't mean to invite him," Eve responded. "The whole point of the party is to separate Claire from Sir Alex, so she can concentrate on becoming better acquainted with her real suitors."

Cecil frowned at Eve. "But you must invite him. How else will he be able to protect you if he remains here in London?"

"I expect Mr. Macklin would be willing to come if I ask him."

Her brother's expression held genuine dismay. "That would be a grave mistake, Eve. No one will take better care of you than Sir Alex, not even Macky."

"I'm certain Macky will be able to provide adequate protection."

"No, Sir Alex is a *Guardian,* Eve," Cecil proclaimed as if that should settle the matter.

She gave him a curious stare. "What is a Guardian?"

Grimacing, Cecil ran a hand roughly through his

blond hair. "I wasn't supposed to tell. I swore to Mr. Verra I wouldn't say anything."

It was Eve's turn to frown. Santos Verra was a jovial Spaniard who owned an inn and tavern on Cyrene, overlooking the harbor. "Cecil, you cannot simply make a statement like that and leave me hanging. What are you talking about?"

The young man jumped to his feet and began to pace the carpet in agitation. "Have you never heard rumors about the Guardians and their heroic endeavors?"

Her frown turned to dawning comprehension. "Do you mean Sir Gawain Olwen's department of the Foreign Office?"

"Yes, but they do far more than simply report to the Foreign Office. I discovered their existence purely by accident two years ago because I sneaked out of the house one night and rode down the coast. When I spied a lugger putting into a cove, I thought it was a band of smugglers. But I crept close enough to overhear their conversation. They had captured two French spies and were discussing what to do when Mr. Ryder returned from his mission. Mr. Verra was there, and so was Lord Hawkhurst, among others. I still don't know how they twigged to my presence, but they caught me, and Mr. Verra made me swear I wouldn't divulge what I had seen. And I haven't. I've kept the secret all this time. But afterward I made it a point to find out everything I could about the Guardians." He gave Eve a speculative look. "I don't suppose it would hurt if I merely repeat what I learned from other sources."

"What did you learn, Cecil?"

"That they are a secret order who follow a noble cause. A league of protectors, committed to righting wrongs and fighting injustice and defending the weak and vulnerable."

Eve regarded her brother in surprise. "And Sir Alex is a member?"

"From what I can tell, yes. It stands to reason that he would be, since he's an expert in weapons and munitions. There aren't many gentlemen with his skills or his experience. I would give my right arm," Cecil added earnestly, "to be able to join their order and perform heroic deeds as Sir Alex does. But no doubt their members must prove their qualifications first before being invited to join."

Eve found herself deep in thought, remembering how Ryder had explained his work for the Foreign Office. He'd said only that he had turned over a new leaf in an effort to become respectable. He'd made no mention that he was a member of a secret league of protectors.

It made sense, though. She had always wondered why when he was near, she felt so safe, so secure. He was a protector at heart.

It was no wonder, either, why Cecil practically worshiped him. For a restless young man like her brother, the lure of a secret league of heroes would be too tantalizing and exciting to resist.

Cecil had stopped his pacing and was watching her intently. "You need to trust Sir Alex, Evie. He knows better than anyone how to protect people in danger. Macky may be a Guardian as well, for all I know, but I don't want you to chance it. You could be risking your life, going to Hertfordshire without Sir Alex."

Eve hesitated. She wasn't disputing Ryder's qualifications in the least. She understood why he inspired fervent loyalty and devotion in her brother. And she agreed to a large extent. Ryder might once have been a mercenary who dealt in danger and death for a living, but now he followed an admirable purpose.

She had always privately believed that class and title and wealth had little to do with the measure of a man, and Ryder was living proof. He was strong and noble, nothing like the shallow pleasure seeker her husband had been.

She was even envious of Ryder. He was someone with responsibilities far more important than hers. He led a life that *meant* something.

Yet he still wasn't the right husband for Claire.

Pushing back her chair, Eve swiveled to face her brother. "Cecil, I admit that Sir Alex is highly qualified to guard me, but I don't intend on inviting him to Hayden Park. It is much more important that Claire be given the chance to make a suitable match."

She was taken aback when Cecil set his jaw stubbornly. "Well, if Sir Alex won't be attending, then I won't either. So you can just scratch my chums off your list."

To her surprise, his tone held real anger. Then to her complete bafflement, Cecil flung the guest list on her writing desk and stalked from the room, leaving Eve to stew over this newest dilemma.

She didn't dare leave her brother here in London

all by himself. Nor did she intend to battle with him over the issue.

No, Eve realized suddenly, she had to take the battle to the source. She would simply have to confer with Ryder. He was a reasonable man—usually. She would ask him to renounce any intention of courting Claire.

Better yet, she would make him see that *he* had to be the one to disillusion her sister. The girl was no longer listening to her, Eve knew very well. Therefore, Ryder would have to make Claire abandon the wholly imprudent notion of a union between them.

When she appeared on his doorstep, Eve was not surprised that the first thing Ryder said was "Where is Macky?"

She couldn't fault him for taking her to task, since she should not have come alone, yet she had actually forgotten about the danger. "I left him across the square because I wanted to speak to you in private."

A muscle flexed in Ryder's jaw, but he escorted her into his study and gestured for her to take a seat. Eve preferred to remain standing, however, so Ryder settled one hip on his desktop. "Now, Countess, what is so urgent that you must disobey my direct order?"

"I expect you know. It is my sister. I hoped you would talk some sense into Claire and convince her to give up this foolish idea of marrying you."

Ryder's eyes held some emotion impossible for her to read. His pose was relaxed, lazy even, as he crossed his arms over his chest. "Lady Claire has all the right qualifications to be my wife."

Eve felt herself stiffen. She had hoped Ryder would be reasonable, but it seemed she had some serious persuading to do. "Perhaps she *is* qualified, but Claire deserves better than a marriage of convenience."

"As you suffered."

That was as good an argument as any, since she wasn't about to explain the true source of her discontent to Ryder. "Yes, if you must know . . . as I suffered." When he remained silent, Eve tried earnestly to stem her anxiety. "Ryder, you know very well that you and Claire would never suit."

"Why not?"

"Well, for one thing, you are much older than she is."

He arched a dubious brow. "My age wasn't an impediment when you were making up a list of potential brides for me."

"Perhaps it isn't a deterrent for other young ladies. But as a husband, you would be too intimidating for a gentle girl like Claire."

He smiled, a cool, dangerous smile. "Claire knows I would never hurt her."

"Not intentionally, of course. But you are far more experienced than she."

"Physically experienced, you mean."

"Yes."

Ryder was watching her with an intensity that was unnerving. "Let me see if I take your meaning. You are afraid I am going to debauch your sweet, innocent sister."

"No . . . not debauch—"

"That is what bothers you the most, isn't it? The thought of my bedding Claire. So you are riding to her rescue."

Eve gave him a look of vexation, not wanting to admit how close Ryder's conjecture had come to the truth.

"You aren't perhaps jealous, are you?" Ryder said in an amused drawl.

She opened her mouth to issue a denial and shut it again. She refused to confess that jealousy was also driving her. "No, certainly I am not jealous. And in any case, my feelings have nothing to do with the matter. I am interested only in seeing that Claire marries a man who is her ideal match—and you most assuredly are not."

A lazy smile touched his lips. "What you are really saying is that I'm not good enough to marry your sister. I am mortally wounded, love."

"No," Eve insisted, "that is *not* what I am saying. I have no objection to your marrying anyone but Claire. But since she won't listen to me, it will be up to you to discourage her."

He paused a long moment. "Very well. I will see that she gives up any thought of marrying me . . . on one condition."

"Condition?" Eve said cautiously.

"Come here, sweeting."

She tensed with sudden wariness. "Why?"

"Because I asked you to." His gaze was a bold and steady challenge, capturing hers and holding it without effort. When he simply waited, Eve reluctantly obeyed, moving to stand before him. She watched in fascination as Ryder reached up to brush her lips with his fingertips.

When she flinched at even that light touch, his sensual mouth flickered at the corner. "Have no fear, I won't attack you the way I did yesterday."

There was a spark of indulgent teasing in his eyes, yet it didn't reassure Eve. "What condition?" she repeated with impatience.

Instead of answering, he tucked an errant tendril behind her ear, letting his fingertips skim the outer rim with the gentlest of caresses.

Eve stood perfectly still, suddenly unable to move. How had Ryder managed to shift the subject so completely? Indeed, how was he able to make her forget why she was even here?

He left off toying with her ear and shifted his hand so that his thumb stroked along her jaw. Eve became aware of an abrupt weakness in her limbs. Her mind was filled with the memory of yesterday's kisses, while her body still wore the burning imprint of his ardent embrace. *Don't think about that,* she ordered herself sternly.

"*What* condition?" she forced herself to say in a voice far huskier than she would have liked.

"That you spend one night with me."

The silence between them was profound. Eve stared at Ryder, wondering if she had suddenly gone daft—or if he had. "I beg your pardon? What did you say?"

"You heard me, Countess."

She bit back a nervous laugh. "You must be jesting."

"Not at all. It is a simple bargain. I won't attempt

to marry your sister if you will spend one night with me in my bed."

"What sort of bargain is *that*?" She took a step backward, out of reach. "The very thought is absurd."

"Not in the least. I'm concerned about you, sweetheart. You have let your fear rule you long enough. I deplore the idea of your going through life afraid of physical intimacy."

Eve hesitated, and Ryder could see her breath quicken as she struggled for an answer. "I am . . . not afraid precisely," she finally said.

"But you have a warped view of lovemaking. I want to show you another perspective. Carnal relations can be quite remarkable with a man who cares enough to give you pleasure. I mean to prove to you that all men are not like your late churl of a husband."

The silence lengthened another dozen heartbeats until finally Eve shook her head. "Ryder, this is outrageous, what you are proposing."

"No, one night of passion. That is my condition. Otherwise I can't agree to put an end to Claire's hopes of marrying me."

Heat flashed in her eyes. "That is blackmail!"

"So it is," he replied, forcing his tone to remain mild. It grated on him, having to resort to such underhanded tactics, but Claire was right on that score. He'd made little progress in his clandestine courtship of Eve, and he would have to change his approach if he ever hoped to succeed. He knew Eve would make any sacrifice for her sister; indeed, she would battle to the death to protect any of her family.

"You are hardly behaving like a gentleman."

His mouth quirked with amusement. "I'm not concerned about being thought a gentleman just now. This is solely about you." When she remained mute, he lifted an eyebrow, feigning innocence. "My interest is purely altruistic, I assure you," he lied. "I intend to help you conquer your fear of men."

In response, Eve squared her shoulders. There was a martial light in her eyes he had never seen before, yet there was also a hint of uncertainty, of vulnerability.

"You needn't worry that there will be a repeat of yesterday, Eve," Ryder said, keeping his tone casual. "I confess it has been a long time since I gratified my carnal desires—not since before coming to London, in fact. But I won't get carried away again, you have my word."

He could see Eve frown as she made the mental calculations, could see the surprise in her searching gaze. Yet he wasn't simply offering an excuse for his boorish behavior yesterday; he wanted her to understand that he wasn't keeping a mistress or dallying with demi-reps or indulging in flings with beautiful widows like Phoebe Ferris-Jones, who kept throwing themselves at his feet.

Clearly the thought startled her. "I never imagined you to be the kind of man who relished celibacy."

Ryder smiled. "I don't, certainly. But I came to London to find a bride, and my social position was precarious enough without being termed a rake as well as a mercenary upstart. Besides, I found no one who interested me."

Eve's brow furrowed dubiously, but all she said was "You cannot be interested in *me,* Ryder."

"Only in an academic way. You are my benefactress, Countess. I would be ten kinds of fool to imperil our association. Oh, my body wants yours," Ryder added lightly. "I think we proved that quite satisfactorily yesterday. But I can manage to control my lustful urges for one evening."

She didn't quite believe him, he could tell. But Ryder refused to back down. He wanted Eve for his wife, yet physical intimacy was possibly the only way to wear down her defenses. If he could win her body, perhaps he could eventually win her heart. He meant to woo her with passion, with sensuality, with every physical skill he possessed.

To that end, he softened his tone when he asked, "Can you deny that you want to know what real passion is, Eve?"

Her lips parted as she stared at him. Eventually she averted her gaze. "I won't find any pleasure in love-making," she murmured in a barely audible voice.

"I can promise you will, Eve. You've just never had the right lover before. I gave you a taste of it in your library, remember?"

He could see she was wavering, and Ryder held his breath. He wanted to melt the ice Eve had encased herself in for so long. To release the fire and the passion he knew were inside her. To make her blossom for him and only for him.

And he suspected that deep down she wanted the same thing.

She had been asleep for too long, and he intended

to change that. At the thought of her sensual awakening, desire stung him with fresh insistence.

"Your body wants mine," he pressed, keeping his voice elaborately casual.

Her unwilling smile was wary and endearing. "I can't seem to help that." She cast a sidelong glance at him. "It isn't fair, you know."

"What isn't fair?"

"How you use my own desires against me."

Ryder hid his relief at her grudging admission, but the tightness in his gut eased a measure. Eve wasn't fully convinced, yet he could see the longing in her beautiful features as her gaze searched his face.

"One night, that is all?" she asked, her tone uncertain.

"Yes, that is all. One night of pure, unadulterated pleasure," Ryder promised, willing his heart to stop pounding as he waited for her answer.

Chapter Nine

One night of unadulterated pleasure. Ryder's outrageous offer echoed tantalizingly in Eve's ears. The prospect was so incredibly tempting.

She drew in an unsteady breath, wondering if she dared accept his scandalous proposal. She didn't think he would actually *force* her to agree, even if he had made it a condition for his capitulation. No, most likely he was acting for her sake. Ryder felt *sorry* for her.

She didn't like being pitied, Eve thought with a spark of defiance welling in her chest. And yet she couldn't dispute his reasoning. She had let fear rule her for too long. The very notion of physical intimacy with a man unnerved her—even if that man was Ryder.

Abruptly Eve shook her head. She couldn't believe she was actually considering letting herself be lured into a romantic indiscretion with Ryder. Other widows might enjoy such wild conduct, but she had her family to think of. Especially Claire.

"I couldn't," she said finally. "I don't dare put my reputation at risk, since the slightest hint of scandal could spoil Claire's chances for a suitable match."

"One night together can be managed discreetly."

Her brows drew together. "How?"

"You can leave it to me. I will arrange matters so that we maintain strict secrecy."

Eve stared into Ryder's dark eyes, trying to resist the danger that beckoned and taunted. He was promising a brief affair conducted in secrecy. And she did want to learn to overcome her fear. . . .

No, she amended, forcing herself to be honest. She wanted more than simply to defeat her fear of carnal relations. The bald truth was, she yearned to experience real passion for once in her life. She had no doubt at all that Ryder could show her.

What was more, this could be her only chance to be with him. Once Ryder chose a bride, it would be morally reprehensible to indulge in any affair with him.

"Come now, Countess," he prodded, his glance holding a hint of wickedness. "Aren't you the least bit weary of being dutiful and proper?"

Eve felt no need to respond to his question; he knew the answer to that as well as she did.

"You deserve a little pleasure in your life. You've sacrificed for your family for years, ignoring your own desires."

That was true, she had repressed all her own desires, all her hopes and dreams. She had never had the freedom to do what she truly wanted. To live her own life exactly as she wished, with no one controlling her every action or demanding that she behave with the strict propriety due her prominent station.

The spark of defiance flared hotter inside her,

spurring Eve on as she argued with herself. Giving Ryder one night did not mean surrendering her hard-won freedom. She would not be turning control of her life over to him. She wouldn't be trapped and powerless again with him.

She would never consider a liaison with any man other than Ryder, of course. And one night together needn't lead to anything deeper or more meaningful. Carnal relations, nothing more. One night of lovemaking.

One taste of passion.

That was all she wanted. She would be satisfied with one night, Eve promised herself.

In the end, his proposition was impossible to resist. Or more truthfully, *he* was impossible to resist.

"Very well," she said breathlessly. "One night. But nothing more."

Ryder had been watching her closely while she debated, but at her answer, his eyes glinted with satisfaction. "Good. I will make the arrangements and let you know."

Eve fought down the panic that suddenly welled in her stomach, battling the cowardly urge to change her mind.

But she wouldn't let herself give in to it, even if she had the vague suspicion that she had just bargained away her soul.

Ryder was as good as his word. He made arrangements for three nights later, saying he would meet her at a side door of her house at midnight after her household was safely abed.

A dozen times Eve almost told him she had reconsidered. But when the moment came, she was waiting for him, wearing a hooded cloak.

Ryder smiled briefly in approval, then guided her some distance from the square to his waiting curricle. He had brought no groom since he wanted no witnesses, Ryder explained—although he *had* informed Macky they would be leaving for a few hours, so that her protector wouldn't panic if he discovered her missing from the house.

Macky, however, was the soul of discretion, Ryder assured her. Which made Eve remember what she had been told about the Guardians. Ryder displayed such casual ease that she suspected he'd engaged in such clandestine activities on numerous occasions before this.

The night was cool and damp, for it had rained much of the day. But the clouds had dissipated by now, revealing a brilliant moon to bathe the two of them in silver radiance.

Eve paid little attention to the beauty, though. Wondering about what was to come, she sat mutely beside Ryder, all her senses on edge, all her nerves thrumming. There was a tightness of excitement in her chest and stomach that held only a slight element of fear. Instead, she was filled with a restless anticipation.

She did not have long to wait. In less than twenty minutes, they drew up before an elegant little house in north London. Eve recognized the district as St. John's Wood, where gentlemen often set up their love nests with their mistresses. Her own husband had done so, Eve knew.

But she immediately crushed the thought, refusing to let distasteful memories of her marriage spoil the evening. In truth, her late husband was the reason she was here tonight. She hoped to overcome the dread and revulsion he had always made her feel whenever he came to her bed.

"The house belongs to an acquaintance of mine," Ryder said when he saw Eve frowning.

"He won't mind if we make use of it?"

"She," Ryder corrected. "Venus owns a number of pleasure houses for the convenience of her clients."

Eve raised an eyebrow. "I gather Venus is a Cyprian?"

"Even more scandalous," he replied, amused. "She's a notorious madam who runs one of the most prosperous sin clubs in London. But she and her servants are utterly discreet, and this place is ideal for our needs."

"Ryder, I think perhaps I may have made a mistake."

"No second thoughts just yet, love. Save them until after you've seen the inside. It's a sight to behold, believe me."

When a groom came out to care for the curricle and pair, Ryder reached up to draw the hood of Eve's cloak more closely around her face to hide her features. Then, after helping her down, he escorted her inside the house.

The decor was indeed amazing, Eve thought as Ryder gave her a brief tour of the brightly lit first floor. The furnishings were tastefully elegant, but every room—the entrance hall, the drawing room, the dining parlor, and even the billiard room—was filled with statuary and paintings of nude lovers in various poses.

The large bedroom upstairs was only a trifle more subtle, for the paintings seemed more appropriate here. Or perhaps it was merely that the lamps had been turned down low.

The effect was actually warm and welcoming, somewhat to Eve's surprise. A fire was burning in the grate—the product of invisible servants—and decanters of wine and liquors stood on a side table, along with a light repast of bread, cheese, meats, and various kinds of fruit.

Eve, however, found her gaze fixed on the high four-poster bed, whose coverings had been turned down to expose black satin sheets.

"So this is what a den of iniquity looks like," she observed, trying to make light of her unfamiliar surroundings. "I have never seen one before."

Just then Ryder closed the door softly, and Eve abruptly tensed. When he came up behind her to take her cloak, awareness tightened her skin and made her shiver.

"I don't intend to pounce on you, you know," he said casually, obviously trying to reassure her and set her at ease. "We'll have a glass of wine first, then decide how to proceed. Are you hungry?"

"No. I couldn't eat a bite." The nervous flutter in her stomach had suddenly become a brutal knot of anxiety.

Ryder led her over to an elegant chaise longue before the fire and made her sit down while he poured her a glass of wine. Returning to join her on the chaise, he handed her the glass. "Here, drink. Perhaps this will settle your nerves."

Eve gave a faint laugh. "I don't think that's possible."

"Of course it's possible." He relaxed back against the chaise, watching her. "We'll take it one step at a time, sweeting. You will have complete control over the entire evening."

She took a gulp of wine, trying to ease the dryness in her throat. When Ryder reached out to take the glass from her, though, Eve felt the tightening of all her muscles in self-defense.

At her obvious alarm, he first went still, then made a tisking sound with his tongue. "You aren't allowed to be afraid of me, love. I promised you a night of pleasure and I fully intend to deliver. My male pride is at stake, you realize."

Hearing the amused note in his voice, she turned to glance at Ryder. The firelight played in his midnight eyes, revealing a tender, teasing glint that she knew was meant to reassure her. Yet she still felt utterly vulnerable and uncertain.

She hated the vulnerability, hated the fear. "I would just as soon get it over with, if you don't mind."

His expression softened, but he shook his head. "Actually, I do mind. I don't like to rush."

Leisurely, as if he had all the time in the world, he took a sip of wine and then gave the glass back to her. Her hands were shaking so badly, however, she could barely hold it. "Look at me, I am quivering like a newborn lamb. Here, please take this."

Returning the wineglass to him, Eve clasped her

fingers together in her lap and sat staring fixedly into the fire.

Setting the glass aside, Ryder reached up to touch his fingertips to her cheek. "It is only I, Eve. You knew me as a callow youth. You taught me to dance, remember? Lovemaking is no more complicated than that."

"Perhaps not for you."

Ryder watched her as she kept her spine rigid, her pose revealing unmistakable fear. She was petrified, he realized. He drew a slow breath, determined to do nothing that would frighten her further. He wanted Eve to know true passion. He wanted to show her every pleasure possible between a man and a woman. And he intended to use every seductive weapon in his arsenal to accomplish it. But first he had to win her trust.

Tenderness burned in him as he studied the delicate firelit lines of her face. "Eve, you have scores of ugly memories, I know. But I promise you, if I do nothing else tonight, I intend to help you banish them."

When she remained mute, Ryder tried another tack. "Years ago on Cyrene, you were the bravest young lady I knew. You're certainly brave enough to face this now."

After a moment she nodded. "I suppose so." Her chin rose as if she were girding herself for battle, and she inhaled a long, uneven breath. "But may we please proceed, Ryder? Delaying is only making it worse."

"All right, then. I'd like to start with your hair. Will you take it down for me?"

She hesitated another moment, then reached up to pull the pins from her hair. Ryder's heartbeat seemed to fill his chest as he watched the rich honey-gold mass spill free.

"You have the loveliest hair," he murmured almost reverently, his hand lifting to touch that shining fall of firelit satin.

Eve didn't flinch from him, at least, but remained completely immobile as he let his fingers glide over the rippling tresses, luxuriating in the incredible texture.

Finally, however, she stirred restlessly. "Now what, Ryder?"

"Patience, love. This is merely foreplay, and it's of paramount importance."

She sent him a puzzled frown. "Why?"

"So you'll quit cowering there, as rigid as a block of oak ready for the woodsman's axe, and resemble something more of a woman who's about to have the most fantastic night of her life."

That brought a hint of hope to her expression, and she acquiesced, although unwillingly. With an obvious effort to relax, she settled back and let him play with her hair. And it seemed that his stroking did seem to help ease the stiffness somewhat.

Eventually Eve risked another glance at him. "I think it might have worked, Ryder. I am not so tense now."

"Good. Then we can proceed to the second step in your seduction."

Her lips quivered with a shaky, endearing smile. "You will have to tell me what comes next. I don't have the slightest clue what I should do."

His heart melted. "The usual procedure is for you to undress. Do you want me to do the honors, or will you?"

"No, I will."

Gritting her teeth, she bent to draw off her slippers and stockings. Then rising, Eve kept her back to him as she removed her gown. She hadn't worn a corset, so she stood shivering in her shift for a long moment before finally drawing the garment over her head.

Ryder caught his breath at the sight of her pale, nude body. "Turn around, Eve," he said softly.

She obeyed, standing regally, too proud to cower.

His breath left his lungs entirely. She was achingly beautiful. From her high, ripe breasts to the triangle of dark gold curls shielding her femininity, she was erotic and sensual . . . pure male fantasy.

Every part of her impacted his senses. Her nipples were exquisite dusky roses, pouting to be kissed, her waist narrow, her hips sweetly curving, her thighs creamy silk.

Ryder stared spellbound, feeling the slow thud of his heart beating in painful anticipation, keenly aware of his loins, where sensation collected, heavy and thick. Eve had no notion of her allure, but she could seduce the moonlight with no effort at all.

His gaze lifted again to her tawny hair as it spilled over her naked shoulders. Then he met her eyes—those blue, blue eyes watching him so warily.

Ryder rose slowly, disciplining his arms that begged

to surround her body. Eve was the only woman who'd ever had the power to make him ache like this.

He took a step toward her, then forced himself to stop. He could see the unconscious longing in her eyes, yet she stared at him as if he was about to hurt her.

God, give me the strength to go slowly, he prayed silently.

He took a long breath to draw air into his tight, aching chest. He was light-headed from wanting her; his body was already on fire with the thought of making love to Eve for the first time. But he had to be careful.

And truly, there was no rush. He had waited half his life for this. Now he would finally claim her after all these years.

A feeling unfolded in him that made it nearly impossible to breathe. His loins were full and aching for her, but it was his heart that swelled to the point of bursting. Inside, he felt a shaft of longing so deep, it was a physical pain. The need to take her flowed through him like liquid fire.

Damn it, man, you have to control yourself, Ryder chided silently. He *wanted* to control himself. Now that the moment was finally here, he wanted it to last forever, to draw it out, to wring every sweet, searing drop of pleasure from their joining.

With infinite care, he stepped closer to take Eve in his arms. Her subtle scent enticed him, sweet and fresh like the wildflowers that bloomed in the meadow where they'd once met.

Barely breathing, Ryder slid his arms around her and drew her close.

For a moment he simply held her, willing his heartbeat to slow. Then reaching up with unsteady hands, he began to stroke her, caressing her hair, her shoulders, the soft contours of her naked back, the curves of her buttocks.

His gentleness had the effect he wanted, Ryder realized with relief. Her rigidity seemed to dissipate, and eventually she leaned into his embrace. After a long moment, Ryder drew back to survey her. Eve had squeezed her eyes tightly shut, but now she opened them. "Ryder . . . I'm afraid . . . you won't find any pleasure with me."

He kept his voice low and solemn. "Right now your pleasure is all I care about. Allow me to show you."

His gaze was riveted on her soft red mouth, and he bent to take it, a tender brushing of flesh. When she didn't respond, he increased the pressure, his tongue sailing lightly across her tense lips, asking her to part for him.

He felt her give way the slightest measure, so he continued with gentle nibbles and nips, coaxing her mouth open.

When finally she obliged, he took her mouth fully, a deep, gentle mating of tongues. At the same time, he moved his hands up her rib cage, curving his palms into her shapely flesh, filling them with her breasts, softly kneading.

In response, Eve arched against the delicious constraint. The soft whimpers she was making were not the result of fear, she knew, but of startled wonder at the pleasure Ryder was making her feel. She was trembling, but the tremors running through her had nothing to do with dread. She felt Ryder's caresses as if in a dream.

She had never tasted a kiss that promised and wooed like this. Never felt anything like the gentle, knowing movement of his hands. Nothing like his enveloping warmth, his tenderness.

When at last he drew back, she was actually disappointed.

"It's my turn to undress," Ryder informed her.

She watched mutely as he proceeded to remove his coat, waistcoat, and cravat, then his trousers and drawers, and finally his lawn shirt.

He stood very still, letting her take in every detail of his body, his gaze heated and compelling as he observed her reaction. Eve forgot to breathe as she stared with helpless fascination.

If any man could be called beautiful, it was Ryder. His chiseled body was perfect, lean and sleek with muscle, rawly masculine. His shoulders were broad, his hips narrow, and his legs long and powerful. She felt the unbidden urge to caress him, just to see if his body was as hard and vital as it appeared.

And yet rising from the nest of curling black hair at his groin was the bold evidence of his sexual arousal, long and huge and swollen. Eve couldn't help staring at that rigid male flesh, which a man could wield like a weapon. Yet she forced herself to remain still. She didn't want to run away, didn't want to be afraid. In truth, she *wasn't* afraid.

It was if he seemed to know what she was feeling. "Come here, Eve. I want you to touch me all over so you can become familiar with my body."

She couldn't deny him anything he wanted. His dark eyes beguiled as she moved to obey.

"Touch me, sweeting."

"Where?"

"Anywhere you wish."

Tentatively she raised her hands, sliding them along the smooth skin of his arms, over his powerful shoulders, where the muscles coiled and quivered.

He was hotter than she expected. His skin felt heated and velvety. In fact, he was hot and hard and vibrant all over. But it was his eyes that smoldered. Her skin burned wherever his scrutiny rested, as if the caress of his gaze was a physical touch.

"Try to relax, beauty."

Strangely the casual endearment did not seem awkward or out of place. Ryder did make her feel beautiful and wanted.

He wanted her, Eve realized, her heart quickening into a fierce rhythm. There was no misunderstanding the heat in his eyes.

A quiet tension crackled between them, filled with unmistakable sexual awareness. Yet she felt no fear when he stepped closer and brought his entire length against hers, making her feel the sensations of flesh against naked flesh, of pulse point to pulse point. Not even when his maleness pressed against the most feminine part of her, since Ryder distracted her by kissing her again . . . a featherlight brush of his sensual mouth that still had the power to scald her.

Her sigh wafted against his lips even before Ryder reached up to caress her again. His sensuous fingers rippled over the tight muscles of her neck and shoulders, then lower to clasp her upper arms.

She stirred restlessly when his kiss ended, but he only trailed his lips downward along her throat. Then he bent his head even lower, to her breast, and wrapped his warm lips around the crest. Eve was shocked by the fiercely pleasurable sensation that streaked through her.

She clung weakly as Ryder suckled first one nipple, then the other, lavishing exquisite attention on the tight, aching buds. When a hoarse gasp came from her throat, he seemed satisfied.

Abandoning his arousing ministrations, he took her hand and led her to one side of the massive bed. Eve abruptly felt a return of her dread, but Ryder merely turned his attention to the bedside table, where a red satin pouch and several vials of amber liquid rested.

Curiously he withdrew from the pouch a small sponge with a thin string attached and opened one of the vials. "This is brandy. We'll soak the sponge and place it deep between your thighs to prevent my seed from taking root."

Eve eyed him with puzzlement. He was concerned about the danger of pregnancy, she finally realized. "I doubt that is necessary, Ryder. I am most likely barren. I never conceived a child in six years of marriage."

"Your husband could have been the reason, if his seed wasn't potent enough."

Her lips parted in a small *oh*. She had never really considered that *Richard* might be the one at fault; that he might have been unable to give her the child she had so desperately wanted, even though he had blamed her for never conceiving.

"I don't want to risk the scandal of getting you with child," Ryder added casually.

"Thank you," Eve murmured. "No other man I know would be so considerate."

"It's time you realized I'm not like any other man, sweetheart."

His tone was light, yet something protective and fiercely intimate shone in his eyes before he concentrated on wetting the sponge.

When he was done, he positioned Eve so that her thighs and buttocks rested against the high edge of the mattress. Then surprisingly, he knelt at her feet. Her face warmed with embarrassment as he gently spread her thighs, but she held herself still and braced her hands behind her on the bed.

When he dipped one finger inside her to probe the very essence of her womanhood, she held back a gasp. Then he slid the sponge deep within her as promised, and she squeezed her eyes shut, the scarlet heat of her embarrassment in stark contrast to the titillating chill of the brandy.

A dozen heartbeats passed before Eve realized that Ryder had gone completely still. When he remained silent, she forced her eyes open to look down at him. He had been waiting for just that, she understood.

Still holding her gaze, he slowly slid his hands up her thighs to her hips, making her grow tense again.

Defensively Eve moved her hands to his shoulders, playing for time. "Ryder . . . you are likely to be disappointed in me. I am not . . . passionate."

He looked up at her through a sweep of black lashes. "You are incredibly passionate, Eve. You just need someone to show you how to unlock it. Now, hush," he commanded softly, "and let me continue with my seduction."

His smile was disarmingly tender. That beautiful smile had the power to enthrall her, Eve reflected. Yet it was the seductive molten darkness of his eyes that held her spellbound.

She obeyed, falling silent. The quiet snap and hiss of the fire was the only sound as gold and black shadows ribboned around them. Then Ryder leaned forward to press a kiss against her belly while his fingers slipped between her thighs.

Eve was suddenly assaulted by sensations. His mouth felt like warm silk on her skin. And the insides of her thighs were unbearably sensitive, she quickly discovered as his caressing fingers slowly stroked upward. So was her feminine cleft. She tried to remember how to breathe when Ryder used his fingers to part the delicate folds. She filled her hands with the thick, silky texture of his hair and held on to him.

Then his mouth moved lower to the curls at the juncture of her thighs and found her intimate center, kissing lightly.

Eve drew in a sharp breath, shocked by Ryder's scandalous act . . . shocked even more by the soft, slow fire seeping through her veins. Her knees trembled, yet she held herself rigid, as if the heat from his touch wasn't pouring through her body.

He dragged his tongue across the swollen bud of her sex, once, twice, making her fingers curl reflexively in the sable locks of his hair. Then he settled his hands at her hips and set about ruthlessly arousing her, nibbling and sucking with gentle thoroughness.

Eve shuddered as a blinding throb of raw sensation took her in its grasp. It wasn't long, either, before a powerful firestorm erupted inside her.

Her hold shifting, she clutched blindly at Ryder, digging her fingers into the muscles of his shoulders as flaming tremors rippled through her body and the world tumbled away.

Her knees nearly buckled, but Ryder held her up. She was barely aware that he had risen and was easing her back upon the feather mattress. But then his shadow covered her, and the stark reality of a man looming over her sent Eve into a cold panic.

Ryder must have heard the strangled sound of fear she made, for he instantly went still. "Easy, love," he murmured softly as he lifted her fully onto the bed. "Nothing will happen that you don't want to happen."

Feeling chagrined, Eve shifted to sit back against the headboard, her legs curled beneath her, and watched as Ryder went to fetch the wineglass. He returned to the bed and slid in beside her, bracing his back against the pillows. When he offered her a sip of wine, she accepted gratefully, a little ashamed of her craven response.

"That was the next step," Ryder said casually. "Preparing your body to receive me. You're naturally dry and tight, so you need some assistance. You'll discover that lovemaking will be much easier now."

When she looked at him with skepticism, Ryder

smiled and took her hand, guiding her fingers to her woman's mound. "Touch yourself if you don't believe me. Feel how wet you are."

Her cheeks warming, she did as he bid. Her feminine entrance was indeed soaked with slick moisture. "How did you know?"

"Experience," Ryder replied, amused. "It's your body's natural response to pleasure. Something you've never enjoyed before. But you should feel little pain now."

"If you say so," Eve replied dubiously.

She started to ease downward to lie on her back, but Ryder shook his head.

"Oh, no, love, I intend to let you take the lead."

"Me?"

"Yes, you. I'm not touching you from now on. If you want to make love, it will be all up to you."

"But I wouldn't know where to begin."

"You can start by caressing me with your hands."

Intrigued by the thought, Eve surveyed Ryder as he reclined back among the pillows. Shadow and light roamed over him, accentuating his lean grace, the powerful lines of his body. The wild, primitive beauty of his form aroused Eve.

Even his masculinity appealed to her, much to her shock. Her gaze fixed on the dark, swirling nest of hair that cradled his hardness. The evidence of his desire stood rigid, flushed, thickly swollen.

"So what do *you* want to do?" Ryder prodded encouragingly. "You have free rein tonight, Eve."

He was giving her complete control, granting her the power to stop or continue as she wished. A maze of emotions rose within Eve, the chief of which was gratitude for his understanding.

"I want to touch you," she murmured.

"I want that too."

Tentatively she reached down to touch his thigh, feeling the slightly rough texture of his skin, the silky fine hair dusting his legs. But when she hesitated to go further, he moved her hand to cover the thick, pulsing heat of him. "Stroke me, sweeting."

She closed her fingers over his arousal. "Like this?"

"Yes." His dark smile told her that was exactly what he wanted.

Tightening his fingers around hers, Ryder showed her how to caress him, tutoring her, demonstrating the way to stroke his manhood with the same slow, lingering rhythm he'd used to pleasure her. Her hand, alternating between shy and bold, obeyed his command.

Eve could tell from his quickened breathing that she was arousing him further. And yet it wasn't enough. She had the oddest yearning to lean forward and press her lips there.

Giving in, Eve bent over him, smelling warm clean skin and musky male arousal. The fragrance was potent to her senses. And when she touched her lips to his rigid male flesh, she discovered that it was not so threatening after all. Instead it was velvety hard, throbbing, magnificent.

At her gentle kiss, a low groan sounded in Ryder's throat. When she glanced up at him, seeking approval, she could see something bright and fierce flare in his eyes. But he kept still, waiting for her to proceed however she wished.

What she wanted was to feel the rest of him. She had the strongest urge to run her hands all over his lithe, hot, muscular body. When she gave into the need, skating her fingers up his tight, flat abdomen to his hard chest, longing caught in her own chest.

It was amazing how touching Ryder like this made *her* want to be touched. Amazing how he made her feel weak and yet at the same time incredibly powerful. How his desire called to something primitive and powerful and feminine inside her. She felt a quivering deep in her belly, a tingling fullness in her breasts, a throbbing dampness between her thighs.

"Do you want to make love, Eve?" he asked, his voice suddenly deep and husky.

"Yes," she answered without hesitation, her own voice just as rasping.

"Then come here."

When he held out his arms, she went into them, meaning to lie by his side, yet Ryder surprised her by drawing her full length on top of him.

Then he eased her thighs apart so that they straddled his. "You may do the honors now."

Her eyes widened when she realized that he wanted her to mount him, since she'd never imagined making love in that position before. She could feel the rigid, heated length of his sex brand her like searing steel. Gamely, though, she braced her palms on his shoulders and lifted herself onto her knees.

She tensed when his hard thickness probed her cleft, yet Ryder merely smiled. "Relax, Eve. We'll go as slowly and carefully as you need to." He held her gaze while his hands went to her hips to guide her with the lightest of touches. Yet she was completely in command.

Barely moving, Eve slowly, slowly, lowered herself upon his swollen member, taking him a little way inside her. She was keenly aware of the heavy intrusion, of the burgeoning pressure that made her breath catch. Despite the tightness, however, there was no real pain. Instead, miraculously, she felt her body straining to open for him. Her own wetness had made all the difference in her acceptance of his penetration.

"Are you all right?" he asked.

"Yes," she answered, finally believing in his promises.

With care he slid in even deeper and made her sit still until her short breaths became less rapid and she grew accustomed to the feel of his huge shaft pulsing inside her.

Then he raised his hands to her breasts, fondling the taut nipples, making pleasure stab through her whole body.

When she arched her back in response, his eyes smoldered. "Now ride me, love." Ryder lifted her up slightly, withdrawing a few inches, before lowering her again, creating a delicious friction that only increased the exquisite pleasure.

He refused to glance away for an instant as he drew her into his rhythm. Something inside Eve quivered and soared, while a whimper formed in her throat. She felt the heat of him inside her. He was hot, so hot, and so was she. She was shivering at the burning lash of pleasure.

A fire blazed in his eyes, she could feel the scorching flame. What she hadn't anticipated, though, was the fiery hunger in herself. She felt wild, reckless, as if a Gypsy had taken over her proper, well-bred body and filled it with the hot aching glow of need.

"Let go, Eve," Ryder whispered hoarsely. "I want you to come again and again and again for me."

A glorious warmth spread through her, pouring deep inside her. Her body had come alive with fire; her skin was aflame.

In some dim part of her mind she was aware of the wanton sounds of urgency and need tangling in her throat.

"Yes . . . come apart for me."

His rasping voice faded to a far distance as the shattering climax caught her in its power and swept her up in a crescendo of brilliant sparks.

Her breath expelled in sobbing gasps when finally she collapsed upon him, Ryder held her clasped tightly to the inferno that was his body. The next moment, however, a shudder went through him, racking every part of him.

"I can't hold back," he said in a ragged, breaking whisper. His body convulsed with explosive passion, yet even in his quaking climax, he took care not to hurt her as he emptied himself inside her in deep, shuddering pulses.

It seemed an eternity to Eve before her senses returned. Unable to speak even then, she lay sprawled bonelessly on top of Ryder, breathing in the musky maleness of his skin, feeling the cool night air sift over her own fevered skin.

Awe was her chief feeling. She was frankly stunned by the beautiful experience he had given her. It had been glorious and wrenching at the same time.

She had always been entirely passive during carnal relations, lying rigid while trying to marshal her defenses against the pain. Yet Ryder had shown her a different way. His passionate, ravishing tenderness had brought her completely alive after she had been numb for so long. Sensations shimmered through her like glowing firelight. So much feeling.

Too much.

Eve shuddered with a hot pulse of emotion that shook her to the core. Absurdly a choking knot formed in her throat.

She had been afraid for so long. Trapped and helpless and vulnerable. But it was as if Ryder had set some part of her free. All the years of denied emotion, of repressed feeling, were over. She was afraid no longer.

She closed her eyes against the rush of joy and swallowed her tears. Nothing could ever make her afraid when Ryder's arms held her so tenderly. She'd never felt more protected in her whole life than at this moment. Nothing had ever made her feel so cherished. So sheltered. So wanted.

After a long while she raised her head to gaze deeply into his eyes. "I've never felt that . . . wild before," she whispered.

"I'm glad."

The tenderness in his eyes set her heart thudding once more. Then he reached up to brush a sweat-dampened tress back from her face, and his hand lingered there to caress her cheek.

Eve was suddenly struck with a hard rush of sexual awareness. *Their bodies were still joined, his maleness to her femaleness.* Beneath her palms, his chest muscles rippled with mobile suppleness, while in her feminine center, she felt Ryder growing, lengthening to fill her once more.

Heat flared to life in her body, igniting the yearning again. Eve still felt unsure of herself, however, so her tone was tentative when she murmured, "Do you think we could try again?"

With tender laughter, Ryder eased her back upon the satin sheets, keeping himself firmly positioned between her spread thighs. His body covered hers, his weight pinning her down. Yet this time she welcomed the primal feeling of being dominated by a powerful male.

Miraculous, really, Eve thought as she gazed up at him.

She shivered, not from the chill but from the fever in Ryder's eyes. The emotions she'd sensed churning beneath the surface that afternoon long ago when he'd kissed her on Cyrene were still there in the shimmering dark depths.

He wanted her, she could feel it in every nerve of her body. And she wanted him—with a desperation she had never in her life felt before.

This was true passion, Eve realized. This was desire. She finally understood it.

She was overwhelmed with longing, the need to feel Ryder driving deep into her, to feel his huge, hot shaft filling her. The thought of him moving inside her, completing her, made her heart labor even harder.

"Ryder . . ." she whispered. "Make love to me."

"Gladly."

He stared down at her with searing intensity as he cradled her head in his palms and sheathed his body as deeply as he could go.

"Wrap your legs around me, Eve," he commanded softly. "That's right. Now grasp my buttocks when I'm thrusting into you so you can control the tempo."

He was still leaving the power in her hands. Still giving her the choice. She smiled softly in gratitude and slid her palms down his sleek back to his taut buttocks.

He captured her smile with a kiss as he began to move, driving slowly forward, then withdrawing, then sinking in again. It was only moments before they were both wrapped up in the consuming pleasure of each gliding thrust.

This time was different from the first, though—more powerful, more urgent, building with relentless force. Soon his kisses no longer coaxed and wooed but took with elemental hunger. His body plunged into her again and again until finally Eve arched and cried out his name. He was shaking as violently as she when the fierce climax overwhelmed them both.

Afterward, they lay tangled in each other's arms, her head on his shoulder. The night air was cool on their damp flesh, so Ryder drew the sheet up to cover them both. But the tremors that still shivered across his skin had less to do with the temperature than with the searing passion that had claimed him.

At last he knew. Knew what it was like to hold Eve and touch her as he'd always wanted. What it was like to be gloved by her, to fill her, to breathe in the scent of her skin after lovemaking, to drown in pleasure and contentment.

The fantasies he'd woven of her were nothing compared with the reality. Reality was infinitely better. The fulfillment had been sharp, violent, intense. Even more incredible than his most vivid dreams.

It was pure heaven, Ryder thought as his fingers drifted languorously over her silken body. Her golden hair, tumbled and tangled from his hands, spilled over his chest, caressing him as he'd always dreamed of it doing. Right at this moment, if he never drew another breath, he wouldn't care.

They had fitted together so perfectly. He hadn't meant to make such fierce demands on her body when she was so unaccustomed to such harsh usage, yet she seemed utterly content now. And he couldn't regret a moment of it. He had awakened Eve sexually, giving life to a staggeringly passionate woman.

She had scored his skin with her nails, but no pain had ever felt so pleasurable. Ryder relished her abandonment. He wanted her passionate, begging for what he burned to give. Wanted to make her feel the same raw hunger, the same torment that he felt, the same obsession.

Yet he didn't want just her passion; he wanted her love. Didn't just want her making love to him. He wanted her loving him.

Taking her body was not good enough for him. A hundred times wouldn't be enough to satisfy his feverish longing. He had to have her heart.

He wanted it more than breathing.

Burying his face in her fragrant hair, Ryder held

her more tightly, wishing he could simply absorb her. The desperate need for her was sated for the time being; the tightness in his heart had eased. But he knew the urgency would never completely lessen.

He would never be able to let Eve go now. Never be able to control this fierce want, this yearning to bury himself so deeply he could never pull free.

Somehow, some way, he would make Eve feel the same unquenchable yearning for him.

Chapter Ten

He brought her home shortly before dawn. After slipping upstairs to her bedchamber, Eve undressed and climbed into bed. For a long while she lay there dreamily as remembered images of her night with Ryder swirled in her mind: The tenderness and the heat. How she had trembled in his arms. The way his hands had drifted over her skin as though she were something lovely and precious. The stunning way he had branded her with the fervor of his body and the fire of his mouth.

He was an expert at making her come alive in ways she'd never known were possible in her entire six years of marriage. Ryder had given her experiences, made her feel sensations—desire, passion, fulfillment—more vivid, more overwhelming than she could ever have imagined. He had seen things in her she had never seen in herself.

Eve closed her eyes, hugging the splendid memories to herself. The marvel of the wonderful night made her throat ache. And when she finally slept, her dreams of Ryder were touched by a wild enchantment.

She woke an hour later, feeling a twinging ache

between her thighs from her unaccustomed carnal exertions. As she rose and rang for a bath, Eve smiled a shy, secretive smile. Her discomfort now was nothing like the painful rawness she'd felt every time after her husband was done with her, but merely a pleasurable reminder of Ryder's incredible lovemaking.

Several times last night, he had offered to stop in order to give her body a respite, but she hadn't wanted to waste a moment of their interlude. She had been so wanton, so needy, she felt positively wicked.

Yet she also felt free and intensely alive.

She'd never felt alive as a woman before, Eve realized. Never like now. The sense of power Ryder had given her was liberating.

It had been the most intense experience of her life. For a brief moment Ryder had turned her world upside down. She hadn't expected to wake up with this happiness unfurling inside her, though. She felt giddy and foolish and tingly all over.

Until disappointment suddenly washed over her. Now that their night was over, Eve reminded herself, she had to return to reality. Ryder had fulfilled his pledge to help her overcome her fear, so there was no reason for any further physical intimacy between them . . . even if she caught herself yearning for it.

There was not even the issue of her sister to come between them, since Ryder had confessed he had no real desire to marry Claire, but had only used the threat as leverage to convince Eve to let him show her passion.

Eve had been lying beneath him, gasping for

breath after their final bout of lovemaking, when Ryder raised his fingertips to stroke her flushed cheek.

"You can't seriously think I feel any romantic inclinations toward your sister," he murmured, gazing solemnly down at her. "Claire is lovely and sweet, but a mere girl—like a younger sister to me. I can't begin to picture her as my bride. Nor does she have the slightest intention of wedding me. She only made the suggestion in passing because she feels comfortable with me and would rather be spared the ordeal of finding herself a husband."

Eve couldn't be upset at Ryder for coercing her to do what she had wanted all along. And if she were wise, she would admit it was just as well that their illicit liaison would be so short-lived.

She couldn't risk the scandal of being discovered with Ryder. But more important, she was afraid of creating any deeper intimacy between them. Ryder stirred her emotions as well as her blood, and she didn't dare become any more involved with him. Especially when he was set on taking another woman for his wife. It would leave her much too vulnerable.

No, Eve resolved as her abigail helped her to finish dressing, she would have to be content with their one magical night together.

When she came downstairs, however, she discovered that Ryder was already ensconced in the morning room along with her siblings and the aunts. Eve's heart began to hammer when she saw him sitting near the bay window, immaculately dressed in a well-tailored blue coat and buff pantaloons.

She tried to look away, afraid that her family

would guess what scandalous acts she had been engaged in with Ryder. But he caught and held her gaze, as if wanting her to remember who had held her and caressed her and driven her wild for much of the night.

Instantly Eve was flooded with the delicious memory of their joining. He had been inside of her, a part of her, melding in the most intimate way conceivable.

Eve shook herself sternly as she advanced into the room. When she breathlessly apologized for sleeping so late, however, Beatrice asked in all innocence, "Are you sickening for something, my dear? You look a trifle flushed."

Ryder responded with barely a hint of a smile, but Eve did her best to ignore him. Then he leaned back in his chair, stretching his long legs and crossing them at the ankles while clasping his hands casually over his stomach.

Suddenly all Eve could think about was the incredible tenderness of his hands, hands that were loving and gentle and relentless as they drove her to a peak of passion she had never before experienced and might never feel again.

"No, I am well, Beatrice," Eve prevaricated, scolding herself. "I have merely had too many late nights at balls and parties, I expect."

Deliberately Eve crossed the room and settled at her writing desk to attend to her correspondence, feeling more comfortable with her back to Ryder.

Yet Cecil wouldn't allow her to remain excluded from the conversation for long. They had been discussing the upcoming house party at Hayden Park,

Eve learned shortly. When Cecil asked her how the plans were going, she explained that she had sent out two dozen cards of invitation and received acceptances from most.

"You forgot to send Sir Alex a card," Cecil prodded, "although no doubt it was merely an oversight, since he doesn't need a formal invitation."

Eve shot her brother a quelling glance, knowing he was deliberately stirring up trouble. "Sir Alex was not sent an invitation because I don't think it appropriate that he attend."

"Oh," Ryder said. "Why not?"

Swiveling in her chair, she forced herself to look him squarely in the eye. "Because everyone will think you are courting Claire, and the notoriety will do her reputation no good. You have become such a favorite with the gossip rags that even your smallest action is commented upon. Moreover, it will hurt Claire's standing with her other suitors if they believe you are competing for her hand."

"I can go merely as a friend of the family."

"I think it best if you don't come," Eve insisted.

When Ryder simply studied her intently, she felt her cheeks grow warm. She didn't want to explain why she was so reluctant to have him attend the house party.

The truth was, she was unnerved by the reckless, rebellious emotions Ryder made her feel . . . the passion, the wanton desire, the secret yearning. Her explosive reaction to his slightest touch made it dangerous to be in such close proximity of him for a full sennight. Much too dangerous.

She wasn't being cowardly, Eve told herself firmly.

She was simply removing herself from temptation. She hoped that an entire week apart from Ryder would allow her to bring her errant feelings for him back under control.

"I don't like the idea of you being away for so long without protection," Ryder observed when she didn't answer.

"Mr. Macklin has agreed to come. His protection should be enough."

She was pleased at how easily Beau Macklin had slipped into their routine during the last few days, as if he had always been a part of the household. Macky normally adhered quite properly to his role of footman, but when he was "on duty" with just the family present, he regaled them with tales of his days in the theater, which frequently had them shaking with laughter. Even Drucilla relaxed her imperious attitude when subjected to Macky's infectious wit.

Eve wasn't surprised by his success. He appeared younger than Ryder by several years, yet she suspected Macky's roguish charm, combined with his curling chestnut hair and handsome visage, made him a great favorite with females of any age.

"Nevertheless, I will be attending," Ryder said with the cool assurance of a man who inevitably got his own way.

Eve pressed her lips together, deciding this was not the best time to argue the issue. Feeling a little helpless, however, she couldn't stop wondering how her life had suddenly spun so far out of control.

Since the recent attempt to kill her, she was still peering nervously at shadows, despite the precautions Ryder had put in place. She couldn't even switch rooms in her own house without a footman accompanying her and watching over her every step.

The routine Ryder had instituted included his meeting with his men each day to review Eve's social plans, which he changed frequently without warning, so she wouldn't seem too predictable. Additionally, Ryder insisted that Eve alter all her regular habits and keep her calls and outings to a minimum, and most critically, that he be present whenever guests were permitted in the house.

It was her lack of control that unsettled Eve even more than the threat to her safety. In the year since Richard's death, she had been able to manage her life much to her satisfaction—and those of her relatives as well. But Ryder had changed all that. From the moment he'd moved in across the square, she had continually been caught off guard.

He had insinuated himself into her life, running completely tame in her house. And the prospect of enduring the further enforced intimacy of a house party with him was a little dismaying.

Given Ryder's persistence, though, Eve acknowledged, it was possible she would lose that battle, just as she had lost the one over her fear of passion.

If she was forced to invite him, she would have to make certain that they returned to a professional footing by including some of the ladies on his bride list. She might even go so far as to include Phoebe Ferris-Jones, Eve thought a trifle morosely. The flame-haired widow could be counted on to keep Ryder occupied with her pursuit of him. Or perhaps she should invite her friend Lydia, Lady Keeling. Lydia was still keenly interested in becoming Lady Ryder.

As for the other younger debutantes on his list, Eve decided it would not be wise to include them, since she had no desire to provide competition for Claire.

Just then, the Hayden butler brought in the morning post on a silver salver and presented it to Eve at her desk. Thanking him with a smile, she sorted through the letters and invitations.

"Are any of those for me, my dear?" Beatrice asked, rising from the settee to come peer over Eve's shoulder.

"Yes, there are two for you and several for Drucilla. And one for Claire."

As Eve stood to deliver the missives to the other ladies, she saw Beatrice adjust her spectacles, the better to read. But the day had turned gray again, so there was no sunlight streaming through the tall windows. Muttering under her breath about her failing eyesight, Beatrice struck a flint and lit the lamp on the desktop just as Eve was returning to her chair.

Suddenly, right before Eve's shocked eyes, the lamp's glass casing exploded, scattering drops of flaming oil over everything in a three-foot radius, including the elderly aunt. As the right sleeve and skirt of her muslin morning gown caught fire, Beatrice screamed in terror and spun in a frantic circle, trying to evade the flames.

Before Eve could even think what to do, Ryder had leaped across the room and pushed the shrieking old lady to the carpet. His reflexes swifter than thought, he grabbed a woolen throw rug from a nearby armchair and flung it over Beatrice's prostrate form, trying to smother the flames.

At almost the same instant, Macky came racing into the room and began beating out the small fires ignited wherever else the flaming oil had landed.

Both men succeeded in accomplishing their tasks, stamping out the final smoldering sparks, but Beatrice was still whimpering hysterically. Jolted out of her paralysis, Eve rushed to her side and knelt beside the terrified woman, the stench of burning muslin acrid in her nostrils.

Struggling to control her own fear, she gathered Beatrice carefully in her arms, crooning soft assurances over and over again as she smoothed back the aunt's silver hair. "It's over, my dear. We're here. Nothing more will harm you."

Her quiet murmurings had only the slightest calming effect. Covering her face with her hands, Beatrice burst into tears and lay there, huddled in a fetal ball in Eve's arms, rocking back and forth, making pitiful little mewling sounds.

Looking up, Eve met Ryder's concerned gaze over the elderly lady's trembling form. A coldness seized Eve when she realized how near to disaster they had come. The danger was over now, but Beatrice could have been burned alive if not for Ryder's swift action.

Eve closed her eyes, nearly sick with relief.

"We should get Lady Beatrice upstairs to bed," Ryder said quietly when her whimpers finally died down, "so that her burns can be examined."

"Yes," Drucilla rasped hoarsely, hovering over her sister. Her usual elegant features were white.

And Claire and Cecil stood back a few steps, looking as helpless as Eve felt.

Unburdened by the same helplessness, Macky stepped forward with alacrity. Bending, he picked Beatrice up in his arms as if she weighed no more than goosedown.

"Shall I take her to her bedchamber, my lady?" he asked Eve.

"Yes, please."

Claire moved to Macky's side and took the elderly lady's limp hand. "I will come with you, Aunt Beatrice," she said softly.

When Ryder helped Eve to her feet, she started to follow Macky just as Drucilla and Claire were doing.

But then Drucilla paused and turned back to Ryder, her voice still shaken. "You saved my sister's life, Sir Alex. I don't know how we can ever thank you."

Ryder shook his head gravely. "You needn't thank me, Lady Wykfield. I regret we didn't prevent it from happening in the first place."

Drucilla pressed her lips together and swallowed hard, as if choking back tears. But then she stiffened her spine regally and turned to march from the room in Macky's wake.

Managing a fleeting smile of gratitude for Ryder, Eve accompanied the others upstairs, where she rang for Beatrice's abigail and the Hayden housekeeper, who had some skill with medicinal remedies. Macky was banned from the room while the ladies helped change the injured aunt's gown and administer to her burns with cold compresses and various ointments to relieve the pain, as well as laudanum to help her sleep. The skin of her right arm and shoulder had been singed, but the damage could have been far, far worse.

When Beatrice had finally dozed off, Eve left Drucilla and Claire there to keep her company while she returned to the morning room.

The burnt stench greeted her when she entered, but she saw at once that the shattered glass had been removed and an effort made to clean up the worst of the damage. A swift glance told her that the charred carpet and her scorched cherrywood writing desk would have to be replaced, but the rest of the room remained untouched.

As expected, the mood was grim when she joined the three men—Ryder, Macky, and Cecil—and answered their inquiries about Beatrice's condition.

"Her burns are not serious," Eve said, "but she is frightened half to death."

"It is hardly any wonder," Cecil responded. "She could have been killed."

Eve looked at Ryder. "What in God's name happened, do you have any idea?"

"I can guess. Someone spiked the lamp with a wax capsule of gunpowder so that heat would make it explode. When Lady Beatrice lit the lamp, the wax melted and the powder ignited. Ingenious, really."

Eve frowned, wondering how Ryder knew about such things—until she recalled that he was an expert in munitions.

"The perpetrator had to be someone familiar with your habits," he added. "Someone who expected *you* to light that lamp."

Puzzled, Eve stared. "But one of our footmen usually attends the lamps and lights them in the evening."

"But you rarely use this room after dark. The lamp could have been rigged weeks ago, when you first came to London, stationed here prepared to explode if you struck a flame to the wick."

Her brother muttered an oath. "Good God, Eve, if you had been sitting at your desk, your face could have been hopelessly scarred. Or you could have even been blinded."

At Cecil's gruesome conjecture, Eve felt her stomach clench, frightened by the notion that she could be so vulnerable in her own home. This second accident in London had been deliberate and had been meant for her. Yet she had been spared while her gentle, elderly aunt had suffered in her place.

Eve suddenly felt fury surge through her, her dread supplanted by the fiercer instinct to protect her loved ones. It was one thing for an unknown assailant to threaten *her* life, but quite another when her family was endangered.

Setting her jaw, Eve nourished the spark of defiance igniting in her breast. Perhaps her assailant truly wanted her dead, but she refused to surrender meekly. And she would die before she allowed her sister or her brother or the aunts to be hurt again. She would have to fight the threats somehow. But how?

She wasn't alone, Eve reminded herself, her gaze returning to Ryder. He was highly skilled at fighting unknown enemies. She was supremely grateful to have him on her side.

"So how do we proceed from here?" she asked with growing determination.

"We'll interview your household staff immediately, trying to discover who might have entered here and fixed the lamp to explode—or who might have been seen in the morning room where he didn't belong."

"Do you really believe it was one of the servants? But they have all been employed here or at Hayden Park since before my marriage."

"Someone had access to this room and knew exactly what to target to put you in danger. The other day you identified three potential suspects. The most likely is still the estate steward you fired, but we can't ignore the possibility of it being your overamorous neighbor, Viscount Gyllford, because you rejected his suit. Or even the new Earl of Hayden—the uncle you said wanted you off the estate because of your interference in his business affairs. Any of them could have engaged one of your servants to carry out his orders. Or it could be someone else we don't yet know about."

Biting her lip, Eve fell silent. She was glad Ryder knew how to go about exposing a criminal, for she didn't have the slightest idea.

"I suppose," she murmured, "we should begin by interviewing our butler, Dunstan, since he came to London with us from the Park. The housekeeper, Mrs. Farnley, lives here even when the family is not in residence, but Dunstan will be familiar with all the servants at both locations."

"Good," Ryder replied. "I'll want a list of their names. I also want a list of everyone you can remember entertaining here in this room since you came to London. What about Gyllford? Did you receive him here on any of the occasions when he called?"

"Yes," she replied thoughtfully. "At least twice that I can recall. But he had no opportunity to be alone. The family was always here."

"Well, let's start with the list of your servants so I can have my own people begin investigating."

Eve gave Ryder a curious glance, wanting to ask him about his "people"—whether he meant the society of Guardians Cecil had told her about. Realizing this was not the time or place, however, she merely fetched pencil and paper from her damaged writing desk to begin making the lists Ryder wanted.

While she was thus occupied, Ryder and Macky combed the town house top to bottom, searching for any more possible traps lying in wait, but they found nothing remotely suspicious. Afterward, Eve and Ryder questioned the entire London staff. Normally the interviews would have been conducted in the morning room, but since it was closed for repairs, they were held in the housekeeper's office.

No one, however, had any clue as to who might have tinkered with the lamp. Nor did they appear to know why anyone would want to harm Lady Hayden or the rest of the family, for that matter. In fact every last servant seemed appalled at the very idea and aghast at what had happened to sweet, gentle Lady Beatrice.

Their lack of results from the interviews was frustrating for Eve but wasn't surprising, since Ryder had warned her this was only a preliminary step in finding the culprit.

What did surprise Eve, however, was that Ryder not only let her participate but insisted on her conducting the inquiries, since she knew all her servants and their histories. And after every interview, he wanted to know her evaluation of each employee.

She couldn't imagine her late husband condoning her involvement or seeking her opinion. The last thing Richard had wanted was for her to have a thought of her own. It was just one more indication of how different Ryder was from the late earl.

At the conclusion, Eve was sitting alone with Ryder in the office, having just offered him the list of staff members and notes she had taken, when he caught her hand with his own.

"You are not going to Hertfordshire next week without me," he said calmly, holding her gaze. "Macky is good, but I don't trust anyone but myself to guard you."

Eve nodded solemnly, no longer inclined to argue about his attendance at the house party. There was no question now that Ryder would accompany them. Her own personal objections to his presence seemed trivial in light of Beatrice's accident. Certainly they all would feel safer with Ryder to look after them.

"I *would* feel better if you came," she admitted, extricating her hand from his. With a gesture of her head, she indicated the list he was placing in his jacket pocket. "How do you mean to proceed? Do you intend to get the Bow Street Runners involved?"

"No, I have my own resources. I've already sent

two of my men to Hertfordshire to find out what they can about your former estate steward. And being in the country next week will give me a chance to do my own investigating."

Eve couldn't pass up the opportunity to satisfy her rabid curiosity. "You said you would have your own people investigate the accidents. Do you mean the Guardians?"

Except for the slightest sharpening of his gaze, Ryder gave no overt sign that she had hit a nerve. "What guardians?" he asked casually.

"The society that Cecil said you are a member of."

Ryder's mouth twisted the slighted degree. "I thought your brother could be trusted to keep confidences to himself."

"Please don't blame him. He was only explaining why you are so skilled—because you belong to this league of protectors."

His dark eyes became shuttered. "If I do, you'll understand why I'm not at liberty to discuss it."

Eve sent him a faint smile. "Yes. But I confess, the knowledge is reassuring. And I am very glad Cecil knows about your order." She paused, then added earnestly, "My brother admires you greatly, Ryder. It is amazing, really. For the first time in his life, Cecil has expressed an interest in something other than his own gratification. He wants to be worthy of joining your league. He has even talked about seeking a post with the Foreign Office in the interim, but I want him to finish his schooling first."

When Ryder remained silent, Eve rose from behind the desk. "Well, I had best go check on Beatrice. She is probably sleeping, but Drucilla and Claire will be comforted to learn the steps you are taking to rout our assailants."

She left Ryder sitting there in her housekeeper's small office, a frown knitting his brow. He would have to have a serious talk with the Honorable Cecil Montlow, Ryder thought darkly, for disclosing the existence of the Guardians. But confiding the secret at least had reassured Eve.

Cecil's faith in him was well placed, Ryder reflected without any false modesty. He was considered the most dangerous of all the Guardians, not only because he possessed any number of lethal skills, but because of his experience dealing with assassins and cutthroats. His familiarity with their treacherous methods gave him an advantage his colleagues in the order lacked.

He trusted his ability to keep Eve safe. And he intended to protect her, despite her reluctance to have him at her party.

Briefly Ryder shut his eyes, remembering the clutch of fear to his heart when he'd seen the lamp explode in a ball of flame, leaving Beatrice writhing on the floor in pain and terror. That could so easily have been Eve, he was horrifyingly aware.

He'd felt such rage toward the villain who had committed such a vile act—the primal response of a man's need to protect his woman.

Eve was his woman now, whether she knew it yet or not. He would give his life before he would let anything happen to her.

It was frustrating, though, fighting a shadow. The thought of spending an entire week living under the same roof as Eve and being unable to touch her was also damnably frustrating.

He wanted another night with her. Wanted all his nights with her. Just remembering the feel of Eve's soft, silky body writhing beneath his, her ripe breasts straining for his touch, her slender back arched in the throes of ecstasy, made his arousal stir.

Deliberately, Ryder quelled his inappropriate hunger. Under ordinary circumstances, the upcoming house party would be a priceless opportunity to woo Eve. But nothing was ordinary about her being a target for murder. And he would have to keep his mind focused on safeguarding her if he hoped to stop the perpetrator before the treacherous bastard struck again.

Chapter Eleven

It was precisely one week later that Eve found herself gazing impatiently out the window at the perfectly manicured lawns of Hayden Park as she waited in the vast entrance hall for Ryder to accompany her on her late-afternoon errand.

The enormous manor, which was built in the grand Palladian style and boasted more than seventy rooms, bespoke great wealth and taste. The centerpiece of the sumptuous, landscaped grounds—a large ornamental lake surrounded with willows and brightly flowering rhododendrons—was home to a flock of elegant black swans. Beyond the lake to the left, Eve could just glimpse the charming stone bridge that spanned a rapidly flowing stream and led to the dower house, a much smaller, less formal manor built for the dowager countesses of the Hayden earls.

Eve fought back her restlessness as she watched the swans gliding on the sunlit water. Her house party had begun well. Conducting a large affair such as this—with over two dozen guests, mostly people from her usual set—was nearly effortless for Eve. Not only had her mother trained her well for the role of a nobleman's lady, but she'd gained vast experience as a hostess by entertaining lavishly for her husband during the six years of her marriage.

All manner of amusements were offered for her company's pleasure. Lawn games such as bowling and cricket and pall-mall. Boating on the lake. Carriage drives and horseback rides. An alfresco picnic. Evening entertainments such as cards and dancing and poetry readings, and even an amateur theatrical of a one-act comedy, complete with costumes, planned for the end of the week.

Tomorrow they would visit the charming ruins of a nearby abbey, and later in the week, they would hold a faux fox hunt sans fox or hounds, with a horseman to stand in for the fox. And finally would come Drucilla's birthday celebration on the final night.

Eve knew she should be congratulating herself on her success. The gathering was a transparent excuse for her to subtly play matchmaker, and for the past three days, she had striven to see that Claire was paired with her favorite gentlemen admirers. It was unreasonable to expect to be able to foster a match in this short a time, but her sister did seem to be growing more comfortable with her swains.

And fortunately, Eve's duties as hostess kept her busy enough to take her mind off the threats to her life. Their remaining few days in London had passed without incident, thankfully. And coming home to the Park had been a relief. But Eve still felt the strain—an anxiety that she had never before been subject to in all her time living here at the Park.

She was truly glad to have Ryder here to protect

her. As were her relatives. Both aunts had heartily endorsed his plan to accompany them to Hertfordshire.

Ryder, it seemed, had won over the aunts entirely. They were so grateful to him for saving Lady Beatrice's life that they'd relented completely, going so far as to call him a true hero. Whereas before he could do no right because of his disreputable past, now he could do no wrong.

Drucilla had even been heard to remark that "Sir Alex is not Quality, but perhaps that is not so important"—a comment that would have been heresy only a short month ago.

Claire and Cecil had delighted in Ryder's presence as well. And Claire had expressed relief that Macky had come with them, saying that she not only felt safe with him, but that he made her laugh.

Thus far, Ryder had performed his role as Eve's bodyguard unobtrusively but with unrelenting seriousness. He'd examined every inch of the manor house and the surrounding buildings and stationed his own footmen inside to guard her. And he wouldn't allow her to set foot outside without him, not even to stroll down to the lake or walk to the stables in the company of trusted servants. Ryder didn't seem to understand why she fretted at the strangling restrictions, saying he considered her safety paramount.

He had accompanied Eve yesterday morning when she'd ridden out to visit the home farm with her new steward, John Baggot, early enough that she could return before most of her guests were even awake. This afternoon she intended to pay a brief visit to the cottage of one of the farm tenants, whose wife had been delivered of a baby son after a difficult labor that had lasted nearly two days.

At this moment, most of her guests were resting or refreshing themselves in their rooms before dinner, and Eve was glad to have this brief time to herself so she could attend to her other duties as mistress of a large estate.

Just then she looked up to see Ryder descending the sweeping staircase. Her heart quickened when his dark gaze swept over her stylish green serge riding habit.

"I apologize for the delay, my lady," Ryder said with a brief smile that set her pulse racing even harder.

As he reached the bottom step, a footman jumped to attention and rushed to open the front door. But Eve was very aware when Ryder placed a hand on the small of her back to guide her outside to where their horses stood on the gravel drive, held by a groom. Ryder, not the groom, lifted her up into the saddle, and then mounted his own horse before setting out with her down the long drive.

"Sorry to have kept you waiting," he murmured when they were out of earshot of the servants. "I was waylaid by the duchess."

Her grace, the elderly dowager Duchess of Gower, was one of Drucilla's contemporaries, and as the highest-ranking guest, she thought it her right to monopolize Ryder's time.

Not surprisingly, Ryder had become a valuable addition to the house party, so charming and attentive to all the ladies that they regularly sought his company. And if she were to be honest, Eve reflected with a spark of irritation, that was a prime source of her dissatisfaction . . . that Ryder paid more attention to everyone else than to *her.* Even if she *had* purposely swelled the ranks of females on her guest list so she wouldn't be tempted to initiate further intimacies with him.

In the end, she hadn't been able to stomach inviting the Widow Ferris-Jones. But Lydia, Lady Keeling, had gratefully accepted her invitation. And Eve had felt compelled to invite at least one other lady on Ryder's list of potential brides, since he'd had to delay his matrimonial plans for her sake. She had settled on Lady Susan Rumbotham, an elegant, striking noblewoman of impeccable lineage and breeding.

She could see, however, no sign that Ryder showed either Lydia or Lady Susan any particular favoritism. But he showed *her* no special partiality, either. In fact he virtually ignored her except when he was acting as her bodyguard.

He was there only to protect her, of course, but Eve had hoped for a little more warmth from Ryder, if only because of their long-term friendship.

It was ironic that he was treating her precisely as she'd wished him to. She had planned to keep a strict distance from Ryder, but his mere presence in her home kept her nerves at a fever pitch. She'd never expected such difficulty pretending dispassion or concealing her wanton feelings for him: the irrepressible longing to see him, the shivery excitement of being with him.

And it was utterly impossible to forget the magical hours she had spent with him making love.

The only time he showed her any particular notice was when the dull-witted Viscount Gyllford, the owner of the bordering estate, came to call. His lordship had not only followed her from London but had shamelessly invited himself to various events of her house party without the slightest hint of embarrassment. Short of ordering him to go away, Eve was obliged to tolerate his boorish imposition.

Cecil, who was not so forgiving, bristled every time the viscount showed his face. "That fool fellow's nothing but a jackanapes, Eve," her brother had complained. "You should throw him out on his ear. If I had the execrable manners to force myself on your company uninvited, you would lock me in my rooms with nothing but bread and water for a week."

Ryder, however, was pleased for the chance to observe the nobleman in person, since Gyllford was one of their three current suspects. Any subtle display of possessiveness Ryder showed whenever Gyllford was near her was certainly not due to jealousy, Eve knew, but out of concern that the viscount might be the culprit they were seeking, since she had firmly refused his marriage proposals.

At that dark thought, Eve firmly shook herself. She had vowed she would try to forget her troubles for the next hour, yet here she was, wasting her few precious moments of freedom.

It was a glorious afternoon, with sunshine spreading golden warmth over the countryside. Late spring was a perfect time to be in Hertfordshire.

Glancing back over her shoulder, Eve found herself admiring the pleasing prospect of the house.

The formal front lawns were graced by precisely clipped hedges of yew and boxwood, but the long sweeping avenue where she and Ryder rode was flanked by tall horse chestnut trees covered in blossom and lined with banks of rhododendrons blooming scarlet and pink and cream.

Before reaching the end of the gravel drive, they turned off onto a tree-shaded lane and rode across the stone bridge. When shortly they came to a grassy hill that just begged to be conquered, Eve's spirits rose instantly.

She was delighted for the chance of a neck-or-nothing gallop; she'd always loved being on horseback for the sense of freedom it gave her. And although she disliked admitting it, she was glad to have Ryder to herself for a short while, even if he hadn't spoken two words to her since leaving the house.

She was keenly aware of her silent riding partner, partly because this moment reminded her of their last summer on Cyrene. Seven years ago, however, they had shared a comfortable companionship whenever they rode across the island together. Unlike now, when all Eve could think about was her memories of their one enchanting night together.

Deciding to put an end to her absurd musings, Eve gestured at the hill. "Shall we race to the top?"

Ryder raised an eyebrow. "Do you really think you can win?"

"I know so."

"Lead the way, my lady."

Eve did, bending low and urging her mount into a gallop. Ryder was right beside her most of the way until they reached the crest, where Eve pulled ahead by a nose.

She drew up, laughing. "You did not let me win on purpose, did you?" she demanded of Ryder.

"Of course not. I wouldn't be so magnanimous."

"You used to let me win when we raced on Cyrene."

"Never. Even when you were eleven, you had the best seat on a horse of any female of my acquaintance."

"Cecil calls me a bruising rider for a lady, which is a high compliment, coming from my brother."

"A pity you're merely a woman. The cavalry could use your skills."

She laughed again—a melodic, husky peal of amusement that went straight to Ryder's heart.

"I miss those wonderful days on Cyrene," she admitted wistfully.

"So do I," Ryder agreed wholeheartedly.

Of one accord, they turned their horses and began to descend the far side of the hill at a much slower pace. In the distance, Ryder could see the valley and the home farm below.

When they'd visited the farms yesterday, Ryder had noticed how eagerly the estate tenants had welcomed Eve back. Everyone she passed had smiled brightly at her, curtsying or bowing and tugging a forelock. And she was full of warmth and concern for their well-being.

Ryder had learned even more about Eve from her new steward, John Baggot, who praised her not only because of the improvements she had made in productivity on the farms but also because of her heartfelt generosity to the estate workers.

Reportedly when her husband the earl was alive, Eve had quietly gone behind his lordship's back to ensure their welfare. And since the earl's passing last year, she had openly involved herself with the running of the estate, much to the relief of her people. To them, Lady Hayden was considered little short of a saint.

Ryder couldn't help reflecting about it as Eve rode beside him, her carriage graceful and elegant as always.

She was in her element here at this grand estate. For the past three days, he'd watched her with her genteel company. She was the supreme hostess, gracious and charming, putting her guests at ease, taking care of their smallest complaints and anticipating their wishes before they even knew to express them. And then he'd seen her deal with her tenants. She was the perfect lady of the manor, bred to the nobility, born to rule.

Yet he knew another side of her. The deeply passionate side she had shown no one else, not even her bastard of a husband.

His gaze wandered over her, drinking in the vision. She possessed a golden beauty that was both ethereal and earthy all at once. At present she wore a small shako hat that left most of her chignon uncovered. The sight of her hair catching the dance and fire of the late-afternoon sun took his breath away. Worse, it sparked an intimate image of Eve naked, hot, needy, desperate, as she'd been during their one night together.

Ryder felt his loins harden at the memory. No other woman could make him instantly, achingly hard without even a touch. And *with* a touch. . . . Her slightest caress could make the fire in him blaze up until it raged out of control.

It was something of a relief to Ryder when they eventually came to the neat row of tenant cottages. Eve drew up before the last one and slid down from her horse before he could come to her aid.

Without hesitation, she went to the front door and rapped quietly. A moment later, the door was opened by a hulking figure of a man. The weary lines on his face disappeared the moment he recognized Eve.

"Milady!" he exclaimed in delighted but hushed tones, giving her a deep bow.

"Hello, Zachery," Eve said just as quietly. "I don't want to disturb Peg, only to see how she is faring."

"You honor us, milady. Please, come in. Peg will be right glad to see you."

He stepped aside to allow her entrance. When Ryder followed, Eve introduced them. "Sir Alex, this is Mr. Zachery Dowell, the new father."

When the farmer tugged on his forelock, Ryder nodded amiably. "I understand congratulations are in order, Mr. Dowell. A boy, is it?"

"Aye, a strapping boy," Zachery replied, beaming. "We've named him Benjamin. M'lady, you can see him for yerself, if you'll come this way."

When Zachery led her to a rear room, Ryder hung back in the doorway. The small bedchamber was already crowded with what appeared to be three other farmers' wives, who greeted Eve with glad faces.

The new mother was still abed, exhausted after her ordeal. The babe was sleeping in her arms, wrapped in a blanket, his puckered red face untroubled by his adoring audience. Ryder watched as Eve took the chair beside the bed and greeted Peg quietly.

"What a beautiful son you have," she said gazing down at the tiny infant.

"Aye, he is at that," the woman murmured proudly.

"I brought little Benjamin a present." Eve fished in the pocket of her riding jacket and withdrew a wooden rattle tied with a blue silk ribbon. "For when he is a bit older."

"Oh, my lady, 'tis so generous you are. You shouldn't have troubled yourself so. But your gifts are much appreciated," Peg hastened to add, as if fearing to appear ungrateful. "The roast chicken was heavenly"—she pointed across the room to the basket of delicacies Eve had sent from her cook—"and the blanket you gave him is so soft." She stroked the lamb's wool that wrapped the child, then shyly offered, "Will you hold him, my lady?"

"I would dearly love to," Eve answered softly.

Bending forward, she carefully gathered up the small bundle and cradled him to her breast. When Benjamin mewled softly and screwed up his face, Eve slowly began rocking the tiny infant. Almost instantly he settled back into contented sleep.

Eve smiled, a picture of elation that squeezed hard at Ryder's heart.

"I would have loved to have had a son like this of my own," Eve murmured in barely a whisper.

"Mayhap God will bless you with one someday," said Peg.

"I'm not certain it will ever happen, for that would mean I would have to marry again—" Eve broke off, as if suddenly realizing where she was. When she cast Ryder a swift glance, he saw that a faint blush had risen to her cheeks.

"Well," she whispered, leaning forward to return baby Benjamin to his mother's arms. "I don't want to keep you awake, Peg. You need your rest."

"Thank you for coming, my lady. Especially when you have all those lords and ladies to see to."

Eve dimpled. "If truth be told, I was glad to escape for a short while. And it was a joy to see Benjamin. I would not have missed it for the world."

When she had said her farewells to Zachery and the other women, Ryder accompanied Eve outside, where he gave her a leg up and then mounted his own horse.

She was unusually quiet as they rode away from the cottage, he noted, suspecting that her thoughts were back in the small bedchamber with the tiny infant.

After a long while, Ryder couldn't stop himself from commenting. "You really don't intend to wed again?" he prodded. "You could have children of your own if you remarry."

Her smile grew wistful, then sad. "I doubt it. I think I told you I am probably barren." Almost instantly, Eve visibly shook herself and sent him a bright smile. "And even if I am not, the possibility of having children of my own is not worth the aggravation of enduring another husband."

At her blithe pronouncement, Ryder felt a sharp ache stab at his gut. She was using her possible barrenness as an excuse not to risk remarrying, he knew very well. "Was your marriage that terrible?" he asked grimly.

Eve's shoulder lifted in a light shrug. "No, not by any normal standards. I had a perfect, privileged life, much like a fairy-tale princess. And Richard was no ogre." Her mouth crooked in a wry smile. "I felt guilty sometimes, wondering what was wrong with me. How dared I be so unhappy? Of course I would never have confessed how miserable I was to Richard. He had lived up to every detail of the bargain I and my parents made with him. He gave me everything money could buy."

Ryder felt his hands tighten on the reins. Eve had allowed him another glimpse into her heart, but that glimpse only chilled him. He wanted badly to exclaim that he was nothing like her late husband, that he wanted to give her a child if she would only consider marrying him.

He wanted children with Eve. But if it never happened—if she *did* prove to be barren with him as she had with her husband—he could bear it as long as she was his wife.

But she was speaking now, her words drowning out his dark thoughts. "I am quite content now, Ryder. I am living a fulfilling life where my small contributions actually mean something."

"True," he forced himself to say. "You are not a useless ornament any longer."

"Exactly. The only thing I have to wish for is that Claire makes a match that ensures her happiness and that Cecil finds some sort of gainful interest that will keep him out of trouble. Once they are settled, I shall be perfectly happy."

"Are you certain of that?"

She gave him a curious glance. "I beg your pardon?"

"Once your brother and sister have flown the nest, you will be alone except for the aunts. A life with only those ancient ladies for company sounds deadly dull." Ryder slowed his horse to a halt, requiring Eve to do the same. "Are you sure you want to spend the rest of your days living a passionless existence?"

Eve found herself staring at him, wondering how she could answer. Before last week, she would have said yes—*emphatically* yes—she wanted to live her life without passion.

But that was before she had spent one glorious night in Ryder's arms. Before he had taught her what real passion was.

Without replying, Eve tore her gaze away and urged her mount forward. Yet Ryder's question echoed in her mind for a long, long while. In fact they were approaching the dower house before Eve became aware of her surroundings again.

This house was where she would live if the new earl ever took up residence at the Park. When her husband was alive, she had sometimes used it as her own private retreat so that she could have a few moments completely to herself, where she didn't have to be the ideal wife Richard had demanded as her part of their marital bargain.

When she reached the drive, without conscious volition, Eve halted her mount. Her heart started pounding at the daring, scandalous thought that had entered her head.

She looked at Ryder, who was eyeing her curiously in return. "There are no servants at the dower house just now," Eve said slowly, her breath uneven. "They only come here twice a week to dust and air the bed linens."

He waited politely, allowing her the chance to expound.

"Would you care to stop here for a moment?" she finally ventured.

Ryder's gaze sharpened for an instant before his expression turned bland. "Is that a proposition, sweeting?"

"Yes . . . I suppose it is," she answered boldly.

She felt her face warming at his scrutiny, but she wouldn't look away. The flagrant truth was she wanted to experience Ryder's incredible passion again. Wanted to surrender to her own wicked desires. Ryder made her want to throw caution to the winds. To rebel from her proper, staid, genteel existence.

Admittedly it had been a torment to remain apart from him this past week, to pretend she didn't want him when she did. For days now, she had tried to fight her powerful yearning for him, but she didn't know how much longer she could hold out.

It was almost a relief to realize that she needn't try any longer. She had an opportunity to be alone with Ryder now. Undoubtedly he would think her a shameless wanton, but she couldn't control her longing to experience a few moments of uninhibited bliss in his arms.

Eve held herself still as she waited breathlessly for his answer. She wasn't as poised as she appeared; indeed, she was trembling inside.

Ryder had told her he found her desirable. But what if he no longer felt that way? What if he didn't wish to make love to her?

"Then I accept, my lady."

His lazy reply reassured her completely. He had the devil in his eyes, pure charm in his half smile. Eve felt all her nerves clench in anticipation.

Without speaking, she led the way down the drive to the rear of the house and halted beside the gate of a stone wall.

When she would have dismounted, however, Ryder shook his head. "Allow me, love."

He swung down from his horse and came around to her side. Reaching up to grasp her waist, he lifted her down effortlessly and held her against him for a moment, his hands lingering on her hips.

The careless smile he gave her made her feel as if they were sharing an intimate secret, while those potent dark eyes sent desire pooling between her thighs.

Eve felt herself shiver as she stared up at Ryder's handsome features. He was danger, he was excitement. He was utterly irresistible.

Before her knees gave way, she forced herself to step back and turn toward the gate.

They left the horses to graze and entered the sunlit gardens, where roses and other fragrant flowers bloomed in charming profusion. Silently Eve followed the path beside the stretch of lawn to a rear entrance of the house. Her hands were shaking as she pushed open the door and Ryder followed her inside, into a small parlor.

The interior was cool and dim with all the draperies drawn shut, but she felt flushed and fevered.

When she heard Ryder close the door behind him, Eve turned to face him. He was not as poised as he appeared, either, she realized. His dark eyes seared her, setting her heart racing and making her keenly aware of the liquid ache of yearning gathering inside her.

She couldn't wait to touch him. She whispered his name and moved into his arms, pressing her body urgently against his.

Suddenly they were both wild with lust and longing. His touch was not entirely gentle as he captured her face in his hands and covered her mouth with his.

Their kiss was explosive, the want too fierce for much gentleness.

Eve had never felt such raw, reckless hunger.

She reached up to grip his sable hair, overwhelmed by the sheer, overpowering need to be one with him, the frantic heat. She was hot and only Ryder could cool her; only he could satisfy the burning need inside her, assuage the ache between her thighs, in her throbbing breasts.

She could feel his hands covering the swells beneath her riding jacket and she moaned, arching into his possessive touch. His fingers made short work of the buttons and pushed back the lapels, only to find too many layers of fabric. While his fingers sought her taut nipples beneath her shirtwaist and corset and chemise, his searing mouth left hers to trail flaming kisses down the arch of her throat.

Almost desperate now, Eve searched blindly for the front placket of his breeches, her fingers fumbling to unfasten the buttons she had to fight the reckless urge to rip apart.

When she set his rigid phallus free, Ryder inhaled a harsh breath, but his lips continued to ply her throat as he pulled her skirts up to her waist, baring her feminine flesh. Her skin burned against his naked arousal as it probed her wet, silken folds.

"I want you, Ryder," Eve rasped in a pleading whimper.

At her hoarse admission, he broke off his caresses, his gaze flashing to hers, hot and glittering. His eyes seemed to blaze with an inner fire, a dangerous fire, as he lifted her up and drew her legs around his hips, locking her to him. Spinning her around, he pinned her back against the door and swallowed her moan as he kissed her fiercely again.

His mouth was wild, devouring, with a primal need that had flared out of control as he thrust inside her and slid home to the hilt.

The sudden, explosive possession was too much. The thrill of his entry, the breathtaking shock of his bigness, made her cry out.

Ryder froze. "God, Eve . . ." he breathed against her lips, obviously struggling for control.

"No, don't stop!" Eve exclaimed when he started to withdraw.

She found his mouth again, desperately holding on to his back, needing to feel the plunge and slide of his thick shaft inside her.

Willingly he surged into her, answering her demand. Eve arched to meet him, straining wantonly into his arms.

The sensations heightened to a wild song in her veins. Their rhythm became frantic, his body moving fierce and strong against hers, her hips jerking eagerly up to meet his thrusts with a sharp, fevered wanting.

His heart pounding, Ryder could barely contain his savage hunger, Eve was so wild around him. He strained to keep his explosive need in check, but there was no finesse left in him.

It was a primal mating, a soul-searing union between a man and his mate. He felt jagged and feverish, driven to satisfy this craving Eve had set burning deep inside him. A craving more powerful than the beat of his heart, than the need to breathe.

In another moment, rapture, savage and blinding, ripped through his body at the same time Eve shuddered and spasmed in his arms, her tight sheath clenching around him as he spent himself in long bursts.

Ecstasy left them clinging in an aftermath of fire. Gasping, Eve melted back into him, while Ryder locked his knees to keep from sagging to the floor, his harsh breaths loud in the quiet parlor.

He could scarcely believe what had just happened. Eve had welcomed him into her body with an eagerness and abandonment that had stunned him. It was a moment of intimacy so intense, so pure, he knew he would never be the same again.

"Are you all right?" he asked finally when he could speak.

"Mmmm . . . marvelous."

Ryder exhaled a slow breath into the curve of her neck. Marvelous didn't begin to describe the bliss he felt. He was still holding her up, her legs wrapped around his thighs, in a position that must be uncomfortable for her, but he didn't want to move.

He would like to have been strong and noble and keep a safe distance from Eve, but her invitation had been impossible to resist. He'd been frantic to get inside her.

At his sudden realization, Ryder silently swore at himself. They hadn't used the sponges. Yet he couldn't bring himself to regret it. If he had gotten Eve with child, she would have no choice but to wed him.

She didn't seem to share the same concern, however. Her face was buried in his shoulder, and after a moment she gave a rueful laugh. "I'll warrant you never expected me to throw myself at you like that."

Ryder strove to keep his tone light. "No, but I won't take it personally. It stands to reason that you would want a moment of abandonment, since you've been repressed your entire life. I'm honored that you chose me to slake your passions."

She raised her face from his shoulder. Her cheeks were flushed from their lovemaking, but there was a shy smile on her lips as she looked steadily at him. "We could go upstairs, Ryder. There are five bedchambers on the second floor."

His gaze settled on the window, on the quiet garden outside. He was still aching with need, with unsated hunger, his craving for her in no way quenched. "I have a better idea."

Slowly withdrawing from between her thighs, he let her slide down his body and set her on his feet, but he kept her captive there as he removed her hat and loosened her hair from its pins so that it fell free around her shoulders. Then Ryder took her hand and led her outside to the secluded garden.

"I want to make love to you here," he explained when she gave him a questioning glance.

He slipped off her jacket and then shed his own, along with his cravat. But there he stopped. The high stone walls offered total privacy, but if a servant should happen along, he didn't want Eve's lithe, lush body to be seen by any eyes but his own. Besides, there was something erotic about making love to her with all their clothing on.

Sinking onto the soft grass to lie on his back, he drew Eve down beside him. He wanted to love her more slowly this time, amid the sunshine and flowers. If he closed his eyes he could imagine this was the sensual paradise of Cyrene, with a cloudless blue sky overhead, the heat shimmering around them alleviated by a cooling sea breeze.

But he didn't want to close his eyes. He wanted to drink Eve in.

Sunshine was tangled in her hair. Ryder reached up to capture a tress where it glimmered with soft brilliance. The bright strands felt cool and silky against his fingers.

When she smiled, he watched her, spellbound.

Eve was golden honey and sunshine, vibrant and alive and unbelievably beautiful. And when she smiled down at him with that beguiling siren's smile, his heart lifted with pure joy.

Carefully, not daring to break the spell, he drew her over him so that she straddled his bare loins, with her naked thighs on either side of his hips.

She was still smiling softly. When she reached down to touch his lips with her fingertips, the simple caress sent a surge of pure emotion through Ryder. Rich, dark emotion so powerful he was drowning in it.

His throat tight, he lay beneath her, gazing up into her blue eyes, aching with desire so raw that he felt on fire. It was as if the warmth of her seeped into him and saturated his soul.

Then she bent to him. Their kiss was hot, slow, searing . . . and the fever started again, swift and enveloping—and as inevitable as the rising of the sun.

Without breaking the kiss, Eve eased herself down over his rigid flesh. She was primed, silky soft, yielding, and she gloved him so tightly, it stole his breath away.

When she began to move above him, another hot wave of desire ripped through him. He could no longer fight the need, the ache that consumed him. His hands roamed frantically over her body, his teeth clenching against the heat swelling inside him. It was white hot, burning him alive.

Eve's back arched as she took him deeper into her center . . . and then came the incredible release—a sudden sunburst of joy as they crested together. The sky blazed bluer, the sun burned brighter in that instant. The hoarse shout Ryder gave as he climaxed was literally ripped from deep inside his soul.

Afterward, they lay there bonelessly, savoring the rapture of their joining. Eve had collapsed upon him, and Ryder had no strength left to move.

She left him defenseless, filled with a longing so potent it made him feel helpless. He would never stop wanting her like this, with this wild, insatiable, soul-deep hunger. He had never felt this connection, this bond, with anyone but Eve.

He could feel the words of love rising to his lips, words he didn't dare speak. He loved her with a fierceness that he'd never fathomed feeling for anyone. Yet he didn't know how to make her accept that love.

All I want is your heart, your soul, for the rest of our lives, he wanted to say.

But it was too soon.

He wanted her heart and soul and body. Wanted her warmth and laughter lighting up his days. And he wouldn't settle for anything less.

For now, however, all he could do was chip away at Eve's defenses, one passionate moment at a time.

Chapter Twelve

Bright sunshine lit the cavalcade of carriages that left Hayden Park late the following morning, heading for the ruins of a medieval abbey some nine miles away. Eve rode in the first barouche, whose front and rear hoods had been folded back, along with Ryder and the aunts.

Trying to ignore the handsome man lounging in the seat opposite her, Eve raised her face to the sun, reveling in the beautiful day. Her spirits were higher than they had been in weeks.

It was foolish, perhaps even dangerous, to be this happy, she knew. And truly, she had no reason to be so lighthearted. Her life was still in peril. And her interlude with Ryder was merely a temporary affair. A relationship based on nothing more than mutual pleasure.

Yet after yesterday's lovemaking, Eve found it utterly impossible to pretend indifference to Ryder. All last evening during dinner and the entertainments afterward, she'd been keenly conscious of his every move. All night long, her dreams of him had been wild and delicious. And this morning—at breakfast and then later when the guests and servants were sorting themselves out to climb into the various conveyances—Eve had been aware of the delicious heat curling in her body whenever she simply glimpsed at Ryder.

It was probable, she acknowledged reluctantly, that to some degree she was suffering from the malady that poets lamented: sheer infatuation. She had read about the feverish madness that could take control of the senses, the blind yearning. She just had never expected to experience the symptoms herself.

She'd never known how brazen she could be, either. Yesterday at the dower house, she had given in to her carnal cravings, greedily offering herself to Ryder and becoming a wild utterly abandoned sexual creature she didn't even recognize.

It was shameful to enjoy her wantonness so much. Yet she couldn't stem the relentless feelings of excitement and desire that rose in her whenever she merely thought of him.

Ryder thrilled her, made her feel emotions so shattering they brought tears to her eyes. He could make her come apart.

And she believed now that he reciprocated her feelings, at least in small measure. Yesterday she'd felt the raw hunger in his touch, in his searing embrace. His kisses had been devouring, possessive, intense; the look in his eyes demanding, hungry, hot.

And at this moment, when she met Ryder's dark gaze across the short space between them, she felt a surge of pure unadulterated lust.

Flushing, Eve forced herself to look away. A man shouldn't have such power over a woman. Even more shameful was how badly she wanted to make love to him again. Having to wait to see Ryder alone was a torment. They were surrounded by dozens of people, so that they couldn't even carry on a private conversation.

Which was why he had resolved to ride with Eve this morning. Not only to offer her protection but also to apprise her and the aunts of the status of his investigation. Drucilla in particular wanted to be informed of every new development in uncovering the identity of their assailant, although Beatrice, who was still recovering from her burns, was content to leave the search solely to Ryder.

Eve herself was of two minds. On such a bright, sparkling morning, it was easy to dismiss the danger she was in. And yet a part of her was grimly determined to hear Ryder's report.

After the barouche got under way, Drucilla focused her penetrating gaze on Ryder. "Now then, Sir Alex, you may tell us what progress you have made on ending this nightmare."

"Not as much as I would like, my lady," Ryder said, leaning forward to reply. His own trusted coachman was driving, Eve was aware, but he kept his voice low, presumably to avoid being overheard by anyone in the following carriages.

"Do you still consider our former steward the chief suspect?" Eve asked quietly.

"Yes," Ryder answered. "I've questioned your current steward at length about Tobias Meade, and I've learned a bit more from your other servants and some of your tenant farmers. Plus, I've had my men haunting the taproom of the village tavern in order to listen to the local gossip. But other than having poor management skills, Meade seems to be fairly harmless. He was not well liked, but thus far, no one considers him capable of initiating so violent a revenge as murder."

"Do you even know where he is living now?"

"My sources tell me he left here with his wife Mabel six months ago, directly after being fired, but his friends claim to have no idea where he's gone. I have men searching in Kent for him now. Meade reportedly came here from Kent to apply for the position of steward. I've reviewed all the estate accounts you gave me, on the chance of uncovering his character references, but unfortunately, your husband didn't keep any detailed records of employee transactions."

"Yes," Eve murmured. "Richard concerned himself with the Park as little as possible."

"And what of our cousin, the new Lord Hayden?" Drucilla interjected. "Do you still think him a suspect?"

Ryder shook his head. "I can't see him as our culprit. He's elderly and not in the best of health, and is even less interested in running the estate than his predecessor. And while he might like to rid himself of Lady Hayden after the headaches she's caused him by championing the estate tenants, that isn't strong enough motive for murder. Your neighbor, Lord Gyllford, however, can't be ruled out until I can examine his circumstances more thoroughly. He might indeed be the vindictive sort, offended enough by Lady Hayden's rejection to seek reparation for his wounded vanity."

Eve glanced back over her shoulder at the carriage directly behind them, which held the twins and Viscount Gyllford, in addition to the Duchess of Gower, Lady Keeling, and one of Claire's beaux. Gyllford, Eve acknowledged, was still imposing himself shamelessly on her company. If he was angry at her because she had turned down his offers of marriage, he wasn't showing it, yet he continued to pursue her with the persistence of a rat terrier.

"I haven't decided if he's as thickheaded as he appears," Ryder added dryly, "or merely an excellent actor."

"I don't believe his obtuseness is an act," Eve said, biting back a smile.

Drucilla pinched her lips together, but refrained from insisting that Gyllford would make Eve a fine husband, as she would have in the past.

"So what do you intend to do next?" Eve asked Ryder.

"I'll focus my efforts on discovering where Meade has gone so I can interrogate him. Simply letting him know we consider him a suspect might be enough to warn him off. But to be truthful, I'm beginning to think that none of our initial suspects fits my notion of your assailant."

"What if we never find him?"

The hard smile that touched Ryder's lips held grim anticipation. "We'll find him, I promise you. I'm not about to stop searching until we have our culprit behind bars."

"You enjoy the challenge, don't you?" Eve asked, struck by the sudden insight. "You relish the danger."

Ryder's smile abruptly faded. "The challenge, yes, but not the danger when it involves you. I would just as soon have this over with."

With effort, Eve quelled a shiver. She would very much like this to be over with as well.

And she found herself in agreement with Beatrice when the elderly dame spoke up to say quietly, "Perhaps we can discuss a more agreeable topic, Sir Alex. It terrifies me to think that this madman could strike again at any moment."

Since that was the consensus among the ladies, the conversation turned to the success of the house party, and the aunts discussed the various guests until they finally arrived at their destination.

Emerging from a narrow lane among the beechwoods, the line of carriages swept onto an emerald green meadow and came to a halt. The massive monastic ruins stood in a picturesque setting on the banks of the River Quinn, surrounded by verdant wooded hills. Eve had always been enchanted by the timeless charm of the place.

"Oh, how lovely," Eve heard her friend Lydia remark in the carriage behind her.

"Indeed, it is," Claire agreed.

Cecil gave a derisive snort. "It's the history that's fascinating. Cistercian monks built this abbey in the twelfth century during Henry II's reign. The timber roofs have all disintegrated and some of the walls are falling in, but the church tower is mainly intact. A pity the crumbling steps are too dangerous for ladies to climb, since the view from the top is spectacular."

"That is regrettable," her grace the Duchess of

Gower proclaimed, "since I have a fondness for splendid views."

When Ryder had assisted Eve down from the carriage, she scanned the impressive buildings. The roofless walls stood three stories tall, with an even taller tower for the church.

"There are some fine stone carvings in the church nave," Eve said to Lydia, who was being assisted down by Macky, "and in the refectory where the monks took their meals."

As proper for his role as footman, Macky had perched at the rear of the carriage carrying the twins, with the responsibility for looking after them. A dozen other servants had been sent on ahead, charged with setting up a picnic luncheon under the shade trees by the river for the guests after they explored the abbey ruins.

The chestnut-haired actor helped Claire down next. Eve's attention was caught when Macky bent and whispered something in her sister's ear that made her laugh.

Eve exhaled a soft sigh of exasperation. Not surprisingly, Claire seemed more at ease with her hired protector than with her real suitors, but she was pointedly ignoring the very gentlemen who were the reason for the house party.

But then Eve was forced to forget her sister in favor of seeing to her obligations to her numerous guests. Due to the large number, the company was divided into three smaller groups, with Hayden employees acting as guides, including Eve's steward, John Baggot, her gamekeeper, and her chief gardener.

There was much congenial laughter and conversation as the guests set off across the beautiful grounds to explore the ruins. The monastery was made up of a church, the monks' living quarters, and a cloister. To the sides and rear of the abbey proper were various medieval farm buildings—what once had been stables and storage barns and cottages.

Without being conspicuous about it, Ryder shepherded Eve and her family into Baggot's group. Eve kept Lydia beside her so that she could add to the steward's detail of the abbey's history.

They first visited the cloister, where the monks had prayed in solitude, entering through a doorless arch, since the timber doors had long since rotted away. As they left the cloister, Eve glanced through one of the narrow lancet windows. Beyond the remains of the stable she could see the riverbank where her servants were setting up the alfresco picnic.

Next they explored the living quarters—the small, barren cells where the monks had slept, the larger refectory, and the kitchens. The storage rooms, Baggot informed them, led to the cellars below, which were linked to the rest of the abbey by a labyrinth of underground passages.

Finally they moved on to the church, where Eve pointed out the stone carvings in the long nave—the narrow central hall that was the main part of the church.

When Lydia wished to view the entire tower, Eve accompanied her outside, with Ryder close behind.

"It is a wonder the walls have stood all these centuries," Lydia said admiringly, looking up at the layers of masonry above her head.

"I know," Eve agreed.

Lydia turned to examine the tall rock monument at the foot of a distant hill. "What are those ruins, do you know?"

Shielding her eyes from the bright sunlight, Eve followed her friend's gaze. "That is a pagan marker commemorating a Saxon victory in battle," she answered. "Apparently the slabs were too massive for the monks to move, so they were forced to tolerate them."

Smiling, Lydia brought a hand to her throat. "This has truly been fascinating, Eve, but I'm afraid all this sun and fresh air has made me thirsty. Do you suppose your servants have finished setting up the picnic yet?"

"I expect so. Shall we see what they have brought us to drink?"

They were on the opposite side of the abbey from the river. Intending to cross through the church, Eve turned with Lydia to retrace their steps along the wall, heading toward the arched doorway where Ryder awaited them.

Just then she heard an odd sound above her head, followed by Ryder's sudden shout as he raced toward her. "Eve, move!"

Startled, she glanced up, only to realize that a shower of stone rubble was hurtling down on them.

"*Eve!*"

She heard the raw fear in Ryder's voice as with sheer desperation he lunged and shoved her and Lydia out of the path of the rubble an instant before it crashed down in a foot-high heap of swirling dust and rock.

Both women struck the ground hard. Beneath her, Lydia gave a scream while Eve cried out at the sudden pain in her right ankle.

"God in heaven, Eve, are you all right?" she heard Ryder demanding. He was kneeling over her as she lay there in stunned silence.

"I think so. . . ." A heavy stone had caught her leg, Eve realized, but the damage could have been much worse. "Lydia?" she asked, easing her weight off her poor friend.

Lydia was trembling, and her chin was bleeding profusely, but she gave a shaken nod.

"I need to go after him," Ryder said urgently, pointing upward.

Him? Dazed, Eve looked up to see that part of the crumbled wall around a lancet window was missing. The wall had suddenly fallen. *Or been pushed.* "Someone tried to kill me again," she rasped.

"*Yes.*" His grim tone was practically a snarl.

Eve shook herself, finally understanding that Ryder wanted to pursue the perpetrator but wouldn't leave her side until she reassured him. "We'll be fine . . . go!"

"Stay here!" he ordered before lurching to his feet and sprinting for the doorway.

After helping Lydia to sit up, Eve fished in the reticule looped around her wrist. Drawing out a handkerchief, she held it to Lydia's chin to stem the bleeding.

Her friend was shaken but recovered her composure in a few moments. "That was q-quick thinking by Sir Alex, Eve. He saved both our lives."

"Yes. He was better prepared this time."

Lydia stared in horror. "It has happened before? Is *that* what you meant when you said someone tried to kill you again?"

"I'm afraid so."

"Dear God, Eve. . . . Are you hurt?"

Leaving the handkerchief to Lydia, Eve inspected her right leg. Her jean half-boot had cushioned most of the blow, but when she probed, her ankle hurt. And when she tried to stand, she could put weight on that foot but could walk only with a limp.

"My ankle isn't broken, just bruised, but I will need help walking. We will wait for Sir Alex," Eve said, easing back on the ground.

It was perhaps another five minutes before Ryder returned. He was furious, Eve could tell instantly from his expression.

"Any luck?" she asked.

"No. Someone was up there on the wall walk, watching you, but he was gone by the time I arrived. When I followed the stairway down to the cellars and searched the underground passageways, I found wet footprints where someone had recently moved through muddy water. The prints led to the rear of the abbey and came up in the cloister, but from there, it would have been easy to slip out through any of the openings in the walls."

"And if he went that way," Eve speculated with rising anger, "he could have hidden himself in any of the ruined farm buildings or disappeared into the woods by the river."

"Yes," Ryder said tersely. "Or returned to the picnic grounds and melded into your servant staff."

"If so, then it could indeed have been one of the servants."

"Perhaps. But it just as easily could have been anyone who knew we were visiting the ruins. The whole countryside knew your plans for the house party. He could have arrived here long beforehand and lain in wait for you, in the hope of finding you alone. Regardless, there's no question he's becoming more brazen. He could easily have been seen."

"What of Lord Gyllford?" Eve asked.

"I intend to discover if he went missing from his group for any period of time."

"You suspect *Lord Gyllford*?" Lydia asked in a high, shocked voice.

Ryder offered her a reassuring smile. "It's unlikely he's the culprit, although he is one of several people who might have had motive and opportunity to hurt Eve. But it would be best not to mention this incident to anyone, Lady Keeling, if we hope to eventually flush out our criminal."

"Of course," Lydia said uncertainly.

"Can you ladies make it to your carriage?" he said, changing the subject. "I will escort you home and then return so I can start questioning your servants and guests."

"But I don't *wish* to go home, Ryder," Eve said stubbornly, her anger swelling at the helplessness her assailant made her feel. "I have no intention of acting the coward, particularly when it would only alarm my guests and cause unnecessary delay in your inquiry."

She saw Ryder's jaw harden, but she cut off his argument before he could voice it. "And I won't call off the picnic and give that villain the satisfaction of thinking I am surrendering to his tyranny without a fight. Besides, I doubt he will make another attempt today."

"*Another* attempt?" Lydia asked, dismayed.

Eve gave her friend a rueful glance. "I am so sorry you were dragged into the danger, Lydia."

"No, no . . . I am fine, truly. But it is appalling to think that someone is actually trying to kill you. You must be terrified."

"I am, a little," Eve said, managing an ironic smile. "But I am becoming more inured to the feeling. How is your chin?" she added, forcing herself to show a pretense of calm.

"Better, I think." Lydia held the handkerchief away so Eve could examine the wound.

"Yes, it *is* better. The bleeding has stopped. But if you would like to go home now and have this tended to, I will have my coachman take you."

"No, I don't want to put you to so much trouble. And I have been looking forward to the picnic."

"Very well, then," Ryder capitulated, though obviously not happy about Eve's decision. "We will stay for the remainder of the picnic." He helped both ladies to stand. "We'll explain your injuries by saying that you met with an unfortunate accident. You both encountered a crumbling step and tripped."

"How clumsy of us," Eve said wryly, trying to make a jest.

Yet she had never felt less like laughing. Now that the immediate danger was over, she felt a little weak from shock, as well as a burning fury that she once again had been turned into a victim.

She truly had no desire to face the inevitable fuss her family and guests would make when she and Lydia returned bruised and bleeding. But there was no hope for it, Eve thought with a regretful sigh.

With Ryder's support, she was able to walk slowly back to the picnic spot. From a distance, the scene looked elegant and civilized in contrast to the rustic charm of the setting. White damask cloths covered the tables where a feast had been laid out, complete with baskets of strawberries and hothouse pineapples and even a succulent roast goose, while crystal goblets and fine china sparkled in the sunlight.

It seemed highly incongruous to Eve, when she had just escaped another near-fatal accident, thanks to Ryder. Most of the guests were already lounging on blankets beneath the beechwood trees as they were served champagne and punch by her servants.

Studying the crowd, Eve felt herself shudder. Her murderous assailant could be right here, looking quite innocent and proper and very much a part of the celebration.

Or he could still be lurking in the woods, observing her at this very moment.

Her gaze flickered to the woods, then returned to the gathering. She saw Macky frown when he spied her limping across the grounds on Ryder's arm. The two men exchanged a significant glance, and she was sure Macky realized something was amiss.

Then she felt Ryder give her hand a reassuring squeeze, and she glanced gratefully up at him.

"Ready for your performance?" he asked, his tone still holding a brusque hint of disapproval.

"Yes." Grasping his arm more tightly, Eve squared her shoulders and feigned a smile, bracing herself to face her jovial company when the last thing she wanted to do was pretend to enjoy an alfresco picnic.

Chapter Thirteen

Four hours later found Eve alone in the small ladies' parlor she favored when she resided at Hayden Park, staring blindly out the window at the swans swimming lazily on the lake.

Defiance had been her chief emotion for the remainder of the afternoon. She was furious that another cowardly attempt had been made on her life, and even more furious that her friend Lydia had been caught in the middle of the treachery aimed at her.

Her family was horrified. Beatrice had wanted to disband the house party at once and send Eve somewhere far, far away, where she could be safe.

Eve refused to be cowed into hiding, however. She was determined to quell her fear, even if she risked grave danger by remaining.

Ryder's grimness was palpable. As soon as they returned to the Park, he had sent to London for more reinforcements. And he planned to redouble his efforts to discover where the former steward, Tobias Meade, and his wife Mabel might have gone after being turned off the estate.

But Ryder was clearly worried about future attempts on Eve's life. He'd alarmed her further at the picnic when he insisted on filling her plate himself, murmuring in a quiet undertone, "I don't want you eating or drinking anything that is not a communal offering straight from your cook."

Eve had stared at him. "You are concerned I might be *poisoned*?"

"It's only a possibility, but you need to be careful. And after this, you will remain at home, where I can better protect you."

"But I have guests to entertain."

"They will have to get along without you."

"What about the hunt tomorrow?"

"You won't be attending. You are too conspicuous at public outings and make too easy a target."

Eve had refrained from arguing with Ryder at the time, even though she had no intention of cowering at home and letting her devious assailant dictate her every move.

Alone in the parlor now, however, Eve shuddered. Her defiance was fading quickly with nothing else to occupy or distract her. In the peaceful lull before the dinner hour, the house was too quiet. She could hear her chaotic thoughts, could feel her nerves shredding. She hated the feeling of helplessness, of powerlessness. She had no command over her life anymore, just as during her marriage. All her hard-won independence had been ground to dust.

Just then she heard the door open behind her. Without even looking, she knew Ryder had joined her. She sensed his comforting presence at her back, a moment before she felt his warm hands come to rest on her shoulders.

Eve exhaled a deep sigh when he began rubbing lightly, kneading the strain and tension from her tight muscles.

"Come with me to the dower house," he said quietly. "You need to get away."

She squeezed her eyes shut. How did he know her so well? How had his instincts become so keenly attuned to her?

The truth was, she desperately wanted to go with him, wanted to escape her fear and responsibilities for a while, even if it would be scandalous. She couldn't help feeling frightened and on edge, but she was sick of being afraid and wanted to restore some measure of control over her life. Her guests were currently in their rooms, resting before dinner, so she wouldn't be missed.

"Yes," she answered simply.

Her defiant mood returned as she accompanied Ryder to the stables, where a groom harnessed the gig for her. And she felt a renewed sense of freedom as they drove the short distance to the dower house.

Halting the vehicle in the drive, Ryder tied the horse and then came around to lift Eve down, taking care to set her down easily so as not to aggravate the soreness of her twisted ankle. As he took her hand and led her inside the house, she realized that she felt safe with Ryder.

No, Eve amended silently. Ryder made her feel so much more than just safe. She needed him, she wanted him. And for the next hour, she was determined to forget her fears, to pretend nothing else existed but the two of them.

"This way," Eve said, preceding him upstairs to

the bedchamber she normally used when she retreated here.

Decorated in elegant shades of ivory and yellow, the room was bright and airy, with late-afternoon sunlight streaming through the lace curtains. Eve went straight to the windows and threw open the sash, letting in the sweet fragrance of the gardens below. The same gardens where she had made love to Ryder so passionately only the day before.

When she turned and saw that Ryder had already begun to undress, her heart skipped a beat. This Ryder was familiar to her, since he had removed his coat and cravat. In shirtsleeves and breeches, he brought to mind images of that long-ago lazy summer on Cyrene, the last of her girlhood.

In silence, they slowly undressed each other, wanting to draw out the moment.

When they were both nude, Eve stood before Ryder unselfconciously, reveling in her newfound confidence. She noted the way his eyes flared and darkened at the sight of her, and knew her own expression was similar.

He made such a picture of male beauty that she couldn't speak. His magnificent male splendor took her breath away.

Her gaze swept over his powerful torso and lower, to fix on his phallus that jutted proudly against his belly. Mesmerized, Eve stepped toward him, yearning to feel his hard flesh filling her, driving into her.

When Ryder drew her against the incredible lean hardness of his body, the heat and hunger gathered inside her in an unbearable need. If she didn't have this man, if he didn't ease the ache within her soon, she would perish.

"I want you," she confessed in a whisper as he bent and touched his lips to her throat.

"The feeling is mutual, I assure you, beauty."

"Ryder, kiss me."

Obeying, he put a finger under her chin and brought her mouth against the burning heat of his. Eve sighed in delight at the tender ravishment of his kiss. But it wasn't enough.

When his hands came up to cup her breasts, she stopped him. "No, I want to do this. Please?"

His smile was all sensual charm. "Do you mean to seduce me, my lady?"

"Yes," she returned boldly. "I want to pleasure you this time."

As if sensing her need to take control, Ryder acquiesced without protest. "By all means, indulge yourself."

She *did* want to indulge herself. Ryder had given her a great gift; he had opened her to passion. And she wanted to repay him.

But more important, she wanted to incite the same passion in him. To make him yearn for her the way she had begun to yearn for him.

Moving to the bed, she turned back the yellow chintz coverlet and the linen sheets, then directed him to lie down. He obliged, lounging back against the pillows, somehow managing to look both relaxed and dangerous at the same time. The contrast between his naked masculinity and the soft white bed was riveting.

Her mouth going dry at the delicious sight, Eve

climbed up after him to kneel between his spread legs. For a moment, she hesitated, gazing down at him—the expanse of his chest, his taut belly, the powerful sprawl of his thighs, the swollen, jutting erection that reached almost to his navel.

Her heart started beating in wild anticipation. She was determined to make this man, dangerous as he was, feel the same hot, uncontrollable pleasure he aroused in her.

Leaning over him, she trailed her fingers along one flat male nipple to his abdomen, marveling at how silky and hot his skin felt. Ryder tensed when she closed her fingers over his arousal, and his eyes turned even darker, but he lay still while she explored.

Eve felt shy and brazen and emboldened all at once as she slowly dragged the tips of her fingers over his sex. She could see Ryder's jaw tighten when she teased his heavy sacs, pulling lightly.

Then bending, she pressed her lips against the swollen head of his shaft. He sucked in a breath as she began to nibble on his scalding hot flesh, yet she wasn't satisfied. She wanted to do more than just kiss him—although she wasn't quite certain what to do next.

When she paused, his hand came up to rest on her hair. "Take me in your mouth."

Eve obeyed, feeling a delightful sense of feminine power when his body went rigid at the first touch of her mouth. His taste was highly arousing all in itself, and she wanted more.

Following her instincts, she set about indulging her desire, taking him deeper into her mouth, sucking lightly, absorbing his scent and taste greedily, finding immense pleasure in the strangled groan he gave as his hands clenched the sheets on either side of him in an effort to remain still.

"Eve."

Pausing in her erotic ministrations, she raised her head to glance up the length of his body. His gaze was devouring, possessive, intense. "You are driving me mad," Ryder rasped, his voice hoarse.

Eve smiled in satisfaction. "It is only fair, since you do the same to me."

His hands came up to fondle her breasts, eliciting a sensuous gasp from her. "What do I do to you, sweeting?"

"You make me feel wild . . . fearless. I need to feel that way just now, Ryder."

His dark eyes softened. "I know."

For a moment as she met his gaze, she couldn't move. She hadn't exaggerated in the least, Eve realized. Ryder made her feel wild and reckless, her senses out of control. And she imagined that she was making him feel the same way. He seemed just as aroused as she was, the look in his eyes demanding, hungry, wildly hot.

As their gazes locked, Ryder couldn't move. Arousal beat a fierce, driving pulse in his veins as he regarded Eve. She was every man's dream temptress, yet this was his dream come to life. Her hair was a bright waterfall cascading down around her face in a tumble of gold fire, curling around her taut nipples and lush breasts. It was her eyes, however, that held him spellbound. His heart thundered wildly against his ribs as he read the emotion there in the blue depths. Passion. For him. His sleeping beauty had awakened.

Scarcely daring to breathe, Ryder tightened his fingers on the sheets, fighting the urge to reach for Eve and draw her up to him, not wanting to spoil the precious moment. He was determined to let her have her way with him.

His fortitude was rewarded when she bent to him again and slid her lips down over his cock. After another few minutes, however, when her tender sensual assault brought him near bursting, he could bear no more.

Taking over, Ryder put an end to her ministrations; grasping her shoulders, he lifted her up and rolled over her, pressing her down among the pillows.

"I thought *I* was seducing *you*," Eve said in breathless surprise.

"You were. You are. But now it's my turn to torment you. Now, hush, love."

He bent to her, covering her lips with a light kiss before finding the silken column of her throat. Surrendering to his demand, she twined her arms around his neck to draw him closer.

A sigh of desire and need whispered from Eve as his lips moved lower, down over her collarbone, nuzzling her pale skin, savoring the smooth, hot texture, relishing the honeyed taste. Her ripe breasts were straining for his touch, and when he found one sweet mound, she arched harder against him, offering him the budded crest. He took it tenderly between his teeth, nipping her, suckling her taut nipple, making her whimper. At the erotic sound, Ryder could feel a throbbing ache shoot like fire through his loins.

His hand slid down along her belly and between her bare thighs, seeking and caressing. She was already hot and aching for him, he realized with elation.

A tremor rocked him when her hips surged to greet his stroking hand. He knew he should go slowly. And in other circumstances—some distant time in the future—he might be able to manage it. He would make love to Eve for hours, slowly arousing her, lingering at each plateau and savoring her response, drawing from her the deep sensuality that she had always repressed in herself.

But just now Ryder couldn't force himself. He wanted to make her burn for him as fiercely as he was burning for her.

Easing his lower body into the cradle of her thighs, he filled his hands with the silky masses of her hair and captured her mouth again, this time with fervor.

She gave a throaty moan and squeezed her eyes shut, nesting him in her damp, feminine softness, inviting him into her body. Her back arched as he probed her sleek, wet entrance with his shaft. Needing to claim her, he began the slow, blissful slide.

It was exquisite torment for them both. By the time he thrust into the hot, quivering core of her, Eve was gasping.

Filled with a fierce tenderness, Ryder sank more fully inside her, heavy and hard and deep, absorbing her, his body buried in hers. He felt bathed in heat, trapped in a web of raw need.

"God . . . what you do to me," he uttered between gritted teeth.

He locked her hips hard against him and began to move within her, setting an urgent rhythm. He felt as if he were drowning in her scent, her fire.

Her breath was harsh now, as was his. As if she could no longer control her longing, Eve began to writhe beneath him, a look of ecstasy claiming her features as the pleasure spiraled higher and higher. Ryder grasped her hips harder, urging her on, intensifying his own pleasure as well as hers, till they were both mindless with it.

Their climax was fierce and powerful, erupting through them in an incredible firestorm, their harsh cries smothered by clinging mouths.

The experience left them both shaking and struggling for breath.

In the aftermath, Eve felt the wetness of tears sting her eyes. For a long while, she lay unmoving, cherishing the way Ryder remained cleaved to her, his body part of her own. This was what it was like to feel so close to someone that he seemed like another part of her.

Her union with Ryder was so much more than physical. Only he could set her on fire with merely a touch. Only he could give her what she inherently craved, this soul-deep, burning passion that seared away all loneliness and fear and replaced it with contentment and bliss.

Eve closed her eyes, wishing she could control the throat-aching tenderness he aroused in her. What made him so wondrous to her? What made passion burst wild and free inside her when she was with this man?

Ryder made her feel alive, made her feel joyous—

She went totally still at the shocking realization. Ryder made her feel happy. *How utterly amazing.*

She usually focused her matchmaking efforts on linking couples who presented the greatest promise of happiness, but she had never expected to feel it for herself. At least not happiness with a man.

Of course, Eve chided herself, she knew what was driving her. It was perfectly reasonable that loneliness and physical need could be powerful forces under specific circumstances, such as the ones that existed with Ryder now. But clearly she had let her cravings get out of control. Her need for him had grown to unmanageable proportions.

That kind of need frightened her. She had waited far too long for her independence, had endured too many years in virtual servitude, to risk surrendering to a passion that could very well be ephemeral. And even if she doubted Ryder would ever treat her like chattel, there was no question of a marriage between them.

Ryder wanted an heir. He had told her that was a chief reason he was planning to marry—claiming it was time he settled down and set up his nursery.

But what if he could possibly be right? What if she wasn't barren? A fierce ache lodged in her throat. She wanted Ryder's child. But it was likely a beautiful fantasy, nothing more. One she had no business even considering.

Alarmed by her thoughts, Eve suddenly sat up,

refusing to look at Ryder while she murmured, "We had best return. My guests will be missing me."

If her sudden coolness puzzled him, he didn't let on as he helped her to dress. But then as he was lacing up her corset, she stiffened at the hot press of his lips on her nape.

"What is wrong, Eve?" Ryder asked softly.

Turning in his arms, she forced a smile before planting a light kiss on his mouth. "Nothing is wrong. And you had best not entice me any further, or we will never get back in time to change for dinner. I have my reputation to consider, remember?"

The wicked gleam in his eyes renewed the ache in her throat. "Very well, but only because I care about shielding your reputation. Nothing else could induce me to leave that bed when you've barely begun my seduction."

Eve gave a small laugh that she meant to be reassuring. She pinned up her hair while he was dressing and then carefully made up the bed, wanting to leave behind no trace of their lovemaking for the servants to find.

With one last glance around the chamber, she negotiated the stairs on her still-sore ankle and then accompanied Ryder out the front door, where the horse and gig awaited.

They both came to a halt when they spied a gentleman on horseback riding along the lane at the end of the sweeping drive.

Eve's heart sank when she recognized the tall, bulky figure of Viscount Gyllford, and sank even further when the nobleman noticed them as well. As he turned his horse into the drive, she quelled the urge to reach up and check for signs of dishevelment.

"Lord Gyllford, how surprising to see you here," she forced herself to comment when he reached them.

"It is more surprising to see *you* here, Evelyn." His frowning countenance held suspicion and an unmistakable dislike directed at Ryder.

Eve had no choice but to brazen out the encounter. "I was showing Sir Alex the gardens of the dower house. He is considering purchasing his own country estate and is interested in various methods of landscaping."

"I can fathom why he would be eager to sniff the blooms," Gyllford remarked snidely.

Feeling Ryder go rigid beside her, Eve placed a calming hand on his arm and managed a sweet smile as she gazed up at Gyllford. "I hope you will join us for the pretend fox hunt tomorrow morning, my lord. But then since you are not one to stand on ceremony, you won't feel compelled to wait for an invitation."

Gyllford's jaw clenched a moment, but he inclined his head with a terse smile of his own. "I thank you, Evelyn. I will be there, certainly."

Eve allowed Ryder to assist her into the gig and lifted her hand in farewell at Gyllford, who stared after them as they drove down the drive.

She remained silent, nursing her anger and dismay, until they were out of earshot. "This is precisely what I feared would happen, my being seen alone with you. I have no doubt he suspects what we have been up to."

"It's none of his business how you conduct yourself with me or anyone else," Ryder remarked. "But his suspicions hardly matter. What does matter is your safety. I told you, you won't be attending the hunt tomorrow."

Eve felt herself stiffen. "Ryder, I realize my life is at risk, but I don't intend to abandon my houseguests. I have a responsibility toward them."

"And I have a responsibility toward you. If you ride tomorrow, I may not be able to protect you."

"I am willing to chance it. I have no intention of remaining locked at home like a caged animal. I endured enough of that during my marriage." Eve broke off, realizing how high and shrill her tone had become.

"Besides," she said more reasonably, "curtailing all my outdoor activities won't ensure my safety, you know that very well. The danger is almost as great just sitting at home. And you are capable of protecting me in any setting. I have every faith in you."

She saw Ryder's jaw tighten, yet he didn't reply. When he remained stewing in silence, Eve quelled the urge to justify herself further. Ryder didn't understand why she couldn't bear to be caged as she'd been during her marriage, or why she was driven to rebel against his controlling strictures . . . because they too closely resembled her late husband's domineering rule.

Eve exhaled a weary sigh. Perhaps being caught out by Gyllford was fortunate, for it reminded her that she had let her relationship with Ryder go much too far, just as she'd feared it would. She had been a fool to let it go on for so long.

There could be no further intimacies between them, she knew. They simply could not continue a passionate liaison that would lead to nowhere.

Even if ending it would be infinitely harder, Eve realized with dismay, now that she had admitted to herself how much Ryder was coming to mean to her.

Chapter Fourteen

"So, Sir Alex," Claire murmured curiously, "how fares your courtship of Eve?"

Ryder could scarcely hear the question over the jovial chatter in the crowded stableyard.

Clearly Eve's guests considered a foxless fox hunt a delightful entertainment. The participants were milling gaily about the yard, quaffing mulled cider in the pleasant late-morning air and waiting for their mounts, while grooms scurried to and fro, leading saddle horses and harnessing carriages for those guests who preferred to act merely as spectators.

Ryder watched the commotion with barely concealed disapproval. Moments ago Eve had again dismissed his admonition to remain at home, even knowing such prominent exposure put her at greater risk.

"My courtship is proceeding well enough, minx," Ryder said, having no intention of expounding further. "I could ask the same of you. How fares your own campaign to find a husband?"

Claire made a wry face. "Lamentably, I fear. I don't mean to complain when Eve has gone to such great trouble for me, but I cannot drum up interest in any of my suitors, even the ones who claim to be positively dying of love for me."

They both watched Eve a short distance away, calmly giving instructions to her head groom in the midst of the chaos. Macky stood nearby, keeping a protective eye on her as well.

"You have known Mr. Macklin for a long time, have you not?" Claire queried.

Her tone was casual, but Ryder sensed more than mere curiosity behind the question. He'd observed Macky and Claire together more than once this past week, and wondered if there might not be a romantic interest blossoming between the two of them.

Claire clearly favored Macky's company over that of her wealthy highborn suitors. And Macky seemed in unexpected danger of becoming enamored of the quiet young beauty, much to Ryder's amazement. The former actor had always claimed he would never bestow his affections on a single lass when there were so many to be sampled. But it appeared Macky was reconsidering.

"I've known him for a number of years," Ryder replied with caution.

"Then you can vouch for his character?"

"Wholly and completely. It would be hard to find a better man anywhere."

Claire nodded with satisfaction. "I thought so."

Ryder eyed her with faint amusement. "Do I detect a budding romance in the wind, my lady?"

Her violent blush betrayed her. "Honestly, I do not know. I am not at all certain how Macky feels about me."

"But your affections are becoming engaged."

"I . . . well . . . I must admit they are. He certainly is the most *interesting* man I have ever met." She stole a glance up at Ryder. "I have not said anything to Eve, for I doubt she would understand. Mr. Macklin is not the kind of suitor she has in mind for me, and she wants so badly for me to find a husband who is the right match for me. And of course I could never tell the aunts, for they would consider him entirely unsuitable. In any event, until I know my own mind—and Mr. Macklin's—there is no point in making known an association that may lead to nowhere."

"Your secret is safe with me, sweetheart," Ryder said as her twin brother strode across the stableyard toward them, leading his mount.

Since Eve had persuaded Cecil to play the "fox," he was wearing a fox-fur stole around his neck. He was also looking highly uncomfortable and trying his best to ignore the teasing directed his way by some of the younger male guests.

Coming to a halt before his twin, he gave Ryder a sheepish grin. "I look like a damned fool, I know. I never should have let Evie talk me into this. We would have done better to hold a real hunt."

"We ladies would beg to differ," Claire responded. "A pretend hunt is much better than galloping after a braying pack of hounds only to execute a poor little fox."

Cecil scoffed. "There is nothing poor about a fox. They are vermin who raid henhouses and terrorize sheep and prove an all-around nuisance."

Their argument was interrupted when Eve called

for silence. A hush fell over the stableyard as she explained how the game was to be conducted.

They would give the fox a five-minute head start. Then the hunters would mount up and ride to a nearby meadow where the hunt would begin, led by a Master of Hounds, who was being played by one of the young nobleman guests, Lord Trafer. The object was to corner the fox and retrieve the stole from around his neck. Meanwhile, the elderly ladies, including the aunts and the Duchess of Gower, would be conveyed in carriages to watch the hunt from a rise that offered an expansive view of the countryside.

"I fear that is my cue to depart," Cecil muttered, turning to mount his horse.

As he rode away, his twin called after him to wish him good luck, and so did Eve.

Eve looked grimly determined to enjoy the morning, Ryder noted. She kept a smile pasted on her face, even when she had to suffer the attentions of Viscount Gyllford, who assisted her into her sidesaddle. The nobleman was clearly too obtuse to realize his gallantry was unwanted, but Ryder had to give him credit for persistence if not brains.

There was much laughter and revelry as the riders set out en masse a short while later. Ryder remained a few horse-lengths behind Eve, while Macky rode near Claire as her groom and another of his footmen accompanied the aunts in their carriage.

When the hunters reached the designated meadow, an excited hush fell over the crowd as they scanned the woods surrounding the field. The excitement intensified when they spied a glimpse of the "fox" hiding in a distant glade. Playing his role as Master, Lord Trafer sounded the cry and they were off amid shouts of glee and laughter.

The leaders, including Eve and Lord Gyllford, maintained a brisk pace, while the others settled for a more leisurely canter.

Ryder stayed with Eve as they dashed across the countryside, taking hedges and ditches and streams in their path, but it required all his skills to keep up. Despite his anger at her foolhardiness in attending the hunt, he found himself admiring her superb horsemanship as her mount effortlessly soared over a wooden coop ahead.

The gray gelding landed smoothly on the other side, then suddenly let out a squeal of pain and flung his head up. Looking wild-eyed, the horse gave a great buck, as if trying to unseat his rider. When that failed, he whirled in a dizzying circle, heedless of the other participants coming up behind him.

Eve had lost the reins when she was thrown onto the maddened animal's neck, Ryder saw with grim dismay, and she held on for dear life when the gray changed tactics and bolted into a full gallop. Her mount was running away with her, he realized, his heart plunging to his stomach.

Before he could get free of the crowded field, he heard Lord Gyllford shout, "Hold on, Evelyn! I will save you!"

Spurring his mount into a gallop, Gyllford took off after her, which only frightened her panicky horse further. Ryder breathed an oath and then a prayer as he followed in their wake.

Eve was still clinging to the gray's neck, desperately hauling on one rein, trying to turn the crazed animal in a circle in a futile effort to slow him. But they were heading directly for a stretch of ash trees that lined the riverbank, making Ryder keenly aware of the new danger. Even if she could manage to hold on, plunging into the dense woods at this speed could be deadly.

Making a swift decision, Ryder veered to his left and raced across the next field in an attempt to cut her off. To his everlasting gratitude, he caught up to Eve a dozen lengths before she reached the tree line.

Galloping neck and neck alongside her, Ryder leaned out and scooped Eve up by the waist and hauled her to safety in front of him.

Without the painful weight on his back, the gray came to a halt just before reaching the woods and stood there, shaking and blowing heavily and rolling his eyes.

Eve clung weakly to Ryder, trying to catch her breath, while his terrified heart pounded in relief.

Gyllford thundered up behind them, breathing hard and scowling at Ryder. "There was no need for you to act," the nobleman said plaintively. "I would have rescued her."

Astounded by the absurd declaration, Ryder sent Gyllford a scathing stare, then scowled at Eve, as angry at her for putting herself at risk as at himself for allowing it. "Damnation, I told you not to come today! You could have been killed! Are you all right?"

She swallowed hard and then nodded. "I don't know what happened. One moment we were taking the fence, and the next, my horse went mad."

"I know," Ryder said grimly. "Something made him bolt like that. Stay here while I check him out. Don't *move.*"

He felt Eve stiffen at his harsh command but gave her no chance to argue. Leaving her on his mount, he swung down and crossed to the gray, who hung his head now, trembling in exhaustion and sweating profusely. At his approach, the horse suddenly became alert and tried to skitter away, but Ryder caught the reins and spoke soothingly to the animal while gently stroking his sweat-dampened muzzle.

After a moment, the gray quieted enough to allow an examination. Ryder ran his hands carefully over the horse's steaming body and legs, searching for injuries. When he found none, he unfastened the girth so he could inspect the sidesaddle and pad beneath.

The horse had gone rigid in anticipation of pain, Ryder noted, and as he gingerly lifted the bottom pad, he could hear other guests riding up, inquiring worriedly after Eve.

"Stay back," Ryder warned sharply at the same time Eve held up her hand to keep the hunters from startling her horse further.

Returning to his task, Ryder saw blood soaking the gray hide, and when he probed gently, he felt the sharp edge of metal. Grasping the offending shard tightly with his fingers, Ryder yanked it out before the horse could do more than squeal.

Ryder held up the bloodstained metal to the sunlight, his jaw hardening as he examined the instrument of torture. An inch-long nail had punched through the rear of the saddle pad, deep into the horse's flesh.

It must have been hidden cleverly, Ryder surmised, so that at the start of the ride, there was no danger. Eventually the point had worked its way through the pad, and when Eve took that last jump, her weight in the saddle had driven the nail downward, which had set the horse off in a paroxysm of pain.

"Someone planted that dreadful thing beneath my saddle?" Eve demanded furiously.

Looking up, Ryder replied with derision. "Obviously. The intent must have been to cause you deliberate injury or worse."

Eve gritted her teeth, her gaze shifting to survey the crowd of spectators, who were gaping in various degrees of shock. Wondering if her assailant was among their numbers, she felt a renewed stab of fear—a fear obviously shared by her friend Lydia and her sister, Claire.

"Oh, Eve, not again," Lydia murmured in horror while Claire eased her horse next to Eve's and took her hand comfortingly.

"Who the devil could have done such a dastardly deed?" Lord Trafer demanded.

"I don't know," Cecil ground out. He had come out of hiding when the entire field had chased after his sister instead of himself. "But by God, if I get my hands on the bastard, I swear I will darken his daylights."

"You will have to stand in line," Ryder interjected savagely.

"What do you mean to do now, Evie?" Cecil

asked. "Do you want to continue the hunt? You don't have a horse to ride."

"By all means we should continue," Eve said, still shaken.

"You will *not* continue," Ryder declared. "You will return home, where you should have remained in the first place."

Her jaw set mutinously. "I suppose I must, since I have no mount. That poor animal must be returned to the stables so his wound can be cared for. I see no reason, however, to spoil everyone else's pleasure."

"I will accompany you home, Evelyn," Lord Gyllford offered.

"Your assistance isn't required, your lordship," Ryder retorted. "You've helped Lady Hayden more than enough for one morning."

Gyllford sent Ryder a nasty look. "And you have overstepped your bounds, Sir Alex. I won't have you addressing me in that offensive manner."

"Beg pardon, Lady Hayden," a low voice called out.

When Eve and everyone else turned their attention to the liveried servant who had ridden forward, she recognized Ned Hitchens, one of her best footmen. Ned and several other male household servants had been pressed into service as grooms for the morning.

"What is it, Ned?" Eve asked.

"I think I might know who done it . . . rigged your ladyship's sidesaddle, I mean."

"Who?" Ryder demanded, stepping closer.

"That gentleman there," he said, pointing at the viscount. "Lord Gyllford. I saw him fiddling with the saddle pad on her ladyship's horse before she mounted. At the time, I didn't ken what he was doing, but now it all makes sense. He planted that nail there."

Eve felt a ripple of shock. Even though her first impulse was denial, she couldn't dismiss the accusation, since Gyllford was a chief suspect in the previous attempts on her life. It was only pure chance that he'd been spied in the act this time by one of her trusted servants.

Lord Gyllford, however, sputtered and looked indignant. "That is totally absurd!"

Ryder moved toward Gyllford, grimly eyeing the viscount as he stiffly sat his horse. "*Is* it absurd?"

"Why, of course! That fellow is a liar."

"Why would he have cause to lie?"

" 'Tisn't a lie," Ned insisted. "I saw you, milord. You put that nail there."

"I do not have to listen to these ridiculous accusations," Gyllford exclaimed, gathering his reins to turn his horse.

"On the contrary," Ryder said, grabbing the bridle to prevent his escape, "you'll explain why you would deliberately put Lady Hayden in mortal danger."

One look at Ryder's dark expression evidently convinced Gyllford he wouldn't escape without answering the accusations. "I certainly did not mean to put her in danger," the viscount retorted. "She was never supposed to be hurt. I would have saved her before it came to that. Indeed, I tried to, but you intervened before I could reach her."

"You mean to tell me," Ryder rephrased in a lethal

tone, "that you staged that scene because you wanted to play the damned hero and rescue her?"

"Yes, blast you, I admit it. Now release my horse this instant, or I cannot vouch for the consequences."

Eve stared in revulsion. Lord Gyllford had confessed to engineering a potentially fatal accident with her horse. It stood to reason that if he was responsible for endangering her this time, he was responsible for the other attempts to kill her.

Ryder evidently shared her conclusion, for his expression turned savage as he bit out, "I'll show you consequences, Gyllford."

Eve drew a sharp breath as Ryder reached up to grasp the lapels of the viscount's riding coat and haul him from the saddle.

The nobleman almost fell, but Ryder jerked him upright.

"Keep your filthy hands off me!" Gyllford said, recoiling.

"The devil I will. She could have been killed, you bloody bastard!" Ryder let fly a blow to the jaw that sent the peer reeling to the ground, which made their audience gasp in collective alarm.

When Ryder reached down again and found a stranglehold on Gyllford's cravat, Eve knew she had to intervene before Ryder did something irrevocable. Still weak from her mad ride, she slid off her mount and hurried over to the combatants.

"Stop, Ryder." Catching the arm that had drawn back in a threatening fist, Eve held tight. "You cannot kill him."

"Why not? He almost did the same to you."

"I know. And I am just as infuriated. But this is not the time or place for revenge."

His head jerking up, Ryder stared at Eve, his dark gaze locking with hers, glinting with dangerous lights. A growl of disgust sounded in his throat as he released Gyllford's neckcloth, but he remained where he stood, glowering down at the nobleman. "This isn't the first time you've staged your deadly little incidents, is it?" Ryder said through gritted teeth.

Still cringing on the ground, the viscount licked his split lip. "What the devil do you mean? Of course it is the first time."

"Don't lie to me again. I'm just looking for an excuse to perforate your liver."

"I am not lying, you fiend!"

"*Get up,*" Ryder ordered.

"Why?" Gyllford asked warily.

"I'm taking you somewhere we can be private."

The viscount glanced around the watching crowd, apparently realizing he had been shamed before the entire company. Just then Eve noticed both aunts and the duchess hurrying across the field on foot. Apparently their carriage had reached the nearby lane in the middle of the fight.

Spying possible reinforcements, Gyllford lifted his chin in defiance, his bluster returning. "You are mad, Sir Alex, if you think I will go anywhere with you."

"Do you want to wear your teeth or carry them?" Ryder responded tersely. When Gyllford remained silent, Ryder added in a dangerous tone, "You *will* come with me, your lordship. I have a good number of questions that need answering, and I don't intend to continue this public spectacle. Macky, tie his hands in front of him."

Macky stepped forward with alacrity, pulling off his linen stock to supply a binding.

"No!" the Duchess of Gower protested. "You will *not* shackle the Viscount of Gyllford like a common criminal."

Ryder returned her scornful gaze without blinking. "I'll thank you not to interfere, your grace. He is very much a common criminal."

The duchess gave a huff of indignation at having her demand so summarily dismissed. "I *will* interfere, sir! How dare you raise a hand to your noble betters! You have no right."

Ryder's smile never reached his eyes. "A noble title does not excuse attempted murder," he replied, his tone unrepentant.

"Murder?" Gyllford exclaimed. "It was no such thing! It was a foolish mistake."

Eve stepped forward, impatient to question the viscount and discover how he had arranged the previous attacks on her. "Lord Gyllford's cuts need tending," she said, adopting a soothing tone for the benefit of the duchess's wounded sensibilities. "I am certain Sir Alex will be kind enough to send for the doctor when he escorts his lordship home."

Her grace remained unmollified, and when Ryder took the stock from Macky and began binding Gyllford's hands in front of him, the elderly noblewoman fairly exploded. "This is *intolerable*!"

Lord Trafer seemed to agree. "I say, Sir Alex, you cannot mean to take a peer prisoner."

When Ryder gave no reply but grimly continued his task, the duchess's wrath rose to apoplectic proportions. "Lady Hayden, I cannot believe you would condone such disgraceful behavior as this! I am deeply offended and refuse to remain in your company a moment longer. I shall return to the Park and order my bags packed at once."

Pivoting on her heel, the duchess stalked regally back to the waiting carriage, leaving a discomfiting silence in the wake of her scathing dramatics.

No one else was brave enough to intervene as Ryder finished binding the viscount's hands, but Lord Trafer sent him a look of disdain before turning his horse to follow after the retreating noblewoman. Immediately, two of Claire's other suitors did likewise, clearly signaling their displeasure.

Eve glanced around at the remaining crowd. "Please, won't you all continue the hunt?"

Cecil shook his head. "Don't think anyone is in the mood for games just now, Evie. We'd best just all return to the Park."

Seeing agreement in the expressions of her other guests, Eve nodded. "Very well, then. Have Dunstan see to refreshments when you arrive home."

Most of the company took their leave, riding slowly back the way they had come. When Lydia would have remained with her, Eve said gently, "Please go with them, Lydia."

"Are you certain you are all right?"

"Yes, I'm fine, especially now that we know who has been behind these attacks. It is a relief, actually."

Lydia did as she was asked, and the crowd disappeared, leaving Eve and her family alone, along with a handful of servants as well as Ryder and his prisoner.

Eve asked Ned to lead the gray back to the stables while she rode his horse home. She wondered if Ryder intended to make Gyllford walk, but Macky brought the viscount's mount over to him.

"Do you need my assistance with his lordship?" Eve heard Macky ask Ryder.

"No, I can handle him on my own. You'll escort the ladies home," Ryder ordered.

Drucilla, who had made no move to return to the waiting carriage, sent Ryder a chill glance. "It seems we no longer have need of your services, Sir Alex, now that the danger is over." Her gaze shifting to Eve, she spoke in a cutting voice. "It is your prerogative, my dear, of course, but I think you should ask Sir Alex to leave before he drives away all of your guests and Claire's suitors as well."

Before Eve could say a word, Cecil jumped to his hero's defense. "You cannot mean it, Aunt Dru! Sir Alex saved Eve's life!"

"He saved her, true, but at what cost? It was barbaric, beating Lord Gyllford half to death before all our acquaintances."

"To death? It was only a single blow!"

"But he was set on doing worse damage. You know the saying 'Blood will tell.' In this case I believe the adage has proved all too true."

Without another word, Drucilla picked up her skirts and turned to cross the field to the carriage. Even Beatrice looked uncomfortable before she hurried after her elder sister.

Ryder's jaw, Eve saw, was knotted tightly as he addressed Macky. "Take Lady Hayden home and don't let her out of your sight."

Eve found her voice then. "Ryder, I intend to come with you."

"You won't. You'll go home where you belong."

She stiffened at his gruff tone, and when he went to his horse, Eve followed, catching up to Ryder before he could mount. "I think I have a right to hear Gyllford's explanations. I have been terrorized for weeks, and now that it is over—"

"It may not be over."

She stared at him. "What do you mean? Surely there is no longer any need for caution now that Gyllford has been exposed."

"Gyllford may not be the perpetrator." Ryder cast a dark glance at the viscount before lowering his voice to say grimly, "Odds are he is guilty, but I can't be certain until I have solid proof or a confession. Before I'm done, I mean to drag an admission out of him and persuade him to give up his cohorts. Until then, I want you safe."

"But, Ryder—"

He cut her off impatiently. "Devil take it, Eve, for *once* just do as I tell you. If you had remained at home as I asked, you would never have been in such danger today. You were nearly killed."

Her mouth dropped open. "Are you blaming *me* for what happened?"

"In part. Now, go home and stay there until I tell you differently."

Eve went rigid. "I will do no such thing! I have had enough of cowering . . . *and* of taking orders. I won't have you dictating to me as if you owned me."

She saw the effort Ryder made to bite back his savage anger. "I am not dictating to you—"

"You *are*!" She was reacting from pent-up fear and frustration and anger, yet she couldn't stop the words from spilling out. "You do *not* control me, Ryder, no matter how much you have done for me and my family. Furthermore, I believe Drucilla is right. You should leave the Park before you drive away all our guests and Claire's suitors."

She might as well have struck him; the pain that flashed in Ryder's eyes was unmistakable. But he kept his lips pressed tightly together as he stared down at her with brooding stillness. "You are taking their side," he said finally.

His tone was ice cold, but Eve was too irate to take warning. "I am taking no one's side but my own. Of course I am grateful to you for saving me once again. You have done your duty exceedingly well, and I sincerely thank you. But I must ask you to go."

His dark eyes bored into hers until she felt as if he were digging down into her soul. "Of course, my lady," he said with only a hint of savagery. "I should never have expected anything different from you."

Ryder swung up on his horse, anger in every line of his hard-muscled form. "I will keep you informed about what I discover from Gyllford."

Eve watched, still fuming, as Ryder caught up the reins of his prisoner's horse and rode away. She had not taken anyone's side.

But perhaps that was the problem: She had not

sided with Ryder against the world, as he had always done with her.

It was doubtless still a source of bitterness for him that he had spent his life on the outside looking in, being condemned for his birth and breeding. And now she was banishing him in favor of such supercilious noblewomen as Drucilla and the duchess.

Of course she hadn't meant it, a voice inside acknowledged.

She started to call after Ryder, to retract her angry dismissal, but he was too far away by now to hear.

Eve gazed after him in dismay, unable to ignore the shameful feeling that she had betrayed him in some irrevocable way.

Chapter Fifteen

He wasn't angry, Ryder told himself, forcibly unlocking his jaw. He wasn't bitter because Eve had reacted with such irrational fierceness. Yet her demand that he leave her house party had cut deep.

He came alongside the viscount, who was sitting his mount in mutinous indignation, a bloody gash marring the corner of his flaccid mouth. Sweeping out one arm to indicate the way, Ryder said tersely, "After you, your lordship."

Awkwardly, the viscount picked up the reins with his bound hands and turned toward his estates some five miles distant.

Ryder kept pace with the nobleman, his thoughts brooding. He didn't regret his violence or that he might have driven her exalted guests away. His fury at Gyllford for putting Eve's life at risk had been entirely justified. He had, however, been too sharp with her. She hated being controlled, being told what to do, although she was doubtless using his actions as a convenient excuse to avoid further intimacy between them.

Perhaps it *would* be wiser for him to leave for a time, Ryder mused, to let her resentment cool. If he could be sure the danger to Eve was over, then he would be willing to make himself scarce.

If he *did* leave, his courtship of Eve wouldn't be over by a long shot. He would no longer keep it clandestine. He was tired of the subterfuge with her, tired of the secrecy. When he returned, he would simply lay all his cards on the table and make his intentions known to her. He would tell Eve that she was the only bride he would ever want so she could begin to come to terms with his feelings. He would court her openly.

Ryder shook himself abruptly. Just now he had a job to do: discovering the depths of Gyllford's involvement in the attacks on Eve. He couldn't simply assume the nobleman guilty of causing the other incidents or convict him out of hand, no matter what his natural instincts were.

If Gyllford wasn't responsible for the other assaults, as he claimed, then Eve's assailant would still be out there somewhere, waiting to strike.

"I suggest you consider your story carefully, Gyllford," Ryder spoke up warningly. "But before we're done, you will tell me everything about your role in the past attempts on Lady Hayden's life, including who carried out your orders. You could not have been directly culpable, for you weren't present for at least one of the incidents."

"I don't know what the devil you are raving about," Gyllford replied sullenly. "I know nothing about any other incidents." He fell back into mutinous silence, and Ryder resolved to let him stew.

When a half hour later they came in sight of the viscount's immense manor, Ryder drew rein, intending to finish their discussion before reaching the house, where Gyllford's retainers could come to his rescue.

"This is far enough, your lordship."

The beefy nobleman looked deep in thought, but he bestirred himself to speak when Ryder's fierce gaze settled upon him. "I have been considering, Sir Alex. You were justified in drawing my cork. It was dreadfully wrong of me to put Evelyn in danger, not to mention ungentlemanly."

Ryder's mouth curled in distaste. "Allow me to commend you on your perceptiveness, even though it's damned late in coming."

The nobleman flushed. "I know that now. And I am grievously sorry."

"Then oblige me by explaining yourself. Why in hell's name did you do it?"

"It was jealousy, I suppose. Evelyn looks up to you as a hero, and I wanted her to see me in the same light."

Ryder found himself staring. "You can't be so witless as to think you could frighten her into marrying you after she's already rejected your suit."

His flush deepened. "A female can always be persuaded to change her mind."

"By terrorizing her?" Ryder retorted scathingly. "I seriously doubt that is the way to a woman's heart."

"I see that now, of course. But I swear on my life that was the first time. I had nothing to do with those other accidents you accused me of perpetrating." Gyllford winced as he licked his split lip, then frowned. "Have there been many others?"

If he was dissembling, it was difficult to tell, Ryder thought. "Quite a few. Two months ago, she was shot at in the woods here at the Park, and then she was nearly maimed by a wolf trap. Then three weeks ago in London, she was pushed in front of a team of draft horses. The next week, a lamp exploded in her morning room. And yesterday at the ruins, she was almost crushed beneath the rubble when part of the wall came crashing down on her. Then the burr under her saddle today. Perhaps even you are bright enough to see why you might be considered a suspect, my lord," Ryder said with acid dryness.

Gyllford looked genuinely horrified. "Good God, no wonder you were so outraged. But on my honor, I never would have hurt her! *Never!*"

Either he was the best actor in the realm, Ryder reflected, or he actually had no knowledge of the assaults.

"Let's say for the moment that I believe you," he said finally. "Who else could have done it?"

"How the devil should I know?"

"Well think, man. You know Eve as well as anyone, having been her closest neighbor all these years."

"Not well enough to guess who might have had wished her ill. Everyone admires and esteems her."

"What do you know about her former steward, Tobias Meade?" Ryder asked. "Would he have been irate enough to seek revenge against her for terminating his employment?"

Gyllford's frown deepened. "I suppose he might, at that. He was certainly bitter enough. Indeed, he applied to me for a post afterward, but I wouldn't have him on my staff and risk his ruining my land as he did Hayden's." The viscount's gaze hardened on Ryder. "Why don't you interrogate him the way you are doing me? He is the much more likely culprit."

"I intend to. Just as soon as he can be located." His men had questioned anyone who might know Meade and his wife Mabel. This morning, just moments before the hunt, Ryder had received a report regarding the steward's expected destination after his firing—to live with Mabel's relatives near the large town of Hertford some thirty miles away. He'd immediately dispatched a man to ascertain if Meade could be found there. If so, then Ryder meant to visit him personally.

"You could always ask Hitchens," Gyllford offered. "He might be privy to Meade's intentions."

"Ned Hitchens? The footman who saw you rigging Eve's saddle?"

The nobleman's face turned darker with spite. "He's the one. Hitchens is Mabel's godson, didn't you know?"

Ryder felt his stomach give a lurch at the odd coincidence. "No, this is the first I've heard of the connection. How did you discover it, Gyllford?"

"I believe Meade mentioned it when he came to me for a job. In fact, it was through Hitchens that Meade knew to apply for the empty post at Hayden Park several years ago in the first place."

Ryder eyed him with skepticism. "This isn't just a way to strike back at Hitchens for fingering you or to direct suspicion away from yourself?"

Lord Gyllford drew himself up in renewed indignation. "My good sir," he huffed, "I am growing extremely weary of having my word doubted."

Ryder hesitated to reply, all his instincts suddenly screaming at him. If there *was* an association between the footman and the former steward, then Hitchens was a possible suspect who had been completely overlooked, despite all their questioning. Was he in truth Eve's assailant? He'd had the opportunity and perhaps the motive. Certainly it was seeming more and more likely that Gyllford was simply a brainless dolt rather than a devious murderer. . . .

Filled with an abrupt sense of urgency to act on his hunch and change course, Ryder realized he needed to return to the Park at once and have a serious discussion with Ned Hitchens.

With a nod, he gestured in the direction of the viscount's manor house. "You'll make your own way home from here, your lordship."

"I am glad you have forgiven me," Gyllford breathed, looking relieved.

"Did I say that?" Ryder replied in a silken tone. "You will return home and pack. You will be traveling tomorrow for the Continent for an extended stay of undetermined duration. I don't want you anywhere near Eve for the next several months at least."

Gyllford stared. "You can't simply order me out of the country!"

"It is your choice, of course, but I assure you, you will regret making the wrong one."

The viscount licked his dry lips again at the implied threat. "You wouldn't dare lay a finger on me!"

"Never underestimate me," Ryder said softly.

Gyllford evidently thought better of challenging the warning, for he gritted his teeth. "Very well, damn you. I have been wanting to visit Paris since Bonaparte's fall, anyway."

"I will rely on your honor," Ryder said dryly, "to keep your word."

From a special inner pocket of his riding coat, he withdrew a deadly-looking knife that he frequently carried with him.

The viscount's eyes suddenly widened in alarm, but he heaved a huge sigh of relief when Ryder merely reached out to slice through the binding at his wrists.

"I will convey your apologies to Lady Hayden and explain why you had to depart so abruptly," Ryder said.

As the nobleman rode stiffly away, Ryder wheeled his own horse and headed back toward the Park. His mind was whirling furiously, forming a plan so he wouldn't alert Hitchens precipitously.

When Ryder arrived, several carriages stood in front of the mansion, preparing for departure, which doubtless meant the duchess was making good on her threat to vacate the premises.

He dismounted and left his horse with a groom. When he entered the house, he found Eve in the entrance hall, looking on as her butler directed the bustling servants. Macky stood nearby, watching over her protectively as commanded.

Ryder half expected Eve to order him from the house, but when she saw him, she merely gave a stiff nod. "What did Lord Gyllford have to say for himself?"

"I'll be happy to tell you in private," Ryder said. He had scanned the hall for Hitchens, but there was no immediate sign of the footman. "I want Macky present, and your butler, as well."

"As you wish," Eve replied, although clearly puzzled. "Dunstan, will you join us in the blue parlor?"

"Certainly, my lady."

Eve preceded them down the hall to the parlor and closed the door behind them, shutting out the commotion. The august butler appeared impassive as usual until Ryder explained what he had learned from Gyllford—about Ned Hitchens being Mabel Meade's godson. Then Dunstan's expression grew grave while Eve drew a sharp breath as she mentally made the connection.

"So you think Ned Hitchens might be behind the attacks on me?" she asked Ryder.

"It's possible. He had the opportunity to arrange all your accidents. He was present the day you were shoved into the street, remember?"

"Yes. We had sent him to the carriage with our parcels."

"But he could easily have doubled back in time to cause your fall. And he had access to your London house, specifically the lamp on your writing desk. He knew all your plans for the house party, and he was with the serving staff when you visited the ruins. I think it was merely a bizarre coincidence that Gyllford decided to stage an accident for you this morning. Hitchens saw him and used it to his advantage."

"But *why*?" Eve asked, still bewildered. "Why would Ned wish me harm?"

Ryder shrugged. "That is far less clear, but if he's guilty, as I'm beginning to suspect, it's likely Tobias Meade commissioned him out of revenge, just as we first surmised."

"So what should we do?"

Ryder turned to the butler. "Where is Ned Hitchens now?"

Dunstan replied with alacrity. "He should be upstairs, assisting the duchess's servants with her trunks. I saw him perhaps ten minutes ago, after he returned to the stables with her ladyship's injured horse, when he reported to the servants' hall to receive his next assignment. Do you wish me to have him summoned, Sir Alex?"

"No, I don't want to alert him to our suspicions. I'll look for him myself. But I would like two of your strongest footmen to accompany me, in case he tries to run."

"As you wish, sir."

Together with Macky and two strapping footmen to assist them, Ryder quietly searched the upstairs floor while Eve followed a safe distance behind. But Hitchens was not where he had been assigned duty, nor was he to be found in the servants' hall off the kitchens.

"Where are his sleeping quarters?" Ryder asked the butler as they left the kitchens.

Dunstan led them up two narrow flights of back stairs to a small chamber Hitchens shared with three other menservants. Upon seeing the room, the butler came to an abrupt halt. One cot was completely bare, and so was the cabinet where clothing and belongings should have been.

"Looks like the wily bugger has cut and run," Macky muttered for Ryder's ears alone.

Ryder nodded grimly, realizing the footman must have gotten wind of the search and gone into hiding. Yet his disappearance only reinforced the suspicion that he was the likely culprit. And at least now Ryder had a focus for his energies.

"Hitchens can't have gotten far," he told Macky, "even if he was mounted. We'll ride after him—search the entire district if we have to. Meet me at the stables."

Macky nodded and left quickly. There was no need for further communication between them, since they had worked together for so long.

Eve was awaiting Ryder in the corridor, so he drew her aside and answered her question before she could even ask it.

"It looks as if Hitchens has just taken off. Macky and I intend to search for him."

Her gaze was troubled as she met his. "Do you mean to go alone? Don't you need assistance? My servants—"

"The men I assigned to protect you will be enough, and we'll move faster on our own. I want you to stay in the house—and make certain the twins and the aunts stay close as well. Until we find Hitchens, I don't want any of you leaving."

"I understand," Eve said gravely. "But please, be careful."

Ryder's mouth twisted in a grim smile. "I will."

Leaving her, he returned to his own bedchamber, where he fetched two pistols and checked the priming. Thus armed, he bounded down the stairs, heading for the side door that led to the stables.

Eve stood near the door with Dunstan, determined, Ryder surmised, to see him off.

Before she could say a word, however, the door burst open and Cecil came stumbling in, half supported by a bleak-eyed Macky.

"*Eve!*" the boy shouted, until he saw her. "Oh, God, Eve."

Cecil was bleeding profusely from the temple, Ryder saw, and his face was anguished, almost as much as Macky's. Ryder felt his stomach muscles knot while Eve turned white.

"What in God's name happened?" she demanded. "How did you get hurt?"

"I was bashed on the skull by three men." He was nearly in tears. "It was all my fault. I should have protected her."

"Protected whom?" Ryder asked sharply, although he had the sickening feeling he knew.

"Claire." Cecil held out a bloody, crumpled note in his palm. "They demanded ransom. God, Eve." Cecil offered it to his sister. "They took her. They took Claire!"

Chapter Sixteen

Raw fear coursed through Eve, turning her body cold. Barely able to breathe, she took the note from Cecil's outstretched hand and read the barely legible print.

Lady Hayden, if you want your sister to live, do not try to find her. I want 1,000 guineas. Gather the money and wait to hear from me.

It was signed Ned Hitchens.

Eve was glad when Ryder moved to support her elbow, for she wasn't certain she could have remained standing on her own.

He scanned the note she handed him, then said tersely, "Cecil, sit down and tell me exactly what happened."

After Macky had helped the boy over to a footman's bench, Cecil explained in a stumbling recitation.

"We were checking on the injured horse. C-Claire has such a soft heart that she wanted to make s-sure he was all right, but she knew better than to go alone, especially since Macky had told us to remain in the parlor, so she asked me to accompany her. She was feeding the horse an apple when suddenly these men came up behind us. One covered Claire's mouth with his hand so she couldn't scream and another hit me and I b-blacked out, but when I came to, Claire was g-gone and that ransom note was pinned to my coat."

"How many men?" Ryder demanded.

"Three, I think. But there could have been more. It all happened so quickly. The ones I saw were dressed as ruffians, and they spoke poorly . . . the Cockney you hear in London stews."

Ryder's gaze settled on Macky. "What more can you add?"

Macky's expression had grown savage, as if he was barely keeping control of himself. "The head groom found Lord Cecil lying facedown in the straw in the gray's stall and alerted me. No telling how long he had been out before that, but Hitchens would not have had time to carry out an abduction himself. It must have been planned in advance, and his cohorts carried out the deed on his behalf." Macky's fists curled in rage. "If only I had suspected—"

"You weren't to blame," Ryder returned harshly. "I was."

Eve saw Ryder's jaw clench as he glanced around at the gaping spectators. They had attracted a crowd by now, and a hushed silence had fallen over the hall.

"Let's find some privacy," he muttered, ushering Eve and Cecil down the hall and into the nearest room, which happened to be the library.

Macky followed, but before he shut the door, the

Hayden butler approached Eve. Silently and proficiently, Dunstan had acquired a clean cloth from somewhere, and he pressed it into her hand. "For Lord Cecil's head wound, my lady. I will have the doctor fetched, if you wish."

"Yes, please do, Dunstan."

Crossing to the chair where Cecil had collapsed, Eve knelt in front of her brother, trying to stem her desperation as she dabbed the cloth against the ugly gash at his temple.

She was grateful, however, when Ryder took the cloth from her and made her sit in the adjacent chair while he ministered to Cecil's wound himself.

Eve raised a shaking hand to her own temple. She felt dizzy and nauseated, her stomach churning so fiercely she thought she might faint.

"What do we do, Ryder?" she forced herself to ask. "Hitchens's note said we shouldn't try to find her."

"We'll find her," Ryder stated grimly.

"I will pay whatever he demands . . . whatever he wants."

"That may not be advisable."

"W-what do you mean?"

"You and your family will never be safe until he is apprehended. Moreover, even if you pay the ransom, there is no guarantee that Claire will remain unharmed."

"Oh, God." Her voice broke, and she buried her face in her hands. "I wish they had taken me instead of Claire. Why could they not have taken *me*?"

"Because you were too well guarded. And Hitchens

knew that abducting your sister would cause you more pain than physically harming you."

"I am so very sorry, Evie," Cecil repeated, his own voice almost a sob. "It was all my fault. I should never have let Claire go out to the stables. Macky told us to stay in the house—"

"You could not have anticipated what Hitchens intended," Ryder said sharply.

"True," Macky suddenly burst out, his own anguish apparent. "And if I hadn't left the lass alone, she never would have been taken."

Eve was feeling a similar guilt. If she had listened to Ryder in the first place, if she had done as he'd told her instead of arguing with him and defying his orders, her sister would likely be safe.

Scalding tears stinging her eyes, Eve gazed blindly up at Ryder. "So how do we get Claire back? We *must* hurry. She may be injured already."

"They won't hurt her yet, not when it might spoil their chances of obtaining the ransom payment."

"But I know she is terrified."

"No doubt she is." Hearing the fury in his voice, Eve returned his gaze. His eyes were harder, blacker, more piercing than she had ever seen them.

"We won't wait to hear from Hitchens," Ryder bit out, "but we're at a disadvantage, since we don't know where to begin looking for him. We could turn the entire countryside upside down and possibly never find him. But Macky will lead a search of the district, including the village of Braughing, while I ride to Hertford in search of your former steward. If Hitchens is acting on his behalf, then Meade may know who the other ruffians are and have information about their scheme that could prove invaluable in unearthing them."

Cecil bestirred himself to ask, "You mean to seek out Meade and interrogate him, Sir Alex?"

"Yes, and make him divulge whatever he knows of Hitchens's plans. Reportedly, Meade is living with his wife's relations near Hertford, which is less than thirty miles away. If I can locate him and compel him to talk, I should make it there and back before nightfall."

Eve drew a shuddering breath as she stared up at Ryder. She couldn't bear to think of what Claire was enduring at this moment, how terrified she must be. But her sister would have absolute faith in Ryder, and she did as well. If anyone could recover Claire unharmed, it would be Ryder.

A numbing calm overtook Eve. She felt a terrible guilt that her sister had been seized when she herself should have been the target, yet she couldn't afford to indulge in guilt or fear just now, not until her sister was safely returned.

"Ryder . . . I want to accompany you to visit Meade." When he hesitated to reply, Eve hastened to add, "*Please*. . . . I couldn't bear to sit here and do nothing. And I know Meade. I might be more effective in getting answers from him than you could be."

"You might," Ryder agreed. "Very well, you may come with me."

"What can I do to help, Sir Alex?" Cecil asked in a small voice. "I *need* to help, too."

Ryder smiled fleetingly at the boy. "You'll remain here to coordinate our efforts. With all of us going various ways, we'll use this room as a command post, and you will be in charge. Meanwhile, Cecil, you'll have the doctor examine your head. I have no doubt it is hard as a rock, but blows such as you took can scatter your brains for long afterward."

Forcing a grim smile, Cecil nodded, satisfied.

The mention of a command post made Eve wonder how Ryder meant to organize the hunt for Claire with so few resources at his disposal.

"What about your league?" she asked. "The Guardians? Could they help find Claire?"

When Macky shot Ryder a swift glance, Eve remembered that she wasn't supposed to know about their order of protectors. But Ryder answered her question anyway. "I've already summoned half a dozen of my fellow Guardians from London. With luck, they'll arrive here this afternoon before we return from Hertford. It will be Cecil's responsibility to bring them up to date about our crisis. And to make certain the aunts don't ban them from the house," Ryder added with acerbic dryness.

"Ryder, I am sorry about—" Eve started to say, before he cut her off.

"It hardly matters now, Countess. Why don't you ask Dunstan to have your traveling carriage harnessed and then fetch your cloak? We may not return before nightfall."

Eve rose at once, even though her knees were still ridiculously weak, glad to be given a task to perform.

Just as she crossed the library, the door was flung open and Drucilla swept in, followed by a white-faced Beatrice.

"Dunstan told us," Drucilla rasped in a voice that was barely audible, "the dreadful news about our dear girl." The haughty dame was actually shaking as she went to stand directly before Ryder. "Please, you *will* save her, Sir Alex, will you not?"

"I intend to do my utmost, my lady," Ryder replied grimly, handing her the bloody cloth. "Perhaps you will see to Cecil. I have urgent matters to attend to."

"Of course." Before he could leave, however, Drucilla laid a trembling hand on his arm. "Dunstan also says that you learned about our dreadful footman from Lord Gyllford. If you had not pressed him, you might not have discovered that Hitchens was our villain all along."

"Yes," Beatrice added in her soft voice. "It seems we have learned a valuable lesson, Sir Alex. Perhaps there is a time for violence after all."

"I was too harsh before, I see that now," Drucilla insisted. "Can you ever forgive me?"

A muscle worked in Ryder's jaw, but he managed a calm reply. "Of course, my lady. Now if you will excuse me, every moment counts."

Turning, Ryder joined Eve at the door, where she impatiently awaited him. If the circumstances weren't so dire, she reflected as she preceded him from the library, she might even have found humor in Drucilla's about-face. They had wronged Ryder, and so had she.

But Ryder didn't appear in any mood to discuss forgiveness, judging from his dark expression, Eve decided as she went to fetch her cloak and prepare for the long drive to Hertford.

* * *

His brooding silence continued during the entire journey to Hertford. Her traveling chaise made great speed, expedited by changing horses twice at posting inns. But for well more than three hours, Eve was left to struggle with her own desolate emotions alone.

What would they do if they couldn't find Meade? They would have no leads to her sister's abductors whatsoever.

She wanted to sob out her fear on Ryder's broad shoulder. She wanted him to put his arms around her, to reassure her that her sister would be all right. Yet she knew she didn't deserve his consideration. Not after the way she had treated him this morning, rebelling against his dictates when he had only been concerned for her safety.

She was ashamed to think of it now. She had asked him to leave her house, despite all he had done for her, for her entire family.

Eve wanted the chance to win his forgiveness, to regain his respect. And she certainly couldn't begin by falling apart in front of him.

As the interminable minutes wore on, however, a disquieting insight dawned on her. She had misunderstood Ryder's silence, Eve realized as she stared at his profile, grim in the sunlight spilling through the carriage window. He blamed himself for what had happened to Claire.

It was only natural that he would. He was a Guardian, and he had pledged to keep her and her family safe. He would consider Claire's abduction his personal failure.

Reaching out, Eve slipped her gloved hand in his larger one, not only seeking comfort but hoping to comfort him. "We will find her," she murmured, managing the semblance of a smile. "I have every faith in you."

Ryder squeezed her fingers once, briefly, before turning his face away, focusing his gaze out the carriage window as he cursed himself silently. Eve's brave smile pierced his heart; she was trying so hard to be strong. His own chest, however, was so heavy, he could barely breathe.

He would never forgive himself for failing to protect Claire. And his guilt would be a thousand times worse if he couldn't bring the girl back safely.

A short while later, the carriage slowed, and he knew they'd arrived at the outskirts of the town. Hertford was much too large for all the inhabitants to know one another or to be aware of every newcomer. When they halted at a local tavern, Ryder had Eve wait in the carriage while he inquired about Mabel Meade's relations. Four more stops were necessary, however, before he learned anything pertinent.

Upon returning to the coach, Ryder directed the coachman before climbing in beside Eve. "Meade and his wife are indeed living at a farm belonging to her parents. It is a few miles beyond the next crossroad."

Eve nodded, the fragile look of strain in her eyes evident.

"Are you certain you want to accompany me?" Ryder asked. "You could wait here in a private parlor instead."

Her spine suddenly straightening, she steeled her shoulders as if preparing to do battle. "I wouldn't miss it."

He wouldn't deny her the chance either, Ryder realized. He intended to make Meade confess whatever he knew about his wife's godson—and all his instincts were telling him that Eve would prove to be an asset in wringing any information out of the former steward.

From the moment they arrived at the farmhouse, Ryder knew his instincts were right. They were admitted by an elderly woman, who identified herself as Mabel Meade's mother, and then shown into a rear room, where a tall, thin man with stringy hair was lounging at a wooden table, staring morosely into a tankard of ale.

An expression of surprise and alarm claimed Meade's features when he looked up to see Eve sweep into the room. "You!"

"Yes, it is I, Mr. Meade."

Tobias Meade was clearly the worse for drink, for his reactions were slow as he struggled to his feet, and his words were slurred when he asked in a barely civil tone, "What brings you here, milady?"

Even though Ryder had moved to stand beside her, Eve took command of the conversation. "I think you know, Mr. Meade. I want my sister."

His expression became hooded. "I don't have her."

"But you know exactly who does."

Meade eyed her insolently. "If I did, you would be the last person I would tell."

Ryder took a threatening step forward, but Eve held up a regal hand. "I don't care about the attacks on myself, Mr. Meade. All I care about is my sister. I will give you one chance to tell us everything you know about Ned Hitchens."

"Why should I tell you a thing, milady? You ruined me, turning me off without a character."

"We won't discuss the fact that you deserved worse for your appalling stewardship," she replied, her tone scathing, "perhaps even criminal prosecution. I simply want to know about Hitchens's plans. I am prepared to make it worth your while to tell us." Reaching into her reticule, she withdrew a roll of banknotes and tossed it on the table. "Here is five hundred pounds, twice the yearly income you claimed as our steward."

The man's thin mouth twisted in a smirk. "You don't expect me to betray my wife's kin, do you?"

At his taunting question, fire flashed in Eve's eyes and her spine straightened. She was every inch the aristocratic lady of the manor, Ryder saw. A woman of power and substance with centuries of blue blood in her veins, groomed from birth to be a member of the ruling class.

Meade evidently recognized her authority, for he retreated a step, cowering a little, simply from her air of command.

An icy smile curled her lips. "I have no doubt you are involved in my sister's abduction, Mr. Meade. If you help us, you won't hang. You will merely go to jail."

"You can't pin that on me," he muttered. "I had nothing to do with it."

"So you refuse to cooperate?" Her chilling smile remained as she gestured toward Ryder. "You have not met my good friend Sir Alex Ryder," she said with acid sweetness. "He intends to make you reveal what you know about Hitchens. You should see how he dealt with the last man who crossed him. The poor fellow's face will take months to heal."

Meade sent a worried glance at Ryder but drew himself up, blustering with false bravado. "He doesn't scare me."

"You never were very bright, were you?" Eve said coolly. "You *should* be frightened, Mr. Meade. If not of Sir Alex, then of me. I could leave you to him, but frankly, I would rather have the satisfaction myself."

From her reticule, she withdrew the pistol Ryder had given her for protection and aimed it directly at Meade's heart.

If her unexpected move surprised Ryder, it certainly startled the former steward, for he took an abrupt step backward, holding up his hands defensively as he stared in fear and fascination.

"Mr. Meade," Eve said calmly, "my sister's life is dearer to me than my own, and certainly dearer to me than yours. As I said, I will give you one chance to tell us what you know—or I will begin shooting you limb by limb, before putting a hole in your miserable chest. Now, what will you choose?"

Chapter Seventeen

Eve tightened her grip on the pistol, aiming at Meade's left shoulder as she waited for his answer.

"I suggest you do as Lady Hayden says," Ryder drawled into the tense silence.

Meade's eyes flickered briefly to Ryder. He swallowed hard before returning his worried gaze to Eve. "You cannot shoot me, milady. It would be murder."

"That hardly concerns me now." She steadied the hand holding the pistol, preparing to fire.

"All right! I will tell you! Put away that gun and I will tell you what you want to know."

"No," she responded. "You will tell me now. Why has Hitchens been terrorizing and attempting to kill me? And why did he take my sister hostage instead of me?"

Doubtless concluding that she wasn't bluffing, Meade ran a hand roughly through his greasy hair. "You were never supposed to be killed. Only scared a little."

"For revenge?" Eve prodded.

"Aye. In the beginning I just wanted to make you pay for the humiliation you dealt me. And maybe to scare you into leaving the Park. So I hired Ned to arrange a near accident or two for you. They were never supposed to be fatal."

"But the incidents in London *were* almost fatal."

"Because the bloody fool thought that was what I wanted—his way of squeezing more money from me. He thought I would pay him to hurt you. But when he went so far, I washed my hands of him."

"Why did he abduct my sister? For the ransom payment?"

"I know nothing about any of that, milady."

When Eve briefly waved her pistol, Meade threw up his hands. "I don't know, I swear it! I saw Ned only once since he came back from London. It was three days ago, and he never told me a thing about what he was planning. Certainly nothing about any abduction."

"What did you discuss when you met him?" Ryder interjected.

"He asked me for blunt. Seems he hooked up with some London ruffians and owes them more than a few quid. I couldn't give him sixpence, though, since I'm dished up myself. When Ned threatened to squeal on me about those accidents he caused, I told him to bugger. . . . er, push off."

"So he concocted an abduction scheme and targeted Lady Hayden's sister?"

Frowning, Meade scratched his head. "Stands to reason. I had no notion he was that desperate. But if he plotted to bilk her ladyship of money, I'll wager he wants some of it for himself. Ned's always hated having to serve the hoity-toity gentry, and he talked about what he would do if he was rich. Securing a fat ransom would allow him to leave behind this life and settle down elsewhere."

"What can you tell us about his possible intentions? His habits, his usual haunts . . . where he and his cohorts might have taken Lady Claire? If they were clever, they would have chosen a location that couldn't readily be spotted, but one close enough to Hayden Park to provide easy communication."

At Ryder's question, Eve held her breath, praying her former steward would offer some clue they could follow to find Claire.

Meade's frown deepened as he thought for a long moment. "Now that you mention it. . . . There's a gristmill located a few miles beyond Braughing on the River Quinn. It belongs to Ned's cousin's family. He might be holed up there. Do you know it, my lady?"

"Yes," Eve answered hoarsely.

Meade's sullen expression softened. "I am indeed sorry about your sister. She always was a sweet young lady, and I don't like to think about her coming to harm."

"Your apology is a trifle late, Mr. Meade," she returned, feeling a surge of anger at this drunken fool who had set in motion the events leading to Claire's abduction.

"Well, I hope you find her."

Ryder spoke again, this time tersely. "You will be assisting us, Meade, before you're incarcerated on the charge of attempted murder."

"But I told you, I'm not to blame!"

"Your action against Lady Hayden was criminal, and you'll pay for it in jail. But first you will accompany us to the Park. If Hitchens is not at the mill, then we'll need to look for him elsewhere, and you know him better than anyone."

The steward nodded bitterly. His glance shifted to the table, to the roll of banknotes Eve had tossed there. "Can I keep the money, milady? It sure would prove useful."

Eve bit back her scornful reply. "You can use it to support your wife while you are in jail."

Meade nodded again. "I'll fetch my coat and tell the missus."

She felt Ryder's hand touch her elbow. "Wait for me in the carriage," he said, guiding her to the door.

He remained to keep an eye on Meade while Eve returned to the coach. When her groom had assisted her inside, she sank wearily back against the leather squabs. Moments later she heard Ryder directing Meade to climb in the driver's box with the coachman, while her two grooms took the footman's perch behind.

She was glad Meade wouldn't be inside the carriage with her and Ryder. She could not have stomached looking at him. The mere thought of what the scoundrel had done made her hands clench into fists.

Yet her anger was no match for the fear that swelled and twisted inside her. An icy cold filled her entire body.

She sat there shivering as Ryder climbed in beside her, but she didn't ask him to comfort her as she wanted to. When she felt her shoulder brush his, however, she gratefully absorbed his heat, letting it chase some of the chill away from her soul.

Her body jolted when the coachman whipped up the horses to set an urgent pace home.

"Do you think Meade could be right?" Eve asked Ryder, bracing against the rocking of the vehicle. "That we might find Claire at the mill?"

"I'd say there's a good chance."

"So we'll go there at once and search for ourselves?"

"Yes, as soon as we stop by the Park to gather weapons and reinforcements. It's on the way to the mill."

Biting her lower lip to hold back the sudden hot sting of tears, Eve nodded. It would be an endless journey home. She was aware of every second the clock ticked away; every excruciating moment they delayed increased the danger to Claire.

Thank God Ryder was here. She could not have faced this nightmare alone—even though just now she felt intensely alone.

He seemed to sense her need, for after a pause, he slid an arm around her shoulders. "I was glad to see you put my pistol to such good use, Countess."

Knowing he was trying to rally her spirits, Eve managed a faint smile. "I decided Beatrice was right. There is occasionally a time for violence, and this was one of those times."

Ryder couldn't bring himself to respond, but as he watched, Eve's smile faded to a bleak and lovely mask. She brought a hand up to cover her mouth, obviously struggling to maintain her composure. Then her face crumpled with anguish, as if a wave of crushing despair were washing over her.

"I'm sorry. . . . I don't mean . . . to be such a

weakling." Her breath cracked on a sob, and she curled into him, burying her face in his shoulder as her control gave way.

Her fear for her sister had finally taken its toll, Ryder knew, reluctantly encircling her with his arms as her desolation spilled out in a flood. Her tears—the raw emotion in her sobs, her agony—lacerated his heart.

He cradled Eve while she wept, the thickness inside his chest nearly crippling him.

"You aren't a weakling," he muttered hoarsely against her hair. And she most certainly wasn't. Eve was a remarkable combination of opposing forces: spun glass and steel, fragility and strength, beauty and toughness. She was everything he'd ever dreamed of having—and he sure as hell didn't deserve her.

His throat convulsed, and he had to close his eyes. If he failed to save her sister, Eve's entire life would be shattered. And there was nothing he could do but offer her false promises.

He could only hold her and touch his lips to her hair and fight to control his own strangling emotions.

Eventually her sobs subsided, and the only sounds were the rapid pounding of the team's hooves and the creaking of the swaying coach. Ryder continued to hold Eve as an occasional tremble shuddered through her until she raised her tear-stained face to his. When her lips touched his jaw, seeking, Ryder went rigid.

He felt her mouth, hot and open, against his skin and knew she was kissing him in a primal need for comfort. But he couldn't help her that way.

"Not now." Extricating himself from her clinging embrace, he gently pushed her away and fished in his pocket for a handkerchief. "Here, this will have to do."

His voice vibrated with gentleness, but the pain that shot through Eve at his rejection was so fierce, she felt it like a blow.

Taking the handkerchief, she retreated to her corner of the coach and stared out at the passing countryside through a fresh blur of tears. *Ryder didn't want her.*

The realization shouldn't hurt so much. He had always been perfectly frank about his feelings for her.

Yet she felt more for him than she'd ever allowed herself to admit. She wanted his respect, craved his good opinion, but deep within the recesses of her heart, she yearned for something far, far more.

She had been so very blind.

Sniffling into her handkerchief, Eve glanced over at Ryder. He was staring broodingly out the window, as remote as a distant star.

It was ironic, really. She was supposed to be a skilled matchmaker, yet she had failed disastrously to recognize her own perfect match when it was staring her in the face. Only now was she coming to recognize the depth of her feelings for Ryder, when it might be too late to influence the outcome. Ryder felt nothing more significant for her than friendship, and it might be impossible to hope for anything more.

The bitter thought left Eve feeling hollow and empty, lonely and cold.

Yet she couldn't leave it at that, she thought defiantly. She couldn't act on her feelings now, not with Claire in such danger. But once her sister was safe . . .

Taking a shuddering breath, Eve wiped her sodden eyes. A sense of infinite calm spread through her as she focused her thoughts on the difficult task ahead.

They would rescue Claire first, and then she would determine what to do about Ryder.

Eve remained lost in her thoughts for the long journey, until her traveling coach drew into the Hayden Park stableyard and she spied all the commotion. A large crowd of men had congregated in the yard, bearing pitchforks, shovels, and blunderbusses. She recognized many of them as her tenant farmers, but their presence startled and alarmed her.

"What has happened?" Eve urgently demanded of her head groom, who had opened the carriage door and let down the steps.

"Naught, my lady. Everyone has heard what befell Lady Claire and came to offer help."

"Aye, milady." Zachery Dowell, the father of new baby Benjamin, stepped forward. "We hope to lend our might on behalf of you and Lady Claire. We couldn't just sit by and do nothing. Please, milady, just tell us what we may do to help. If you mean to mount a rescue, then we could come in handy."

Her throat constricting with fresh tears, Eve managed a shaky smile of gratitude. She hadn't expected an entire army of farmers to come to her rescue, but it was truly heartening to see. "That is so good of you . . . all of you." She glanced up at Ryder beside her. "Sir Alex is in charge. He will have to decide how to proceed from here. Whatever we do cannot put my sister in further danger."

Nodding solemnly, Zachery tugged his forelock politely at Ryder, who indicated the prisoner in the coachman's box. "I'd like you to take charge of Meade for the time being."

" 'Twould be my pleasure, yer honor." His fingers tightening around his gun, Zachery eyed the former steward with grim dislike before addressing Eve again. "However you can use us, we are at your disposal, milady."

"Thank you, truly."

Just then she saw Macky working his way through the crowd. "Has there been any news of Claire?" she asked urgently when he reached them. "You didn't find her?"

"No and no," Macky said grimly. "But six of our friends are here from London."

Eve presumed he must be referring to Ryder's fellow Guardians, but Macky forestalled her questions by asking one of his own. "Did you learn anything from the steward that might lead us to Lady Claire?"

Ryder answered for Eve as his hand pressed the small of her back to guide her toward the house. "We have a strong possibility. Let's collect our friends and we can discuss our exact plan on the way."

Chapter Eighteen

Her heart pounding, Eve crept silently through the dark glade beside Ryder, following the course of the River Quinn. There was barely enough moonlight to prevent her from stumbling, although the illumination was better when they reached the edge of the alder woods.

When Ryder paused, pointing, she could see the gristmill beyond a wide stretch of open road, a massive wooden structure built three stories tall. Light spilled from two middle-floor windows while an armed, roughly dressed sentry lounged at the front entrance door, yawning occasionally as if bored or half asleep.

The fact that the mill was occupied by at least five armed men had been discovered an hour earlier when Ryder and his fellow Guardians had reconnoitered. But wanting the element of surprise, they had resolved to wait until dark to mount a rescue of Claire, rather than storm the building and risk her being caught in the cross fire.

They'd kept determined vigil since, prepared to charge at the first sign of threatening activity. Commanded to remain back out of sight, Eve had paced the entire time.

Her nerves were thoroughly shredded by the time Ryder came to fetch her, and now, when a menacing shadow emerged from the darkness of the woods, she jumped and nearly gasped out loud. Ryder, however, didn't twitch a muscle except to lay a calming hand on her shoulder.

"It's only Macky," he murmured, barely breathing. "Don't be alarmed."

He had obviously been expecting to meet Macky. Eve drew a steadying breath as behind her, Lord Thorne moved to confer quietly with the other two men. She'd been only a little surprised to learn that the charming fair-haired viscount was a Guardian.

Ryder's other colleagues from London had spread out some time ago to surround the mill. Additionally, he'd positioned several dozen of her retainers behind them, creating a human net in case Hitchens and his cohorts tried to escape. In military parlance, they were establishing a perimeter.

Cecil had been allowed to participate, overseeing the force of tenant farmers; a responsibility meant to help him prove his courage and assuage some of his guilt for allowing his sister to be abducted from right under his nose. Assuming the rescue was successful, Eve reflected with increased foreboding.

"None of the thugs have changed positions," Macky informed them.

The casements on all three floors stood open against the warmth of the night, Eve saw, yet with the vast expanse of exposed ground surrounding three sides of the mill, a clandestine assault—sneaking up upon the kidnappers quietly enough to disarm them all at the same moment—would be highly difficult.

The only other possible approach, Ryder had said, was to swim in. The River Quinn ran alongside the west wall of the mill, directly under the giant waterwheel that turned the massive millstones inside. The wheel was stationary just now, so they couldn't count on noise to camouflage their arrival. The last thing Ryder wanted was to panic Claire's abductors and give them time to harm or even kill her.

And so he had chosen to lure Hitchens and his cohorts into the open.

Her stomach churning, Eve murmured a silent plea for success as Ryder led her former steward forward to the edge of the wood.

When Ryder nodded, Meade called out loudly to the occupiers. "Ned? Ned Hitchens? 'Tis I, Tobias Meade. Are you there, lad?"

Instantly the man guarding the entrance whirled, aiming his pistol in the direction of the shout. Eve went rigid, afraid even to breathe. Myriad rescuers' weapons were trained on the mill, but they wouldn't risk firing except as a last resort.

The silence seemed deafening. She could hear nothing more than the ripple of water from the river and a breeze rustling the alder limbs above her head.

Finally the outline of a man's shoulder appeared in one of the second-floor windows and a voice responded, "What do you want, Tobias?"

Eve thought she recognized the voice of her footman, Ned Hitchens.

"You need to surrender peacefully, lad," the steward warned. "The game is up."

"You must be daft if you think I will give up now. I intend to make them pay. Only a few hours more and I'll be a wealthy man."

" 'Tis you who is daft, my boy. Sir Alex Ryder is here with a score of his armed friends, and he's not inclined to pay you any ransom."

There was a long, grim silence until Ryder stepped forward. "He's right, Hitchens. You have no way out."

Ned gave a harsh laugh. "And you've no way to stop me, Sir Alex. I want my money. If you don't deliver, I will kill Lady Claire! I swear it!"

Eve bit her knuckles to the bone, tasting blood, as Ryder spoke out in a deadly dangerous tone. "If you harm her, you won't leave here alive. Think hard, Hitchens. If you surrender now, you will likely get off with prison or transportation. Otherwise . . ." He let the word hover in the night air as he took another step into the open.

"That is far enough!" Ned shouted. "If you come an inch closer, I will slit her throat! Her blood will be on your hands, Sir Alex."

It took all of Eve's willpower to hold back her whimper, but she dared not distract Ryder from his purpose.

"What of your confederates?" Ryder asked with incredible calm. "Do they get a say in their fate? Greed is one thing, but I doubt they want to take part in the murder of a genteel young lady. If they do, I can promise they won't live to see prison."

When the mill's occupants remained silent, Ryder addressed Ned's cohorts. "You others in there, I have no quarrel with you. I want Hitchens. So I will offer you a chance to leave. Now, immediately. Otherwise there will be no escape. You have one minute to decide."

Eve held a painful breath, praying the ruffians would choose to flee.

A moment later, her prayer came true. She heard the sound of running feet a moment before three shadows spilled out of the mill, like rats fleeing a sinking ship. A fourth rat, the sentry who had been guarding the door, followed them, racing east across the open expanse to disappear into the dark woods.

A fierce curse sounded from the window above when Ned Hitchens realized he was being abandoned.

"Your cohorts won't be able to assist you now, Hitchens," Ryder called out. "You had best come out with Lady Claire."

Suddenly Ned's silhouette disappeared from the window. As Eve waited in tense silence, she found herself clenching her hands so tightly, her nails drew blood.

A moment later, Ryder muttered an oath beside her and pointed upward at a different window on the topmost floor. Her gaze following his, she saw the dark figure of a man hauling himself through the window, out onto a narrow ledge above the immense waterwheel. Ryder had warned them that Hitchens would likely have determined an escape route in the event he needed to get away quickly.

Before she could blink, Ryder muttered, "He's mine," and sprinted across the clearing toward the giant wheel, followed swiftly by Lord Thorne. Macky ran toward the mill door, accompanied by two other

Guardians intent on rescuing her sister inside, Eve knew.

Eve forced herself to remain where she was, having solemnly promised she wouldn't interfere with the rescue or put herself in the very kind of danger they were trying to rescue Claire from. But it was excruciating to merely watch as Ryder reached the wheel.

Grabbing hold of a wooden slat, he hauled himself up and began to climb, evidently intending to apprehend Hitchens before he could escape. For if the footman gained the river and managed to swim downstream, his pursuers could easily lose him in the darkness—a result Ryder was determined to prevent.

Eve caught her breath as his grasp slipped, suddenly realizing that the wheel paddles would be treacherously wet and slimed with algae. Then a gunshot rang out, the report sounding like thunder in the quiet night.

It was all she could do to bite back a scream, for Hitchens stood on top of the wheel, looking like an avenging devil as he trained two pistols down on his pursuers. He had fired one of them at Ryder, who was halfway up by now, and then threw the empty pistol at Ryder's head, trying to dislodge his precarious hold.

But Ryder ducked and kept on climbing, with Lord Thorne only a few steps behind him.

Her fear for Ryder was like a live thing gnawing inside her. She couldn't bear for him to be hurt or killed. But she clamped down on her dread, telling herself that Ryder had experienced this kind of danger a thousand times before.

What was more, *he had to do this.* This was his calling. The essence of the man he was: a protector, a fighter, supremely skilled and dedicated, prepared to risk his life for his cause. She couldn't interfere, Eve knew, a welling of pride and love breaking through her fear and squeezing at her heart.

"Stay back or I'll shoot!" Hitchens warned, waving the second pistol threateningly down at Ryder, who had halted momentarily under cover of a slat.

"Give up, man!" Ryder growled in return. "You won't escape."

The next instant, Eve saw Lord Thorne throw something upward and caught the glitter of steel before the knife blade buried itself in Hitchens's right thigh.

The footman screamed in pain and bent over to clutch his wounded leg, discharging the pistol harmlessly in the process. Ryder leaped upward, hauling himself up onto the final paddle as his stumbling opponent turned to flee.

He caught Hitchens around the ankle, bringing him down hard and rousing another scream as both combatants nearly fell off the edge of the wheel. Somehow, however, Ryder managed not only to hold on but to wrestle himself on top of the captured villain, laying him out flat and drawing back his fist to deliver a blow.

Suddenly Ryder froze. His head came up and whipped around, as did Lord Thorne's. Both men were staring at the mill.

It was then that Eve smelled the acrid scent of smoke, but it took another instant for her to realize the cause of the golden-red glow coming from beyond the second-floor window.

Hitchens had set fire to the mill, inside where her sister was being held.

Claire. Dear God.

Macky had already gone in, determined to rescue Claire, but he might not reach her in time. . . .

Panic filling her, Eve blindly began to run for the entrance.

From his precarious position high above her, Ryder felt his heart clench in dread as he watched Eve race into the burning building. The instant he'd smelled smoke, he understood the danger. Not only could the mill go up in a fiery blaze, but explosion was an even greater threat, since storerooms filled with sacks of grain and flour were highly combustible. Everything and everyone inside would be demolished.

A surge of desperation and fear rushed over Ryder. Instinctively he loosened his grip on Hitchens as he met his friend Thorne's grim gaze.

"Go!" Thorne ordered. "I'll handle this scum."

Ryder abandoned his prisoner and began to climb down the slippery paddles. Smoke was billowing out of the windows now, and he had not a second to waste. The woman he loved was prepared to risk her life for her sister, but he couldn't allow either one to die.

He made it down in record time, dropping the last few yards to land with a jolt. He leaped for the open door and plunged inside. The fire had been started on the floor above, but thick smoke already hazed the large bay where drays and wagons were driven in to be loaded and unloaded.

Bounding up the first set of steps he came to, Ryder immediately felt the heat and spied flames spitting from a doorway farther along the corridor. His throat closing from the acrid smoke, his eyes stinging, he ripped off his coat and wrapped it around his forearm so as to ward off fire, then took a deep breath and lunged forward.

Just before he reached the doorway, Eve backed out, to his vast relief. She was doubled over, her body heaving from great racking coughs, but there she stopped, refusing to go any farther, even when Ryder took her arm and tried to lead her to safety.

"I won't leave her!" she cried, then shouted hoarsely to the occupants inside the burning chamber. "This way!"

Two Guardians staggered out next, but it was only when Macky emerged, stumbling and carrying the limp figure of Lady Claire, that Eve permitted Ryder to pull her down the murky corridor.

Forcibly he guided her down the stairway and through the loading dock to the wide door, where he pushed her out into the less deadly night air, shouting, "Head for the woods! We'll see to Claire."

Not waiting to see if she obeyed, he returned for Macky, who reluctantly gave up his precious burden, since Ryder had more strength.

Wheeling, Ryder rushed the unconscious Claire outside, intending to take her as far away from the burning mill as possible. With Eve a few steps ahead of him, he ran for the shelter of the trees.

He made it a third of the way across the clearing

before the explosion erupted at his back. Thrown forward by the force, Ryder barely managed to stay on his feet and keep hold of Claire, protecting her with his body.

Behind him, Macky was not so fortunate. When half the door blew off its hinges, splintering in lethal fragments, Macky caught the brunt of the blow with his shoulders and head. Out of the corner of his eye, Ryder saw his friend pitch forward to land facedown in the road.

Grimly clamping down on his dread, Ryder kept moving, away from the roaring fire. Reaching the edge of the glade, he laid Claire gently down in the grass and bent to check her breathing.

"She's still alive," he muttered, swamped by an enormous surge of relief. Drawing a knife from his coat pocket, he sliced through the rope her abductors had used to bind her wrists while Eve knelt beside her, alternately sobbing and coughing as she began chafing her sister's hands and face, trying to revive her.

When the girl suddenly moaned and began coughing, weakly struggling for breath, Eve gave a helpless whimper. "Thank God."

Claire's hacking cough finally quieted enough for her to gaze up at Ryder. "I knew you would come for me," she said simply.

Ryder couldn't manage to return her faint smile. "I need to see to Macky," he said gruffly.

Eve nodded in understanding. "Go, please . . . I will stay with Claire."

He covered Claire with his coat and got to his

feet. When he was gone, Eve gazed back down at her sister. "Did Hitchens harm you in any way?"

"No, except that he kicked a lantern over on purpose, the horrible fiend. And his friends tied me with ropes."

When Claire raised her arms, Eve saw the raw, bleeding flesh at her wrists.

The sight tormented her. "Oh, Claire, I am sorry you had to endure that horror."

"I am all right, Eve, truly," the girl insisted in a rasping voice before another fit of coughing seized her.

When she recovered, Claire turned her head to peer at the inferno that had been the mill, where swarms of farmers were attempting futilely to douse the fire with river water carried in shirts and coats and hats. "Where is Macky? I thought . . . I saw Mr. Macklin kneeling before me. Was I dreaming?"

"No, dearest," Eve replied. "He saved you from the fire. But then there was an explosion."

When she cast a troubled glance in the direction of the mill, Claire demanded, "Was Macky hurt?"

"I fear so," Eve said.

"I need to see to him."

"Of course, as soon as you are able to stand."

Macky, who had been dragged across the road, away from the heat of the flames, regained consciousness just as Ryder reached him.

"What of the lass?" he demanded, lurching to his knees. There was terror in his voice, and he didn't relax until Ryder responded, "She's safe, thanks to you."

Reassured, Macky collapsed back onto the grass. His face was scraped raw, Ryder saw, and he was bleeding from two places on his head and a nasty gash on his left arm, but he still retained enough energy to swear a string of accomplished oaths as one of his fellow Guardians began to attend to his injuries.

As he lent assistance, Ryder glanced back across the clearing. He felt his heart wrench at the sight of Eve's expression in the flaming glow of the mill fire. She was still crying silently, her beautiful face smudged by smoke and streaked with grimy tears, a reminder of his failure. Claire's rescue didn't absolve him from the fact that he had neglected to protect her in the first place.

He was only vaguely aware that several people had surrounded the sisters, including the doctor who had come in the event Lady Claire needed medical attention. She would be in good hands now.

It was then that Cecil came rushing up, demanding to know what had happened to his twin. When Claire smiled up at him, the boy fell to his knees and grabbed her in a ferocious bear hug that startled a laugh out of her but soon had her protesting that he was crushing her.

When Eve warned him to take care, Cecil merely reached out and hauled her into his hug as well, drawing Eve close while burying his face against Claire's hair as he muttered a heartfelt prayer of thanks over and over again.

The emotional reunion, filled with elation and relief and unquestionable love, sliced at Ryder's heart, since he didn't deserve to be part of it. All three siblings were laughing and crying now as they celebrated Claire's narrow reprieve from death.

Unable to share in their joy, Ryder turned his face away, leaving Eve and Cecil to minister to their sister.

By the time Macky's injuries were bandaged, Ryder was able to glance around at the devastation. The blaze was dying down, but it looked like a battle scene.

When he spied Hitchens, Ryder felt himself struggle anew with the fierce desire to kill the bastard with his bare hands. Thorne had managed—regrettably—to bring the footman down from the waterwheel before the explosion.

Hitchens was now trussed up tightly as a Christmas goose, with several armed farmers guarding him and prodding him none too gently with their pitchforks.

All in all, the outcome could have been infinitely worse, Ryder acknowledged, but the fact was little comfort.

He had only a moment to dwell on his dark thoughts, however, for he caught sight of Eve moving toward them. She and Cecil were helping Claire make her way slowly over to where Macky lay.

When Claire saw the extent of Macky's injuries, she gave a murmur of pity and protest and promptly knelt beside him. "Oh, your poor face. To think you were wounded so terribly saving my life."

Wincing, Macky managed a grin. "It was nothing, my lady. I was glad for the chance to play the hero."

She stroked his brow, then gave a little sob.

Macky's expression dissolved into dismay. "What is this, tears? Are you weeping over me?"

Claire took his hand in her own and brought it to her lips. "I couldn't have borne it if you had been killed."

"Oh, my beautiful lass, you're safe. That's all that matters."

With no apparent concern for his injuries or for anyone who might be watching, he pulled Claire down into his arms. Ryder saw Eve give a start as Macky tendered her sister a passionate, ardent, heartfelt kiss that left no question as to his feelings for her.

When he finally released her, Claire stared down at him in breathless wonder, while Macky stared back with the same spellbound awe.

After a moment, he peered sheepishly around at the spectators, then sent an apologetic glance at Eve. "Might as well be hanged for a sheep as a lamb," he muttered. "This may be the only chance I'll ever get." His hands reached up to cradle Claire's face tenderly. "I would be honored, lass, if you would consider marrying me. I am not such a grand prize, but I love you witless."

The joy that overcame Claire's expression conveyed her answer before she even replied; her sooty, tearstained face looked beatific. "Yes, I will marry you, Macky. And gladly."

Her twin didn't appear in the least surprised by this turn of events, but Eve looked startled. "Claire . . . This is not the time to make such a momentous decision. You have just experienced a traumatic ordeal."

Claire smiled up at her. "I know. But strangely, my ordeal is precisely what made me realize just what is important to me. I know it is not quite what you planned for me, Eve, but Macky is the husband I want, suitable or not. I love him."

Evidently rendered speechless by her sister's declaration of love, Eve gazed down helplessly at Claire. "I knew you were fond of Mr. Macklin, but I had no idea your affection had gone this far."

"Well, it has. It was quite unexpected, but it happened before I was even aware of it."

"Claire, you should at least wait until you are more recovered from the shock. There is no reason to make a hasty decision."

At her response, Ryder found himself clenching his teeth, suspecting Eve's dismay was likely due to the vast difference in the lovers' stations in class and fortune. He wanted to come to his friend's defense, but Macky broke in before he could speak.

"Yes, my love. Her ladyship is right. I want you to be very certain you wish to marry me."

Claire regarded him indulgently. "I won't change my mind."

Eve reached down to help her sister to stand. "We will settle this later. For now we need to get you home to bed."

With weary amusement, Claire wrinkled her nose. "And a bath first, if you don't mind."

Eve managed a faint smile. "Of course."

Rising to his feet, Ryder addressed Cecil. "You did well tonight, lad. Do you want to help me finish the job and see the felons incarcerated, or to escort your sisters home?"

"Oh, finish the job, most certainly," the boy declared. "I haven't had this much excitement in the whole of my life." Cecil caught himself and flashed an apologetic glance at his sisters. "Do you mind? Now that you are both safe, I can stop worrying and enjoy this bang-up adventure."

When Eve smiled in wry exasperation and told him he could go, Cecil raced off.

Without commenting further, Ryder escorted the ladies some distance along the road to where Eve's carriage now awaited with her coachmen and two of Ryder's armed men acting as grooms. He handed Claire inside but detained Eve for a moment by grasping her upper arm.

"Don't forbid the match," Ryder said, his voice low and testy. "A man's worth is not in his title or fortune."

She stared up at him, as if surprised by his acrimony. "I know that."

He took a slow breath, attempting to control his irrational anger. "Macky is a good man."

"I know that, too. I just want Claire to be certain she is making the right decision. Marriage is too enormous a commitment to enter into lightly." When he gritted his teeth, Eve smiled tentatively up at him. "Ryder, I haven't had the chance to thank you for every thing you did . . . for saving my sister."

He didn't respond. He didn't want Eve's gratitude; gratitude was a mere crumb compared to what he wanted from her.

But now was not the time to take issue with her,

Ryder realized. The skin beneath her eyes had the violet smudge of exhaustion, reminding him that she had experienced a terrifying ordeal herself.

"Take Claire home," he said more gently.

"What will you do?"

"Escort our culprit to the local authorities and supervise his incarceration. It will likely take all night."

"But you will return to the Park when you are finished?" she asked. When he hesitated, Eve's tone softened. "Please, Ryder. I know the aunts will want to thank you personally for what you have done."

"I don't care about their thanks."

"I . . . understand."

Involuntarily his fingers curled around her arm as he stared down at her, fighting the urge to draw Eve closer and kiss her the way Macky had done with her sister. This might be the last chance he ever had to taste her lips, to feel her warmth against him. But then Ryder forced himself to release her and step back. "Perhaps when I've dealt with Hitchens."

Eve looked as if she would say more, but she merely searched his face for another long moment before finally turning and climbing into the carriage with her sister.

Shutting the door after her, Ryder watched the vehicle pull away. His dark mood had plunged even further now that the battle was over, even if he could declare himself victorious. Tonight he'd witnessed how deeply Eve loved her sister—so much that she was willing to sacrifice her own life to save her. Eve protected those she loved with the brave, determined fierceness of a lioness, and she would fight to the death if it came to that.

He wondered if Eve could ever come to love him that much. It was possible it would never happen.

The reflection brought a sudden emptiness to Ryder's chest, as if his heart had stopped beating.

Abruptly he spun on his heel and headed back to the scene of destruction. He would have to decide soon whether he should keep pursuing Eve. She was everything he'd ever wanted and needed, but what about her? She might be happier living her life without him.

Perhaps he would do better to leave altogether and return to Cyrene. Ryder felt his stride falter. The thought of leaving Eve was like a knife in his chest; he wondered how he would survive walking away.

But at the moment, he didn't have the luxury of indulging his feelings of despair. He had the fate of his prisoner to deal with and a good deal of work ahead of him.

It would be quite some time until he could try to settle his own fate.

Chapter Nineteen

The interior of the coach was blessedly dim, allowing Eve to hide her despondency from her sister. Her spirits should have been soaring after Claire's safe rescue, but instead she felt strangely forlorn.

The truth was, Ryder's terse dismissal had upset her greatly. She had seen his brooding eyes as he stared down at her. His dark perusal had lingered upon her face, as if he were committing her to memory. As if he might never see her again.

Disquiet had clutched at her throat when he refused to answer her question about his plans. Eve was almost certain Ryder didn't intend to return to the Park. His belongings were there, but he could always dispatch a servant to pack for him. He needn't come himself. In truth, there was no reason for him to have anything more to do with her; now that Hitchens had been apprehended, she no longer needed Ryder's protection.

The very thought left her feeling bereft.

Yet what did she expect when just hours ago she had baldly demanded that he leave? The possibility that he would actually do so left a hollowness in the pit of her stomach.

Just then Claire interrupted her dark reverie to say tentatively, "I know you are worried for me, Eve. You think that I am not in my right mind just now after the ordeal I suffered. But that couldn't be further from the truth. I know my own mind. What is more, I know my own *heart*."

With effort, Eve roused herself from her despondency. "I *am* worried for you, dearest. It alarms me that you would make such an irrevocable decision so hastily. Won't you at least consider the possibility that you have confused your feelings of friendship and affection for Mr. Macklin with love?"

"But I haven't confused my feelings, Eve. I have never been less confused in all of my life. I love Macky. And I believe him when he says he loves me."

Eve hesitated, feeling helpless. "Perhaps you do love each other now, but you both must be absolutely certain that marriage is what you want. Your life will be an utter misery if your feelings for each other dissolve shortly after the wedding ceremony. What is worse, you will have no way out. A married woman is legally her husband's possession, and you will be totally at his mercy."

"I trust Macky," Claire said with conviction. "He would never abuse my trust."

"But you have known him only a short time. Not even a month."

"I realize that. But sometimes you just *know* if a person is right for you." The soft smile in Claire's voice was unmistakable. "Macky is right for me, Eve. I know it here." She pressed a hand over her heart. "It may not be logical. And it may not conform to all your tenets of matchmaking. But then love is not always rational, you must admit."

When Eve remained silent, Claire peered at her in the dim light thrown from the outer carriage lamps. "Have *you* never considered the possibility that the heart can recognize its soul mate?"

The question disturbed her. "I suppose it is possible. But Claire, it happens so rarely."

"But it *does* happen. Macky makes me *happy,* Eve. It is as simple as that." Reaching out, Claire took her hand. "You said that was precisely what you wanted for me—the chance to find happiness with my chosen mate. Well, I have found it. If you want me to wait to marry Macky, I will, but I won't ever change my mind about loving him. And I would like your blessing for our marriage."

Eve felt her throat tighten with poignant tears. She could actually *feel* Claire's happiness. There was a joyful serenity about her sister, a serenity that belonged to a mature woman rather than a nineteen-year-old girl.

She would have to be satisfied with that, Eve acknowledged. Claire would very likely know true happiness married to Macky, and that was all she had ever wanted for her sister. Her most ardent dream was that Claire would make a marriage based on mutual respect and caring, with a husband who would cherish her as she deserved—and it seemed she had found such a match with Mr. Beau Macklin.

"Very well," Eve replied, her tone softening. "If you are both positively certain that you love each other and that your feelings will last, then you have my blessing, and gladly."

With a laugh, Claire threw her arms around Eve's neck, hugging her tightly. When she drew back, her eyes were shining. "I want you to be happy too, Eve. You deserve it, if anyone does."

"Yes, well . . . perhaps happiness isn't in the cards for me."

Sinking back against the cushions, Claire gave a tired sigh. "At least you needn't be concerned about me any longer. Now that you don't have to make a match for me, you can see to your own future. And you can concentrate on finding Sir Alex his ideal bride."

At the sharp stab of pain in her breast, Eve turned to gaze blindly out the carriage window. When she didn't reply, Claire prodded, "You do still mean to continue helping him, don't you?"

Eve cleared her throat of the gravel that had suddenly lodged there. "Sir Alex doesn't need my help any longer. He will likely choose one of the candidates on his list, and that will be the end of it."

It was a moment before Claire spoke again. "Do you really want him to wed Lady Keeling? Or, God forbid, Mrs. Ferris-Jones?"

"No," Eve said rather too sharply.

"Why not?"

She forced herself to clamp down on her emotions. "I didn't mean to imply that he shouldn't wed Lydia. She will make him a good match." Eve managed a dismissive shrug. "Don't mind me, I am just blue-deviled. It has been a long and terrifying day"—she paused, smiling wryly—"although I'm certain it was much worse for you."

Claire's lips curved in her own secret smile. "I

suppose it wasn't too terrible, considering what came of it. But I had hoped . . ."

"What did you hope?"

"That you would find happiness with Sir Alex."

Feeling her heart jolt, Eve turned to stare at her sister.

"Don't you care for him just a little, Eve?"

Yes, she cared. More than she had ever imagined possible. But after this, Ryder would likely return to London and proceed with his plan to marry.

Eve felt her jaw clench. She couldn't bear the thought of his taking another wife, couldn't bear his being with any other woman but *her.* She didn't want to face the thought of living forever without Ryder, never knowing where he was, what he was doing, or if he was even alive. Without Ryder, a future of unbearable loneliness awaited her. The emptiness that swelled inside her now was proof enough of her feelings.

Claire was still waiting for an answer to her question. "Well, do you care for him?"

"Yes," Eve whispered, "I care for him. More than I ever realized."

"I knew it!" Claire clapped her hands together with glee. "I hoped you would come finally to love him. Oh, this is famous, Eve! And I know Sir Alex will be overjoyed to hear it. He has been waiting forever for you to see him as a possible husband."

Eve gazed back in startlement. "What are you talking about?"

"Sir Alex loves you, Eve, I'm sure of it."

"He . . . *loves* me?"

"Yes. I suspect he has loved you for years."

Eve's mouth worked, but she remained speechless out of shock. "What makes you say so?" she asked finally.

"Simply from watching him all these years. All the time you were married and living in England, he couldn't hide his eagerness to hear how you were faring. His eyes got this certain look whenever your name was mentioned."

"What kind of look?"

"A sort of needy . . . yearning, I guess you could say. As if his greatest dream had been denied him. And every time he sees you now, his eyes soften and fill with a special tenderness."

Her own eyes opened wide. "Are you certain, Claire? You aren't mistaken?"

"No, I am not mistaken. Didn't you ever guess how deeply he felt for you?"

"No, never." Ryder had always kept his feelings for her carefully masked, his expression carefully neutral, even when he was lavishing the most incredible passion on her. She'd always thought the passion he'd shown her, the poignant tenderness, had been out of sheer kindness.

How could she have been so blind? But she knew the answer to that question, Eve reflected. She had been so set on her own self-protection that she'd never given a thought to Ryder's desires, his needs. Was it possible he truly loved her? That he had done so for years?

"Trust me, Eve," Claire insisted with a hint of smugness. "He loves you. Why else would he have put up with Cecil and me for so many years and gone to such lengths to take us under his wing? It was for your sake, not ours. I knew weeks ago that he wanted to marry you. As soon as he came to London, in fact. But I told him how crucial it was to go slowly with you."

"Slowly?"

"He only requested your help in finding him a match so he could court you without threatening you and arming all your defenses. His search for a bride was mere pretense."

"But *why*?" Eve asked, bewildered.

"Because you had adamantly vowed you would never marry again, and he feared—we both feared—that you would reject his suit out of hand and possibly never speak to him again. He likely would have offered for you weeks ago, but I convinced him to wait. He wants to marry you, Eve. And I would wager any sum that you are the only wife he's ever wanted."

Eve stared at Claire, startled and gratified by her sister's revelations. The spark of joy in her heart, however, was immediately tempered by the remembrance of her own actions today. Ryder might have loved her before this morning . . . but it was just as possible she had driven him away.

With shame Eve recalled how she had insisted that he leave the house party so she wouldn't have to face any further intimacy with him.

Claire broke into her dire reflections. "You don't mean to reject him now, do you, Eve? Surely you aren't afraid to wed him?"

Eve shook her head mutely. No, she wasn't afraid to wed Ryder. She knew with absolute certainty that he would be nothing like her late husband—

authoritarian and cold and controlling. Ryder was passionate and caring, concerned for her feelings and protective of her without treating her as a mere possession or a beautiful object to be displayed. Instead of caging her, he treated her as a real flesh-and-blood woman. A capable, thinking woman deserving of respect. A woman who could be his lover and his life's mate.

Slowly her headshake turned to one of amazement. To think that she would actually consider taking another husband. But then she had never been in love before.

She'd never believed it was possible for her to know true love. To experience the kind of blissful passion she had secretly yearned for. But she felt it with Ryder. He filled the emptiness inside her, made her feel joy. When he was with her, she felt genuinely *happy.*

Perhaps Claire was right. Perhaps it was as simple as that.

A tentative smile flickered on Eve's mouth. She wanted to secure that happiness. She wanted a future with Ryder, wanted him for her husband. A marriage based on true love.

"You will have to tell him how you feel, Eve," Claire insisted. "You have given him little reason to hope you would welcome his offer of marriage. But if you love him, you must tell him."

"Yes," Eve agreed in a low voice.

"I think Sir Alex will make you an ideal husband."

She suspected he would. Yet she wasn't so certain she would make him an ideal wife, not after rejecting him the way she had. Dismay caught at her throat.

She was afraid she couldn't begin to measure up to him. Ryder was a hero, worth more than any hundred noblemen combined. Perhaps *she* was the one who needed to prove her worth to *him*.

But regardless, Eve acknowledged, one thing was certain: If she wanted to grasp happiness, she would have to be the one to act.

She fell silent again, yet this time it had nothing to do with melancholy. A burgeoning hope swelled in her heart. She had a great deal to ponder.

Just then the carriage slowed to turn, making Eve glance out the window. As they swept along the drive to Hayden Park, she could see the manor house ablaze with lights. The aunts and servants had undoubtedly remained on high alert, awaiting their safe return.

Eventually the carriage drew to a halt in the stableyard. Moments later, Eve ushered Claire inside the house by way of a rear entrance door, so they wouldn't be seen by their houseguests, who by this time would be in the drawing room enjoying an evening of music and cards.

The butler, Dunstan, was the first to greet them, but Beatrice and Drucilla came hurrying down the corridor almost immediately, no doubt having been summoned by a footman standing watch.

"Oh, you dearest girl," Beatrice exclaimed, embracing Claire warmly. "Thank heavens you are safe."

Drucilla was less effusive because of the smoky grime covering Claire's gown and hands, but the elegant dame still kissed the girl's forehead tenderly. "Did those dastardly villains harm you in any way, my dear?"

"No, Aunt Drucilla—other than tying me up and hefting me about like a sack of grain and starving me half to death."

Drucilla pursed her lips. "Regrettably after so shocking an event, we cannot avert a scandal, but perhaps we can minimize the effects so that your reputation is not *entirely* ruined. Once you have washed and changed, you will join our guests in the drawing room to prove that you are unscathed. Otherwise all your suitors are likely to abandon their courtship posthaste."

Claire smiled. "My reputation won't matter to my choice of suitors, Aunt."

Eve, not wanting to precipitate a battle just now by announcing Claire's engagement, interrupted. "Dunstan, Lady Claire is famished. Will you have a supper tray brought up to her chamber and then arrange baths for both of us?"

"Certainly, my lady. And may I say on behalf of all the staff, how pleased we are that Lady Claire is safe?"

"Thank you, Dunstan." As she directed Claire toward the rear stairway, Eve sent Drucilla a pointed glance. "We have Sir Alex and Mr. Macklin to thank for her safe deliverance. We owe both gentlemen an enormous debt of gratitude."

Returning a haughty look, Drucilla waved an aristocratic hand in surrender. "I am not too obstinate to admit that I was much too hard on Sir Alex,

Eve. And I hope he returns shortly so that I may offer my most abject and humble apologies."

"I hope so as well," Eve murmured fervently before turning to mount the stairs after her sister.

She wanted to put Claire to bed at once, but Drucilla was right on that account; they needed to put in an appearance immediately if they hoped to preserve any shred of Claire's reputation. After they bathed and changed, they would spend the remainder of the evening in the drawing room with their guests, attempting to minimize the damage. Nothing could lessen the scandal of Claire's abduction, of course, but at least she hadn't been forced to spend the night in the company of those villainous thieves.

And as she'd said, Macky wouldn't care a whit about her reputation. Not if he truly loved her as he claimed.

At the thought, Eve felt her spirits lift for the first time in countless hours, optimism tangling with the knots of anxiety in her stomach. If indeed her sister's future was happily settled, then she was free to concentrate on her own future. She knew exactly what she wanted now. Like Claire, she knew her own heart.

The question was, how should she proceed?

Undoubtedly she would have to confess her love to Ryder and convince him that she wanted to be his wife. But she was a successful matchmaker; she should be able to devise her own match to her satisfaction.

Eve felt a strange calm wash over her, much as she'd felt when her sister had been in such grave danger. As if she were girding herself for battle.

It didn't matter if Ryder failed to return tonight, or if he left Hertfordshire for London to pursue another bride, or even if he'd fallen out of love with her. She would just change his mind back again.

And she wouldn't stop until she had won Ryder for her husband.

Chapter Twenty

Dawn had just broken when Ryder at last reached his bedchamber at Hayden Park. Entering, he shut the door behind him, then came to an abrupt halt. Across the room, rose-gold fingers of sunrise speared through the open draperies, illuminating the peacefully slumbering woman curled up in a wing chair near the window.

Ryder's heart suddenly began hammering in painful surprise. Eve had evidently fallen asleep while waiting for him. She wore her nightclothes—a blue brocade wrapper over a white batiste nightdress—while her golden hair spilled down around her shoulders in tousled disarray.

At the sight, Ryder felt his breath catch in awe. Pale sunbeams caressed her face and hair, making her appear part goddess, part angel.

He watched Eve for an endless moment, unable to move. When eventually she stirred and opened her eyes, his fists clenched at his sides with the effort of keeping his pounding heart in his chest where it belonged.

"Ryder," she murmured softly, meeting his gaze in the hushed silence of the room.

"What are you doing here, Eve?" he asked, his voice hoarse.

"I . . . wanted to speak to you in private, so I waited for you here in case you came to collect your belongings." Her blue eyes searched his face questioningly. "Must you remain way over there?"

Ryder kept rooted where he stood, reluctant to cross the room to her. During the long night, he'd found the opportunity to wash away the soot and grime from his hands and face, but the acrid scent of smoke still clung to his hair and a shadow of stubble darkened his jaw. He was in no condition to come near Eve's fresh loveliness.

He responded by taking a mere step toward her. "You know it would be damning to your reputation if you're caught in my bedchamber. You are inviting scandal just being here."

Her mouth curved in a faint smile. "I don't care about a possible scandal or my reputation. I couldn't let you leave without telling you how I feel about you."

When his eyebrows rose questioningly, Eve uncurled her legs and stood. But there she remained, her fingers plucking nervously at the skirt of her dressing gown.

"How you feel about me?" Ryder repeated, not daring to breathe.

That ghost of a smile flickered across her lips again. "Claire said something very profound this evening. She wants to wed Mr. Macklin because he makes her happy. Until then I could never quite describe my feelings for you, but I realized that was exactly how I felt. You make me happy, Ryder. Incredibly so. What's more, you satisfy something deep inside me. You soothe the lonely ache"—Eve brought her fingers up to her breastbone to cover her heart—"here. The simple truth is, I love you."

When Ryder stood there in utter stillness, Eve went on. "The realization has gradually been coming over me. If not for Claire's abduction, I might not have come to my senses for a while longer. But yesterday in the carriage, when we were returning from visiting Hertford, I suddenly understood how I felt about you. I would have told you then, but it was hardly the appropriate time."

"You . . . love me?" Ryder echoed, wonder and hope and doubt all warring inside him.

"Is that so hard for you to believe? Claire says my love is precisely what you have been striving for these past weeks. She says you have feelings for me, Ryder. Is that true? Do you love me?"

"I expected Claire to be more circumspect," he muttered.

"But is it true?" Eve prodded.

His mouth twisting in a sardonic smile, Ryder raked a hand roughly through his hair. "Devil, yes, it's true. I can't remember a time when I didn't love you. I've been madly head over heels for you ever since we first met all those years ago."

Eve's expression held awe, as did her tone. "I never knew."

"Then I succeeded," Ryder said wryly. "You can't imagine how hard I worked to keep from making an utter fool of myself over you. I've never loved any woman but you, Eve. I intended to tell you yesterday, but then Claire was taken and . . ." He closed his eyes, remembering. "God, I felt sheer terror when I saw you run into that burning mill. You could have been killed trying to save your sister. It awed me that you loved her enough to risk your life for her without question."

"I know," Eve said softly. "I felt the same terror and awe when you risked your life fighting Hitchens. It only confirmed to me how deeply, how irrevocably I love you."

Ryder felt his throat constrict as a dozen emotions churned inside him. He had wanted so badly to hear those words from Eve. Wondering if he dared believe, he took another step closer, feeling a strange weakness in his limbs. Knowing Eve might love him was enough to bring him to his knees.

"You truly love me?" he repeated.

"Yes," Eve whispered, watching him. Ryder's dark eyes bored into hers, making her feel as if he were digging down into her soul. Those intense, handsome features were very vulnerable in their masculine beauty.

For an endless moment, his gaze searched her face, holding that same yearning look her sister had described—as if he were surveying the object of his most ardent dreams.

It was the same for her, Eve realized. Ryder had become the embodiment of her secret dreams. Her every fantasy.

Without conscious thought, she moved toward him, stopping when she was near enough to touch him. She swallowed hard as she stared up at him. "Ryder, it is frightening for me to contemplate marrying again. But it is more frightening to think of living without you. I want to be your wife."

His slashing eyebrows drew together in a frown. "Are you certain? I can think of a dozen reasons why you wouldn't wish to marry me."

"I can't think of a single one."

His gaze burned into hers. "I just want you to be happy, Eve, whether or not that means marriage."

She reached up to touch his rough cheek. "I am happy. I will be with you." His presence brought her desperate happiness.

"What of your craving for independence?"

Eve shook her head. "It took me a while, but I finally realized I was mistaken. I don't want independence as much as love. That was entirely missing in my first marriage. When I wed again, it will be nothing less than a love match. On both sides." She paused. "I was given little choice of husbands the first time, but now I am choosing. I want you for my husband, Ryder. Will you marry me?"

"You are proposing to me?"

"Yes," Eve answered, trying not to feel how hard her pulse was thudding with her own vulnerability. Striving for a lighter tone, she managed the glimmer of a teasing smile. "I believe I can fill your requirements for a bride. Perhaps I could even be the ideal mate for you if I work hard enough."

Ryder's face softened while his eyes flared with tenderness. "You are perfect as you are, Eve." He closed the final distance between them, till his body was flush against hers. "You're sweet and lovely and strong, kind and caring and brave and clever." His voice fell to a lower, huskier timbre as he reached up and cupped her face in his hands. "And you take my breath away."

His lips covered hers possessively, searing her with warmth and desire and heartfelt emotion. When finally Ryder broke off to stare at her, his countenance turned sober again. "I've tried damned hard to become your perfect match, Eve. To make myself suitable to be your husband. For half my life, everything I've ever strived toward has been because of you, so I could win your hand in marriage."

"Then you accept my offer?"

Joy lit his eyes. "God, yes, I accept."

Eve could not doubt that Ryder loved her. The heated tenderness in his gaze made her ache inside.

Raising her mouth again to his, she kissed him lightly as she began loosening the cravat around his neck.

"Umm, Eve," Ryder whispered against her lips, "what are you doing?"

"Undressing you." She wanted to express her own love, to show him how much he meant to her.

But his hands came up to clasp hers, halting her movements. "We aren't married yet. We ought to wait until our wedding day."

"I don't want to wait. I need you, Ryder."

A black eyebrow rose in query. "Your resident dragon Drucilla might object if I seduce you under your own roof."

"For your information, *I* am the one doing the seducing."

"Eve . . ."

Provocatively she drew her fingertip along his

lower lip. "Don't you want me, Ryder?" she asked, already knowing the answer.

A tender smile eased the hard lines of his face and gave him almost a boyish appeal. "What kind of question is that?" He cut off any further teasing with a fierce, marauding kiss that left no doubt about his desire for her.

The intensity of his passion stole Eve's breath. When he raised his head, his dark eyes blazed with a blinding light. Yet she pushed gently at his chest, making Ryder release her. "Not so quickly, my love. We have plenty of time."

Stepping back, she went to the door and turned the key, locking them in. Then she brazenly slipped off her dressing gown. Her thin nightdress clung to her form, showing off the curves of her breasts and hips, intensifying the feverish glow in Ryder's eyes. When she drew the garment over her head, baring her body, the naked hunger on his face made her heart pound. And yet he continued to resist her.

"I still smell like smoke. You should let me bathe first."

"Do you think I care?" Eve shook her head. The scent of smoke reminded her of how Ryder had risked his life for her and her sister. Remembering those agonizing moments, she shuddered, feeling a fierce rush of tenderness for Ryder, the need to cherish him always. "I have been waiting all night for this."

Moving to the bed, she drew down the covers and climbed in, then lay back, completely nude, stretching invitingly in what she hoped was an erotic display. "You have on too many clothes."

Ryder proceeded to undress, but slowly, as if fighting her seduction. His jaw was locked, evincing his struggle with himself.

With bated breath, Eve watched him. Even in the bright morning sunlight, he looked hard and dangerous, his sable hair tousled and his jaw darkly stubbled. His bronzed face seemed all hard planes and angles, in contrast to the other soft, fair-skinned gentlemen of the ton, while his lean, muscular body showed the hard usage of his difficult career. Yet he had never been more beautiful to her. He was, quite simply, breathtakingly male. And there was no doubt that he was fully aroused.

Finally Ryder joined her on the bed. Still reluctant, he lay beside her, bracing himself up on one elbow. "Are you certain about this, Eve?"

Laughter lit her blue eyes as she trailed a fingertip through the swirl of dark hair on his chest. "Entirely, utterly, absolutely certain. If I compromise you, then you will be forced to marry me."

Unexpected delight gathered in his chest. "That will be no hardship whatsoever."

He sucked in a sharp breath when her fingers trailed languorously lower, down over his abdomen to his loins. He wanted to be stalwart and honorable and wait for their formal union in matrimony, but he couldn't summon the willpower. He needed to claim Eve with the same undeniable need she professed to feel for him.

Accepting that his surrender was inevitable, he eased over her, bracing his weight on his forearms and positioning his lower body between her thighs. His powerful arousal settled intimately against the swollen wetness of her cleft, finding her body not only ready but eager for him.

Smiling, Eve reached up to twine her arms around his neck. "I wanted this to be my seduction, so I could show you how much I love you."

"Not this time, sweeting. This is *my* moment. I've dreamed of this a thousand times . . . loving you when you loved me in return. Imagining how you looked and tasted and felt. Now it is finally real, and I want to relish every single sensation."

He bent his head, possessing her mouth in a warm, softly ravishing kiss. She responded ardently, wrapping her arms around him more tightly to draw him closer, hot skin to hot skin.

"Then you *do* want me?" Eve asked breathlessly when he finally raised his head, laughter and love shining in her blue eyes.

"Sweet heaven, yes. I'll want you forever . . . in my life, in my heart, in my bed, under me, over me, around me."

Parting her thighs wider, Ryder slowly entered her. When Eve welcomed him joyously, he was swept with such hunger that his entire body shook.

It was a hunger as primal and fierce as survival. Eve had held him captive for years and would continue to hold him for eternity. Each time he was with her, he lost more of himself to her. She was the fever in his blood, his heart, his life.

Her back arched as he filled her liquid heat, and she gave a whimpering sigh, enveloping him with a shuddering moan of pleasure as he buried himself to the hilt.

Savoring the moment, Ryder held himself still,

gazing down at her beautiful face, knowing the fire in his heart was reflected in his eyes. "I can't even describe what I feel when I'm inside you," he murmured hoarsely. "The contentment, the fulfillment. But I never, ever want to leave you. Never want it to end."

"I feel . . . exactly . . . the same way." Her words were whispers that rose between his heart-stopping kisses as he began the languorous, ever quickening rhythm that would sweep them to paradise.

Together their breaths grew ragged, their need more urgent. Exquisite sensation surrounded them as they moved as one, their bodies straining to meld even closer.

Ryder felt himself drowning in the fervent emotion brimming in Eve's eyes; his chest was so full of love, he thought he might burst.

He did burst moments later when nearly unbearable pleasure broke over them. As her moans turned to gasping sobs, he plunged more deeply, claiming her for his own, branding her, possessing her . . . and Eve reciprocated, giving back his passion measure for desperate, blissful measure.

Their joining this time was a commitment, a pledge to love and to cherish, to entwine their lives together. The shattering conclusion was more incredible, more satisfying, than anything Ryder had ever felt in his life.

For a long time afterward, they simply lay there side by side, drinking in each other's breath, sharing heartbeats and feather-soft kisses.

It was a longer while still before Eve gave a faint

huff of exhausted laughter. "I consider that a satisfactory reply to my proposal."

Utterly sated, Ryder managed to summon a languid, wicked grin. "You are the expert on matchmaking, of course, but I thought the gentleman was supposed to do the proposing to the lady."

"True, but I thought you had waited long enough for me to understand that you were my ideal match."

"How perceptive of you," he murmured dryly. "I've waited half my lifetime for you, Eve."

"I don't know how I could have been so blind."

"It's understandable, I suppose. After your first marriage, you couldn't bear to entertain the notion of being controlled by another husband. And I was willing to wait. But I'm damned glad the wait is finally over."

"So am I." Eve smiled to herself. "Last night I told Lydia of my feelings for you, and she wasn't the least surprised. She said she had always suspected as much, that she never felt she had a chance with you."

"She didn't. I never even considered marrying any of the candidates you kept throwing in my face."

Eve raised herself up on one elbow, staring at Ryder in exasperation. "*I*, throwing? You were the one who coerced me into finding a bride for you. Under false pretenses, I might add."

"I know. But I've never wanted any bride but you, my darling love."

Reaching up, he caught her nape and pulled her down for an extremely satisfactory kiss. Mollified,

Eve gave a contented sigh and snuggled down next to him.

"What shall we do about setting a wedding date?" she finally inquired.

"I am not waiting to call the banns," Ryder said firmly. "We are marrying as soon as I can procure a special license. If you want an enormous wedding after that, you can arrange anything you choose."

"I don't want anything large. My first wedding was in London. It was lavish and pompous and cold and impersonal, attended mainly by strangers. I hated every moment of it."

"We can hold a small ceremony for your family and friends, and perhaps a wedding breakfast afterward."

"I would like that," Eve said softly. "What about once we are wed? Would you mind very much if we lived on Cyrene?"

His thumb came up to stroke her lower lip. "If I have you, I don't much care where we live, but I admit I have a decided preference for island life."

"So do I."

"Then it's settled. We'll live on Cyrene. We can sail as soon as you like—although Sir Gawain would be pleased if I returned to my duties as soon as possible."

"Once Claire and Macky are married, there should be nothing keeping me here." When Ryder's eyebrow rose, Eve expounded. "I have given them my blessing. I couldn't possibly refuse when they claim to love each other so completely."

"What did the aunts say when they learned about your sister's marriage plans?"

"They don't yet know. Claire and I agreed we would break the news to them this morning, but now they will be receiving a double shock when they hear our plans." When Ryder's brows drew together, Eve reached up to stroke the furrow there. "I don't expect they will object too strenuously. Drucilla is wallowing in contrition and wants to offer you her heartfelt apologies . . . just as I want to offer you mine."

"You already have, love, quite convincingly."

With that she received another breathtaking, heart-stirring, passionate kiss. When Ryder finally broke off, it was to glance at the windows, where morning sunshine was pouring through. "You had best return to your own room, sweetheart, so you won't be seen leaving mine by any of your servants or houseguests."

Eve sighed. She yearned to stay here in his arms forever, yet she saw the wisdom of trying to maintain at least a modicum of propriety. "Very well, though I doubt my houseguests will rise early, since they retired so late last night after all the excitement."

Rising reluctantly from the bed, Eve crossed the room to fetch her nightdress and wrapper. Ryder lay back with his hands laced behind his head, watching her dress.

"If you like," he offered, "I will join you downstairs later this morning so we can inform the aunts together about our plans. What do you say that I meet you downstairs for breakfast in an hour?"

"An excellent notion," Eve replied, realizing she was suddenly famished. "I have scarcely eaten anything since yesterday. First I was too terrified about Claire, and then I was terrified to think I might have lost you."

The tenderness returned to his dark eyes. "You could never, ever lose me, Eve. You'll have me forever."

She savored those words as she kissed him deeply one last time—and carried them with her when she slipped out to return to her own bedchamber.

Thankfully the corridor was quiet and deserted. Once she reached her room safely, Eve shut herself in and leaned back against the door, hugging her joy to herself. Her feelings for Ryder ran all the way down to her soul. He filled her aching emptiness, made her complete, and she would do the same for him.

She stood there for a long moment, hearing the echo of his promise. *You'll have me forever.*

Forever. A future filled with years of love and passion and happiness with Ryder. Eve smiled secretly to herself. The blissful prospect was almost too much to comprehend.

Eve had difficulty containing her smile when she went downstairs an hour later, washed and dressed and still thoroughly exhilarated.

To her surprise, the breakfast room wasn't empty as she'd expected. Her entire family was there, along with Beau Macklin. Even more surprisingly, Macky was sitting at the table beside Claire.

What was astonishing, however, Eve realized as she paused in the doorway unnoticed, was that there were no footmen in attendance. Instead, the aunts were performing the honors of filling breakfast plates from the sideboard. It was perfectly reasonable for Claire to be pampered after her ordeal, yet the elderly ladies were serving not only Claire but Cecil and Mr. Macklin as well.

Meanwhile, Cecil was proudly regaling the aunts with tales of how Sir Alex and Mr. Macklin had foiled the villains and saved the day, with a bit of help from himself and the estate tenants. His account was regularly punctuated by gasps of alarm by Beatrice and expressions of amazement and wonder by Drucilla.

Eve smiled to find such harmony existing between them after the difficulties of the past day. Clearly Cecil's pride and excitement were infectious, and Claire's happiness was spilling over. She was literally beaming, while Macky looked a trifled dazed by his good fortune.

When Eve finally stepped forward, Claire looked up and greeted her with delight. "I have told Aunt Drucilla and Aunt Beatrice about my betrothal, Eve, and they have agreed to lend their support."

Taking a seat at the table, Eve gave Drucilla a curious glance. "I own myself surprised."

"It is against my better judgment," Drucilla admitted calmly as she poured coffee into Eve's cup. "But I have resigned myself to the marriage. Mr. Macklin *did* save Claire's life, after all, so he is entitled to our approval." She cast an arch glance at Macky. "If anyone demands to know why she is marrying our . . . *footman,* we will simply tell the truth—that he was posing as a servant in order to capture a vicious assailant."

Eve offered Macky a fond smile. "Welcome to the family, sir. And thank you from the bottom of my heart for all you did for us yesterday."

Macky grinned in acknowledgment. "I couldn't allow this pretty lass to be harmed, now could I?" There was a twinkle in his eye as he laid a large hand protectively over Claire's. "I only thank God that she is safe and that she has agreed to make me the happiest of men."

Suspecting that Ryder might also want to lay claim to that title, Eve couldn't prevent a soft smile of remembrance at his own declarations earlier this morning.

"I say, Evie." Cecil broke into her thoughts. "What is to do with you? You are positively glowing."

"Yes, Eve," Claire added more politely. "Does it mean what I think it means? Have you spoken to Sir Alex?"

Eve nodded. "Yes, we have spoken." When Claire clapped her hands with glee, Eve sent the eldest aunt a penetrating glance. "Drucilla, I'm afraid there is to be another wedding in the family."

"Well, I should hope so," the lady declared. "It will help mitigate the scandal if you and Sir Alex tie the knot."

"Oh, famous!" Cecil exclaimed. "Sir Alex will be our brother! It is about time, Evie—" He suddenly broke off when he spied Ryder standing in the doorway. "Sir Alex!"

When Eve looked up and met his dark gaze, she felt a spark of fire all the way down to her slippers.

"Then we have your consent, Lady Wykfield?" Ryder asked casually, entering the breakfast room.

Drucilla inclined her head regally, as if conferring a great favor. "You do, Sir Alex."

"You realize we don't require your consent, Drucilla," Eve remarked.

"Well, you have it all the same."

"Yes," Beatrice said with a gentler smile. "Eve is very precious to us, Sir Alex. We would not approve of just anyone stealing her away from us. But we are certain you will take excellent care of her, and we will be happy to welcome you into the family."

"Indeed," Drucilla seconded her sister. "If you are agreeable, Sir Alex, we will let bygones be bygones."

Ryder held out a chair for Drucilla and waited until she was seated before he bent to kiss her cheek. "I would like that very well, my lady."

Startled by his show of affection, Drucilla eyed him with distrust. Ryder performed the same function for Beatrice, offering her a seat and then kissing her soft, wrinkled cheek. In response, the younger aunt flushed a becoming pink.

When he had poured his own coffee and taken his place beside Eve, Drucilla eyed Ryder coolly. "I can see how you won Eve's heart, sir. But let me inform you, your seductive wiles will not work with me."

Beatrice lifted her chin in defiance of her sister. "They certainly will work with *me*, Sir Alex."

Ryder returned a slow grin, while most everyone else at the table laughed.

Drucilla cleared her throat, pointedly ignoring

the laughter. "I suggest that we officially announce both betrothals tonight at my birthday celebration. The sooner we put an end to the gossip, the better. This past week"—she leveled a stare at Ryder—"you and Eve have been far too intimate for propriety's sake."

"I think you protest too much, sister dear," Beatrice intervened. "You know very well you wanted them to wed." She gave Eve a mischievous glance. "The truth is, we were concocting a scheme to convince Sir Alex to propose to you."

"A scheme?" Eve repeated blankly.

Drucilla cut off her sister's answer. "Fortunately we will be spared the indignity of resorting to underhanded means."

"What means?" Eve asked, highly curious now.

"It was only to be a last resort," Beatrice said. "We planned to discover you with Sir Alex in a compromising position so that you would be compelled to marry him."

Her eyes widening, Eve remained speechless, torn between astonishment and laughter.

"A compromising position wouldn't be difficult to arrange," Ryder said, his eyes glinting. "I'm certain we could find a way to oblige you."

"That will *not* be necessary now," Drucilla retorted. She turned her attention to her coffee cup. "But I admit, I was wrong to think Lord Gyllford would make a better match for you, Eve. I've come to believe Sir Alex will be an adequate husband for you."

"I've always thought so," Ryder murmured dryly.

"So have I," Cecil declared, polishing off the last bite of his breakfast.

Seeing his empty plate, Beatrice rose to fetch the platter of kippered herring and offered it to him. "Have another kipper, young man."

Cecil flashed her a broad grin. "I say, Aunt Beatrice, I think I could grow accustomed to being treated as a hero."

"You *are* a hero for the moment," Drucilla stated magnanimously. "Not that I expect it to last."

"Oh, it will last," Cecil promised. "I am turning over a new leaf, Aunt Dru. Sir Alex said I might be able to join the Foreign Office if I apply myself to my studies when I return to Oxford in the fall and prove myself worthy."

Drucilla's hand went to her heart. "Pray, don't even mention such dubious ambitions, you rascal. We have had more than enough shocks for one morning, with not one but two betrothals." Turning, she looked intently at Eve. "I do hope you won't regret your decision to marry Sir Alex, my dear."

Meeting Ryder's gaze, Eve saw the blaze of tender affection in his eyes. Knowing the same fierce emotion was mirrored in her own eyes, she slipped her hand in his. "Never," she said ardently, entwining their fingers. "My only regret is that it took me so long to accept his proposal."

"It's my regret as well, love," Ryder agreed, raising her hand and pressing a tender kiss on her palm. "We have a great deal of lost time to make up for."

"But just think what a pleasure it will be," Eve said, her lips curving with the joy she couldn't hide.

"*Eve!*" Drucilla exclaimed, her tone reproachful.

"Pray mind your tongue at the breakfast table. Honestly, this is exactly what I feared—that Sir Alex's mercenary manners would rub off on you."

The glimmer of love and laughter in Ryder's eyes deepened when Eve started to leap to his defense. When he gave a slight shake of his head, however, Eve held her tongue and summoned an appropriately chastened expression to mollify Drucilla.

Nothing could spoil her happiness just now, not even the dowager's long-held disdain for Ryder's common origins and questionable past.

After all, the waiting was nearly over, Eve reminded herself. She and Ryder had an entire lifetime ahead of them. A glorious future as husband and wife.

And judging from the loving way his hand tightened around hers as she met his dark gaze, Ryder shared her joyous anticipation.

Epilogue

The Isle of Cyrene,
September 1816

As he reached up to help Eve dismount from her horse, Ryder's breath lodged in his throat. Golden sunlight poured down over her, setting her bright, unbound hair ablaze.

The waiting was over. She was his bride at last.

She belonged to him.

Possessively, he slid Eve down his body and stood holding her. He'd brought her here for a purpose, to the meadow where he'd first kissed her all those years ago. The afternoon was warm—September was still considered late summer on Cyrene—but the warmth was tempered by fresh ocean breezes coming off the Mediterranean.

To Ryder's mind, the island was a sensual paradise, yet just now it was made even more enchanting by the special occasion.

Eve was truly here with him, just as in his dreams. Smiling up at him, that sweet, aching smile of hers, filled with love and tenderness.

"You don't know how long I have waited for

this," he murmured, his voice husky with desire as he brushed her mouth with his thumb.

"I do so know," Eve replied with a ripple of laughter. "You have told me often enough that I can picture it in my own mind."

Ryder's eyes gleamed. "Then you know what happens next."

"Yes. This is the part where you make passionate love to me."

"Exactly. So why are we tarrying?"

Grasping the quilt from his saddlebag, Ryder left their horses grazing and took Eve's hand to lead her through a glade of willows to the banks of a lazy, rippling stream. While she watched, he spread the quilt on a carpet of grass and late summer wildflowers.

A short while ago, they had slipped away from the lavish wedding breakfast hosted by Sir Gawain Olwen at Olwen Castle. Today's event was actually the second such celebration held in honor of their marriage. The first one in London—a small wedding ceremony and breakfast in June—had been attended by Eve's siblings and the aunts, as well as several of Ryder's friends and fellow Guardians.

The festivities this afternoon had been much larger, resembling more of a feast. Along with many of the island's inhabitants, Eve's parents had attended. While they would never welcome Ryder with open arms, they were prepared to tolerate his marriage to their eldest daughter.

His friends, on the other hand, had welcomed Eve gladly into their ranks. She had fit with perfect ease into island society, while Ryder's fellow Guardians and their mates had made her one of their own.

Eve was admittedly fascinated by the remarkable tale of how the exiled knights and followers of one of England's most legendary kings had settled on Cyrene nearly a millennium ago and founded the secret order, the Guardians of the Sword, with the purpose of battling evil and tyranny and defending the weak. The league had nearly died out during that long dark interval of history, and only in the past century been revived to meet the grave challenges spawned by the bloody French Revolution and Napoléon's subsequent attempt to conquer the civilized world.

The future of the Guardians was still in question, however. The current elderly leader, Sir Gawain, was growing weary of his enormous duties and hoped to retire soon. His intended successor, the Earl of Hawkhurst, who was one of Ryder's closest friends, would have been named long before now, except for one significant problem: It seemed that Hawk first needed a bride. And not just any bride, but one who could carry on the legendary bloodlines of the original knights, as the order's charter required.

But the Guardians' business was not on Ryder's mind at the moment. Instead, his every thought and feeling was focused on his beautiful wife. He and Eve had escaped from the festivities to hold their own private celebration here in the meadow.

They had officially been married for three months now. Three incredible months in which Ryder had experienced the sheer joy of waking up next to Eve each morning. Of holding her and laughing with her and challenging her. Of knowing she belonged to him, just as he belonged to her.

He went to her now and gazed down into her eyes without speaking, aware of how rare and precious it was for a man to be able to live out his most cherished desire. Loving Eve in this sunlit meadow was the fulfillment of all his dreams. She was his life, his future, his every wish come true.

"What are you thinking?" she asked when Ryder remained silent.

"How lucky I am to have you."

Reverently, he placed a hand over her slightly rounded belly. They both considered it miraculous that she was to bear him a child next spring. It wasn't until they'd reached the island that Eve had discovered that her morning nausea during the two-week voyage from England was not due to seasickness, but rather to her impending pregnancy.

"I still can scarcely believe our good fortune," she said softly, marveling.

"It's hard for me to comprehend as well."

He had a family now—and the familial warmth he had yearned for for so long. Claire and Cecil, the aunts, and the prospect of children of their own. But best of all, he had Eve.

"Now for our vows," Ryder prompted. She had indulged his whimsical desire to pledge their marriage vows over again in this special place.

Her smile as warm as the day, Eve allowed him to draw her down onto the quilt. They knelt facing each other, hands clasped. The moment was hushed and reverent as she spoke the simple promise:

"I, Eve, take thee Alex as my wedded husband, to love and honor and cherish forever."

And Ryder responded with the same promise: "I, Alex, take thee Eve as my wedded wife, to love and honor and cherish forever. You're mine to protect, to keep, to hold."

"And you are mine."

His arms wrapped around her fiercely then, and he kissed her with all the pent-up ardor he'd been denying the entire day.

"And now to consummate our new vows," Ryder finally breathed against her lips as he bore her down onto the quilt and rolled over with her again and again until she was laughing in protest.

"You do realize this is wicked, making love out-of-doors," Eve remarked as he began to divest her of her ivory silk gown.

"No one can see us." They were sheltered by the copse of willows and would have ample warning if anyone happened upon the meadow. "But if you want me to stop . . ."

"Don't you dare stop!" she exclaimed, beginning to help him. "Not after arousing me this far."

Drawing down her bodice to bare her luscious breasts, Ryder nuzzled the swelling slopes as his thumbs began to draw slow circles on her nipples. "Have I aroused you, love?"

"You know you have."

"You aren't nearly as aroused as I would like. I want you panting and writhing and whimpering for me."

"That will come soon enough," Eve assured unevenly as he cupped her breasts. "I have no doubt."

He bent to take a peaked nipple in his mouth, kneading gently while he suckled her, and he heard her breathing sharpen.

A moment later, however, Eve pressed her splayed fingers against his chest. "No, my darling, this way isn't your dream. I want to enact it just as you described it to me. *I* am supposed to be making love to *you*. Now, lie back and allow me to."

"Very well," Ryder agreed without much resistance. "I'm entirely at your command, sweetheart."

She undressed him first completely until he lay nude, the warm sun beating down upon his bare body. Then Eve rose to her feet to remove her gown and underclothing.

Braced on his elbows, Ryder watched her with heavy, half-closed lids. She moved with a grace that left him aching, all elegance and lush warmth. Sunlight played on her pale skin, on her hair, coloring the rich gold with tints of flame. The bright tendrils wound around the silken globes of her breasts, teasing the peaked buds of her nipples.

Ryder's eyes glistened as he followed her progress, his gaze touching every part of Eve, drinking her in. The sight ravished his senses. Her bare, dusky-tipped breasts. Her slender waist and curving hips. The dark gold curls at the apex of her thighs. The long, lovely legs that would soon wrap around him.

Feeling a sheen of perspiration break over him, he clenched his fists, knowing it would take all his willpower to let Eve maintain control as she did in his fantasy.

"You are incredibly alluring, you know," he muttered as she knelt beside him. "Utterly irresistible."

"So are you."

She reached down to caress his throbbing arousal with a fingertip. The smile that curved her lips was one he relished, playful and innocent, seductive and sinful. Then she curled her fingers around his manhood, making him inhale sharply. When she laughed, delight surged through him, while desire exploded in him with blazing heat.

"Eve." His voice came out as a hoarse rasp. "I don't know how much of this I can bear."

"You must," she asserted with that beguiling siren's smile.

Rebelliously he rose up to kiss her. Before his lips could touch hers, however, she pushed at his chest with both hands, making him lie fully on his back.

"I told you, I want this to be exactly as in your dream. I want to make love to you, Ryder . . . to show you how very much I love you." Her voice was husky, rough silk, stroking his nerve endings, and Ryder let Eve have her way.

She kissed his entire body, beginning with his face and sweeping slowly downward. Her lips teased the line of his jaw, the vulnerable hollow of his throat, his breastbone, searing the part of his rib cage that concealed his hammering heart. She was profoundly sensual, her warm breath pooling on his skin, the cool silk of her hair caressing his fevered flesh.

Finally, however, she eased over him and lowered herself to straddle his thighs. When she leaned forward, pressing her body flush against his, all Ryder's muscles clenched in anticipation of their joining. Her naked skin burned his, while her hair spilled down in a gold curtain around them.

As their gazes locked, the air shimmered with raw passion. When she bent to press another ardent kiss on his bare chest, Ryder gave a harsh, shuddering groan. In response, Eve smiled her soft, beguiling smile.

That smile was his undoing. Needing to satisfy his fierce hunger, he grasped her hips to lift her up, then coaxed her willing body down to receive his hard shaft until she was impaled fully on his rigid flesh. His heart pounded as Eve sheathed him in wet, silken heat.

"At last I am yours," she whispered.

"Yes."

She was bound to him now in the most primal way possible.

Her eyes shone brighter than the sun-rippled sea as she began to move against him, setting an urgent rhythm. Ryder held her waist, urging her on, intensifying his own pleasure as well as hers, feeling her flushed skin burning under his desperately roving hands.

The surge of her hips matched the thundering of his blood; her keening whimpers echoed his harsh groans as she clutched fiercely at his shoulders, throwing her head back in wild abandon. She was all wild, unleashed passion. The passion he had taught her.

"God, Eve," he grated in a ragged, breaking whisper.

As they climaxed in unity, love and wanting came together inside Ryder, pouring through him like honey and sunlight until their whole world dissolved into hot, pulsing brightness.

Afterward, Eve collapsed upon him and lay there unmoving, her face buried in his damp shoulder.

Ryder couldn't move a single muscle, either. He couldn't speak. His throat was too thick, his heart too full. He felt a love for her so strong, it burned with every breath. A happiness so intense it was almost painful.

Somehow, by some miracle, Eve was his bride and she loved him.

"Was that like your dream?" she finally murmured against his skin.

Sated and boneless, Ryder nodded. "It was infinitely better."

"Good."

After a long while, he summoned the energy to roll over her so he could gaze down at her beautiful face.

Her eyes were closed, her expression one of utter contentment. He knew without her telling him so that she felt loved, felt treasured and cherished, just as he meant to keep her for always.

Then as he watched, a slow, sensual smile curled her lips.

"Now what are *you* thinking?" Ryder demanded, his voice still rough with passion.

Eve opened her eyes to fix a slumberous gaze on him. "I was remembering the letter we had from Cecil yesterday. His complaint that Claire and Macky were disgustingly happy."

"Which is just what you wanted for her."

"Yes, but obviously Cecil is feeling left out." She gave a fond laugh. "Or perhaps he is only trying to soften our sympathies by playing the martyr. Can you believe his request that our first child be named after him?"

Ryder grinned. "I could possibly consider Cecil for my son's name."

"But what if our child is a daughter?"

"I suppose we could always name her Cecily or Cecilia."

"I suppose so," Eve said dubiously. "Although I had hoped we might name our first daughter after your mother."

"Truthfully, I like that better." Bending, Ryder pressed his smiling lips against her forehead. "Fortunately we have ample time to decide."

"All the time in the world," Eve agreed, wrapping her arms around his neck and drawing him down for another beguiling kiss.

Read on for an exciting chapter from Nicole Jordan's

Touch Me with Fire

coming in December 2006

Vitoria, Spain
July 1813

Through hooded eyes he watched the woman undress in the moonlight, his carnal hunger tempered by pain. His right thigh, mauled by a volley of cannonshot six weeks before, ached dully, although not enough to make him refuse his hostess's late-night visit to his bedside. He would not ask her to leave. It would be rude and pointlessly cruel to reject her after all she had done for him these past weeks.

Naked except for the heavy bandage on his thigh and the cool sheet drawn up to his waist, Julian, Lord Lynden, reclined against the pillows. Waiting.

With a whisper of black silk, she let the dressing gown fall to the floor, revealing lush, full breasts, with nipples peaked in anticipation. "Do I please you, *señor?*" Pilar asked in soft, throaty Spanish. She moved toward him slowly, her dark eyes shimmering with sexual awareness.

Although not fluent in her language, he comprehended her meaning and replied politely, "Very much so, *querida*. You are exquisite."

He did not greatly exaggerate. The silver light flooding through the open patio doors spilled over her nude body, turning it mysterious and pale. He knew that voluptuous body with a fair measure of intimacy now. This was not the first time Pilar had played the ministering angel, slipping secretly into his bedchamber at night to comfort and soothe him—and to indulge in a few stolen hours of forbidden passion.

The first time had been a surprise. She was a highborn Spanish lady, older than he by several years—a beautiful widow, lonely and hot-blooded. This *hacienda* was her home. Despite the fact that he had helped drive the conquering French troops from her country, she hadn't been eager to let a wounded British cavalry officer billet there, not until she'd learned he was a war hero and an *aristocratico* as well. Even then she'd demanded an extravagant sum for his accommodation.

The cost had been worth it. The opportunity to recover from his injuries here rather than in a wretched field hospital had undoubtedly saved his life. And the attentive personal care he had received from the lovely widow had been an unexpected bonus.

Demonstrating that same attentiveness now, she climbed into his bed to kneel naked on the mattress at his uninjured side. Her gaze was fixed on his lower body, on his arousal rigidly defined by the pale linen sheet.

"You please me also," she murmured with a seductive smile.

Reaching for her hand, he kissed her fingertips lingeringly, one by one, while he held her heated gaze. "I fear the honors must again fall to you," he apologized. Before his wounding, he could claim an advanced degree of sexual prowess, but although his body was mending, he was not in the best condition to perform any demanding feats of athleticism.

His hostess responded by reaching up to touch tenderly the savage wound that slashed across his right cheekbone all the way to his temple. "Leave everything to me, *vida mía.*" Her throaty whisper resonated with promise as she brushed back a tousled lock of his pale golden hair. "I will help you forget your dark dreams."

Doubting, he remained silent.

The warm, moon-splashed room grew hushed. The woman bent over him, scattering kisses along his throat, his collarbone, his bare shoulder, while her hands traced the smooth contours of his naked chest. Before his injuries had weakened and scarred him, he had been endowed with a beautiful male body, graceful and tautly muscled, well toned by years of sporting endeavors, honed to steel by the rigors of a military campaign. His lover's roving, slowly gliding hands expressed her appreciation now, lingering on his belly, flat and hard, circling his lean hips, drawing down the sheet that covered him.

She drew a sharp breath as she boldly revealed his rigid manhood, her gaze riveted by the sight. In the pale light his erection stood blatant, powerfully formed.

"*Magnífico.*" Almost reverently, she took his hard, straining arousal into her hand and caressed it with long, lingering strokes.

Shuddering, he closed his eyes. His desire was insistent and sharp now, dominating the diminishing ache in his thigh.

She continued to tease him, moving her hand slowly up . . . then down. At length, she lowered her mouth to his chest, arousing him further with tongue and lips. When she encountered a hard male nipple, she bit lightly with her teeth.

Reaching up, he closed his fingers urgently on her shoulders, drawing her against him in a wordless command.

She mounted him then. With careful regard for his bandaged thigh, she settled one leg over his hips and lowered herself onto his pulsing arousal, her gasp of pleasure loud in the heated quiet of the room as he penetrated her moist entrance.

"Slowly . . ." he murmured. His hands moved to cup her full white breasts with their tight brown nipples. Restraining her momentarily, he raised his good left knee and braced it against her back to keep her from sliding onto his wounded thigh. "Now," he ordered as he surged deeper into her sleek, hot passage.

Her dark, passion-hazed glance locking with his, she obeyed, riding him slowly, clenching her inner muscles with practiced expertise, her honeyed silkiness holding him tight.

He tensed with mingled pleasure and pain. Shifting his hands, he grasped the smooth mounds of her buttocks and hauled her closer; at the same time he arched his hips upward, swelling and probing deep within her.

Her eyes shut. Her mouth went slack. Soon she threw her head back, and the room grew loud with the ragged moans that tore from her throat. As he rhythmically thrust into her, she dug her nails into his shoulders, whimpering and writhing and grinding her hips against his.

A few moments later, the flame-hot woman above him cried out and her body jerked in a wrenching shudder. Closing his eyes, Julian let the searing release flood through him in a rush of sensation.

Eventually he regained awareness and found her lying limply on his chest. A thin sheen of perspiration covered his body, while pain throbbed in his right thigh. With care, he rolled onto his uninjured side, easing her onto the mattress.

In the dim light, her eyes were half-lidded in languorous contentment, her pale flesh suffused with the afterglow of passion.

Solicitously he brushed his lips against her damp temple. "Forgive me, *querida,* for being unable to pleasure you as you deserve."

She opened her heavy lids, her slow smile sated and amused. "I doubt that I could bear any more pleasure," she replied in thickly accented English. Her glance dropped below his waist. "A wound could not slow a magnificent man like you. It is fortunate, however, that the injury was not slightly higher and to the left."

He laughed, a pained sound as the ravaged muscles in his thigh cramped in protest. With clenched teeth he waited until the spasm passed. Then he kissed Pilar's fingers once more and shut his eyes, wondering if he would be able to sleep without the drugging effects of laudanum.

He forced himself to think of something other

than his injury. Home. His family seat in England. Lush pastures, ripe fields, thick woodlands teeming with game. His longing to see the cool green country of his birth was like a physical ache inside him . . . an ache that turned to fire as he drifted into a doze . . .

The searing heat originated in his right thigh and speared throughout his body, echoing sharply in his right temple and cheekbone. Half blinded by the blood streaming from his brow, he tried to lift himself from the rocky ground and nearly screamed in agony.

Where in God's name was he? Who *was he?*

Recognition of the tumult came slowly . . . the explosive booms of cannon, the crackle of musket fire, the moans of dying men, the screams of horses. An acrid black smoke obscured his vision, but through the haze he caught glimpses of devastation. The hillside was dark with dust and blood, splashed with the scarlet and blue of shredded uniforms.

Ah, yes. This hell was Spain. Vitoria, he remembered. A battlefield . . . one of many he'd seen during the four years since he'd condemned himself to this war. He was Julian Morrow, Sixth Viscount Lynden. Lieutenant Colonel Lord Lynden, second-in-command of the Fifteenth Hussars. His wife was Caroline. . . . No. . . . Caroline was dead. He had killed her. This hell was his penance for causing her death.

His mission . . . to lead a cavalry charge against a French divisional battery. He remembered succeeding, and yet he must have taken a volley of cannonfire at close range.

He lay where he'd fallen, on a rocky hillside, sur-

rounded by the piteous moans of wounded men and horses. The battle still raged around him. Mortar shells shrieked overhead and burst, the thunder of artillery fire rolling and echoing around the hilltops. The suffocating stench of powder smoke burned his nostrils and throat, while his mouth filled with the coppery tang of blood . . . the acid taste of fear.

Fear. He was afraid to die.

No, not afraid. Simply not eager. He wanted to live after all. Surprising, considering how zealously he had courted Death for the past four years. He truly wanted to live. Ironic to discover it only now, when Death stared him in the face. His right thigh was a mangled, bloody mass of torn flesh.

He knew he should try to stanch the flow of blood, but the effort was too overwhelming. Abandoning the struggle, he slipped back into oblivion . . .

Voices, snatches of conversation drifted toward him in the darkness. Something about his leg. He tried to open his eyes, but he couldn't manage to weave his way through the labyrinth of pain and fever fogging his mind. The harsh pain dulled his senses, weighted his eyelids . . . while images floated in the fuzzy corridors of his mind . . . haunting images of Caroline . . . her lifeless body lying amid the stone ruins. He let himself slip back into the dark world where the pain was not so fierce.

"Please, *señor,* lie still. You will hurt yourself."

He came awake with a start. At first he didn't recognize the darkened room, but the dense night air was warm with the musky scent of lovemaking, and the cool hand on his brow was one he remembered from his weeks of convalescence. The Spanish widow. His hostess.

"You had the dream again, no?"

He closed his eyes, trying to ignore the question, trying to shut out the haunting memories.

"What are these dreams, *vida mía,* that torment you so? Who is this Caroline? You cry her name in your sleep."

He didn't answer, yet his thoughts would not be silent. *Young, beautiful, unfaithful Caroline. As blond and blue-eyed as he was himself. A member of the nobility as he was, raised to wealth and privilege, indulged and fawned over. They made the ideal couple, until their last fierce argument had ended in her death . . .*

The woman beside him ran her tongue lightly, provocatively, along his naked shoulder, and slid her arm around his lean waist. Pouting as if jealous, she glanced up at him, her dark eyes flaring hot with a familiar emotion.

"I shall drive away your nightmares," she murmured, pressing her nude, voluptuous body against his in an unmistakable invitation.

He had not planned on taking her again tonight. Certainly not with such force. Definitely not with her beneath him, a position which placed a severe strain on his healing thigh. But she was a willing body. And she had black hair, not blond like Caroline's. She could help him forget, at least momentarily.

Her gasp was loud and startled when he rolled over her and plunged his rising maleness between her open legs, but then her eyes widened in pleasure as she caught his savage rhythm.

Roughly he buried his hands in her hair and drove into her, slamming his body against hers, thrusting hard, over and over again, as if he could exorcise the devils in his soul. In response she clung to him, whimpering raggedly, her climax coming swiftly, with racking power.

His own violent release followed shortly. His breathing was harsh, his body glistening with sweat when he gave a final shudder and collapsed against her, his leg wound throbbing like fire.

Far from being offended by his fierceness, though, she stroked his spine soothingly, offering comfort, whispering endearments in soft Spanish, until he eased his body away and rolled onto his back with a groan. "Forgive me, *querida.*"

"There is nothing to forgive." But instead of drifting back to sleep, she kissed the damp skin of his shoulder and slid out of bed in order to dress. "I must go. It will not do to have the servants find me in your bed."

Julian made no protest.

When he was alone once more, he lay there and stared at the ceiling, remembering the past, thinking of the events four years ago that had brought him here.

Murder. That was the allegation whispered behind his back.

He was never officially charged, of course, since there was no proof. He was too wealthy, too wellborn, and too high-ranking to be arrested for murder on only circumstantial evidence. Lady Lynden's death was ruled the result of a riding accident. Yet the rumors, fanned by her lover's grief, persisted.

The rumors were not unfounded; Julian had been unable to refute them with any degree of honesty. He was to blame. He had killed his wife.

In the end it was his own guilt that had decided him. To punish himself, he had gone off to war—bought a commission in the cavalry and joined the Peninsular Campaign in Portugal and Spain against Napoléon's invading forces.

Not caring whether he lived or died was a decided asset in war. Ironically, his indifference had often been mistaken for courage, his reckless deeds hailed as heroic. He had driven himself relentlessly, desperately, only to discover he could never toil hard enough, never ride swiftly enough to escape his guilt and self-recrimination. He couldn't fill the aching void in his soul. There was nothing left in his life. No joy, no passion, no fire. Nothing but dreams of his late wife. Nothing but his guilt. . . .

The sunlight streaming into the room made him wince as he slowly came awake. He was lying in bed, naked except for the bandage that wrapped his injured thigh. Feeling a familiar touch on his leg, he groaned softly and squinted against the bright light.

Will Terral, his batman and personal servant, was leaning over him, scowling as he probed the bloody bandage.

"I never would have taken you for a fool, m'lord, but you've proved me wrong. The scab has broken open."

Julian bit back a savage retort. His exploits last night *had* been imbecilic. And his batman had a right to criticize. Will had saved his leg from the "butcher" field surgeons, later nursing him through the worst dangers and the long bouts of agony that followed his injury . . . feeding him, changing his bandages, forcing him to drink bitter-tasting nostrums. Once, the terrible wound had putrefied and had to be drained, the mortified flesh cut away. But Will eventually had triumped with his simple home remedies and the same poultices he used for his master's horses. Julian had emerged from the ordeal a gaunt, pain-racked ghost of his former self.

And now, just when he was beginning to recover his health, he had set back his progress in exchange for only a transient moment of forgetfulness.

Still grumbling, Will changed the bandage, then brought water, razor, and soap in order to shave his patient. Looking in the hand mirror afterward, Julian hardly recognized the man he had once been. His skin was tanned from the summer months he'd spent fighting, but beneath the tan waxed an unhealthy pallor. Worse, his once-handsome face was disfigured by the savage puckering scar that slashed across his right cheekbone, upward toward his temple. It was probable, as well, that he would always limp. And yet he was grateful to still have the leg. He had survived, thanks to Will, and with that he would have to be content.

His batman was not so content. As Will gathered up the shaving equipment, he muttered for perhaps the hundredth time, "I'll be right glad to see the last of this Papist country," before he stalked from the room.

Julian lay back wearily, contemplating his future as he had frequently during the past weeks. He would be invalided home to England unless he asked to remain here in Spain. Did he want to make such a request?

He knew Will's feelings on the subject. Not only did his faithful servant wish to return home, but Will didn't mind saying, regularly and frankly, that his lordship had wallowed in guilt long enough.

Perhaps his batman was right, Julian reflected. Perhaps it *was* time to end his self-banishment and go home. Perhaps he had suffered enough. He had lost his wife, his friends, his good name, the life he once knew. . . . In four years he hadn't found the redemption he'd sought. And he was so weary of war, of death, of pain.

Gritting his teeth, he slowly sat up and swung his legs to the floor, then reached for the crutches that stood beside the bed, prepared to endure once more the torture of forcing the knotting muscles of his thigh to function.

But he was girding himself mentally, as well. He had finally come to a decision.

He had punished himself long enough. His penance had been served.

It was time that he returned home and faced the ghosts of his past.

Don't miss this steamy romance from NICOLE JORDAN!

WICKED FANTASY

Antonia's charming wit and vibrant beauty make her England's most sought-after heiress. But it's her fiery spirit and awakening sensuality that make infamous adventurer Trey Deverill yearn to possess her. Deverill sweeps Antonia into unforgettable passion. But a treacherous plot threatens their lives and their chance for the grandest adventure of all: true love.

"Seduction, masked balls, houses of ill-repute and the stirrings of first love swirl into an intoxicating mix. Once more Jordan proves that she well deserves her reputation for delivering both steamy scenes and an emotional punch."
—*Publishers Weekly*

READ A SAMPLE CHAPTER
AT www.ballantinebooks.com

Available now in paperback

 Ballantine Books